The Parrot's Tale

by

Miller Caldwell

ISBN – 978-1-910256-05-3

Contents

Author's Disclaimer

Those who read my books no longer ask whether the characters in my books are real. They prefer to ask whether such bizarre events in my life actually happen.

The locations in The Parrot's Tale are mostly real as are some of the situations and characters. You will recognise many characters and places in Dumfries and Galloway. The rest are composites of real places, events and people and just now and then figments of my imagination which I think are real. This disclaimer keeps me one step ahead of a punch on the nose.

The African Grey Parrot is a native of West and Central Africa. Experts regard it as one of the most intelligent birds in the world. The parrots' overall gentle nature, and their inclination and ability to mimic and often understand speech, have made them popular and unique pets.

A missing person is a person who has disappeared and whose status as alive or dead cannot be confirmed, as their location and fate is not known.

1
Missing

Four years earlier
2011

Little traffic and fewer people stirred outside that damp early night. Frank Dunbar, the local Your Move building society manager, had endured a long busy day sorting house schedules and preparing mortgages. His final duty of the day relaxed his tired mind as he walked along with his loving black Labrador, Bobby, and entered Moffat Road. Frank was aware of a car at the top of the road which stopped for only a brief moment. Some distance lay between him and the vehicle but he had seen someone get out of the car: yes out, not in. He did not see who it was. He had his black plastic bag poised to collect Bobby's dropped offering at that precise moment. A steady drizzle made human recognition impossible, let alone the car registration. Frank thought it was a mid-grey car but the make eluded him. The police gained little evidence from his statement.

This mid-week leaf-kicking October evening would be seared into local minds. Morag, a popular school pupil, had disappeared. To all concerned, it was inexplicable.

After visiting a school friend she had walked to the bus stop to travel to her Georgetown suburban home in Dumfries. But the bus came and went without her. Something must have happened on Moffat Road. Her distressed parents could be told nothing else with certainty.

Within an hour, police were starting to make door-to-door enquires and combing the road for any clue. Her school friends were mystified as were the police. One police officer in particular was in painful distress. He was at home with his wife Alison, pacing the carpet up and down, waiting for the telephone to ring. It was their daughter who had not returned home that night.

'Harry Dynes, please,' called the senior staff nurse loudly, casting her eyes over the anxious patients gathered in the casualty reception area.

A rocking motion got Harry to his feet. His free bus pass served as a bookmark. He slammed his book shut and returned it to his gabardine coat pocket. In truth he was disappointed not to have read more of the Napoleonic war novel before being called.

He had not taken well to the tie-less collar era. His light-blue shirt sported a dark-blue tie with golfers' swings in abundance, a sporting memory already more than a decade gone in his life. Grey flannels under his coat hid the unintentional unzipped fly as his polished leather shoes shuffled towards the nurse.

'Give me your arm. Take your time, Harry,' said the nurse in her smartly pressed blue tunic.

'Hmm,' thought Harry. 'She might have just as well mentioned 'Old Boy' in her request. He smiled weakly. She knew the ropes. He didn't. Instead he absorbed this bouncy, voluminous black-haired professional with a designer white serviette balanced on her head at a rakish angle. He was out of his depth in this clinical atmosphere.

Wavy grey hair made Harry look distinguished but an occasionally sagging back categorised him more severely. Some people charitably questioned his age, but he found that irksome. It was something he could do little about. The empty booth received him. The polished linoleum floor and flat-heeled shoes enabled the black-stocking nurse to arrive behind him like a shadow.

'Doctor will see you soon, Mr Dynes,' she stated, as she stretched up to close the curtain.

Harry noticed her pinched waist, strangled by a broad black belt with an outsized silver buckle. With a twirl she disappeared, leaving him to reflect on what had brought him to Casualty.

This sterile room, clinical and lifesaving, was an unfamiliar setting. Three boxed packets of different sizes of hygiene gloves hung on the wall facing him. On the side wall, above a hospital bed, a series of wires and tubes dangled. Fortunately his treatment would not involve such paraphernalia. Then he saw a piece of white plastic, partly obscured by a bin, on the floor. Someone's aim was not true. It must have been an oversight. Identifying it puzzled Harry, but only for a moment.

'Good afternoon to you, Mr Dynes. Now what have we got here?' asked the white-coated, stethoscope-swinging Irishman, Dr Joe Hamilton.

A man of considerable height and charm, he had come to Dumfries from his troubled land and settled more than two decades ago amid the rolling sheep-splattered hills of Dumfriesshire. He loved his work and had seen every unfortunate condition imaginable needing his professional attention in A&E. His glasses rested high on a thatch of tight rusty-brown curls.

Harry raised his swollen and bent left index finger.

'Aha! A finger not looking so good. Tell me about it.'

'Well, actually, it's really rather daft,' Harry admitted to this melodic-tongued doctor.

'Oh don't worry. I've heard all sorts of mishaps I can assure you.'

'Okay, I clean my parrot's cage weekly. He watches me from the scullery floor. It's a heavy base; it has to be, of course. I saw him approach the stand when I was scrubbing it and so my eyes wandered. Then thud! Down came the base with my finger trying to hold it up. When I recovered it, it quivered, shaking as if dancing The White Heather Jig. Then I noticed I couldn't straighten it. Painful, too.'

The doctor raised Harry's fist to inspect his finger. 'You'll need an X-ray first, just to see if there is any piece of bone which may have come away. Then I will see you when you return.'

It took ten painful minutes then Harry returned with his x-ray.

Dr Hamilton dropped his glasses down from his curls and raised the X-ray to the light.

'It's what we call a mallet finger, Harry. I'm going to have to put your finger in a splint.'

Harry looked at the tray of jumbled plastic devices. An aperture at the top end exposed the fingernail and at the bottom it was cut back on the other side to enable sticking tape to hold it in position. It seemed ever so familiar. The doctor selected one and secured it around his damaged finger.

'How does that feel, Harry?'

'Yes, quite comfortable. Not too big and not too tight either. Yes, that's fine.'

'I'll apply the sticking tape then. Remember to use a short ruler or something to support the finger when washing it. That's important. Keep yer pointy finger straight at all times. And here's a roll of tape to keep you going. Now, I'll see you in two weeks' time.'

'Fine... thank you... umm... on the floor over there in the corner behind you, by the bin. Is that another splint?'

Dr Hamilton spun round in his swivel examination chair to focus on the corner.

'You are right.' He completed 360 degrees in his chair. 'That shouldn't be there. The cleaner must have overlooked it.'

'Can I have it?' asked Harry.

Dr Hamilton hesitated. He doubted if he had ever had such an unusual request before.

'It's been used, I presume. I can't return it to the tray. But why would you want a second splint, anyway? I've never seen one broken. In fact, they are indestructible.'

'Exactly,' said Harry. 'It's not for me, you see.'

'Really?' Dr Hamilton remained perplexed.

'No, it's for my parrot Kofi. He's always looking for a new toy to play with.'

Dr Hamilton smiled and shook his head. He knew he had been defeated. He hadn't seen that googly arriving.

'Here, let me wash it first. It sounds as if you and your parrot have fun. There you are, make it a present from the NHS. Now, do you need an ambulance home?'

'An ambulance? No thanks. I came by bus.'

Seated on the No. 5 bus to take him back to the town centre, Harry looked at his left index finger protruding from its new covering on his clenched fist. The index finger pointed instructions. It was authoritative. It emphasised a point: undoubtedly the most important of fingers. Then a chuckle emerged from his seat, momentarily distracting some other passengers. What message would he be giving, had it been his middle finger, damaged, erect and pointing upwards? His resultant smile stretched from one cheek to the other. He didn't mind passing pedestrians who might see him this way. He could not have been happier.

On the second bus, the No. 1 to Locharbriggs, he saw his undone fly. Gosh, who had noticed? He fumbled to close the zipped opening. The bus dropped him off at

Marchmount, on the Moffat Road. As he walked the last few hundred yards home to his detached red-brick house, he thought about putting the kettle on, sitting down with a cup of tea and relating his hospital experiences to Kofi, his African Grey Parrot of some thirty-five years. And of course, the present from the NHS would be offered. Now they would both have a splint. Just how would Kofi react to his?

Clink... cluck... thud: back home. A smattering of mail lay on the hall floor. Harry bent down, gathered the letters with the aid of his plastic digit and made his way to the kitchen to boil the kettle.

'That's me back. Be with you soon and guess what? Yes, a toy for you today, Kofi.'

That would usually warrant a reply from his caged bird. But Harry did not hear him. He filled the teapot, and opened two of his letters, recycling three others addressed 'To Whom It May Concern'. He shook his head. If they could not address him by name, he assumed it must be junk mail. One letter was a receipt for his annual subscription to his Probus Club, and the other a utilities statement which his standing order would have addressed. He poured himself a mug of Tetley tea, took a digestive biscuit from his Edinburgh Castle shortbread biscuit tin and entered the lounge to relax with Kofi.

He noticed the parrot's cage was open.

'Oh dear, yes, I must have forgotten to close it before I went to hospital,' he murmured.

'Kofi, where are you?' he asked in a high-pitched funny voice.

The silence began to disturb him. He laid down his mug of tea and went upstairs.

'Come on, Kofi. Where are you? In here? No... Ahhh, I guess in the spare bedroom? No.'

And neither was Kofi in the bathroom, where he often watched Harry shave. Harry stood still for a moment, listening for any slight movement that would betray the parrot's whereabouts. He concluded Kofi was not upstairs.

He descended with a degree of urgency. Then he noticed the inside conservatory door gaping, and his worst fears were summoned from an agitated and over-burdened mind. His throat tightened. He walked through the glass room and in horror saw that the outside conservatory doors were open, too, sufficient for the exit of a curious parrot.

Bristles like those of a nailbrush stood erect on the nape of his neck. Tears gathered in a congregation of sorrow, as his world decayed before his eyes. The consequence of the open door hit him hard. Open! Yes, open to the wide, wide world. Kofi had joined the birds in the sky.

2
When Harry met Kofi

Tema, Ghana
West Africa 1978

The Dawhenia project was a large-scale government farming enterprise in Ghana. Irrigation from the tributaries of Lake Volta created fertile land. The military dictatorship of the pugnacious General Ignatius Acheampong paid twenty-two young farmers at irregular times an inadequate fifteen cedis a week to work hard on the project. It caused poverty and left almost nothing to save or send home to their rural humble families, as the Ghanaian custom required. Operation Feed Yourself: a Government fiasco here and elsewhere. Harry visited as Secretary of the Tema Welfare Association, when he learned of their grievances.

'We've had noooo pay at all for de last two months,' said Yaw, a skinny young man with a torn T-shirt and dirt-stained trousers. He had bare feet.

The workers had downed tools as a result of their treatment and although that made the authorities aware of their plight, the military government's way to manage the situation was brutal. Soldiers arrived with batons and started to beat the young farmers, demanding to know who their leader was. The farmers refused to divulge the information and as a result bones were battered and broken, as were their spirits. Their demoralisation was plain for all to see.

'Okay, let's try to make your lives a little bit better, eh? Come and give me a hand,' Harry requested.

They helped him off-load soured kenkey dough, ripe plantain, tins of evaporated milk, several tins of sardines in tomato sauce, a bag of rice, and a hot chocolate drink called Milo. Chocolate pebbles in bags were distributed too, as a treat. Harry took the most seriously injured farmers to Tema General Hospital but not before promising to come back soon.

The Tema Welfare Association had funds for the needy, and there were many needy people in the industrial town of Tema. But the committee approved Harry's wish to help the unpaid farmers of the rural Dawhenia project on the outskirts of Tema.

During a weekly game of squash with some of the expatriate community at the Tema Beach Club, Harry learned of the Ghana Rubber Plantation in the far west of the country. It needed a regular workforce. The problem seemed to be that the plantations were in a deeply forested area far from towns where young people wished to meet. No employee seemed to last more than a week. Harry went to bed thinking about this situation.

The following morning he telephoned the managing director of the Pioneer Rubber Plant, a frosty expatriate German bachelor.

'Herr Ziegler, I can get you at least twenty-two hard-working men for you.'

'Don't tell me zat, Mr Dynes. I can't get the Ghanaians to vork for me. Zey all want the good money I can pay for a week's vork but they spend it all on drink and they don't come back the next week. You didn't know that, did you Mr Dynes?' said the second-generation German agriculturist in Ghana.

It was the talk of the villages that his father's start-up capital in the cocoa farming business was thought to have come from the proceeds of Nazi loot. He did not dissuade those who believed his father's dubious past. They retained their concerns. He had a horsewhip but no horse. He used an open blade to trim his fingernails but grew a lengthy beard. The beard was almost insignificant, lost in his huge frame, the result of his love of the Ghanaian Tata beer. He was a complex individual, a single man and one who did not suffer fools gladly.

'The men I have in mind are not like that at all. They are good agricultural workers. I know each and every one of them. Are you willing to take them on?'

'I pay ninety cedis a veek, free board and lodgings, and a cook to feed zem at night. Okay, we will see. Send them to me and you will find zem back with you in a week. I tell you. I know what I am saying.'

'I'll arrange for them to get the bus to Cape Coast on Saturday. Can you collect them from there?'

'Collect them at Cape Coast? I can collect them from Timbuktu if you vish. Of course I collect them… if they come. Don't be wasting my time though. Don't take me for a fool, Mr Dynes.'

'That's a deal then. Let me get them prepared.'

'Be careful, Mr Dynes, you are making me think you have some real farm vorkers!'

'Believe me, Herr Ziegler, I am not wasting your time,' said Harry.

Harry returned to the Dawhenia project two days later. The men sat around in the shade of a sprawling Beelzebub tree but got up when they saw Harry's car.

'Gentlemen, I have work for you. What do you say about free board and lodgings into the bargain?'

'Ehee... dat sounds good,' said one man.

Heads nodded and the man next to him, in faded torn trousers and well-worn flat sandals, smiled. The other men gathered close like tealeaves from a draining teapot.

'You will also have a cook to provide a solid meal at the end of the day,' Harry teased them.

'Even better, eh? Dis, man, means da business is coming. He be good. But do we get paid?' a voice from the rear of the group asked.

'Yes, I've kept that till last.'

'Better than the fifteen cedis a week we are meant to get here?' asked another in growing anticipation.

'It's enough to live on, enough to send home to your families, enough to save and enough to spend on a weekend, no less. Well, as long as you don't drink too much. How does that sound?'

'Too good to be true,' said another broadly smiling man, snapping the fingers of both hands in excitement.

Harry looked at them as they stared at him. He leaned forward and lowered his voice.

'Then... if I said ninety cedis a week, what would you say?'

A gasp of astonishment greeted the suggestion.

'Eh... he say ninety cedis?'

'Yea, man, ninety, he say so.'

'Well, I assure you these are the conditions. If General Acheampong wants the land to be farmed, the rubber trees to be planted, latex tapped and collected, then sent abroad to make good foreign cash, he must pay you well with no delay and pay with regularity. This is what I have secured from the Managing Director who, I warn you, is a hot-headed German.'

'We don't mind that. At least he won't beat us like the soldiers. But tell us true, you really mean ninety cedis a week?'

'It will be hard work. You will be up early, work in the cooler part of the day, and he'll make you work hard to earn your pay, but yes, I promise, ninety cedis a week it will be. He might even pay more if you stay long enough.'

'So how do we get there with no money? And even if we had some to pay the fare, when could we go?' asked Kwabena with an expression of excited anxiety.

'Don't worry. I've arranged that. This Saturday morning at 6.30 a.m. the bus will leave Kortu Gon Presbyterian Church compound in Tema's Community One. Your fare is paid. I'll be there to see you off. The bus will take you to the large coastal town of Cape Coast and you will be met at the lorry park by Herr Ziegler.'

'Cape Coast? I've never been there. Wow, I'd like to see that historic fort town,' said Kwabena.

'You should be able to see the slave fort from the lorry park. Herr Ziegler will have transport to take you to your lodgings and he will teach you the work. Good luck. I am sure you can make a good job of this. But I advise you not to tell the Government soldiers that you are leaving. If they hear, they might return,' warned Harry.

That Saturday all twenty-two men reported to the Presbyterian Church compound in Community One. At 6.45 a.m. the bus set off from Tema. An hour later, Harry telephoned Herr Ziegler.

'They are on the bus, Herr Ziegler.'

'How many?'

'Twenty-two.'

'All twenty-two? I am beginning to believe you, Mr Dynes. I hope zey will vork hard.'

'Treat them well and they'll do the work for you.'

'We will see, mein Freund, if twenty-two vill arrive at Cape Coast first,' replied Herr Ziegler.

'Let me know if they don't, won't you?' asked Harry.

Five months later, not long after his fiftieth birthday, Harry and his supportive wife Maggie were packing for the last time to return to the UK. Generous presents from colleagues and friends were packed into a heavy wooden crate of hard kaku redwood planks. They were looking forward to their voyage home after Harry's twelve years as a maths teacher and secretary of the Tema Welfare Association.

Maggie had supported him in his work and found time to run a ladies' English and accountancy class. In her Ghanaian cloth and headscarf, she threw herself into the culture of the country. She also organised a team of Ghanaian wives to make fufu and kenkey dough balls, and from the groundnut's sizzling frying pan, sweet kelewele with ginger. These fried plantain slices were sold each night in the lorry parks as workers returned home after a hard day's work in the harbour or in one of Tema's many blossoming light industries. Profits were shared amongst the wives to supplement family incomes.

A few unwelcome stowaways lay undetected in their crate. Cockroaches were devious. They, like the Dynes, awaited news of the Oti River's departure date and time. This Black Star state-owned cargo boat was docked in the port of Tema loading hardwood timber. It was a long process, making the departure date to Amsterdam uncertain.

Last-minute farewells were placed on hold. Days passed with no news of the departure date, yet knowing one might be announced at the drop of a hat – um, perhaps on reflection at the drop of a coconut from a palm tree to the beach below, which was far more common.

During this period of uncertainty Harry noticed a young man, dressed in long colourful striped trousers, a smart multi-coloured ironed shirt and a clean pair of flip-flops, approach his home. He was carrying a large covered box with extreme care. Harry opened the door, puzzled.

'Do you recognise me?' the young man asked.

Harry looked him up and down.

'Er, should I?' he said.

The young man smiled, his white teeth showing brightly against a healthy fresh young skin.

'Sir, you found me work at the Ghanaian Rubber Plantation in the western region. Do you remember?'

'Ah yes, you are Kwabena, aren't you?'

'Indeed I am, Mr Dynes, sir.'

'Come in, please, and tell me about the work.'

Kwabena entered Harry's home, oozing excitement. He stumbled, fighting to steady the box.

'Easy, Kwabena, take your time,' said Harry.

Kwabena smiled as he regained his balance. He slipped off his rubber flip-flops and entered the sitting room, bowing to Maggie who responded with a smile. He seemed almost out of breath and his eyebrows were arched as if to announce something of significant importance. But when he opened his mouth he stuttered, seemingly overcome by arriving safely here with his box.

'W-w-well... you were right about H-h-Herr Ziegler. He is strict, but an honest man.'

He placed the box on the floor as if it contained a fragile ornament.

'I mean, he is a harsh man, but a fair one too. He pays us every Friday; we have fine accommodation and a really good cook, just as you promised. We are all happy there. We send money home to our families as well, as you also said. We get time off which we never had at Dawhenia. That's why I can visit you, to tell you how much all of us farmers appreciate what you did for us.' He rubbed his hands together.

'I'm pleased to hear it has turned out well for you all. Now, twenty-two set off from Tema. Tell me how many are left?'

Kwabena laughed. 'We are twenty-seven now. Yes, twenty-seven.'

'Five extra? How come?'

'Some of us have brothers with no employment and Herr Ziegler agreed for them to join us. He felt that if one brother worked well, so would the other brother.'

'Sounds a good policy to me. So in a nutshell, it's been a good move for you all?'

'Yes, it has been.' Kwabena's demeanour changed in a flash. Gone was the smiling face and the arched eyebrows fell in anguish.

'But there is one sad thing.'

'What's that, Kwabena?'

'We heard you were leaving.'

'Yes, I'll be in London for a couple of years. Then I'm certain to return to Scotland.'

Kwabena smiled with embarrassment. He bent over and brought the box up to the table.

'We would like you to accept this small gift.'

He took off the cover to reveal a wire cage. Inside, sitting on a perch as if anxious to discover what might be in store at the end of a long journey, was a young African Grey Parrot.

Harry's mouth gaped open. Maggie frowned, as if thinking it was a most inappropriate gift as they prepared to leave the country. Harry noticed her expression. But he knew it was not polite to refuse a gift.

'You wish me to have this parrot?' he asked.

'Please. Yes, it is our present to you. We came across it in the forest last Friday. Its mother had been shot.'

'Shot?'

'Yes, hunters use bows and arrows to shoot adult

parrots for their red tail feathers. They say they're used for juju medicine.'

'Last Friday? Oh, I suppose that makes him a Kofi.'

'It does indeed. The Friday-born are always named Kofi in Ghana, as you know. And you know that a parrot often lives for eighty years?'

Maggie's attitude softened as the parrot stared at her with an air of intelligence.

'Eighty!' said Harry. 'Wow, I'll be one hundred and thirty by then!'

'I hope so,' said Kwabena, smiling. 'I hope so.'

3
Help, Get Me Out of Here

Kofi had disappeared. There was no report of either sight or sound of him anywhere. Harry searched the garden again and called his name. Instead of the usual inevitable response, silence reigned. Within his heart, Harry knew his friend of more than thirty-five years had vanished. But he would not give up hope. He still felt confident that Kofi could be found. He was, after all, unique, quite unlike any other native bird.

First he emailed the Dumfries Standard, with copies to the Annandale Herald and the Stewartry of Kirkcudbrightshire papers for good measure. Even if Kofi had not flown as far as that, people from these towns would read about his disappearance and might be alerted to a possible sighting. An attachment went with each message showing a picture of Kofi on Harry's hand as if they were in conversation on happier days. An elderly man with the loss of his sole companion: very emotional, he thought. That would surely touch local readers' hearts and lead to Kofi's capture.

The police had to be informed too.

'Good afternoon. I suppose it's a missing... um...no, a missing... missing item perhaps, that I am reporting. You see, I've lost my parrot, an African Grey Parrot. His name is Kofi.'

'A missing pet is in a category of its own, sir. When did you last see him?'

'Just before I went to hospital earlier today.'

'That's very interesting. We've had a report of a red-tailed bird flying around the Accident and Emergency Department about 5 p.m. this afternoon. Perhaps he went looking for you. Had we heard from you sooner, we could have got you to him earlier. I would head that way. I am sure he will come to your call.'

Harry's spirits were raised. His face was a picture of confident expectation. Kofi had been located.

'That's great news,' he said in relief.

'Yes, I hope so. I think you had better get around the hospital grounds before it gets dark,' said the police telephonist encouragingly.

'Don't worry, I'm on my way! Yes, wonderful news,' said Harry, replacing the hand set.

Light was fading by the minute. Harry's pace quickened as he walked around the wooded hospital grounds calling Kofi's name. As he did so, he looked up at the branches for any movement. A gentle breeze made it difficult to focus on trees as they shivered in their stateliness. Nearby patients in the mental hospital opened their windows to follow Harry's strange behaviour with increasing interest. When they heard him talk to the trees, they were somewhat amused.

When Harry called 'Kofi', they replied 'Coffee' in unison. The residents of the wards, who understood the nature of mental illness only too well, identified one of their own in the grounds and informed the staff that a bed mate must be missing. They had seen him walking in the grounds, looking up at trees and asking for coffee.

Who could this be? A quick head-check revealed no patient missing. Nevertheless, a clear case of delusion had surfaced and the man should be sectioned with absolute care if deemed necessary. The concerned charge nurse threw his lit cigarette out of the back door into a puddle and summonsed his colleague.

'Alan, go out and see what this is all about, the guy outside. There's something not quite right.'

'Okay, I'll get my jacket.'

'I'll get Dr Jamieson to prepare a detention certificate. It looks like one for us.'

Alan, a prematurely receding red-bearded folk singer and violinist, was in his twelfth year as a psychiatric nurse. He came from mid-Nithsdale where he'd grown up with his mother and drug-dependant sister. His father had committed suicide when Alan was only six years old. He'd withdrawn into himself as a young boy and turned to his violin to give him comfort and confidence. Now an accomplished player, he played fiddle at ceilidhs. He played regularly at social events throughout the year. He also indulged his patients and they never tired of his tunes. Alan, the gentlest of men.

His nonchalant, hands-in-pockets approach seemed most appropriate. He confirmed the patients' earlier reports. Indeed, this man was asking for coffee from the trees. He was much older than Alan had expected. Little force would be necessary to apprehend him.

'Are you all right, my friend?' he asked.

'Yes, thank you.' Harry registered a friendly face. 'I'm searching for Kofi. Kofi... KooooFi...'

'Which ward were you in?' asked the nurse, with his hands on his hips and a puzzled look on his brow.

Harry recalled his earlier visit to the hospital that day but wondered what relevance this could have to his search. The impertinence of the man! Nevertheless Harry felt he should respond to the searching question.

'Er... the Accident and Emergency Department, in fact,' he said. 'That's where I was this morning.'

'A & E, that's right. Come on then.'

The nurse took Harry gently by the arm. Harry was surprised and cautious.

'Where are we going?'

'Let me get you a coffee inside. It's getting dark and there's a chill in the air. I'm sure you could do with one. I'm ready for mine.'

'A coffee?' Harry smiled, regretting his initial thought about the man. He could do with a coffee and a loo break. After all, the man seemed obliging enough.

'Yes, over there. That's my office,' directed a rather relieved Alan.

'That's very kind of you indeed. Are you sure? I mean, I'm not inconveniencing you?'

'No, not at all, but it's getting late. You should be inside at this time.'

'Yes, you are right, it is getting late. I can't stay long mind you. It's getting past my bedtime,' said Harry.

A plastic mug of hot coffee was brought to him after he had returned from the loo. Soon afterwards, he was invited to take a bed in the ward.

'What! I'm not staying here. I have a home to go to,' he insisted.

'Yes of course, I know you have. But if you want to find coffee in the trees in the morning, it will be very convenient if you spend the night here, won't it?' suggested Alan.

How strange! Such consideration! Harry could not fault his reasoning. And it was certainly getting dark. An early start in the morning would be a good idea perhaps. Indeed, what an inspired invitation. After all, Kofi was an early riser too and he'd be roosting by now. Indeed, an early start. Just what Harry required.

'Yes, well, I... I suppose so. Thank you very much indeed. Do I pay for this hospitality? I've not brought my wallet, you see. It has been all so unexpected, this kind gesture.'

'Don't you worry about that, sir. It's a pleasure having you as our guest. Now, you just slip into some pyjamas. They are lying on the bottom of your bed.'

'Well, I admit I am quite tired. This is very kind of you. It has renewed my faith in humanity, I can assure you.'

Alan smiled at this elderly and ever so polite new patient.

As Harry changed into regulation blue-striped hospital pyjamas, he glanced at the row of bed mates. Hands were waving to him. He responded with a similar gesture.

'Good night, coffee,' said one, which encouraged the others; all twelve beds wished coffee a good night too.

'Good night,' said Harry thinking these were strange but friendly bed-fellows.

'Sleep well,' the nurse said, turning off the ward lights. 'The psychiatrist will see you all tomorrow morning at 8.30 a.m. sharp. Be ready for him,' he added, standing at the foot of Harry's bed.

Harry's eyes were closed, but he was not surprised that some of his ward mates would be seeing a psychiatrist in the morning.

The following morning Harry awoke and sat up in bed. The smell of bacon permeated the ward as each tray appeared at the bedsides. After a plate of bacon and a sunny-side-up egg, a mug of hot tea and buttered toast, Harry felt fine, ready to search for and be reunited with Kofi.

He had never been apart from his parrot for any significant length of time. Kofi had gone on holiday with the family in their caravan and if Harry had to be away for any reason, his wife Maggie used to tend to the bird. But Maggie had died six years ago. What would she have made of Harry's carelessness? To have left his cage open was excusable as Kofi often wandered around the house. But not to have noticed that the conservatory door and also the outside door were open was simply unforgivable. Perhaps it was age that had made Harry less observant and more careless. Perhaps his eyes were not as keen as they once were. But his mind was alert. He took some comfort in the fact many eyes would be looking out for his parrot and he knew Kofi would still be around the hospital grounds.

The night staff had crept away from the wards before Harry woke. The day shift replaced them on duty. Harry got dressed and with no familiar staff member present, he made for the door to depart and continue his search. But the door was locked. A robust burly male nurse called Pete, around forty years of age, whose designer beard was so pencil thin that Harry thought some thread had found its way to his cheeks, saw his attempt at departing.

'And where are we off to this morning?' he enquired.

Harry turned round.

'I do apologise. I am sorry. I should have thanked you for last night's accommodation.'

'Ah, so you arrived last night. That will be why I don't have your file yet.'

'I don't think I have a file, unless it's at the Accident and Emergency Department,' said Harry.

'Okay, don't you worry about that. They'll send it over before too long. We'll sort it out.'

'But I was only at A&E for my finger. Look, see!' Harry held his splinted finger aloft.

'Well, I don't know about that splint you've got on but you go back to your bed and get into your pyjamas again. Await the psychiatrist's rounds. He'll be coming soon.'

'You really don't understand, do you? I mean, I'm not mentally ill – ring A&E. They'll confirm I'm not mentally ill. Please get this sorted out.'

'That's right. You are not mentally ill. They all tell me that. Now do as I say, get back into bed,' Pete growled with a don't-argue-with-me frown.

No point in resisting a belligerent and sarcastic stance. Harry's resolve to convince the psychiatrist that it was all a grave misunderstanding seemed to be his last and best option. Then a shudder went through his spine. Perhaps the doctor might detect a distinct case of mental illness in him.

Underneath the blankets he crossed his toes and fingers. What else could he do?

The slow-moving, pre-occupied, age-wizened psychiatrist started at the other side of the ward and proceeded down the beds. Dr Clive ffrench-Blake was as complex as his surname suggested. This sixty-four-year-old medic was dedicated to his profession. Known to be a man of few words, he amazed his colleagues and patients with his rhyming couplets shared at every opportunity that came his way. He had written a dozen books of poetry. Most were of a much higher standard than his off-the-cuff offerings but this is what made him popular in the wards. He was one of a mould, crumbling away with grace and dignity.

Harry would be the last patient he would see on his rounds. Would he be too tired to listen to Harry's account? Harry took great interest in the psychiatrist's progress.

'Pop a pill again today
Another one another day.'

The toothless patient smiled as the pill went over his throat, chased by a tumbler of water.

The next patient awaited his entertaining medication.

'Green liquid, like dishwasher soap
Last resort, but don't give up hope.'

The next patient shook his head. 'No I don't give up on Hope. She's a great lass. I miss her. Ha ha haaaahaha.'

Few saw the humour in his words except Dr ffrench-Blake.

'That's my man.
Laughter gets you feeling fine;
That and a glass of claret wine.'

Pills continued to be doled out like sweets to good boys. Teaspoons of green liquid medication were given to almost all the patients, in the wake of the rhyming psychiatrist. What medication, let alone what rhyme, would await an anxious Harry? Would his anxiety itself be detected and merit such medication?

Never had nine minutes passed by with such anxious slowness.

'*Where's the patient's medical notes?*

If none exists, then let's all take votes.

Ill or not-ill that is the question without the notes...' stated the psychiatrist.

'Not arrived yet, sir. He was admitted late last night,' replied the nurse.

'*To be, or not to be, that is the question:*

Whether 'tis nobler in the mind to suffer... Mr Dynes, is it not?' The doctor looked at the name tab clipped on the rail above Harry's bed

'Yes, I'm Harry Dynes. I was invited to stay here overnight after they heard that I was looking for Kofi in the grounds of the hospital.'

'A clear case of delusion, I suggest, Doctor; that's my diagnosis. We sectioned him just before 10 p.m. last night, as he says,' said Pete, the smug, know-all bruiser of a psychiatric nurse.

The doctor gazed at Harry. Harry smiled back somewhat inanely.

'I wonder. Mr Dynes,

Tell me about your search?

I myself would look for a perch,' said the doctor with a wink.

'He's been my companion for over thirty years. I've had him since I lived in Ghana. But he escaped yesterday. I think he's looking for me as much as I am looking for him.'

'Yes, I'm sure he is,' said the doctor.

The nurse thought he had heard sarcasm in the psychiatrist's words. But his diagnosis was surely to be confirmed to his satisfaction any second now.

'So you are indeed *the* Mr. Harry Dynes?'

'Um, yes... I suppose so. I don't know any others. Yes, that's me.'

'The local radio news this morning had a piece about you and your missing parrot,' said Dr ffrench-Blake.

'Really?' said Harry

'Really?' said nurse Pete.

'Yes, really,' said the psychiatrist. 'Mr Dynes has no notes because he doesn't need any notes, nurse.'

The nurse was crestfallen.

'It's time to bid you farewell, Mr Dynes.

Your parrot awaits and I think it pines,

and good luck with your search.'

The nurse's eyes widened; he gulped and his gaze fell to the wooden floor. If only it would open up. What a blunder! A blunder that even questioned his competence to work in a psychiatric hospital. His next few weeks were lived under a cloud.

4
Two Lost Souls

John Reid had retired from the police force two years ago. Each morning after his slice of toast he swallowed his Lexapro with the last mouthful of his lukewarm Yorkshire tea. Much of the structure of his day had come apart. Gone were the regular shift patterns and in their place were bed hours, dreaming hours, and occasional spurts of energy in which he attended to the necessities of each day. Some days, the postman was his sole contact. Yet the postie was always on his way to another delivery too soon, and was too quick to engage John. Outsiders could see that all was not right. The lawn had grown to almost pencil-length height.

The local news came on air, on his kitchen-window ledge-perched digital radio. The voice seeped into the dining room where he was gathering his toast crumbs with his knife. An item caught his imagination. He rushed though to increase the volume.

An escaped parrot? Poor man. Widowed? He must be depressed too. His mind focussed on what he had heard. He poured himself another cup of tea and bit into a Cox's Orange pippin, then turned the radio off.

Leaning towards the stocky build of a light heavyweight, depression had plagued John since his retirement. Very occasional long walks helped. So too did his pride and joy on two wheels but social contact opportunities remained few. Was it his acrimonious separation or having been in the police that kept people away from him? He did not know.

But a mission in his mind occupied much of his daytime thinking and night-time dreaming. Thinking was not, however, action. Action was John's biggest hurdle. At night an ice-cube-rattling whisky enabled him to sleep. He knew it was a pernicious devouring circle. He longed to break it and find greater meaning to his life. Finding the key to his greatest conundrum had so far been damned elusive and soul-destroying.

Yet this news item caused him some creative anxiety. The engaging discomfort was real. He felt a solution might be at hand. It was the missing parrot that had initiated positive thoughts, which were emerging in a previously dormant mind.

Kofi's trail had gone cold. The police reported no more sightings. Harry kept the conservatory open all night, every night. The cage stood open with a light shining on it. But the trap was empty each morning. Kofi's fate remained as mystifying as the consequences of a magician's wand. Harry feared his parrot might find hostility for the first time in his life. A dog or cat getting the better of him, because of the naivety of this house-trained bird.

'What if he can't find food?' he pondered aloud.

Meanwhile Kofi rejoiced in the autumn season. Fruit trees abounded in gardens and the countryside had acorns and conkers aplenty. It seemed remarkable that when daily washing was placed on the line, nobody seemed to look around to see or hear Kofi. If he had been a Blue or a Scarlet Macaw, the detection rate might have improved. To confound it, Kofi would not fly from branch to branch to peck at different apples and pears like most small garden birds. He would demolish the whole fruit, core as well, sitting camouflaged on one branch. No large avian evidence could be traced to him from any garden.

One Saturday morning, while Harry was washing his breakfast dishes, enjoying the warm soapy studs, he received a telephone call. He dried his hands insufficiently to prevent losing the call.

'Hello.'

'Morning, Mr Dynes. I'm John Reid. Hello. We have nay met but I think we should. I'm retired. It was in ma last four years with the police, they made me the wildlife officer. I'd like to help ye find yer parrot, so a would.'

'Really? Just when I was thinking of giving up. That's very kind of you. In fact, I was feeling I couldn't do it all myself. I've run out of ideas. What a pleasant surprise coming out of the blue.'

John laughed. 'Did you mean that? Me a retired policemen, right out of the blue eh?'

'Oh I see. Um... it wasn't intentional,' Harry smiled.

'Maybe so, but it was funny tae me. I've no laughed as much for some time.'

'That's strange. I'm not very good at jokes. Well, anyway, perhaps we could talk about what to do next. As I say, I'm at a loss. Do you know where I live?'

'Aye, I ken. I could be roond this afternoon aboot three? How does that suit you?'

'That suits me fine. Er, sorry... what's your name again?'

'It's John, John Reid, so it is.'

'Till later then John. Looking forward to meeting you.'

John felt good. Harry seemed a down-to-earth likeable sort of soul.

A rumbling announced his arrival that afternoon. John steered up to Harry's front door and parked his sleek MV Butane 800. He dragged his leg over his machine. He removed his helmet and gloves and extended his beefy hand to greet Harry.

'That's a fine mean machine you've got there,' said Harry.

'Aye, ma pride and joy, so it is.'

'Come away in. How about some tea?'

'Just fine. Can you manage?'

'I've got to do everything myself now. Just takes a little longer.'

'I'm in the same boat. Separated last year, so I was,' said John.

'Retired too, you said?'

'Aye.'

'We've got a lot in common,' Harry suggested, despite the obvious age difference.

'Aye, in a way, that's why I wanted tae see you,' said John.

'Milk and sugar?'

'Jist milk, please. You keep a very tidy house.'

'You gave me a couple of hours to get it ready.'

John saw a vase on the window-sill.

'They flooers… fae your garden?'

'Yes, just a few to brighten the room. More show than scent at this time of the year.'

'True.'

John noticed a photo of Harry with two young women on either side of him.

'They your girls in the picture frame?'

'My daughters, yes. Fiona and Laura.'

'Live locally? Can they keep an eye on you?'

'Not practical. Fiona is in Edinburgh, a procurator fiscal. She comes down some weekends. The other one is in Birmingham, a clinical psychologist. Don't see her quite as much, as you can imagine.'

'And her name again?'

'That's Laura in Birmingham. She's the younger daughter. Quite an athlete she is, still playing netball at her age.'

'And how old is she?'

'Laura's two year younger than Fiona. She's thirty-eight.'

'Ah yes, very nice to have two good-lookin' bright girls. It must be great, having daughters,' said John.

He studied Fiona. She was slim with a generous smile on a face showing two deep dimples. Round her neck on a chain were her glasses, taken off for the photo presumably. She looked studious in spite of her smile. Clearly a clever lass. John knew all about submitting reports to the procurator fiscal in days gone by, of young girls with a less solid background, though many were just as pretty.

He moved his head slightly to the right and focussed on Laura. At first he did not see the two-year age gap between Harry's girls. Laura was more robust with a healthy complexion. She had blonde hair and from her ears dangled a chain with a green stone at its end. On her chest rested a chain too, with a locket swinging in her cleavage. A clinical psychologist, thought John. Perhaps that was what he needed to bump-start his lethargy.

Harry brought through mugs, milk, and a plate of ginger nuts along with the teapot.

'Hey, can you manage all that?'

'No problem. Years of practice,' replied Harry.

He stooped to place the tray on a low coffee table.

'I'll let it brew for a moment. So tell me, how did this kind offer of help come about?

'Well, I heard aboot you on local radio, like. That got me thinking, ye ken. Ye see I joined the police service as a cadet at sixteen. It was either that or work for the Forestry Commission, you know. I love the outdoors, like. So I combined the two and jumped at the chance to be the force's wildlife officer when the opportunity came a few years ago.'

'So you were not always the wildlife copper.'

'No, a street cop for most of the time but in the last five years they sure needed a rural cop to deal with everything in the countryside that wis happening.'

'Yes, I think I remember you on street duty. I guess that's why you have a good tan,' said Harry.

'Good tan? Naw, a weathered face. Can ye no tell the difference?'

'No, not these days. Eyes not as keen. Anyway it sounds an idyllic position,' said Harry.

'It was not all fair sailing. You have no idea how cruel some folk can be.'

'In the country, you mean?'

'Aye, animals trapped in vicious clamps, egg theft, poisoning of game and birds, and of course farm theft of livestock and farm equipment. Rural life is as complicated as city life at times. But there were more pleasant duties. Like arranging pet cover when an elderly person finds himself or herself in hospital, or retrieving cats fae roof ledges...'

'Don't fire officers do that?' asked Harry, engrossed in John's past work.

'Och aye... you might think so but when they git the cat down, who do they pass it to? You got it, the wildlife officer. Onyway it was a job I did for forty years and I retired two years ago, so I did. Time is my own but when I read aboot your plight I thought to myself, well, I thought, I ken all the wildlife officers in the country. We attended courses and such like, you see. I'll let them know your parrot is on the run as it were and I'll get some o' their reports in due course if it flies their way. Even although I'm retired, it is probably the best way noo to find yir parrot.'

'You are a godsend, John. That's very good of you. It sounds a great plan. And you're right. Kofi may have flown out of the region by now. So we sit back and await developments, I suppose?'

'Hmmm... we could, but that's no the way I see it, Harry.'

Harry poured the tea. John stirred his drink as if holding a porridge spindle.

Harry lifted his mug to his lips.

'So how do you see it, John?'

'Have you ever ridden a motorbike?'

'Like the one outside?'

'Yeah.'

'No. Only a pushbike when I was young.'

'Then you have a treat in store, Mr Dynes. But not today. We should have a few trial runs to get you in the mood. It's quite addictive, this motor bike riding thing, so it is.'

That this man meant business was clear to Harry. Riding a motorbike at his age might not be a good idea but John had been a policemen; he should be as safe as houses on the roads.

An hour passed as they talked about the countryside, motorbike intricacies, and how Harry had found his parrot missing, as well as how he had first been given him all those years ago. They agreed the next step was a trial bike run but that was for another day, a fair weather day to begin with, at least.

John revved up his bike as he left Harry's home. He stopped at the top of the drive to gauge the flow of traffic. A petite woman with a spring in her step approached from his right. He concentrated on the steady flow of traffic and was not particularly observant. He decided to let her pass by before joining the traffic. He backed off with instinctive courtesy.

'Hello, John,' she said.

John hesitated. A shiver went through his encased body. He raised his mask to his recently separated wife, who stood before him.

'Hello, Alison. How's yer mother?'

'Looking after me well,' she replied.

'Good.'

'And you, you seem to be managing to look after yourself better, getting out and about.'

'Aye, I take the medicine and I'm coping well.'

The conversation was hesitant and their eyes rarely met.

'Where have you come from?' she asked, looking down the residential drive.

'Well, if ye must know, I presume you've heard aboot that elderly man who lost his parrot?

'Yes, in the local paper. I have, yes.'

'Well, wi ma former wildlife officer's hat on, I'm giving him a hand.'

Alison smiled. This was evidence of John getting his life together again which pleased her immensely.

'That's good. I'm pleased to hear that, John.'

John lingered on her smile and the woman he still wished to love, if only she would return home. Separation was not divorce. One was final; the other left the door open. It seemed the door was just a little further open at that moment.

'But I hope you have not told him about Morag. A man of that age would not be able to cope with that sort of stress, especially as I couldn't,' she said.

'Don't go there Alison. No, I honestly haven't mentioned Morag to him,' said John.

'That's a relief. It's good to see you taking a wider interest in life, John.' Her smile revealed the dimple, which he loved so much.

'No, I haven't told him about Morag... yet, but I'll have to tell him soon, so I wull.'

'Why for heaven's sake? Why can't you leave it alone? Come to terms with Morag's death and move on, John? You've got to move on...'

'Just one last chance. What I'm thinking is touring with Harry an' dropping off leaflets, that's all.'

'About the parrot?'

'Aye, aboot Kofi the parrot... and Morag too.'

Alison's eyes tightened. Her heartbeat quickened. Her vitriolic outburst would extinguish any glimmer of reunification, there and then.

'That's it. You are impossible, John. You are obsessed. Christ, why did I ever marry you? Obsessive? You should seek help, John, real psychological help. Don't try and help others, it's not fair on them,' she said with venom. 'Sort yourself out first, for God's sake.'

She strutted past the motorbike, staring straight ahead. John snapped down his visor, and revved up the bike in anger four times before making his departure in the opposite direction.

5
Dirs Gold in Dem Hills

Anthony Dickson, known with malice at school as Tony Dickhead, was thought to be the last of around eight or possibly ten children. Rumours circulated that when his mother was a teenager, she had two children taken from her at birth and later fostered. Adoption followed when no hope of reconciliation was deemed possible by social workers at that time. Tony, being the youngest, lived with his mother and three sisters in a 1759 stone cottage in the second highest Scottish village at Wanlockhead. A brother and two half brothers sat incarcerated. In Saughton Prison in Edinburgh, Billy Dickson had recently lost his appeal and was now serving twenty-one years for the murders of a couple of vagrants who owed him money. Eddie's abode in Barlinnie Prison in Glasgow was where he was wasting his life serving twelve years for multiple housebreaking offences to feed his heroin and cocaine addictions, not to mention his alcohol abuse. 'Fearless Frankie' Dickson meanwhile festered in Dumfries Prison for Social Security fraud, as well as driving without a licence and insurance, theft of a Honda Civic, speeding at 84 mph on the M74, and a couple of breaches of the peace.

This chaotic trouble nonetheless brought some peace to Tony's mother, Ella, as she tried to make ends meet on social security and to bring some semblance of an ordered life into her thick-walled stone cottage, now bereft of the delinquents.

Tony walked to and from his home at Wanlockhead to his primary school at Sanquhar every day, twice a day. Two reasons for this emanated from his mother's latent maturing outlook on life. Ella was fifty-eight but looked almost seventy. Grey unkempt hair fell down her back. Her bathroom was starved of cleansing plastic shampoo bottles. Her locks resorted less to baths and more to encounters with *forest rain* au natural. She had few joys in her life, beyond the occasional bottle of sweet stout. The destructive days of Buckfast at the age of ten, of wine at fifteen and spirits at eighteen, which had resulted in a chaotic and often violent past, no longer prevailed. Yet villagers showed her kindness in pots of seasonal jam and made sporadic visits to drop in second-hand clothes. Ella had little to be proud of in her home other than the fact it was built in the year Robert Burns was born just up the road in Ayrshire, meaning that he must have passed by on his way to Dumfries. It was also rumoured that the Bard had spent a night in the cottage but that was loose-tongued talk, that could never be proved beyond doubt.

The one glimmer of hope she held dear was her daughter, Helen. She had taken on the responsibilities for the younger members as much as her mother had, during her child-bearing years, and this had given her a habit of responsibility. She had been the brightest of the family at primary school and had done well at Sanquhar Academy where she had fallen in love with Willie Craig.

Two years ago Willie and Helen married, and they were determined to break the rotten mould that had festered in and surrounded Helen's home in her early years. Coal merchant Willie took on his deceased father's business and he was also a retained fire-fighter. His sturdy frame, supporting a leather brass-studded waistcoat all day, transformed into a buttoned woollen cardigan at night. His snug slippered feet crossed before the roaring fire as he lay back in his armchair. He earned that comfort after washing the evening dishes and providing a goodnight kiss to Helen without fail.

Tony came to that home in Sanquhar each day after school to have his tea and his homework supervised by Helen. Then on warmer days, between April and October, he returned home to Wanlockhead, several miles away, on foot.

Ella had matured to a satisfactory degree at last, albeit better late than never. Her excessive drinking days were not only curbed but practically gone, save for that stout which provided the necessary vitamin B her body seemed to require. She knew that Tony would be her last child, the child she might rely on when old age came to haunt her. She was determined he would not follow his brothers and half brothers into a life of crime and Helen was the key to that realisation.

Kofi enjoyed the freedom his flights gave him. Everything seemed so new. He saw people scurry about in the town but saw fewer further out in the suburbs. Rich pickings of autumn were available in great supply. He marvelled about the generosity of garden owners, but felt he was unable to thank them sufficiently with a vocal performance for the apples and kale, pears and plums. Little did he know that inside their homes, people were reading for the first time about his escape.

Kofi followed the River Nith as it wound its way north through rich farming fields. A barn at Dalswinton hosted him the first night. A few cows were in the byre but they paid scant attention to him. He found the aroma of the byre not too appealing so the next morning, even before commuters filled the roads, he flew north again. Taking a rest, he waddled along the banks of the Nith stopping to drink from the fast-flowing, salmon-leaping, trout-guddling noisy river.

As Kofi threw back his head to gulp down some fresh water, he became aware of a flash of reddish brown, like an autumn leaf swept along in a breeze. It came from nowhere but two angry sharp jaws snapped at his plumage in anger. Kofi flew out over the water, instinctively making the sound of a police car, but he could not gain much height. A fox had sized three of his primary wings. He turned to see his assailant. The fox squatted on the pebble shoreline licking the blood that came from the base of each feather. Cover in the wild was risky. That night Kofi had to seek a more open spot and one out of reach of these wild nasty dogs.

The attack had frightened him. He would never let his guard down again in the open. The lost feathers did not pain him but a greater effort was needed to keep a steady course of flight. When he got to a quiet spot with a few lone trees, he decided he must seek cover and recuperate.

At six o'clock Tony Dickson walked home on the verge of the B797. His school clothes had been passed down the line and his shoes, too. They were not in good repair. The left shoe sole in particular flapped like a yacht's pennant in the wind with each step. He had to take off his shoes. In bare feet he continued up the road.

Three miles into the glen, two large areas of grass straddled the road. Here, Ayrshire families came in the summer months with their tents. Children played in the burn and dragged their nets through the water. Minnows and trout fry ended up in jam jars. Few ever made it back home. Those that did were soon given a naval burial down the loo. But families came back year after year and exaggerated stories filled the classrooms in the autumn terms. While some children spoke of their holiday in Cannes where they saw famous celebrities and monokinied beach walkers, others recalled Lanzarotti where the paella plate was enormous, crawling with luscious crustaceans. But for the holidaymakers at the foothills of Leadhills the stories were about late-night star gazing; fishing for arm-length salmon, and singing at night by smoky campfires lit to deter the famous Scottish midges.

It was on a tree near this pastoral spot that Kofi preened his remaining feathers and rested in safety.

Clop, clop clop. Tony approached with his shoes on again. He sat down on the bank of the river and removed his shoes once more. He lowered his heel into the cool rushing water and felt his blistered heel's searing pain ease. Kofi saw the difficulty and pain he was in.

Tony began to sob. He had still four miles to walk. It would soon be dark and he felt as miserable as a soggy scone.

Kofi had not understood the fox. He'd had dogs occasionally visit his home. Harry would stroke them. They held no fear, yet this dog had caused him pain. Animals were unpredictable, he concluded. He was also missing the care and interest human companionship offered him, and young Tony did not look like a threat.

Kofi flew down on to the bank opposite Tony.

'Hello, hello, helloo,' he said.

Tony looked up to see the African Grey Parrot.

'Hello!' he replied. A wide smile came over his face. He was no longer alone.

'I'm Tony. I'm Tony,' he said.

'I'm Kofi, I'm Kofi.'

'Hello, Kofi.

Kofi felt confident enough to greet Tony so he flew down beside him. Tony offered his hand. Kofi accepted and climbed up his arm.

'Can you be my friend? Eh? Will you?'

Kofi cocked his ear. Tony stroked his head and Kofi gave reassuring murmurs. Then Tony caressed his back. When his hand stroked his raw wing, it hurt. Kofi let out a screech and flew to the bank again.

'Sorry, Kofi, I didn't mean to hurt you. Come back, Kofi.'

But Kofi did not return that day. He returned to the lone tree and slept the night.

The next day as Tony was going to school he passed by and Kofi gave a loud police-car siren sound. Tony was relieved that it was not a real police car and he waved to Kofi.

'Can we still be friends, Kofi, eh? I didn't mean to frighten or hurt you yesterday.' Kofi heard but kept silent. He reflected on the tone of Tony's words.

Tony had not had the papers to read in his home and the search for this parrot had not entered his mind. He continued to wave as he passed by. The school bell would soon be rung in Sanquhar.

During the day, Kofi investigated the stream of the Crawick water. He waddled upstream out of sight from the road. He came across very tough quartz stones in the banks on one side and peat on the other side. The sun shone on the stone. Then Kofi's eye saw a glint of a bright yellow shining stone. He investigated further.

It was shining just beneath the water. But this shining was securely welded in the quartz. Kofi began attacking it with his powerful beak, using it like a pneumatic drill. The glitter made his efforts stronger and he knew that with each day with no flight his damaged wing would repair, while he set to work. Every now and then he stopped to look around. Such a desolate place, he thought, and recalled it as being a somewhat similarly quiet environment from which the fox had appeared. He knew a second time he might not be so lucky to escape, or even survive.

Once more after school and a good meal, with homework completed, Tony set out for home carrying his plastic Tesco school bag.

He had a spring in his step for he had told no one of his meeting with Kofi. The encounter was his secret. No one would have believed him anyway. As the evening shadows

grew longer Tony arrived at the spot he had last seen Kofi.
He sat down.

'Kofi, Kofi... where are you?'

Kofi popped his head up from the bank of the river one
hundred yards further up.

'Hello Tony... hello Tony.'

Tony ran to be near Kofi. He sat down near him,
swinging his legs over the bank.

'What have you been doing all day? Anything?' he
asked.

Kofi returned to the stream. Then, grabbing the stone
he had worked on all day and finally released, he dropped it
in front of Tony.

'What's this, Kofi?'

Kofi walked up to it and pecked at the stone. It fell over,
revealing a nugget of gold. Tony knew from local folktales
and their occasional findings what it was. This was one of
the first gold-rush rivers in the UK and every now and then a
prospector came up with a tiny piece of gold. But this piece
was the size of a bean – a butter bean, no less.

'Wow, you have made me rich, Kofi! Yeah, you are
wonderful, my friend.'

Tony placed the precious gem in his pocket, said
his farewell to Kofi and ran all the way home, despite the
increasing pain in his feet. He was out of breath when he
reached home.

'Mum... Mum... you'll never...'

'Take your time, Tony. Get yer breath back an' sit doon.
Noo, whit's this a' aboot?'

Tony had still to catch his breath. He took his
handkerchief from his pocket and gave it to his mother.

'Av tae wash it, yeah, yer hanky?'

'No Mum.'

Ella uncovered the stone and screwed up her face. What
a way to get worked up over a stone, she thought.

'Turn it over Mum,' said Tony.

Ella did.

'Oh ma Gaud. Whit's this? Where did ye get it?'

'Down by the Crawick water.'

'Hiv you been there a' day. Truanting? Yer no too auld tae get a beatin' if ye have ma lad,' she said with menace in her eyes.

'Naw, it was a bird that gave it to me Mum, honest, so it wiz.'

'Come on, tell the truth. If ye stole it let me know noo. I'm no goin' tae be made a fool o'.'

'No, honest Ma. It was a bird that gave it to me. A parrot. Honest Mum, I'm tellin' you the truth. It wis a parrot.'

'A parrot? Hard tae believe. But if it's true whit yer tellin' me, I'll tak' it tae the Bank tomorrow an' see what they say. You sure I'm no goin' tae be made a fool?'

'No, Mum. That's how I got it, just as I said, honest a parrot gave it to me, cross ma heart.'

Kofi's secondary wings were beginning to grow in again and that gave him some confidence but he liked where he was. He'd stay another few days in this bleak spot where he was unknown, except by one schoolboy, Tony.

Ella Dickson set off to make an appointment to see the TSB Bank Manager in Sanquhar the very next morning.

Mr Bannerman came from a long line of bankers. He was a Glasgow Academical who started banking in the same city. He had been earmarked for greater things within the financial world but some speculative dealing came unstuck and in the tradition of sexually promiscuous Roman Catholic priests, he was sent away to the Ayrshire Styx. His wife followed him to Sanquhar but she found few friends in the town to her liking and so they moved to the coast at Troon from where he travelled every morning. Such a move was resented by his customers as they felt he was not making efforts to be one of their kind. But he was oblivious to their private thoughts. He saw himself as a lynchpin in the town. His attire was not usual, however. His selection of business suits ranged from pin-striped black to pin-striped navy blue; his black shoes were always polished until he could see his self-satisfied smile of community prominence in each toe-cap. A gold ring on his finger, a gold watch on his wrist: and when he smiled, a row of gold fillings flashed. He liked gold and knew its value.

He had a lazy eye, which seemed to linger in conversation. It made ladies uncomfortable at times. He had arrived eight years ago with jet-black hair. Now it was grey and at the rear of his head; baldness was on the move forward.

The Manager was advised that Mrs Dickson was in the bank. He would be expecting a formal request for a loan in all likelihood and he would almost certainly not be going out of his way to give a loan to any one of the Dickson family. His discretionary powers had a baseline and the Dicksons fell short of it by some considerable distance.

'Guid morning,' Mr Bannerman,' began Mrs Dickson in a nervous manner.

'Good morning, Mrs Dickson. What can I do for you this morning?' he replied, dealing with her professionally and with dignity, but nonetheless his conversation with her retained an atmosphere of rigid disapproval.

'Well, it's this.' She handed over the stone wrapped in an old newspaper.

Never had a client appeared before him with a newspaper-wrapped stone. He wondered if a threat might materialise.

'And may I inquire what this is, if not a stone?'

'My son Anthony brought it home yesterday.'

Mr Bannerman lifted the stone. He turned it around in his hand. Then he saw it shine.

'I see… if this is… a gold nugget…' he began.

'Aye, it is. Does it need tae be insured or will the Bank do that fur me?'

'What the Bank can do is have this stone valued first. We have to see what we are dealing with, you realise?'

'Aye, of course. So you can put it in a safe till we ken its price. Then can I sell it?'

'It may have to be auctioned or the State may claim it. I'll have to make investigations and these will take time.'

'Aw'right. So I'll leave it wi' ye jist noo. It wull be in safe hands here I think, naw?'

'That would be the best solution. I assure you, I'll take great care of it, indeed Mrs Dickson.'

As Ella left the bank, Bannerman opened the office windows to air the room. There was perhaps not such a need to do so today but whenever he had dealt with the other members of the family in the past, this ritual was observed and deemed most necessary.

Ella called into Helen's home to share the happy news. When Tony arrived later that afternoon he was delighted the bank now had his stone and it would be valued. That would be sure to make his mother feel so much happier and even more prosperous.

The coal truck was loaded and ready to head up to the hills. Tony and his mother joined Willie in the front and they set off in a laboured second gear up the narrow, twisty road to Wanlockhead. Sheep on the road made the lorry stall three times on the way up the glen. Tony strained to see Kofi at his usual spot but he was not there.

The following evening a police car came up to the village. Eyes peered from the cracks of curtains but were not surprised that it was heading for the Dickson household.

Constable Simon Morrow and Sergeant Steven Pinker had been to the Dickson home many times before but never to see Tony.

They parked outside the cottage. Morrow took off his hat before entering and lowered his head more than a foot and a half. He was six feet seven inches tall. But as height was no longer a requirement he had been paired with Sergeant Pinker who was five feet five (and allegedly a half) inches. Morrow was a long-legged, fair-haired cop with a recent bruise under his right eye.

Pinker, the elder of the two, had a limp from a bad-tempered five-a-side match at police headquarters the previous week, and glasses which looked like Nana Mouskouri was missing hers. He was nearing his thirty years' retirement and over the years had made it his work to ensure there were fewer and fewer Dicksons in this historic auld sleepy village.

'Mr Bannerman, the bank Manager at the TSB, tells us he has a significant quantity of gold held on your behalf, Mrs Dickson. Is that right?' asked Pinker.

'Oan my behalf, aye. He's gonna value it fae me.'

'And how did you come by the gold?'

Meanwhile Sergeant Morrow looked around the room.

'Mind if I go upstairs Ella? Just for a wee look?'

'Aye, mind the ladder, it's no sturdy, an' there's nae drugs so dinnae send that spaniel o' yours up again,' she replied.

'The gold? Just how did it come into your possession, Ella?' persisted sergeant Pinker.

'Tony brought it to me. He foond it oan his way hame fae school the aither day.'

'And how did he come across it? Bought it with his pocket money, did he?'

'Less o' yer cheek. I niver got ony pocket money as a kid and neither daes he,' she growled.

'So how did Tony get the gold? Will I ask him myself?'

'Ye can an' he'll say the same as he telt me. It was one o' they, ye ken, parrots that gied it tae him. That's whit he telt me and make nae mistake Tony is nae like ony o' the aithers. '

'Come on, Ella, we're no takin that as yer answer. One last time, who gave Tony the gold?'

'If he's lying tae me, I'll skelp his bum till it's raw red. I'm no havin' him turn oot the way o' the aithers.'

'So where's Tony the now?'

'He's roond at his freend's hoose.'

'And who's that?' asked Morrow.

'Billy Naismith.'

Sergeant Morrow took his mobile phone from his tunic pocket. He didn't need to search his contacts for long. The Naismith number was already stored and appeared promptly. He dialled.

'Is Tony there? It's Sergeant Morrow. Tell him tae come home, noo. Got it...? No, no, I'm no tellin you whit it's aboot. None o' yer business. Jist send the kid hame noo.'

Three minutes later Tony came through the door. He had no idea that he had done wrong until he saw the wrath in his mother's eyes.

'So young man, where did ye get the gold?' asked Sergeant Morrow.

'The parrot gave me it,' Tony replied with his honest face on show.

'Well, we're no believing this story of yours and you'll have tae come up with a better reply. We can wait till we hear whose hoose has been broken intae. We'll soon hear. Perhaps it would help if you took Mrs Dickson outside for a minute, Constable Pinker.'

'Make it quick then. I'm no havin the neebors talkin,' said Ella.

The front door closed with a thud.

'Now, Tony. Yer a young boy about tae grow into a big man. Ye dinnae want tae land up in the jail like the rest o' yer brothers now do you? Eh. Do you?'

'No, I don't.'

'Eddie's still inside for hoose breakin'. Yer family are experts daen that. Thank God you're the last in line till the next generation comes along – an' that won't be long, I'm sure,' he said.

'I'm not like them,' said Tony with pleading eyes.

'Stop wastin' oor time, laddie. Jist tell us the truth and that'll be the end o' the matter. Noo think aboot what I've just said. Okay? So, how did you get the gold? Whose hoose did ye get it fae?'

Tony could not see how he had committed any offence. He had told the truth. He must continue to do so.

'Honest, no kiddin', I did get the gold from the parrot.'

Sergeant Morrow called in his mother and Constable Pinker.

'He's still sayin' a parrot gave him the nugget. Sorry, lad, I'm havin' to charge you with a theft by finding. Of course it'll be a theft of housebreaking as soon as we have the evidence. Do you understand what I am saying, Tony?'

'Aye but I didn't steal.' Tony looked at his mother for support but it was not forthcoming.

'Get tae bed the noo. I'll speak tae ye later.'

'Noo, Ella don't be laying a hand on him or you'll get charged,' said Constable Pinker.

'Leave the discipline tae me. I can handle him. Tell me, what will happen next then?' asked Ella.

'We'll send a report to the Children's Reporter who will decide whether to have a children's hearing or not. Possibly not, it's his first offence after all and that's a record of sorts for this family.'

Ella's eyes stared at the stone floor. Yet another chapter of crime seemed to have begun in her household.

Harry kept near the telephone. Although it rang, it conveyed concern and support from many of Harry's friends. It was a surprise that there had been no further sightings of Kofi to date.

Meanwhile Kofi's recuperation was continuing. His new feathers were growing, giving him an opportunity to find new pastures, but he was content in the Mennock valley for the time being. He enjoyed the safety of the tree he spent the night on. It was at a height no fox could approach.

A children's hearing was arranged a few days later by the very short-skirted blonde reporter, Delna Gibb. She had been a reporter for four years since her LL.B graduation at Stirling University. The care and protection of children was her remit and she had satisfied herself that there was sufficiency of evidence to have the three-panel members consider the case. She sighed, realising it was another Dickson family member referred. She wondered if this was the next generation or the last of the rotten current generation of offending Dicksons. They met at their offices in Castle Street, Dumfries. There were two women and a man as panel members, Miss Gibb and Larry Godwell, social worker, in attendance, to meet mother and son. Both women panel members wore twin-suit pieces, one in an autumnal brown and the other in dark blue with a bed of pearls bobbling around her heavy bosom. The male panel member arrived in a white coat, which he took off before the hearing started. He was a pharmacist and an evangelical Christian. He had a caring heart, seeing the best in everyone no matter what grounds were laid before each child or parent. After introductions were made, the chairman read out the ground for referral. At each point they asked both Tony and his mother to respond intimating their understanding and their agreement or denial of the charge. They had no difficulty in accepting this was indeed Anthony Dickson and he did live at the said cottage in Wanlockhead. Thereafter there were denials from Tony and his mother. He did not steal the gold. Theft by finding was denied in no uncertain terms.

By a majority decision, the panel instructed the Reporter to remit the case to the Sheriff court for determination. Miss Gibb explained that this was *sui generis* meaning that children's cases were set apart from the general running mayhem of a typical Sheriff court. The press would not be able to attend and if the Sheriff found there was a case to answer, he must send the case back to the children's hearings for their consideration and conclusion of the case.

'Do we get reimbursed for comin a' this way for a two minute hearin'?'

'Yes, of course, Mrs Dickson, your travel expenses and some extra for you to have a meal before you return will be given to you in a moment.' said Miss Gibb, uncrossing her shapely legs.

Three days before the Sheriff Court case for Tony, Mr Ernest Wetherstone, a retired surgeon from Truro, arrived in Nithsdale to observe and record some ornithology, indulging in his favourite hobby. He had already had a week in Northumbria capturing puffins and cormorants at Lindisfarne on his lens as well as well-fed fearless seals. He came armed with binoculars for close range and a larger pair for longer distances. His camera had a sizable zoom lens and was housed in a square bag secured across his right shoulder along with filters and other photographic paraphernalia.

A gnarled varnished walking stick of character with National Trust visitor stickers down the shaft was in his left hand. And in a leather case, he had a telescope to find the high mountain birds of prey.

A knapsack was strung across his right shoulder for his sandwiches of smoked salmon and cucumber, as well as an apple, orange, and a flask of Twining's English Breakfast Tea which he drank morning, noon and night. With his brand-new four-by-fours in mottled green tweed he wore a matching deer-stalker hat purchased from the nearby Drumlanrig Estate shop two days ago.

And then he sank into a wooded copse and descended to make himself comfortable. So he waited, waited, waited and waited to see what fauna this landscape would provide.

That morning Kofi exercised his wing. He flew up the valley and then down to where he had originally mined the gold. In doing so he had weakened the seam. The stream had all day to wash around the bank of Kofi's site of excavation. A smaller nugget began to appear in the quartz gravel lurking in a pool of cold water. Kofi immersed his head and his beak over the bright nugget and waited for Tony to return to give him another shining present. After a few beak excavator-like gouging manoeuvres, Kofi took the precious metal to his tree. There he saw some movement.

Mr Ernest Wetherstone poured some tea from his flask into his dark-olive plastic mug. Then he munched into his Granny Smith apple. His biodegradable apple core was chucked into the foliage behind him. Kofi saw his opportunity to acquire some vitamin C. He flew down as Ernest's video camera took aim.

'My goodness gracious me. Good Lord, an African Grey Parrot! It must have escaped from somewhere. Must get a closer shot,' he thought.

But before taking the remains of the fruit, Kofi dropped his small gold nugget. Ernest looked as the dropped stone rolled to a stop. He picked it up. He knew this part of the world had been the interest of pan-swishing prospectors in the past and so he soon came to a conclusion that he had discovered a small nugget of gold. He was excited. He carefully deposited it in the waistcoat pocket he wore. The retired consultant had no idea an African Grey Parrot was loose in the area and he had no one to tell of this experience. So he continued to spend a further day in the area taking recordings of bird song as well as pictures of red kites, rooks and ravens, black-tailed godwits, long-eared owls and, to his delight, one capercaille.

At the end of his ornithological expedition he spent his last night at the Cairndale Hotel in Dumfries. There he glanced at a local paper to discover an African Grey Parrot was indeed on the loose. He had taken a video of the parrot and he mentioned this visual recording to the hotel bar staff. They asked to see it and he showed them. It was suggested to him, before he left the following day on his long train journey south, he should go to the offices of the Dumfries Standard with his video. They had been running the story of the missing Dumfries parrot until it began to fade over the past few days. The newspaper prepared their Friday edition with enthusiasm.

On Friday, Mrs Ella Dickson accompanied her son to the Sheriff's court in Dumfries. There they met Miss Gibb, dressed in a light-green suit and a blouse with a rather low-cut front. She tottered along in very high black stiletto heels. She led the family into a quiet small waiting room and informed them that the Sheriff would hear the case in chambers, meaning he would conduct proceedings in his court office. Then she left to ensure her two police officers were present to lead their evidence.

At 10.15 a.m. the Sheriff's clerk requested that the family enter the chamber. Sitting behind his oak table was Sheriff Ross Barr QC. He had a reputation of being fair to the accused but fairer to the victims. This lean sporty father of four had spent the hour before the case sipping a warm comforting latte provided by his court secretary, as she did every morning at this hour. The coffee sharpened his wits, he always said. However, as it was Friday, the local Dumfries Standard was out, and it was on his desk as he sipped.

'Please have a seat, everyone,' he said. 'Now Tony, come forward. Tell me about this parrot. Where did you see him?'

'I saw him as I walked home,' Tony said.

'Was there anyone else with you?'

'No, no one.'

'So this is a case of your word against the police, Tony. Well, Miss Gibb I don't think you have lost many cases over the years, have you?'

'I've never lost one case because if I don't think there is enough evidence, or the balance of probability fails, I don't take the case to a children's hearing in the first place,' said Miss Gibb, a little rattled.

'Perhaps the family's reputation clouded your judgement?' asked the wise Sheriff.

'I would doubt that. In fact it did not enter my mind at all,' said Miss Gibb, wondering if the Sheriff did actually have a point, which she had forgotten.

The learned Sheriff produced the Standard and thrust the front page towards her.

'Read on please and when you have finished give it to your police witnesses.'

Miss Gibb folded the paper and read the news.

Tony and Mrs Dickson listened with great attention to the direction the Sheriff had taken the case. But they had no idea why the local paper was connected to Tony's case. And anyway Ella could not read.

'An ornithologist, that's someone who has an interest in bird life, took a video of an African Grey Parrot giving him a gold nugget. It was smaller than your gem, Tony. What I am saying is I believe your story. I believe it was an African Grey Parrot, as you said. I have read about this missing parrot in today's Standard and I am sure you have come across him on your way home from school. The locus was not far from your home: I mean, the place where the parrot was seen. This will please a rather elderly gentleman. The bird's name is indeed Kofi. I believe Kofi did give the gold to you as he did to Mr Ernest Wetherstone, therefore there is no case for you to answer, Tony. The case is dismissed,' said the Sheriff, rising from his seat.

'Well, that's the end of the matter,' said Miss Gibb. 'I'm pleased for you, Tony. The police did not give me a thorough report and perhaps I did think the family name clouded my judgement a little. I'm sorry. You have no criminal record, Tony. I wish you well in your studies at school and I hope the gold nugget will bring you good fortune.'

'And do we get expenses for coming here today too?' asked Ella.

6
The Quests

The story reported in the Dumfries Standard led to carloads of prospectors returning once again to the site near Wanlockhead of the occasional gold find. Riddles sieved the gravel over three hundred yards like the sound of traffic rushing through water after a deluge. The following Wednesday the Standard also reported on the parrot's assistance in proving a child, whose name could not be mentioned for legal reasons, being found not guilty in the Sheriff Court.

Harry was delighted to read that Kofi had not travelled too far. Wanlockhead was on their doorstep and with luck, on John's bike, they would soon catch him and get him back to his domestic life.

The heavy helmet on his head weighed him down. Yet he found it surprisingly comfortable.

'Fits well, but what's the wire for?'

'That's so when we are riding, we can communicate wi' each other, ye see?' said John.

He opened a holdall to reveal a leather cycle suit.

'Here try this oan. I'm sure it's yer size.'

Harry struggled into the glove-tight attire. John produced boots. Harry had to struggle to buckle his boots but the eighty-five-year old (he had quietly celebrated his birthday two days after Kofi escaped) felt twenty years younger. He donned his leather gloves and punched one fist into the palm of the other.

'I told you I've never been on a motor bike before,' he said.

'Dinnae worry. It'll be a trial run. Wait till you feel the breeze, take the curves and get the stares o' the young ladies.'

'The young ladies will be short-changed when I take my helmet off,' said Harry.

'Then keep it oan, silly,' laughed John.

And the trial run lasted three hours. Off to the Stewarty of Kirkcudbrightshire they rode. Harry gained confidence over each mile. They stopped for lunch at the Kippford Anchor by the sea estuary.

'So how does it feel, Harry?'

'Even better than I anticipated. I'm getting used to leaning over as you take the bends. It's a fun experience. Mind you, it's been fair weather so far. Not sure what it will be like in the rain.'

'Not much different as a pillion passenger. But I go slower then.'

'Let's say it's been a success. I'm up for it.'

'Great. Harry, you have cheered me up no end.'

'That's good to hear. Just one thing, though. Can you take a picture of me on the bike with the incoming sea in the background?' Harry handed over his digital camera.

'Sure. One fur your album?'

'No, a photo to send to the girls to show there's life in the old dog.' Harry laughed until his ribs hurt.

John took the photo and showed it to Harry.

'That's a good photo. Very good, John. The girls will appreciate it when I get back.'

'You do that, it will give them a smile,' said John.

'And a surprise, I hope.'

After a bowl of lentil and broccoli soup and a ploughman's sandwich each, they set off homewards.

Just as Harry gained more confidence on the bike, John suddenly braked. His momentum thrust Harry into John's back. He held on tight.

'Bugger it,' said John.

At that moment Harry saw a rabbit scurry past the front tyre.

'A rabbit?'

'Aye, I don't ken why I braked. I niver used tae slow down fur anything, sure I didn't.'

'You mean you used to run over them?'

'Aye, thirs mony a rabbit in the land. They've nae sense, they furry creatures.'

'Phew. I thought I was a goner,' Harry said with a deep breath.

Forty minutes later, they were back home. Harry had experienced an exhilarating time on two wheels. He was ready for more. But first John boiled the kettle as Harry sat down, still in his leathers, to send the photos in an attachment to his daughters.

'I'll take a chequebook on our tours. It might come in handy for some B&B stops, John.'

'Aye,' said John. 'I'll dae the same and I'll pick up a wodge o' cash tomorrow morning.'

As Harry considered what he'd have to pack into his pannier, the telephone rang.

'Are you out of your mind, Dad?'

Fiona was forty: a career girl who had never married but who had a cast of divorced, single, married and widowed friends to fill her Edinburgh address book. She still ran half marathons and attended the gym every week for Pilates and swimming. She also played her clarinet with the Edinburgh City strings. She was a caring soul who lived with her Siamese cat Horace.

'Hi Fiona darling. You mean the bike?'

'I see it's not a stunt. You've got all the gear! And that's Kippford in the background. How did you get there? Have you been riding that bike?'

'Steady, now. Only as a passenger, dear. I don't drive it.'

'At your age, you are driving me daft. Dad, what if you fall off?'

'I won't. John's a retired policeman. He knows what he's doing. I've been out riding for three hours today, you know?'

'I'm not convincing you that it's a bad idea, am I?' said Fiona.

'You wouldn't deny your old Dad one last fling in his life, would you? And of course we're trying to find Kofi.'

'Put that way, no. But do take care. Remember it's almost winter; the days are shorter. The roads can be icy. Anyway, keep me updated, not just about Kofi but also… no suffering in silence in a hospital ward covered in plaster from head to foot, please.'

'I'll be fine, Fiona. Honest darling, I promise. Love you. Bye.'

'She's a great girl that Fiona o' yours. Very concerned about her father,' said John, staring at the carpet.

'Yes, both are.' Harry looked up to see John looking very serious.

'What's on your mind, John? Having second thoughts about your pillion partner? Pillion rider in fact – that sounds better, doesn't it?'

John took a gulp of tea, and nodded to Harry.

'Aye, yir right, Harry. I should've come clean from the start. I do have anaither motive, a personal one, like.'

Harry was taken aback. He sat up and looked at John as he explained himself.

'Four years ago ma only daughter Morag, on the eve of her sixteenth birthday, went missing, so she did. Vanished. Vamoosed. Dead or alive, I've nae idea. The police worked hard on the case initially, they did their best tae solve it. They informed missing persons' agencies, read reports o' similar types o' cases from aroond the country. And I can tell ye there's a significant number o' missing people. A murder squad was initiated and that got me really scared. The mountain rescue folk spent days on the hills in search of her. Tracker dogs were called in too. Even heat-seeking devices were deployed from the air. But oor Morag didnae fit the usual criteria.'

'How dreadful, John.'

'She wisnae a child running away fae foster parents or a children's home, nor was it a case o' domestic violence. She wis a normal loving kid, a wonderful daughter. Oor only child, ye ken?'

'Yes, I'm recalling that now. I read about it a while ago. It was a story that died down pretty quickly, didn't it? I mean not died down, but off the front pages,' said Harry.

Tears began flowing down John's face. Harry was not used to such raw emotion in a man. He offered a tissue.

'Thanks, Harry.'

'Didn't the police find any clues?'

'No. Not one. But I canny blame them. There was nothing tae go on. Ony girl leaving home would surely make plans tae share her aspirations, leave a forwarding address, keep in touch and in all probability return when the money ran oot, like most kids leaving hame. But no. Not in Morag's case. She was a bright lass, heading for uni the followin' year. But she just vanished into thin air.'

'No help from her friends?' asked Harry.

'Her friends could add no insight intae her thinking the day before she disappeared. We had no leads. She was no in a relationship and certainly could no be pregnant. She had an accident when she was seven and that caused her to be unable to have ony children in the future.'

'I'm sorry to hear that.'

'She had no reason to disappear whatsoever. I was not in the CID so couldn't find the time to mount my own investigation and so the pressure mounted. It got nasty, I mean, the friction in the house. When I retired I used to stay on the computer for hours after Alison had gone to bed. I was on the missing persons' websites. It was addictive. I was logging on every half hour to see if there was an update. Hoping beyond hope that Morag Reid's name would surface from the search box.'

'Gosh. I can just imagine.'

'Naw, Harry, I don't think onybody could. Not unless it's yir own kid. The more I checked, the more I needed to check a' the sites. It was like waiting for an expected e-mail that was never sent. It made me tired, of course. The lack of sleep made me angry too. I was losing it. My wife eventually told me that it was more likely that we'd never see Morag again and hearing that, I lost my temper. It was too much for Alison. So she left me last year. She left to live with her mother. I don't blame her in a way but she sees me as obsessive... her words. We are two sides of a coin. There's no halfway.'

'Hmmm...What a dreadful thing to happen. John, I feel for you.'

'Thanks, Harry. A cold case as we used to say in the force.'

'Thankfully it's so rare, although that will be no comfort for you. We hear of such cases in the news only once in a blue moon. I am just so sorry it happened to you.'

'Well, you can see it irks me. I simply do not know where tae start. At first my colleagues on the case told me of girls, often non-English speaking from Eastern Europe, coming for work and tae git a job. But their dreams crashed when there wisnae jobs and they took the oldest job in the world to make ends meet. A better life promised anywhere by anyone and the girls were up for it. Then they went missing from city centres in Glasgow, Manchester and Liverpool. But that wasn't Morag's lifestyle, these were city girls. Even if she's dead, we'd want to find her. We could bury her and come to terms with whatever tragedy befell her. That's the biggest thing for me noo. Closure, they call it. That's what I need, closure. Now I know exactly what they mean. And… I'm pretty sure this misery has been the cause of my depression.'

'I see and I think I understand. You want to get to the bottom of what happened. I don't blame you,' said Harry.

'I knew you wid understand. You see, we are very much in the same boat. We're even a team.'

'Really? In what way?'

'Well, we're both single, we're both searching for a missing loved one, and we are motivated to do our best for their sakes. It's a double or joint quest, isn't it? That's team work.'

Harry thought for a moment. He could hardly disagree.

'I suppose you are right. I could not have put it better myself,' he smiled.

Then a serious furrowed brow emerged. 'But does that mean a crash helmet every day?'

'I think it might come in quite handy,' said John, 'on fair weather days.'

'Yes, we're going to find Kofi and Morag. My, this will be quite an undertaking. Do you realise, on your super bike, our combined ages will be a hundred and forty-two years old?' asked Harry.

'You mean a hundred and forty-two years young?' said John.

Harry punched John's shoulder in fun. John did the Ali shuffle.

Harry wondered if he had taken on too much.

7
A Trail on the Road

Parbold Parrot Painters was a new enterprise in Lancashire. The shop was modest in size, and seemed particularly so when the staff numbered nine in total. No fewer than seven wore the white dungarees with a multitude of splattered paint-stains of many colours on their garb. They worked in that ancient hilly Lancastrian village of Parbold near the M6, but their shop had unusual opening hours. The impression was that the business was just getting off the ground and the painters were busy away from the office most days. Their sizeable white van had a logo for all to see. It was, of course, a parrot. An Amazon Red Parrot, to be precise. It also read: 'We paint anywhere in the country'. And the painters travelled far and wide. The only other distinguishing mark on the van was its expensive number plate.

PA3 10TT was as near the company name as it could be to make it legal and enhance the reputation of the travelling painters.

Kofi's wing was fully functional once more and east he flew. Through clouds he appeared and disappeared like the spitfires of old and when the prevailing winds were in his favour he rested his wings in a fixed position and glided with the ease of a ballerina's soubresaut.

There was much activity at the Annandale Water Motorway Service Station at Junction 16. It was the last Scottish services station for motorists heading south, and of course the second for those travelling north. Gretna had more than a services station to offer as soon as the border was crossed, coming north.

High on the roof of the Annandale Service facilities Kofi took his rest as he observed the desperation of some people running into the services while the same people returning to their cars took their time. It was not comprehensible to him. But as there was a light drizzle, heads were downcast and no one lifted their eyes to see Kofi enjoying his shower.

Cars, vans, lorries and motorbikes came and went, and none took Kofi's interest until a white van appeared with a parrot painted on its side. He watched as four white-coated passengers got out and set off to the service building. With them away, Kofi made his way to the van to inspect this one-dimensional parrot. Two painters remained in the van with their windows down, letting tobacco smoke rise heavenward. Kofi landed on the slippy roof.

'Whaz at?' asked Pete, the youngest member of the party, a scar-faced youth only seven weeks out of Stangeways' Prison for the supply of amphetamines and heroin.

'The noise? It is a bird on the roof,' said Eric, his older brother.

'What a relief, I thought we were nabbed.'

'Ye know mate, if we could harness a homing pigeon, we'd be able to fly our drugs and not have to travel up here every time.'

'Don't worry. We've got good cover with this van. They'd never suspect the load of drugs we've got,' said Eric.

'For God's sake stop saying the word drugs. We'll be overheard.'

'There's no one near our van, Pete, take it easy. Drugs, drugs, drugs, money, money, money, that's why I've got a beautiful home and a lovin' honey,' said Eric, the red-haired and bearded Evertonian supporter.

'Aw shut up you bam pot.'

'Hey, look over there.'

'What?'

'Traffic cops.'

'Okay, let's not wait for the others to return. Lock the car and wind the windows up. A quick piss and we're off. Let the others know the cops are around.'

Kofi flew off as soon as he heard the windows close. He sought a vantage point on a tree near the Battenberg-diced police Range Rover.

Sergeant Mike Ramsay brought two lattes and two jam doughnuts to the vehicle. Mike was a dour practical cop who did his job well and people asked no more. He was as reliable as the daily milk. Tee-total for sure but his doctor worried about his eight cups of coffee a day and this one was already his third.

'That's ma man, Mike. Best part of the day,' said Constable Janet McHattie, a buxom officer who had served twelve years with a couple off for child-rearing priorities. She bundled her hair under her police hat with a blue kirby grip and prepared to enjoy her well-earned break.

The coffee lids were sucked and the first bite of the doughnuts consumed.

Mike and Janet were one of two regular traffic cop cars in the police authority. They were a team with a good record and a good working relationship. Janet wore the trousers and Mike drove the car. They acted like sock and shoe.

'You know why there's a hole in a doughnut but none in a jam one?'

'Sure, that's why I'm a sergeant.'

'No seriously, diyi know?' pestered Janet.

'Because, if you are watching your weight, you buy one with no jam and wi' a hole in the middle. Obvious isn't it?'

'Good theory but no.'

'Okay, smarty pants, what's the answer?'

'They have rings in them so you can tie a few together and by the way... isn't smarty pants on the sexually non-political wing?'

'Maybe, sexy pants,' the Sergeant replied, receiving an elbow in his ribs. 'Okay okay, I get the message... hey wind down your window,' he said in an agitated manner. 'Look, ain't that the missing parrot?'

'Ohh aye, that parrot. Yes, it must be.'

'Leave this to me, let me try and get him.'

'Okay, I'll notify HQ.'

Sergeant Ramsay got out of the car and closed his door without making too much noise, just as the white van was leaving the car park. He noticed the coincidence of a parrot on the Parbold Parrot's Painters' van as he kept an eye on Kofi. He stood under the branch Kofi was resting upon.

'Hello Kofi, hello. Come down and meet me.'

Kofi looked at this man in uniform. He seemed imposing.

'Hello, hello,' he replied.

Mike smiled.

'That's a good parrot. Harry is missing you, you know. Isn't it time you came home to Harry? Are you going to come back with us to Dumfries?'

Kofi cocked his head to digest what was being said.

'Come on Kofi, come to me,' Mike begged with his arm extended.

'Parrot... drugs... parrot... drugs...'

'What? What did you say, Kofi?

Kofi realised this uniformed man had mentioned Harry and wondered if Harry was looking for him, but the officer kept asking him to speak, so he obliged.

'Parrot… drugs... parrot... drugs.'

Mike realised Kofi was not going to oblige. He could not coax him down. He returned to the Range Rover.

'That's Kofi, no doubt about it.'

'Aye, I've notified HQ. They are sending the Lockerbie fire-unit to try and catch him.'

'Not easy. But you know he kept saying something.'

'Aye, I saw you two chatting. So what's the crack?'

'Parrot, drugs, parrot, drugs.'

Their brains worked overtime for a full eight seconds and then in unison they shouted, 'That van!'

Kofi flew south before the Lockerbie fire engine had left its station. It was a short flight. There was much activity at the Gretna Green's Blacksmith's anvil.

Sergeant Ramsay put out an alert to his Police Scotland colleagues in South Lanarkshire for a spot check on the Parbold Parrot's Painters' van, travelling north. They would join them as soon as they could. But first some priorities had to be entertained. They finished their coffees and after a quick loo visit they set off on the speculative tail of the Parbold Parrot's van.

'Hotel Alpha, do you read me?'

'Go ahead Delta Golf.'

'We'll tail till Junction 13. Reinforcements available there, over?'

'Your hunch well founded?' asked the Hamilton-based traffic police.

'As good as they get,' said Janet.

'Okay, then we go for it. Sure we'll need help if there's

a few on board. We'll get that organised. You collie-dog them up.'

'Will do, over and out,' said Janet.

They soon caught sight of the white van. They kept their distance.

'Boys in blue in rear window. Okay, keep calm,' said Walt, the gang leader and Toxteth Liverpudlian driver.

'Let's rehearse again,' said Tom, the No. 1 courier of hard drugs.

'Where are we going?'

'237 Dowanhill Drive, Glasgow.'

'Why?'

'Renovation job.'

'More detail.'

'Three rooms and a hall and all ceilings.'

'Who's the owner?'

'Sheik Yer Manu.'

'Where does he live?'

'Kuwait.'

'Okay, got it? Don't deviate and we're safe. Check the speed.'

'I make it 63 mph.'

'Fine. Relax boys.'

Kofi was drawn to the playing of the bagpipes. Pipers stood around tuning their drones before marching to the appointed venue to give the happy couple an air or two. It was sound rather than tune that attracted Kofi: the very same criticism made by Harry when hearing modern repetitive pop tunes.

Long cars drove up to the blacksmith's shop and deposited brides and bridesmaids, while the registrar, Avril Crosby, looked through her eighteen marriage schedules before lunch. Avril was the busiest registrar in Scotland. That meant smart dressing each day with daily carnations in her buttonhole and perfectly groomed hair. On her days off she was in jodhpurs, mucking out her Cleveland Bay harness horse Frisky, her hair flowing freely restrained only by a silver Alice band. Beach rides along the Solway shore were the ideal solitary contrast to her busy days. On competition days, she guided Frisky's coach around obstacles at the seasonal gymkhanas. The awards on her dressing table reflected her success as a horsewoman.

Second marriages were regularly conducted at this venue. Smartly dressed two-piece suits and suited gents were de rigueur for the wives and husbands-to-be. Widows and divorced couples alike hoped a new start would banish the disappointment of an earlier period in their lives.

But it was inevitable that the services the registrar provided were like production lines. Retired pastors and priests made a comfortable living in tips from the happy couples too.

Danny McGregor and Daphne Pertwee were due to be married at 3 p.m. on the dot. At 2.50 p.m. pandemonium struck Danny. He had lost the all-important wedding ring. His fingers searched every pocket but found nothing. This did not augur well for a successful second marriage. His acrimonious divorce from an unfaithful wife and Daphne's marital domestic abuse had been the backdrop to their union. At this moment, the next chapter of their lives was under severe strain.

Danny retraced his steps searching the ground for one glimpse of gold to resolve his happiness. Then the thought of it having already been discovered and stolen crossed his mind. How could he possibly find a new ring at this late hour? He wondered if he knocked on a front door, a brass curtain ring could be provided. Anything in fact would do. As long as it was symbolic, round and fitted Daphne's finger, any finger.

Kofi had become a particular expert in finding gold in Wanlockhead and an opportunity to find more began to materialise. It came about quite by chance. Someone wanting to steady prenuptial nerves had drunk black coffee. Time had caught up with him so the unfinished coffee lay under a bench in a polystyrene white beaker. A child swinging her legs on the bench accidentally knocked over the beaker and the black coffee began to run. That was when Kofi saw the gold appear as if by magic from the dark-brown flowing stimulant. He flew down to collect the ring in his claw. He returned to a nearby branch to decide who should receive this gift.

Danny returned to the open-sparred bench where he and Daphne had sat for the best part of thirty minutes an hour ago and he kicked the fallen beaker in frustration.

'This is where we were. I remember taking the ring out of my left-hand pocket and looking at it. I was so happy to know that it would soon be on your finger. I was sure I put it back in my trouser pocket. Yes, I must have. Oh, I also remember that half-cup of black coffee. It was right under the bench. Remember I moved along a bit to avoid it? That was why. I didn't want to knock it over and get my shoes wet.'

He sat down with his head in his hands. Tears were not far behind. His day was about to be spoiled. It was 2.57 p.m. Daphne placed her arm around his shoulder. She tried to console him.

'Let's go, Danny. If we tell the pastor I am still sure he can get us married. The registrar has to prepare a certificate of marriage, not a ring of marriage.'

Danny saw the sense in what she was saying but his disappointment was tangible. Having no ring was like an artist without a brush, Andy Murray without a racquet, Lionel Messi without a football.

Kofi had found his recipients. He flew down and perched on the back of the seat. Danny was frightened by his arrival. Daphne was taken aback to see the ring in his beak. Kofi waddled over. Daphne offered a shaking hand and the ring fell into hers.

'Amazing, Danny. Quick, let's go. We can still do it.' It was 2:59 p.m.

Danny was still transfixed by the parrot, despite an ecstatic flow of energy streaming through his veins.

'Come on, Danny.' Daphne grabbed him by the suit sleeve.

As the village clock struck 3 p.m. a somewhat out-of-breath couple presented themselves before the registrar.

'I see you have no best man. Shall I act for him?' asked the clerical collared Rev. Alex Niven.

'I don't know if it's possible but... that parrot, over there on the anvil... could he do the job?'

The van was now flat out shaking at 70 miles per hour. The Land Rover was cruising at the same speed. They continued on with the drivers keeping a constant eye on each other. Then the second police car emerged from a raised vantage slip point.

'Delta Golf... in for the kill. Go, Go!'

It was the signal Mike had been waiting for with relish. It was of course officially still a routine spot check, one that they could bluff their way out of, if nothing was found. Mike placed his foot on the accelerator. The flashing lights were switched on, as well as the siren.

The van could not outpace such powerful police cars so it pulled up on the hard shoulder with Mike at its rear and the Hamilton station car at the front.

'Okay, boys, stay calm and keep to the story, especially if they split us up,' said Walt.

'Good morning gentlemen. Routine check if you don't mind. I'll check the tyres while my colleague will look at your driving license,' said Mike.

David Holmes was a sergeant at Hamilton. He was gay, and was Secretary of the Police Scotland Gay and Lesbian Society. He read the car's papers and smilingly said, 'All in order,' in a soft Lanarkshire accent. The driver looked relieved.

'It's a long way to come to paint, isn't it?' asked David.

'Special job,' said Walt.

'Oh I see, by Royal Appointment perhaps?' said Mike with a degree of sarcasm.

'As a matter of fact, yes. A member of the Kuwaiti Royal family has asked us to work for him in Glasgow.'

'Hmm, you must be very good at your work. I think if you travel this far and you come that well recommended, I might need a team tae paint my hoose. Have ye got a business card?'

'Er... we are getting a new lot printed at the moment,' said the driver.

'Och, dinnae worry aboot the new one, an old one will do,' said Mike with a growing sense of unease.

'Sam... any of you boys got a card?' asked the driver.

None surfaced, and heads shook.

'Okay, I think it would be best if you came outside for a moment. Onto the grass verge, please,' instructed Sergeant Holmes.

The painters' growing tension coiled like an over-wound clock.

The men sat down on the verge. Mike opened the rear door of the van as a back-up police van arrived. He took a fifty pence coin from his pocket and tried to ease off the lid off a tin of yellow paint. It was not a full tin. Dry paint was dribbled down its sides and the lid had a ring of paint to break through. The coin made its way around the rim inching its lid open as slowly as an octogenarian pushing his Zimmer. Finally, as it eased back, Mike's eyes lit up. Bingo! He beckoned for Janet, placing his fingers on his lips.

Janet saw the tin stuffed with twenty-pound notes. David then took a wallpaper tube from the improvised rack on the inside of the van. Its ends were sealed. He took no time in cutting through the tube with his Swiss army knife. A white powder flowed onto the floor of the van.

'Mike to Hotel Alpha... jackpot! Arrest them all. Class A drugs aboard and oodles of bank notes. This is a big one.'

The Parbold Parrot van was seized and the officers high-fived each other as the drug couriers were handcuffed and led away. A police van took the painters to the Hamilton cells.

'Okay, Mike. What was your lead?' asked Sergeant David Holmes.

'No, not a lead. More of a caged bet,' he replied.

'Hmmm.... You can't put "a caged bet" in your report,' David suggested.

'No, of course not. I'll just put intelligence. Yes, that's what it really was. Intelligence, avian intelligence.'

8
Larkhall Lunacy

Reports of Kofi remaining close to Dumfries were encouraging. The local papers had done their part and the radio had followed the stories up in Nithsdale. But no- one reads yesterday's newspapers. Why would they? Without news of his capture, Kofi's freedom might have been slipping from people's minds.

Kofi's inbuilt inclination was to fly south, to warmer climes. With many rests and possibly by sailing on the masts of freighters, he could be back in West Africa within two weeks. He'd be back to his lush vegetation in western Ghana, his alma mater, soon after.

In fact Kofi left Gretna Green and flew due north-east, on the western Atlantic's forceful tight isobars; as a result, he was no longer in Dumfries & Galloway. The Southern Uplands provided sparse parrot food pickings but farm outhouses gave some warmth and an escape from a windy early Scottish winter.   Kofi eyed up the occasional barn owl and tried to snuggle up to his distant relation, twice removed. The owl felt the parrot gave no threat and they accepted each other's company. It did not always work well, however. Kofi learned the owl's quiet murmur when sleeping and so reassured his sleeping partner that all was well. But when he shrieked out, mimicking a human, all hell was let loose.

'God save our Gracious Queen... God...'

Amid the commotion, the barn owl made its escape. Beyond possible doubt, a human in disguise had been identified. Wow, a near disaster, thought the escaping owl. Kofi realised other birds were not so keen on dialogue. Speaking seemed to be a human and parrot thing.

After five days in the inhospitable mountains dominating the southern uplands, Kofi saw the light. In fact he saw several lights. He was approaching the old Scottish village of Larkhall, where the Larkie Loons lived.

Larkhall was not the wealthiest of large Scottish villages but on four fronts, they set a pace few could rival. They had supported Glasgow Rangers by and large, through each successive generation. Through all the woes upward from the third division, the club's red, white and blue scarves flew from bedroom windows. Such was their loyalty. Their second attribute remained their warm generous nature. They had supplied, as the winter approached, a wonderful selection of garden titbits. Groundnuts seemed to grow in profusion in Larkhall. Every garden seemed to have them. Round fat balls dangled in a mesh, and insect- and berry-laden fat blocks abounded. Larkhall could surely feed Kofi all through the winter.

Their third attribute had always been a canny sense of humour. A supporter presumably with a nationalist leaning had painted on a community wall 'Scotland For Ever'. One of the more evangelical nationalist members of the same community had arrived one night with a paintbrush and changed the slogan. It now read: 'Scotland for Ever and Ever, Amen'.

Their fourth attribute was more divisive. In fact it was a failing rather than a virtue. They relished confrontation – indeed, any argument. Following the bitter campaign in 2013/2014 for the Independence struggle for Scotland, funds were more than ever being sought by political parties.

Droves were questioning their loyal Socialist Labour vote which successive members of parliament knew they could take for granted, although they never said so, of course. But these days were gone. Labour could not depend on the loyal socialist vote.

Larkhall retained many partisan pubs. Arguments led to police attendance on many occasions when the wrong element entered with the intention of being refreshed. Divisions came to light. The Scottish National Party was taking hold of local politics and of community minds. Not all were in agreement.

To boost party funds on Saturday mornings, stalls were laid out in the High Street. The Nationalist campaign flew their yellow banners at the top of the street while the Labour party flew the red one at the other end of the long straight street. With more pandas than Tory members of parliament in Scotland, they were not represented at any table that day in Larkhall.

Now this dowdy village came to life when, for the first time, there were two colourful parties in town seeking support. Colour attracted Kofi very much and so he had to investigate further.

'It's going well, team. I see we're getting low on flyers. Hang on, I've more in my garage. I'll be back in a mo,' said pompous Councillor Ivan Goodie SNP. Time and time again Ivan had tried to stand for parliament but he had, with some ambivalence, come to the conclusion that he did not have a national persona or sufficiently charismatic personality for a higher position in the party. In truth, he was often all bluff. Today? Perhaps less so. Local politics would drive him from now on and that is what he was doing so well this morning.

The avuncular Ivan, an overweight local butcher with the Scottish Saltire draped over his shoulders, entered the open garage of his home. He noticed the box in which the flyers were stored had fallen from the shelf above. It lay on the concrete floor with some flyers spilled out into a patch of car oil. The cardboard box was almost empty, save for a few leaflets. The bundle of flyers had disappeared. Yet he knew them to have been there only an hour or so ago. He looked around with growing anxiety. He came to the one and only possible conclusion. The opposition had entered his garage and stolen his yellow flyers. He opened his bin. Well, if that's not where they put them, then where? They must have taken them away.

In Larkhall, before an allegation is made, two preparations were required. First, Ivan rechecked his facts. They were indisputable. Secondly, he went inside for a wee nip of whisky to steady his nerves. This was civil war.

Councillor Goodie returned to break the critical news.

'So how do we tackle the opposition tables?' he asked.

'Turn them upside doon,' said one supporter.

'No, we must be careful. We must retain some decorum, act with reason and firmness. We should inform them that they have been found out first,' said Ivan.

'Okay, I'll get the loudspeaker out,' said Agnes, a petite, retired red-headed lady supporter in green cords.

'Then we can get tore in,' said a young man, up for a fight.

'Steady now, we are the party of the Government of Scotland. Any fracas would not reflect well on the cause,' cautioned Ivan. 'Loudspeakers are the answer.'

Everyone agreed with his suggestion.

As Constable Ewan Smart strolled up and down the High Street, ensuring that traffic flowed past the political tables at each end of the town, a loudspeaker was brought to the table. Councillor Goodie cleared his throat. He contemplated what should be his opening salvo.

Now if a 747 Jet Liner can fly, who could then doubt that on discovering this open garage, with its bright yellow leaflets, Kofi was able to secure his claws around the Dundee jute string which bound a thousand flyers in each block? Flying out of the garage with the grace of any aircraft, he flew heavenward with a vertical takeoff. His beak was working hard. It was a powerful tool. It cracked open chestnuts and walnuts as fast as you can snap your fingers. Yet his beak was also an instrument of fine precision, being able to select a flyer one at a time and dispatch it with grace and purpose, earthbound. He watched as they floated in their descent beneath him, like autumn leaves.

The flyers descended in the gardens and streets. They descended into hands and on pavements where dogs pounced on them. Villagers could not help but see the SNP logo. Councillor Goodie saw his leaflets descend and did not miss the opportunity. He switched on the loudspeaker.

'Some have reservations about our cause, but not now. God is sending these down. It meets with His approval,' he said, and his supporters marvelled at the sight. They wondered how this was possible. Mystified, they applauded and shouted without decorum.

The opposition was dumbfounded. The Nats had stolen a trick on them but how on earth had they managed this? All eyes were heavenward to trace the source of political opportunism. Few could see the tiny speck that was Kofi, the unpaid nationalist yellow leaflet distributor, as he vanished into low cloud.

Kofi tightened his grip on the twine as the piles diminished. The wind had got up a bit and the flight downward was more erratic. As light faded, the yellow campaign leaflets found a new home. Some landed on windscreens, some on top of bins in gardens or in petrol forecourts, and some even stopped a five-a-side game of footie. Once more all eyes looked aimlessly at the sky. In this deeply religious community, surely God had indeed spoken and showed His card in the Independence Battle.

Journalists, always on the lookout for a scoop, or a different angle on a breaking story, were in cloud cuckoo or perhaps cloud parrot land that Saturday.

'Campaign from heaven declared!'

'Is it a bird... is it a plane... can it be Superman?'

Bold and prominent, the banners broke out in the Hamilton Advertiser, the Carluke Gazette, the Bellshill Speaker and the Motherwell Times. The journalists had a field day. And the word got out. On the last item of the news bulletin Sally Magnusson of BBC's Reporting Scotland reported on the mysterious campaign that the SNP denied fabricating in south Lanarkshire. Radio Scotland had created a frenzy of excitement, interviewing people in Lanarkshire's proud town. Larkhall had never had it so good for so many, while so disastrous for so many others. But even they accepted that bad publicity was better than no publicity and they took pride in the attention being shown to the town as shopkeepers heard their tills ching-ching.

The news item captured the country's imagination. The Herald and Scotsman daily papers published stories about the missing parrot. Some had gleaned more about its antics in Wanlockhead and at Gretna. It was a story hitting journalists from many different angles. Not unexpectedly, the Scottish Parliament, which never missed a trick, got in on the act. Many tuned into Thursday's First Minister's Question Time in the debating chamber. They were in for a treat. It was bound to be lively as usual but even more so that day.

'Would the First Minister confirm or deny that he has sought divine intervention in their fund-raising campaign?'

Presiding Officer: 'Mr Salmond.'

Alex Salmond rose to his feet amid much applause and cheering from his benches.

'Mr Presiding Officer, the leader of the opposition claims I have divine intervention powers. I am surprised I do, but am truly grateful to have been guided by the good

Lord. Can she be a bit more specific about her concerns, if any? What point is she making?'

'I am sure it has not escaped your notice, Mr Salmond, but divine intervention in the form of a dove or other such bird should not be the domain of politicians but left to the clerics of the land.'

The members of parliament waved their papers as if they were flying and guffawed at the opposition's attempts to address the happenings in Lanarkshire.

'Order, order... order... Mrs Lamont, continue,' the Presiding Officer demanded.

'Thank you. As I was saying, the house cannot have helped but notice the press speculating on a parrot delivering his Nationalist message in a staunchly Nationalist Lanarkshire town. Is this not an abuse of an animal's life, if not political shenanigans?'

Mr Salmond rose again with his characteristic smile from ear to ear.

'Mr Presiding Officer, I have no knowledge about how or why this has occurred in Lanarkshire or to be more specific, in the canny toon of Larkhall. Generalisations in politics are frowned upon. Detail, Mrs Lamont, detail please.'

Laughter went on from the government rows. The First Minister continued. 'It was fortuitous to our cause and I dare say we might have been miffed if it had preferred red flyers' (he turned to the Socialists) 'or blue Flyers' (he looked up to the Conservative list MSPs) 'or green flyers' (he looked at the only Green MSP). No, the parrot took the yellow one.'

His supporters laughed with great mirth and the First Minister sat down, pleased with his performance.

'Miss Ruth Davidson,' called the Presiding Officer to the leader of the Conservative Party.

'Mr Presiding Officer, can I ask the First Minister how much the parrot cost to train?'

'First Minister.'

Mr Salmon rose with a smile as broad as the Forth rail bridge. He was armed and ready to fire on all cylinders.

'How can my friend ask such a question? Her party have rented a bigger bird in the sky. Have you not been flying a helicopter over Troon in the west, Aberdeenshire and Royal Deeside in the north, and Morningside in the east with your banner? My bird cost nothing. I ask her how much her bird in the sky cost?'

The parliament split its sides laughing before moving onto more weighty matters.

Harry sat by his radio listening to the growing reports. He knew Kofi was a survivor and he was proving it. Then John came round with a proposal.

9
Breakfast on Air

Kofi had no knowledge of the political upheaval around his activities in Lanarkshire but he had already left the area. Feeling the weather was milder in the west, he was seen briefly in several Glasgow parks. In Queen's Park on the south side, he drank at the boating pond. In Maxwell Park he dusted his feathers in a children's sandpit. There was no end to the pleasures of city life for him. Back gardens still provided his nourishment and there were enough city trees on which to roost at night. School children talked about him in the playgrounds and wrote about him in their essays. They claimed him as a real live personality and one joke around the schools was being spread like wildfire:

'Did you hear the joke about Kofi? He was on a branch when a raven flew on to the same branch. Kofi asked if he had bred any good rooks recently!'

John's proposal was underway. Holding on tight, Harry was beginning to enjoy the motorcycle experience. The noise of the engine and the throttle did, however, seem to act on his bladder. John found a few hard shoulders for Harry to relieve himself. At such times Harry noticed John lighting up a cigarette.

'A smoker, are you?' he asked.

'Aye, a wee bittie, so I am. No' near the bike, mind you.'

'You must have been holding back. I've not seen you smoke before,' said Harry.

'I took it up again last year. I thought it might calm my nerves. I get through aboot a packet a week,' admitted John.

'So not a hard smoker?'

'I hope not. Hope I can keep it at that number.'

'But does it work. I mean, does it help with your nerves?'

'Maybe... maybe not. It's psychosomatic, perhaps. If I want to make it work, it will.'

'Hmmm... I guess chewing gum would do it just as well.'

'C'mon,' said John stubbing out his fag on the damp verge, disappointed to be arguing with Harry on the first day out. 'We've all got a weakness, haven't we?'

'Aye, you're right. But at my age any weakness has long since become the norm.'

Getting back aboard the bike was not easy. Harry seemed to have strained an inner thigh muscle. He chose not to make anything of it.

'You having difficulty?' asked John.

'No, not really. Just tip the bike over a wee bit more for me to straddle the beast.'

They finally made their stop for the night. The Shawlands Hotel near Larkhall was where they arrived and parked their bike at the rear of the premises. Harry took a few moments to relax and let his body come to a halt. He swung his leg over the bike. Then he stood still regaining his footing, his equilibrium. He breathed, unrestricted, and realised how tense his body had been on the bike since the last stop.

They booked two single rooms. Before they ate, they came down to the bar. John ordered a couple of Heineken beers, and when he paid he pulled a picture out of his wallet of his missing daughter, Morag. He showed it to the barman.

'Have a look, will ye? Do ye think you've seen her around here, a while ago perhaps?'

The barman held the photo up to the light. An open-necked black shirt with turned-up sleeves and matching black cords were his work attire. It seemed he was not a consumer of his sales. He was as lean as the straw in the glass of vermouth. He had a ring on his left ear and a natural-born curved upper lip.

'Pretty lass. Natural blonde, too. But no, doesn't ring any bells. I'll pin it up if she's missing.'

'Sure. Aye, that's great. Here's my card if you get ony information. She disappeared four years ago.'

'Four years ago? Guess she'll have changed a bit. Girls and fashion change weekly. Think she passed this way, do you?'

'Maybe, maybe no'. I really don't know. Simply no trace of her,' said John.

'Have the police not been involved?'

John smiled. 'I've just retired as a police officer. It became a cold case eventually. No trace or sighting, not a word at all.'

'Did you know her?'

John's lip trembled. 'Morag wis my daughter. I'm hoping Morag is still my daughter. It's a personal challenge I'm on.'

'Christ! What a shock. Okay, sir, I'll pin her up on the inside door and I'll get back to you if I get a recognition from anyone.'

'Here's anaither card tae pin beside her, if you hear anything... like.'

'Thanks. So that's your father helping you to find his granddaughter?'

John looked over his shoulder. 'Harry? Oh no. He could be my father, mind you, but no, he's my pillion passenger. He's looking fur his lost parrot. I ken, what an unlikely team we are. That's what you're thinking, isn't it?'

'Hmmm... I suppose so. Hey, is he not the guy whose parrot delivered SNP flyers down the road?'

'Aye, I believe so. We heard that on the radio. That's why wur here. Parted for the first time they are. The pair of them have lived together for more than thirty years. '

'Wow, that's something else. Well, at least I can give you the drinks on the house.'

'That's ofy kind of you.'

'The restaurant is ready whenever you are. And breakfast? What time do you want to come down?'

'Nine on the hour I think will be just fine.'

The cycle ride in cool fresh air had strengthened the appetites of the duo. Even Harry had a third course. But there was no need to stay up any longer and no nightcaps were ordered or consumed. John had a final fag in the cool Lanarkshire air. It was still. It was calm. He looked up at the stars. The Dog Star shone brightly. By the time he stubbed out his fag in the gravel and deposited it in a nearby bin, he had identified many stars. In the constellation Aquila he identified the Eagle. But as yet, no parrot had been honoured in the skies overhead. His main focus was on Libra. That was the month Morag was born. Was that her twinkling in the sky?

Both longed for the covers of a solid bed and a good night's sleep. Harry's eyes were watering and it took him some time to undo his leather boots. He rationalised that it was his body's response to the fifty-mile bike ride and nothing else. He eased himself into a warm but not too hot bath. Fifty miles a day was more than enough. After he dried himself he applied some heat-cream onto his inner thigh. He massaged it into the muscle, which caused him some pain.

The heat increased and Harry relaxed. It seemed to be doing some good.

At 9 a.m. on the dot the following morning, the pair arrived in the restaurant once more. A self-service table provided fresh fruit juice and while John poured a bowl of muesli, Harry filled a bowl of stewed fruit.

'Got to keep regular; it's the secret of a long life, you know.'

John laughed. 'Let's sit here by the window.'

The window seat offered a view towards Lesmahagow on the right and on the left a sliver of the Douglas Water. Detracting from this panoramic view was the hotel's car park. John was reassured to see his MV Butane 800 untouched from when he'd parked it the previous night.

'You were late up last night. I heard you come in,' said Harry.

'Aye, star gazing.'

'Know much about the sky at night?'

'Aye, I do. Saw a lot on late shifts and had a colleague who had a telescope. Saw satellites in orbit and got to identify the major constellations.'

'But not the stars in the papers?'

'Horoscopes? Read into them what you like. They're not fur me.'

The full Scottish breakfast lay before John. A plate devoid of egg, haggis and bacon faced Harry.

'It doesn't matter where you are on these islands, they all claim their own breakfasts,' Harry mused. 'An Irish breakfast in Belfast; a Welsh breakfast in Wales; and the full English breakfast down south, but they cannot all be the same.'

'Aye, you are right there, Harry. I ain't got an Ulster fry or an English saddle back Wiltshire sow. And they ain't got a mealy pudding or a haggis. I guess they're not all the same after all,' commented John.

'So what's the plan today?'

'I think we need to speak tae those who saw Kofi in Larkhall first and find oot where he was last seen. That may lead to him.'

'That's a short trip,' said Harry, much relieved.

Twining's English breakfast tea washed down their buttered toast and pills. As they relaxed for a brief moment, a van arrived in the car park. The unmistakable BBC logo was emblazoned on the side. As if to confirm its livery, an aerial and a dish were atop the vehicle.

'I wonder where they are off to?' asked Harry.

'Down south somewhere. They'll be in for a coffee, I bet,' said John.

In the background the crew gathered in the backdoor porch speaking to the hotel barman/owner who had served them the previous night. Their collective gaze turned towards the two at their table. Then, with microphone in hand, and a cameraman at the rear, the entourage approached the breakfast diners.

'Good morning.' Extending his hand to them both Reevel Alderson, a familiar television face, the seasoned cheerful north-eastern-accented BBC Scotland Home Affairs correspondent. His blue anorak and blue and white scarf made him look like a lost football supporter in search of an away-day fixture's grounds.

'We were stopping for a coffee break and the manager told us about you. We hear you are on a mission to find your now famous escaped political parrot.'

'Well, he wasn't political when he escaped from me in Dumfries, I can assure you,' said Harry.

Reevel laughed and turned to face his crew to see them enjoying the moment too.

'Okay, hold it there. I think we can go from here. Lighting okay? Sound, yes? Right, let's start again… and… action,' said the producer.

'Harry, you have come up from Dumfries to search for your missing parrot. How long have you had the bird?'

'Well now, let me see. I got him in the seventies in Ghana. That makes... er... thirty-five years.'

'You must be very upset that he escaped,' said Reevel, stating the obvious.

'You have no idea. Animal lovers are all the same when their pet is missing. Well, it has affected me too, but if we go by reports, he's still alive. At least I know he is surviving. I am hopeful one day he can be humanely caught if I don't catch him myself. If I do, I'll be the happiest man in the world,' smiled Harry.

'And you are searching for him on the back of a motorbike?' asked Reevel.

'Yes. First time on a bike for me. It's quite a thrill.'

'But I'm told you are not alone on this mission. John, how did you become involved?'

'I heard about Harry's plight and thought now that I am a retired wildlife police officer, I could help in finding Kofi the parrot. But I have my own agenda too, of course,' said John, seizing his opportunity for publicity.

'Tell me about that,' suggested Reevel.

'Yes, it's a very personal mission, so it is. I am trying to get to the bottom of my daughter's disappearance almost four years ago.'

John pulled out a photo of his daughter.

'This is Morag when she was fifteen. The last time I saw her.' There was a tremor in his voice.

'Cut,' demanded the producer. 'Camera, a close-up of the photo, please.'

'And... action.'

'And how can you help each other?'

'Well, Harry is not only good company but he's also searching. We have that in common. He's like a father figure for me. He's thoughtful and caring. We just seem to gel but you should ask him the same question. I'd be interested to hear how he sees it, so I would.'

'Well, Harry, what's it like for you?' enquired Reevel.

'Being a widower I don't get to meet so many active people these days. But John introduced himself to me as a wildlife officer. I thought no one could be better placed to track Kofi. Then he told me he wanted to get to the bottom of his daughter's disappearance and I said I'd help in any way. Publicity helps to jog people's minds, you know. So that's what we are doing.'

'Yes but on the back of a powerful motorbike, for someone of your age?'

'Why ever not? It's great fun and John is a seasoned and careful rider.'

'Cut. A shot of them on the bike together and then see them riding off, to conclude the recording. Okay?'

'Can you let me finish my breakfast first? Have a cup of tea yourself, the pot's still warm,' invited Harry.

The manager who lurked in the background told them he'd bring them fresh coffee for the team before they shot the outside film.

'It will take a moment or two to get our things ready,' said John.

'That's fine,' said the film producer.

'So where will you be going today?' asked Reevel.

'We thought we'd get into Larkhall to ask what they saw. That might put our minds at rest if we hear he's looking well. And of course he might still be there,' said John.

With their belongings stored in their side panniers, John supported Harry's efforts to mount the mechanical beast as the hand-held camera prowled around them. Off they went, but the BBC film unit lingered a while in the car park.

'Can't see them making any progress on that motorbike,' said the elegant producer.

'I won't be surprised if that old man falls off that bike. He doesn't look very comfortable, does he?' said the cameraman.

'Let's not hang around. That beached Minky whale awaits us at Southerness,' said Reevel.

10
Bread of Heaven

'This is Kofi without a doubt,' said Harry, reading the Herald's second page. 'A good photo too. Must have been some quality zoom lens to get that one.'

Kofi, however, had left the south side of the city and ventured to the north side where he found a large building which interested him. He had in fact discovered the home of Barlinnie, the human gaol of Glasgow. These prisoners were locked up at night and much of the day except when they were released en masse to exercise in the enclosed yard. Kofi observed this with interest. The offenders walked in the same direction in pairs, going round the perimeter of the yard. Then they disappeared inside one after the other. Once they were all in their cells again, they tried to attract him.

'Pretty Polly... tut tut tut tut... Pretty Polly,' said one prisoner, whose arms were dangling out through the bars.

'Bet itz nae called Polly,' said another.

'Okay, Tizer, Sean, Pete, Wully, Dick.'

'Danny Bhoy, yull niver guess its name. Gui it sum food,' advised the prisoner.

And some offered titbits which interested Kofi somewhat more. But first he flew down to drink from puddles after a cloud burst, causing most bored prisoners to know of his presence. Kofi sought human friendship as it was now lacking from his life and so he flew to a cell window to meet a resident of this large establishment.

Reassuring sounds came from inside and a hand proffered some bread. Now that was not a parrot's staple diet but the gesture was appreciated. Kofi drew nearer to receive the crust. He took it from the prisoner's hand, holding it in his claw while standing on one leg on the window ledge. Suddenly his other leg was grabbed. Fear hit Kofi hard.

'Goat it,' the prisoner shouted with joy.

Kofi was caught. He dropped his titbit in haste and, with one nod of the head, sank his beak into the hand of his captor, drawing blood.

'Ya bugger. It bit me. Ouch ya... oooouch...'

And the bloodcurdling cry of the prisoner was met with raucous laughter from the watchful prisoners. Prison entertainment had surpassed itself that morning. Kofi left wishing never to return to this building but the excitement lingered at the Bar L while one young convict reported to First Aid.

'Ya wanker,' became a chorus. The prison officers allowed them to continue letting off steam. The Bar L's southern wing had a bird in the hand that day.

It was time to leave this strange building and seek a warm friendlier environment. As Kofi prepared for a change of scenery, the motorcyclists arrived in the south side of Glasgow to seek him. A few pedestrians noticed the elderly man riding pillion. But had they seen under the helmet, they would have found a contented rider, even although the men were always a day behind. Kofi, however, had flown east.

The Glasgow to Edinburgh train takes an hour. It takes an hour by car to get to the outskirts of the capital and a further half hour to reach the city centre. But for a well-fed Kofi, with strong wings and strong following westerly winds, it took less than forty-five minutes to see the famous large building on a mountain in the centre of the city. It was not the castle that attracted him but an arc of light as the dimming dusk enveloped the capital on this Saturday afternoon.

The crowded lit bowl, which is universally known as Murrayfield (as opposed to Murray Mound) in the other capital, was hosting an international club final on this occasion. The rivalry was between the Glasgow Warriors and the Cardiff Blues. At stake was the National Club Team's Cup. Tension was plain to see on the faces of both supporting teams in the terraces.

'Cumon Glasgow, git into them. Hud the line. Nae long tae the whistle.'

'*f* Bread of Heaven, bread of heaven, feed me till my want is o'er... Feed me till my want is o'er,' the Welsh responded to encourage the Blues.

'O Flower o' Scotland...'

The reason for their excitement and anxiety was quite obvious. Glasgow Warriors were leading 22-20. There were forty seconds to go. The whistle was at the referee's lips and he was counting in his head to the final whistle. Thirty-nine, thirty-eight, and thirty-seven... twelve, eleven, ten... nine... then he blew his whistle. An alleged collapse of the scrum by Glasgow awarded Cardiff a penalty. That decision led to an outrageous confrontation. The Glasgow captain shouted into the referee's face a foot away from his whistle, stating that it was Cardiff that had caused the scrum to collapse deliberately, to gain a penalty. He remonstrated with anger, raising a fist. It was a foolish action. The referee settled the matter beyond doubt and restarted the game with an additional penalty to the Cardiff Warriors ten paces further forward into the Glasgow half for verbal abuse to the referee.

Cardiff had to score to win and it had just been made so much easier. It was the penalty kick to end the game. The kick was well within their kicker's ability, and the Glasgow Warriors knew it.

Gareth Lloyd Llewellyn Hughes was not just a kicker par excellence. He had already earned twenty-seven caps in his twenty-sixth year, serving his national Welsh side.

What's more this was now one of the easiest penalty kicks he had ever to make under pressure.

The electronic vehicle that brought the ball holder to the kicker had returned to the sidelines. Many of the Cardiff players could not face the moment. They turned their backs on the play and fully anticipated Gareth to score: to gain the result, the victory, the raised arms of blue sleeves, and to boot the Cup itself. Their Blue supporter ecstatic accents would confirm their joy. The stakes were never higher. But they were confident.

Gareth satisfied himself that the ball was steady. He stood up and then walked backwards to a halt. He took two giant steps to his left and bent his back with his clasped hands before him as he had done so for many a sporting year, in honour of Jonny Wilkinson who first devised this camp approach to converting the ball over and between the posts. He looked up at the blue and white goal posts, fading in the night sky. His aim was true. He looked once more at the ball and the beautiful spot on which his boot would strike. A final look at the posts reassured him of the Cup and then, the first step.

As the reliable Gareth approached the ball, he was suddenly aware of a flicker, no more than a slight distraction out of the corner of his eye. It irked him as it flew towards the top of the goal post. Seconds before Gareth struck the ball Kofi perched on the very top of the left-hand post. It was enough for that beautiful spot on the ball to be missed. The ball rose, apparently heading towards victory but as it did so, it faded just past the upright post.

There was a gasp. The final whistle was blown. Then a roar from Scottish voices deafened the stadium and there was a groan of pain from the Welsh hordes that had come north confidently and in expectation. They could not have come closer to taking the booty.

'Can you believe it? Did you see that miss? How could he have missed? What caused it? Did his foot give way?' Brian asked his girlfriend. And the five foot ten, bullet-headed, solidly built Brian McAndrew, who had given up playing front-row prop last year for Glasgow High school, awaited Helen's response.

'Perhaps it was the bird?' Helen suggested.

'What bird? I didn't see one. What do ya mean?'

'I bet there was, you know. I may have got it on camera,' said Helen.

The Glasgow team danced towards the exit.

The Welsh players shook hands with bowed heads.

'Hard luck, Gareth,' each man seemed to say.

'I was distracted,' he repeated in his defence. The press wondered what he meant. By now Kofi had flown on to the roof at Murrayfield. He was unable to be seen as the dark clouds descended.

The Sunday papers' sports sections were full of the Glasgow Warriors' success. The dying moment seemed to outplay the previous eighty minutes of hard slog. What was Gareth claiming in his much quoted saying that 'he was distracted'? The papers invited readers who had watched the game and taken photos of the final kick to check and see if there was indeed a distraction. Or would it be declared a bad sportsman's excuse? It could not of course alter the result. Nor move the cup from the display cabinet of the Glasgow Warriors. That was made clear.

As a result, the story ran for three days. Every day a photo emerged. Most did show a speck of dark material approach the upper post but it was hard to distinguish just what it was.

'Probably a blackbird or pigeon flying by; a really poor excuse in my opinion,' said the Sunday Post editor.

Then, on the Wednesday, Helen sent in her photo by e-mail. The paper contacted her.

'Helen? We will pay you for this photo. We think you've got him. A parrot!' said sports columnist Andy Hubb.

'Really? That's great. I caught a flash of red tail and that made me think it might have been a parrot.'

'And not just a parrot, unless we hear otherwise. It may be that missing Dumfries African Grey Parrot, Kofi.'

'Kofi, the bird mentioned in Parliament, do you mean?'

'The very same. It seems he's now settled in Auld Reekie now. Keep your eyes open, we might see him again.'

Harry bought a Scotsman newspaper from a newsagent in Kilmarnock Road in Glasgow. On a two-page spread that had been brought forward from the back sporting pages, Helen's photo convinced him that it was indeed his parrot.

'John, we are being given the run around. He's on the other side of the country.'

'True, but for me being able tae distribute photos o' Morag is very satisfying. But you have the advantage. Your quarry is being noticed. Morag is in minds o' many noo but still nowhere tae be seen,' said John.

Harry laid his hand on John's shoulder.

'There is a saying in Ghana. Ebeye. It means, it will be all right,' said Harry, 'and it will. I feel sure of that.'

'If I wis a Muslim I'd say Inshallah. God knows how I've been relying on him. Yes, we need a' the help we can get. We're going to find Kofi and Morag, we've got to believe it, so we must.'

'I'm a believer, are you?'

'Aye an' I'm a monkey,' said John, playing his air guitar.

11
Edinburgh Rock

'Climb aboard, it's off tae the capital and let's see what the stir is over there,' said John.

It wasn't a long ride. They stopped for a comfort break at Harthill where John distributed more leaflets about his daughter.

'Watz zat?' asked a youth zipping up his trousers on leaving the gents.

'A leaflet... about a missing girl,' said John, handing the youth a copy.

'Stunner ain't she?'

'Aye, but the photo is four years old.'

'No seen her fur four year?'

'No. She'll be twenty by now,' said John.

'Ye'll nae fin her noo mate but guid luck onyways,' he said, heading out of the services.

The conversation attracted others keen to see what information the flyer contained. Most took a flyer with a grunt or said nothing at all. But John was pleased with their apparent interest.

'Here, Harry, you take these. It's my turn tae go.'

Harry straightened the pile. He began to hold the flyers out.

'Can you help? Have you seen a missing parrot?'

'That's no a parrot mister. That's a bonnie lass.'

Harry chided himself. When John returned though, he was in good form.

'And is it your granddaughter that's missing?' asked an elderly lady.

'No, but I wish she had been. A lass from Dumfries but she could be anywhere now.'

'Then I'll take a few leaflets. I can tell the ladies at the Guild about her.'

'An excellent idea. Thank you very much.'

'Well done, Harry. Don't think any of them would have lost a daughter but they showed a lot of interest. Yea, that wis good. We did well.'

The bike eased through the traffic. Harry appreciated the high vantage point that enabled him to look into vehicles as they passed. Short skirts, one kilted highlander, and many suited men at the wheel. He was not being prurient, just taking advantage of an unusual vantage point that had been denied him over his lifetime.

They crossed over the George IV Bridge and pulled up at the front door of the Cherry Tree B&B in Newington, a city centre district of the capital.

After a good night's sleep, the pair set off by foot to go to the Castle.

'I've a feeling aboot Edinburgh. It's much more open. Glasgow's surrounded by high buildings. I'm hopeful oor paths will cross an' we'll hae Kofi in oor grasp this time, so we will,' said John.

'I hope so. Yes, not just in our sights. Edinburgh seems so much more inviting, like an old friend.'

'Funny that. I mean, it's "Come away in an' sit yer self doon," in Glasgow bit "You will have had your tea?" in Edinburgh,' said John in his best cultured accent.

There, on the historic volcanic battlements, they stood in full view of the Firth of Forth. What's more the air was fresh and crisp and the late autumn sun dispelled any cloud cover. The omens were good. After all, Kofi had last been seen in central Edinburgh. Harry leaned on the battlements and sighed. He had been here before many times. The annual Tattoo had attracted him on many occasions. But that was a nocturnal event. Daylight was needed to find Kofi and that meant moving on. But where?

His thoughts left Kofi for a moment of reflection.

'I had a thought last night, John,' he said.

'About Kofi?'

'No, about Morag.'

'Yeah?'

'I wondered whether those heat-seeking devices could be used.'

John smiled. He knew his friend was trying to help him.

'It may have done in the first few weeks. A decaying body does give off some heat but after all those years, a corpse is so decayed. It leaves few clues until it's uncovered.'

'And then?'

'It will be identification through dental records, length of bones, DNA, that sort of thing. I just don't want it to come to that. I'd not be part of that grim discovery unless I had to.'

'No,' said Harry. 'Of course not. Sorry I brought the subject up.'

'No, I don't mind. It was a reality check for me. I must face up to all possibilities, no matter how grim.' John patted Harry's shoulder twice. 'If only Alison could have heard me say that.'

Harry looked around.

'Stay here a moment. I won't be long,' he said.

John watched as Harry set off at pace and then smiled as he saw his purpose. It made him think. Perhaps he should go too, in a moment.

Harry stood before the urinal and after a moment of strain the flow began. The relief came over him and it was a satisfying moment as he felt the next loo break would be more difficult to find in the city centre. Entering a café defeated the purpose. Forced by convention to have a further cuppa in such situations, the draining process would begin all over again.

Just as he was shaking himself of the last few drops, he became aware of a young man standing close behind him. He wore tattered sandshoes, and faded and torn jeans but that was a current style. A T-shirt advertising Tennent's Lager and a denim jacket with a Hibernian FC badge sewn on to the lapel gave away his allegiance and favourite tipple. His face was pock-marked and his hair dyed as black as the black and white tiles around the latrine. His face was on edge.

'You up for the Tattoo, old daddy?' he said in a threatening manner. It riled Harry. The Tattoo was long finished for the year. Tension mounted. He prayed for someone else to enter the loo. He was no match for a high testosterone-packed youth with an angry disposition. Stalling was his best option. Keep talking.

'No, I'm in search of a parrot and a lost girl in fact. A strange combination, don't you think?'

'The girl, what's her name?'

'Morag Reid, but she's not from Edinburgh. She was from Dumfries. A pretty lass...'

'Dumfries? Morag Reid? I know where she is. She's in Edinburgh now. Didn't you know?

'Really?'

'Sure. So what's it to you?

'It means a great deal to me. You say you know where she is?'

'That's what I said. You don't believe me?'

'Oh yes, yes... I... I... I believe you. You have an address?'

'Yea but... that'll cost you.'

'What do you mean?'

The youth drew closer to Harry. The alcohol on his breath grew stronger.

'What's in your wallet?'

The lad looked behind. Still no one entered the loo.

'C'mon, get it out.'

Harry patted every empty pocket for his wallet with purposeful ineptitude, knowing exactly where it was.

'Stop muckin' about, Granddad. Get the fuckin' wallet out. There it is, I can see it,' said the lad, punching Harry in the ribs.

Harry gasped and bent forward. He took out his wallet and the youth snatched it, turned around and fled. Harry gave an impulsive chase over the first five steps but then realised there was no point. He left the loo just as John made his way into the toilet entrance.

'I've been robbed... robbed, John. That lad over there...' Harry pointed to the youth's denim back.

The youth walked away with haste but not enough as to draw unwelcome attention. As he progressed he stuffed Harry's wallet into his jeans. John saw him. He followed at a quicker pace and then broke into a run. The youth looked behind, fatally pausing. John made as if he was looking beyond the youth and would pass by him any moment. The thief did not associate this running man with his wicked deed. But at the last moment John's velocity turned sharp left and he grabbed the youth on the pavement. Behind them was an old Scottish tenement entrance. John bundled the youth backwards into the 'close' and out of sight.

'Give me his money back, thief,' said John.

'Whit, whit's this a' about? I've nae money.'

John forced his arm behind his back. If only he had retained his service handcuffs, he thought.

'Rob an old man, would you?'

'I didn't rob anyone,' he said in a high-pitched scream.

John tried hard to remember if Harry pointed to the right assailant. He'd try once more, and then if he was getting nowhere, he'd have to let him go. The grip behind his back got tighter.

'Right, I'm gonna rip the trousers off ya. I'll search your pockets. And if you've nothing to hide, then I'll kick yer arse in and we'll leave with no hard feelings. Understand? Right... yer breeches, get them aff,' threatened John.

'Okay... okay, if you let me go,' the youth squealed.

'If you let me go, okay... okay... what?' asked John.

'Och, okay. I'll gie ye his wallet. There's nae much in it onyways.'

John eased his arms back to his front, ready to knee him in the balls if he moved the wrong way.

'God man... that wiz sore.' The youth brought out Harry's wallet and handed it over.

John frisked his other pockets. A reefer, chewing gum. No money. 'Right get the fuck oot o' here, pronto.' He let fly a kick, which only just found the backside of the fleeing culprit. He saw little point in taking him to a police station. His responsibility was for his elderly friend. The thief would sober up in pain and reflect on his act for the rest of the day.

The youth darted out of the close. John walked towards the entrance and looked both ways. No one was showing any interest in the youth or where he had been. He saw Harry on the other side of the street looking the wrong way.

'Harry,' he shouted. 'Over here.' He raised his arm with Harry's wallet in view.

Harry crossed over.

'Good heavens, you got my wallet. Well done. How did you manage that?'

'Police know-how Harry, best not to ask. But tell me, how did you get into that mess with him?'

A café nearby provided comfort and privacy. Harry explained about his confrontation in the Gents over a strawberry-jam-laden currant scone and a fruity, floral, astringent, Darjeeling tea.

The best zoo in Scotland dominates Corstorphine Hill in the Capital. For over a century, species had been captured, displayed, cared for and bred there. The pandas had brought special interest over recent years, especially during the amazingly short window of procreation.

In a close-netted aviary facing south, attractive birds were to be seen. Colourful waxbills, cordon bleu finches, Java sparrows and Bengalese finches abounded.

In the larger stronger cages were the vultures, the grim-looking scavengers of necessity in the African scrub. More colourful parakeets, the Blue and Scarlet Macaws of South America, preened themselves there, and four African Grey Parrots were in the adjoining aviary, quietly talking to each other like friends on a bus. On a nearby external branch was Kofi eyeing up the enclosure and seeing his own breed for the first time since he was orphaned.

It did not take him long to fly down and with his powerful claws attach himself to the outside cage. An African Grey approached Kofi out of interest as they both started to mimic the sounds of Edinburgh's traffic. This communication lasted ten minutes or so. Then Kofi began to descend the cage and got to the very bottom of the aviary. On the internal side was a length of concrete. On the external side was a wooden beam on which were stapled u-nails at the end of the cage wire. With his sharp beak Kofi managed to ease back the staples from the wooden beam and pull the wire back sufficiently for one of the zoo's African Grey Parrots to investigate the developing space between the concrete and the wire. Escape was thus possible.

Once on the outside, the pair of parrots familiarised themselves by pecking at their ceres above their beaks. A bond soon existed. They flew off together over Corstorphine Hill to a residential part of town they seemed to like. Perhaps they had heard the name of Barn Town. It sounded an ideal place to settle. The locals called it Barnton.

At dawn the feathered duo fed on fat balls and apples which still remained on some trees as the keen morning frosts had not destroyed them. There were kale and sprouts to add to their diet and some leeward garden sheds that gave them some protection and comfort. It was impossible to separate them as night fell. They gave each other warmth and company as they huddled together on a sycamore tree branch.

A second night in Newington gave both John and Harry media coverage at the Scotsman newspaper offices and several politicians wished to meet them.

It was with a politician that John's searching for Morag's disappearance was confronted.

'It's been such a while since your daughter went missing. That leads me to think she is either dead or out of the country,' suggested Tommy-after-shave-smelling Nathan Stevenson MSP. This politician was the most dandy of the honoured members' chamber. A decorative top pocket handkerchief corner announced its presence in small white dots on a pink background. His cufflinks protruded from his grey suit. They showed the party's colour of red, white and blue. The Tory made his enquiries.

'Yes, perhaps she is dead, here in Scotland. But someone must hae buried her or disposed o' her body. That would mean a murder enquiry. I may have tae accept that but fur the noo, I have got tae give it a worthwhile shot, tae learn what happened tae her,' said John.

'And out of the country?' asked the MSP.

'I hadnae thought of going south at this stage but the media have given us great coverage nationally as well as locally. I live for the day someone can gee me some, indeed ony news o' Morag, no matter how improbable. And I wake up each morning hopin' it will be that day, so I do.'

'But she may be even further away, you realise,' the MSP said.

'Aye, but even in New York and Los Angeles they are running the story o' an elderly man and a recently retired police officer oan a motorbike oan a journey to find two lost souls. I saw that online. It's a story which has a long way tae run,' said John.

'And will you know when and how it will end?'

'Aye.'

'And…?' asked Nathan.

'That's very personal, isn't it, Harry?'

Harry nodded.

'I see but really. With winter coming along, it's not likely a West African parrot will survive and as for your search, sir, it's been too long. I feel your search is a non-starter, if I may say so,' said the negative and forthright politician.

John's blood was boiling at this self-important politician with the attitude of a heartless man.

'Mr Stevenson, sir. The differences between you and me politically are poles apart and so is oor thinkin'. Ye see, Mr Fancy Pants, the biggest difference is that you've niver lost a child in mysterious circumstances, or ye wouldn't be talkin' the way you do.'

Mr Stevenson saw the anger in John's eyes. But he was well schooled politically. He looked at his watch.

'Well, I have been delighted to meet you, Mr Reid. I must be on my way. I have a meeting in Parliament shortly.'

12
The Storm

The storm arrived unannounced. Fine drizzle began the day. An inconvenience. But not unusual for this time of year. Manageable, folk concurred. At first not a breath of air was detected. Then three days of incessant rain ensued. The temperature was of course mild but no let up of the rain was detected.

Then a deep low advanced, approaching from the west, which covered the entire country.

'I think we need a rest day, Harry. It's been a hard slog so far and it's not a bike day for us,' said John.

Harry looked out of the window.

'You're right. That out there, it's not a fair day.'

'At least we are in the city where we know Kofi is likely to remain. It's got everything for him,' said John.

'Yes, and heavy rain will put him under cover. He'll not fly far in this weather. But he's not averse to a shower or two to freshen up,' smiled Harry.

'Freshen up? I've not heard that expression for a year now,' said John, reminiscing.

Scottish drizzle was purifying. It took its time to drench the outsider but did so in a gentle way. For the two parrots it was time to spruce up and look good. And look good they did at the bottom of Dr and Mrs Simpson's garden in Barnton.

By the second day, the drizzle had been replaced by a steady downpour. Pedestrians feared being splashed by passing cars and cyclists were fewer than usual although the diehards had donned luminous rain jackets, had lights fore and aft, and with ankle socks and cycling slippers paddled at restricted speed through the deepening water, past blocked drains and hidden kerbs.

In the morning, the rain was a real discomfort but by midday it was a considerable worry. There was no let up. Drains were clogged by late autumn leaves everywhere. Garden lawns were saturated, as were the parks. And still it rained, all day.

John looked out of the window in Newington, and scratched his head. He had not seen such a dismal day for a very long time.

'Harry, you know this is a real stinker. It's settling in.'

Harry did not answer. He was taking a midday nap.

John took out a pack of cards and played Patience. But it soon bored him. He took from his wallet his picture of Morag. He kissed the photo and then placed it on his bedside table.

'I'll not let you down,' he said.

Soon the kettle was boiling. It woke Harry.

'I see you've been playing cards.'

'Patience, Harry.'

'Yes, patience is what we need on a day like this.'

On the third day, there was a definite change. The rain was lighter, although still falling, but the low depression from the North Sea was replaced by the isobars gathering in tightly concentric circles like a Catherine wheel.

First they came in short bursts battering the windows and then came more prolonged assaults. Branches were waving as if ecstatically in the streets and the gardens. Then under cover of darkness, the full force of a storm unleashed itself on the ancient capital, the likes of which had not been seen in many a citizen's living memory.

Roof slates flew in the air like autumn leaves descending to break car windscreens and setting off alarms. But they could not be heard clearly in the evening din of fire engines, ambulances and police cars in an orchestra of chaotic disharmony.

The two parrots gripped their branch securely and withdrew their heads into their warm feathered necks. Mothers reassured young children that it would be all right in the morning. Only sleep would relax them. But they had no confidence in what they had said to their children. Fathers fiddled with absorbent material to ensure no water might seep into the family home as they slept.

On the advice of the BBC reports, action was required. Click, click, click… off went computers, the lights in rooms, the kettle, the microwave, the bread maker and the television. Numerous iPlayer and mobile phone recharging points were switched off too. It seemed like a never-ending job. Eventually with covers over the ears and with Radio Scotland news kept on as an exception and set for forty minutes, sleep was sought to dispel the angry elements battering every home.

The storm was not, however, ready to pass by. It still had a sting in its tail. Nothing that the weather forecasters could describe was comparable with the assaults on homes and property experienced that night in Scotland. Many lay in bed fearing what they would find in the morning. The more pessimistic feared that there might be no morning ever again. If the chimneystack fell from the roof, and many had been constructed more than one hundred years ago, it had nowhere to go except the basement. What a way to die. The full force of a winter storm had hit the country. It eased a little by 4 a.m. and by 8 a.m. the wind had dropped to strong breezes. It was time to discover what the storm had done to the land.

'Hi, Dad, how's it been for you?' asked Fiona's voice on Harry's mobile.

'Well, we've had a few days of it. Flooding, winds devastation. But we're okay. Guess you're fine on the second floor in Viewforth?'

'Windows rattled, streets strewn with slates, branches and the contents of spilled bins everywhere, but no damage personally. I got off lightly, I think.'

'Yup, I know you are only a couple of miles away but there's no way you can visit. The streets are impossible.'

'True. Can you hear the noise in the background?'

'No, what's that?'

'It's the saws cutting trees. They are getting through them like a knife through melted butter. The main roads will soon be clear. You're not going out on that bike, are you?'

'No dear, no biking in this weather. No roads to negotiate on two wheels.'

'Any signs of Kofi yet?'

'We still suspect Kofi is in the capital but where after the gales I have no idea. Will speak to you when I have more news. You take care of yourself.'

'Will do. Love you, Dad.'

'And love to you too, darling.'

Harry returned to lie on his bed. He was not used to sleeping in the morning. But it satisfied his tired frustrated body on a day of restricted action.

A lorry was reported to be on its side on the Forth Road Bridge; the old bridge at Kincardine had been washed away; sea walls had been breached at numerous seaside towns with particularly severe damage reported at Ayr and Arbroath on west and east coasts respectively.

News was coming in about deaths and casualties. Trees falling on cars had claimed no fewer than seventeen lives around the country; three children had drowned in a local park in Irvine; a Douglas fir tree had fallen on an old folk's home in Methil, killing four residents. A fireman was killed at Kirriemuir when his tender overturned, and the Nith had burst its banks in Dumfries and flooded the town centre, which it had never done before. Troon's seafront had flooded right up to Fullarton Drive with the Royal Troon Golf Course: a very large puddle.

The River Clyde had reached Hope Street and roof damage in Shawlands closed off main arterial roads, the likes of which some had not seen since the hurricane of January 1968.

Yet at Brodgar there was much excitement as the high winds and rain had washed away much land surface and revealed even more early settlements awaiting proper archaeological evaluation. Orkney, the land of ancient surprises, as ever.

And in Barnton, Mrs Simpson surveyed the damage. A cherry tree was down on her lawn, uprooted. Twigs were everywhere. Remarkably her drive was clear of major debris but this did not mean her husband could get his car out to work. The outside road resembled wholemeal spaghetti made of branches, devoid of a sauce. Driving was impossible for everyone. People walked to work climbing over fallen trees. Cyclists were as rare as daytime owls. Walking was achieved with extreme care. Many had phoned in to work to say they had so much to clear but no one answered their pleas or considered their requests to stay at home.

If the front garden would require a morning's work to clear the debris, the back garden would take a week. Everywhere Mrs Simpson looked there was damage. The gazebo was a pile of broken glass and shattered wooden boards; the garden hut was on its side, demolished. Garden implements and flowerpots lay strewn around the garden, like the debris from a blunderbuss. Thoughts of compensation were in doubt as Mrs Simpson intuited how her insurance company's small-ink information would refer to exclusions, especially such obvious acts of a most fearful and vengeful climatic God.

Three trees had been laid to rest on her back lawn and would need professional clearance. They would take time. She held her head in her hands. Never in her fifty-six years had she seen such devastation and it was everywhere. She turned towards the kitchen with the thought of a comforting hot coffee in mind. But what was that? Were her eyes deceiving her? What was that glimpse of red amongst the debris?

She walked towards its source, her low heels sinking into the saturated lawn. There was more than a red end to notice; it was, with absolute certainty, a grey parrot, lying on its side with its feathers quivering in the wind. She knelt down to look at it better. Its head was seeping blood over dried blood and its wing was clearly broken. After a moment gazing at its eyes it was obvious. No life was detected.

She recalled the recent stories of a missing parrot and its antics and so felt obliged to keep it so that the search could be concluded. She brought the feathered carcass into her scullery where an empty shoebox awaited. She placed old newspapers in the box. She gently laid the bird to rest, covering it with the white tissue paper once hiding new shoes. Then she remembered more about this bird.

'Bless you, Kofi. You are at rest,' she said.

She placed the lid on the box covering Kofi up. But how could she report this find? Would the police be interested on such a devastating day? It was worth a call.

Harry was shaving when the telephone rang.

'I'll get it, Harry,' said John.

'Hello?'

'Inspector Thomson here. Is Mr Dynes there?'

'He's shaving right now,' said John.

'Okay, I'll be over in about half an hour. It's not easy getting around at present. And I'm sure he'll not be going out in this weather.'

'I can imagine your work's cut out for you today. Is it anything serious, Officer? Can I pass on a message?'

'I'll tell him when I arrive.'

John replaced the handset. He wondered how serious it might be for an Inspector to take time off in these present conditions, just to see Harry.

'Who was it, John?' asked Harry.

'It's the police; they are coming for you, so they are,' joked John.

'For me? What about?'

'Time will tell. Is there anything you have not told me?'

'Er... can't think of anything yet.'

'A murder, a tax evasion? Or perhaps you were the victim of a crime? Remember anything?'

'Me? No way. Clean as a whistle, I think.'

'Perhaps they've found Kofi.'

It was a thought Harry had not considered but it raised his hopes all of a sudden.

'You might be right, you know. You might be right. I reckon you've hit the nail on the head. Why else would he want to see me this morning? We'll just have to wait and see.'

Just under an hour later, Inspector Thomson strutted up the stairs and knocked on the door. He was in full uniform. A wisp of grey hair sneaked out from under both sides of his checked black and white ribboned hat. He held a shoebox tied securely by a knotted piece of string. A shadow of beard clung to his ashen face. He had been up all night.

'Good morning, gentlemen.'

'Come in, Inspector. What a night, eh?' said Harry.

The Inspector moved into the room with a box under his arm.

'Indeed. I don't need to tell you how it's been over the last few hours. We've had quite a storm. Most of us battened down the hatches and survived. Unfortunately, many have lost their lives in this maverick weather, all over the country. And of course, the death toll does not just include humans.'

Neither Harry nor John spoke as his tone deepened. They knew more was on the Inspector's lips and they dare not interrupt his flow.

'A Mrs Simpson in Barnton rang me this morning. I am afraid to tell you she found your parrot... in her back garden. She was quite distressed. It seems he was killed by falling branches. I'm sorry, Mr Dynes, truly sorry.' He laid the box down on a coffee table.

Harry gasped as he realised what the box contained. Words were gone from his lips. Instead a hard gripping caught his throat. John moved beside him and placed his arm round his shoulder.

'It will be a dreadful shock for my friend, Officer. The parrot's been his constant companion for almost forty years.'

Harry peeled away from them and began to head for his bedroom.

'I never thought... I'd outlive him. (Sob) I could never... (sob)... (sob)... imagine this would be... how he might die.' He closed the door behind him. An anguished pain was heard through the door as the years of love and attention he'd given to and received from Kofi washed though his mind.

'I knew this would be a great shock to you both. I thought you might like to bury him at home,' said the Inspector.

'Aye, of course, we will and you can call the whole search off noo. I'll tell the press and get back to Dumfries to bury... to help Harry bury him in the garden.'

'I am sure he'll appreciate that,' said Inspector Thomson.

'In a way, that's one quest over. Perhaps we can focus on my daughter noo. But not today. I'll take care of Harry, Officer. Rest assured he'll be fine after a few hoors. Ah ken him well.'

The bedroom door opened and a sad-looking Harry emerged with damp eyes behind a white handkerchief. He stared at the shoebox.

'He's at rest in the box. I am sure you will want to say your farewells,' said the Inspector, handing the box to Harry, who took it and sat down, thanking the Inspector.

'Harry, Kofi is at peace there. Sit down here and see how restful he is,' said John.

Harry smiled at John and then looked up at the Inspector.

'Thank you, Inspector. You have some dreadful jobs to do, I can imagine just so well and… after this storm, there will be plenty more sadness for others like me, I'm sure.'

Inspector Thomson nodded as he thought what his afternoon duties would be and if and when he'd get a few hours sleep.

'I'll leave you then,' he said. John showed him to the door. On the doorstep they chatted in low voices about their police connections for a few moments. Harry could not hear their conversation. Then John shook Inspector Thomson's hand.

Harry's preparation was ready. He untied the string knot. He put the lid to one side with care and precision. He approached the discovery with reverence.

The front door closed with a quiet click, causing the knocker to sound a moment later.

Harry eased back the tissue paper in which Mrs Simpson had carefully covered Kofi. He gazed at the lifeless body, the body of his best friend. More tears came to his eyes again following faster than the Nith in spate. He lifted the bird and kissed the grey soft feathers on his head. It seemed Kofi had lost some weight. Then his tears dried up and his mouth opened wide. These muddled feelings which had consumed him since the box arrived became clearer now. He turned the parrot onto its back.

'Wait, come here, come back, this is amazing, come here,' he shouted.

John opened the front door and shouted for the Inspector to return. He arrived out of breath having taken two steps at a time to the door.

The Inspector looked at John. John shrugged his shoulders and invited him back into the lounge.

'This is *not* Kofi,' Harry said.

'Really?' said the Inspector.

'No, most certainly not Kofi,' said Harry.

'Are you sure, Harry?' asked John.

'Look at his foot. See. He's been ringed. Kofi never had a ring. That ring will identify this bird. It will show it's not Kofi,' said Harry with a smile on his tear-stained face. He replaced the bird in the box and washed his hands. Then he moved towards the kettle and filled it.

'Don't tell me there are two African Grey Parrots on the loose,' said John.

'It seems so. Anyway, time for a cuppa strong tea? I need one,' said Harry.

'I'd ask for something stronger if I was off duty after this discovery, but yes, I've time for a strong cup of tea,' said Inspector Thomson.

The shoebox was tied up securely once more.

'Well, if there are two parrots, then I'd better take this one back with me. It's no longer a dead parrot. It has become a production,' said the Inspector.

Harry chuckled away with happy abandon.

'What's got into you then?' asked John.

'Ah, a production, yes, a production again,' said Harry, recalling the day when Kofi was cited to Ealing

District Court. When Harry told the Inspector this story he laughed till his ribs rattled. In his convulsions he spilt some tea over his dark-blue trouser leg as he pondered over the precociousness of parrots.

Harry brought him a paper kitchen towel to dry himself.

'Dearie me, thanks.'

'That's a story I've nae heard, Harry,' said John.

'John, I'm sure I could tell you more of Kofi's antics if my memory didn't play up from time to time,' he replied.

'But I'll tell you this, Harry. This is the happiest wake I've been to,' said John.

'Make it as happy for me when my time comes then.'

'Aye, okay then Harry. Thirs nothin' like a happy funeral, is there?'

13
Local Developments

The telephone was answered promptly.

'Sergeant McNish? Inspector Thomson here.'

'Yes, sir. You have a problem?'

'A puzzle more than a problem. Can you identify a ringed parrot?'

'If it's ringed I'll identify it. Almost impossible if it's not.'

'Yes, I see. Come over to HQ. The bird's here. Deceased of course.'

Sergeant Mark McNish was a six foot eight inches tall Highland policeman who gave Gaelic lessons in his spare time at the University of the Third Age. A piper in the police Scotland band he was also an amateur ornithological photographer both on and off duty. His precise clipped tones of his Highland heritage left no room for ambiguity. He put on a pair of plastic hygienic gloves and picked up the bird. He turned it over.

'Not badly damaged. If it had been found sooner, it might not have died.'

'Thank goodness Harry Dynes saw the ring. It was a close shave. We could have been burying the wrong bird,' said the Inspector.

Mark consulted the appropriate UK ringing of birds register.

'No, it's not on that register.'

'Perhaps it's a foreign bird?' asked the Inspector.

Sergeant McNish looked over his glasses at the Inspector. It wasn't a joke. Of course it was a foreign bird. What else did he think it was?

'There's a special category of zoo entries. I'll try that now,' he said.

He ran his finger down a column. His finger lingered halfway down the third page. He checked the ring again.

'It's a local parrot. It's definitely not Harry Dyne's parrot.'

'Definitely?' asked the Inspector

'Yes, sir. It belongs to Edinburgh Zoo. Job done.'

An extensive internal inspection of the parrots' aviary confused the zoo staff. There was no break in the overhead wire and the door locks had been secure. Of course the bird count was not done regularly so the initial escape could not be pinpointed by time. An external inspection of the fence was ordered. One area was out of bounds. The side at which Kofi unpicked the fence was surrounded by bushes and debris. No human could get access easily and none tried. It was therefore a mystery how this parrot had escaped and when that had happened. But which parrot was it? Questions mounted. Was it a chick when it left? How long had it been in the zoo? The Zoo Director could not answer any of these questions. Nor did they occupy Harry's mind. The telephone rang.

'Hi, Dad. Is the storm over yet?'

'Much calmer today, Laura. What was it like in Birmingham?'

'Nothing to talk of. The isobars were all over the east coast of Scotland so I knew you were in the eye of the storm.'

Harry told Laura about the police visit and how he had almost accepted Kofi's death; unless new information came, he was hoping Kofi had survived. But he did not let Laura know just how much energy had been sapped from his body over recent days.

He was laboured, not wishing to start the day. John noticed his lethargy.

'In a way, that was a big disappointment, that ringed bird. But it doesn't mean Kofi is not still around, does it?' asked John.

'John, I feel rundown and tired. Let's return to Dumfries. It'll soon be Christmas.'

John thought for a moment. He looked at Harry's demeanour. He saw in his companion, a man who had aged over their days away from home. Mid-winter was doing him no good. And they were no nearer capturing Kofi or his daughter.

'You are right, Harry. Let's pack up for the time being. We've achieved nothing, yet we've achieved a hell o' a lot,' he said. 'We've made many contacts and gained quite a number o' supporters and friends, so we have. Kofi will be found, of that I'm sure. The media will tend tae that. But he won't be found by us, in all probability.'

'That's true but you don't mind going home?' asked Harry.

'Why should I? After all we've had more publicity than a publicity agency could muster for Morag and we have all the wildlife officers around the country with Kofi on their radar. Returning home won't stop their searching. If they find him we can return to the central belt at any time. We should keep that in mind. And Morag is beginning to make people talk. I think we deserve a cup before we pay-up and leave,' said John

'I'm all for that,' said Harry.

An hour later as the light gradually faded they left their Bed & Breakfast in Newington and made their way through Morningside onto the A701 south. It was a cold night with a shadow of a full moon. With little cloud covering, the temperatures dropped. Harry's leather cladding, warm gloves and visor face covering rebuffed the chilling friction. Each mile was a mile nearer familiarity. But it was a slow ride. In the countryside even the main roads had a branch or two to clear. That was expected and gave Harry a chance to relieve himself; after clearing some branches, John had a fag. Harry stood in perfect silence waiting for John to finish smoking. The clouds thickened, obliterating all stars. The stars were out for another hemisphere to wonder over that night. But the cloud kept the frost and ice at bay for the travellers.

Kofi was sad to have lost his companion. He felt the cold getting underneath his feathers. He needed to find a source of warmth. He found the necessary conditions emanating from Edinburgh Royal Infirmary. Warmth escaped from metal funnels onto the hospital roof. Sheltering from the prevailing chilly winds, Kofi settled down for the night against the metal funnel, content, dry and warm.

It was just before 10 p.m. when John dropped Harry off at his home. He helped him dismount the bike. He wanted to ensure Harry was safe inside before he left. The front door did not open with ease.

'I've been away too long. The door is jammed,' said Harry.

'Let me try.'

John used his shoulder to good effect.

'This will take you a week or two to get through, Harry.'

'What's that?'

'Mail. Fan mail, I suspect. A few Christmas cards an' odd bits and pieces but the rest looks like messages of support. Maybe even a few letters of proposal. I had better leave you tae it. Hadn't I?' suggested John.

'I can't possibly open any this evening. I think a warm bath and a good night's sleep is what I want.'

'And I do tae. But I'll come by tomorrow and see what you need by way of provisions. How does that sound, eh?'

'John, we're a team, aren't we? You'll always be welcome here. In fact, let me give you a front door key. It was Maggie's but I'd like you to have it now.'

John placed the key in his pocket. He did not need to answer. Instead he drew near to Harry and gave him a hug.

'Till tomorrow, old boy.'

Harry closed the door. By the time John's motorcycle had reached the end of his drive, the bath water was already running.

When John arrived home that night, there was a letter awaiting him from Morrison's store in Dumfries. The letter invited John to have a table in the store on Saturday, to advertise Morag's disappearance. That pleased John so much he wondered if he might skip his Lexapro in the morning. It also gave him a couple of days to prepare. There was also another letter, a brown envelope of A4 size. It had a postmark from Police Scotland Glasgow.

'Hmmm, that's good of them.' He smiled at the letter's contents and then brought it to his lips where he kissed each photo with love. His third cigarette of the day emerged from his packet as the kettle was announcing its presence. Coffee and fags kept his weight down. Not what any self-respecting GP would recommend but John found these aids relaxing as he read his mail unhurriedly.

On Saturday he arrived at Morrison's to find a table and chair set out at the entrance of the store. Jack Gibson, the rotund, smiling, moustached manager, greeted him. He was of a similar age to John.

'Mr Reid, welcome. I hope you will have a good response today.'

'Thank you. It was very kind of you to arrange this. I jump at every opportunity as you might imagine but I had not thought of doing this.'

'We are community-spirited here at Morrison's. If this venture falls in place, it should jolt our customers' memories. But to be honest, I have a personal interest too.'

'Really?'

'Yes, my daughter Gail was in Morag's class.'

'Gail... Gail Gibson... I'd be lying if I said I remembered her.'

'Actually we don't call her Gail. She was always called Googy and the name's stuck to this day.'

'Ah, Googy. Yes, now I remember. It's all coming back. A tall girl with lovely black hair, not so? I remember her well. Morag had her round to our house in the past. What's she doing now?' asked John.

'Yes, that's Googy. She's finished her third year of medicine at Glasgow. How they grow.'

'Aye, how they grow indeed. You know I received an enhanced age compatibility photo of Morag from the police in Glasgow.'

'Let's see.' Jack studied the photograph. 'It's amazing what they can do. She really does look like a contemporary of Googy. How do they do that?'

'Latest technology they have up there in Pitt Street.'

'I'd better display both. I hope at least one of them will prompt recognition,' said Jack.

'You mean all three then. Don't forget the picture of Kofi. That should attract them to the table. Then concentrate on Morag. That's the way to reach them.'

'Let's hope so. Tell you what. I'll get them laminated. Keep fresher that way. Then I'll set them up for you, okay?' said Mr Gibson.

'Brilliant idea, yea, go for it.'

John's leaflets were well received but few stopped to speak to him. He consoled himself with the fact his presence would settle in their minds and he prayed for just one person to add to his knowledge of Morag's disappearance.

Understandably, children were more interested in asking about Kofi.

After lunch, which was selected from the nearby store fridge, he was brought a cup of tea. He held it cupped in his hands mesmerised by the flow of shoppers entering the store. A middle-aged woman approached the table and stopped before John.

'Hello. I am sorry for your loss. I do hope your daughter will be found soon.'

'Thank you. That is kind of you to say so.'

The woman offered her hand. John shook it, feeling it was a gesture of sincere sympathy.

Out of focus above the handshake John glimpsed his wife Alison, as she scurried past by with her trolley.

Their hands separated.

'I'm Elly-Anne Jones. I'm an author. I have been following your progress with that other gentleman on your bike, Mr Dynes. Picking up the story from the papers and from the radio, I could not help but become engrossed. I wonder if you would be offended if I wrote about this story in a novel.'

Elly-Anne Jones was Welsh. Her name almost gave her away but she had been in south-west Scotland since her marriage to a local farmer and the valley accent of her youth had all but vanished. She had that farm scent about her. Sweet, not unpleasant, but most certain of all, she was not an urbanite. Many of her books were about the farming life, filled with romance. But they also featured animals and that was her second love. It was natural that Kofi's story had interested her ever since the first newspaper report of its missing.

'A book?'

'Yes, a book!'

John was taken aback at first, but then came to realise a book could travel further than all his motorcycle trips.

'Well, I should have tae ask Harry but I guess he'd agree. It would be exposure for Kofi too.'

'Oh yes. It's very much a double quest. I've mentioned it to Neil Scott, my literary agent. He thinks it's a good project. He likes the idea of a double quest. He sees it as a pretty rare and captivating story. It's what we call a crossover genre.'

'Crossover genre?' asked John.

'Books, they have to be categorised. You know, thriller, comedy, chick-lit, that sort of thing.'

'I see. It's certainly no' a chick-lit,' said John, laughing.

'No, it won't be. Crossovers are not so common. It means that they are suitable for the teenage market as well as older adult readers. Kofi's story would entertain the younger reader who would also want to know about a missing teenager. The story holds up for the adult market, too, as they would identify with Harry's age and loss. That's why it's a crossover. And that's why there are not so many of them around.'

John noticed his separated wife Alison again as she returned down the aisle. She glanced at his table and then turned away to the vegetables. The awkward moment had gone. Elly-Anne noticed his absent gaze.

'You follow me? A crossover?'

'Ah yes. You seem to know what you are talking about. It's all a bit beyond me,' John confessed.

'I hope to come and see you and Harry if I may. You know, to get some facts right. I'll also contact his daughters if he doesn't mind.'

'His daughters?'

'Yes, I gather he has two. They would be good for getting the overall picture about him.'

'Oh yes, that's right,'

'So I'll be in touch. Bye'

'Okay, thanks. Till next time,' said John.

Alison arrived with a trolley full of provisions.

'I see you can still pull the women,' she said.

'You were never a jealous woman, Alison, don't start now,' John replied.

'Making any progress?'

'Yes, and on all fronts,' said John with a smile.

Alison was quick to correct his grammar.

'You mean both fronts, John?'

'Both for two; all for three,' he said.

'I don't follow.'

'Well, I've now got a computer image of what Morag would look like today. I'll send you a copy if you like; aye, I'll post it tae ye. A novel about oor venture is about to get off the groond and Kofi's antics are well recorded now. He's alive after the storm and hitting the headlines. It may be only a matter of time now before he's captured. That's what they call a win/win/win situation.'

'Lucky you,' Alison said with a smile, adjusting her shoulder bag. 'You're looking well too.'

'Thank you. I'm getting the balance to my life again.'

'I'm pleased to hear it. Keep it up.' She set off with the trolley.

'Send my love to your mother,' said John, feeling it an appropriate way to end the conversation, although he had not gone out of his way to see his mother-in-law since the separation.

Harry was indeed pleased to hear about the book development. He promised to buy himself a diary. He felt sure his life again needed some organisation, some structure. Well, a diary or perhaps a secretary. The thought dwelt in his mind.

14
A Court Summons

Elly-Anne's hair was tied back. Featherings of grey wisps escaped over her ears. Her writing days did not require enhanced grooming but this meeting was important to her. Her sharp pencil and the professional black leather folder showed she meant business.

'Mr Dynes. You have had this parrot for some time. When did you first notice its antics?'

Harry recalled that it had been as soon as they had returned to the UK. Kofi had been nearly one year old and by that time Maggie was as fond of him as Harry was. He sat back, contented. Mugs of Darjeeling tea sat on mats steaming mystically, while he reminisced and recalled the moment when he realised he had a very special bird indeed.

Elly-Ann began to scribble as the story unfolded.

Ealing
West London
Winter 1979

Harry, Maggie and Kofi sailed on the Black Star liner Oti River from Tema Harbour, made memorable by songstress Mary Hopkin. They were heading for Amsterdam. Remaining in his cage for most of the voyage, Kofi was taken on deck to acclimatise him as each day grew cooler and the African shore less visible. A colder European month of May awaited.

Two weeks later they sailed from Amsterdam to Rotterdam and from there overnight to the UK, entering at Kingston Upon-Hull.

By now Kofi was hand-tamed and he cocked his head to listen to Harry when speech was directed at him. He seemed to internalise conversations with ease.

Harry and his wife found a flat in Pittshanger Lane in Ealing. Harry attended the London University School of Oriental and African Studies as a way to unwind from his years in Ghana. His wife found work at the laboratory of the Government Chemist. At the weekends, Kofi was taken out of his cage and waddled around the flat following his master. But during hours of study in the flat or when Harry was at the university, Kofi sat deep in thought, stationary on his perch in his cage. He watched Harry sit by a growing pile of large books, and he followed the passing traffic on the busy West London Pittshanger lane.

One day in the third week of November, Harry set off to a seminar in heavy winter clothes. He took the Central tube line from Ealing Central and got out at Tottenham Court Road to walk up to the university. On that very day, while he was studying, Kofi had a visitor.

Harry returned after a long day at the university library. He climbed the stairs to his flat. As he approached the front door, he stopped with sudden shock. He gasped.

'Bloody hell,' he whispered.

The front door had been smashed and the lock lay on the hall carpet. Papers were strewn around the hall floor. Harry's senses were heightened; he was on edge. He entered the flat on tiptoes with arms held wide for balance. He stood still to hear if the intruder was still around, pillaging.

'Hello Harry, hello Harry,' Kofi said with delight on seeing his friend after witnessing the ordeal.

Harry's instinct was to place his finger to his lips. He crept forward like a tabby cat to inspect his cage and also

Kofi himself to see if he had been harmed in any way. Kofi bowed his head through the bars, inviting Harry to stroke his feathered scull. But this time Harry did not oblige. He was not sure if he was alone. The burglar must have feared Kofi's powerful beak. And for certain the intruder was less likely to have been an African, or Kofi's tail feathers might have been missing.

He lifted the solid brass Buddha from the mantelpiece and held it ready for throwing at the burglar. He entered each room, still on his tiptoes, seeking his adversary. He could hear his heart pound as adrenaline coursed through his veins. But no one was there. He looked in wardrobes and under the beds. The mess created made it difficult to ascertain what had been stolen. But first the police had to be notified of the break-in.

Harry stroked Kofi's head and cheeks at last but his anger about the mess of the house and the thought of a burglary dominated his mind. To his relief the deed box under the bed was untouched but the top of the dressing table was empty. That was where his wife kept some of her less expensive jewellery. His wallet, watch and course papers had been safe with him that day and no other missing item could be identified after his initial search. Damage to the door seemed the most obvious offence. Perhaps his wife might find other missing items on her return.

Two and a half hours later, Constable Tom Yates and Inspector Ralph Truesdale from the Met arrived. They inspected each room, taking notes and focussing their interest on several locations.

'Nice one here,' said Tom Yates, enthusiastic and personable.

'Yup. I've got a good one here too,' said Inspector Truesdale, pinched-mouthed and imperious, marking the areas with chalk.

'Nice one,' said Kofi.

'Was that your bird, sir?' asked Tom.

'Yes, Kofi picks up what's being said all the time.'

'Okay... I see... what's his name again?' asked Ralph.

'It's Kofi,' said Harry.

'Alright then Kofi, who broke in?' asked Tom.

Kofi cocked his head.

'Are you going to tell me then?'

Kofi returned to his perch and just as the police had decided the parrot wouldn't answer, he opened his lungs and then his beak and sang the first line twice. 'God Save our Gracious Queen. God Save our Gracious Queen.'

'Inspector, do you think Her Majesty is a suspect?'

'Behave yourself, Tom,' he rebuked.

'I'd be obliged, sir, if you did not go near these chalk circles we've made. We suspect we have good fingerprints to examine. The crime boys who do that will be round soon.'

'Well, I guess that's all you can do just now,' said Harry.

'I'll leave my card with you but I assure you the villain won't return; they rarely do. Better report that broken door to your landlord, though,' said the Inspector.

'You're right. I'll do that right away,' said Harry.

'Daaa da daaaaa da da da,' said Kofi with enthusiasm.

'That's a new one on me. I've never heard that one before,' said Harry.

'Daa da daaaa da da da.' Kofi repeated the refrain.

'Never short of a thought, is Kofi,' Harry smiled.

'Wait a minute,' said Tom Yates. 'Daaa da daaaaa da da da. Let me think... yes... I think I've got it. Inspector, I've got your man!'

'What do you mean, Tom?'

'Daaa da daaaa da da da... I belong to Glasgow!'

To emphasise his brilliant piece of detective work, Tom began to sing: 'I belong to Glasga, dear old Glasga Toon, there's nothing wrang wi Glasga fur it's goin' roond and roond... and do we have any Glaswegian housebreakers in this area, Inspector?'

'We most certainly do. It's time to call on Malky Fraser first. I wonder what he has been doing this afternoon. I'm sure he's a good suspect,' said a rather pleased Inspector.

'PC Kofi Dynes did the spadework, sir,' said Tom.

'I think we should promote him to Detective Sergeant Kofi of the Bill, don't you think?' asked Ralph.

'Special Branch, perhaps?' said Tom, his eyebrows raised in fun.

'Given half the chance, he'd tear the stripes off your uniform,' said Harry, laughing.

'Maybe so, Mr Dynes, but he's a sure smart bird, you have to admit.'

Malcolm Joseph Anthony Fraser, convicted thief and burglary specialist of the Royal Borough of Ealing, West London, was a well known law breaker who had served time, lots of times. He had a scar, but not on his face. It travelled from just below his right ear to his Adam's apple. He had worn that distinguishing mark since he was thirteen. His hair was unkempt and his teeth discoloured and at war with each other. He was a man who lacked decorum, dignity and any social delight. He was not married but at least three boys, now adopted out, had his genes. He appeared at the Uxbridge County Court three days later to acknowledge his name and address. Five weeks later he was back at court and his defence agent indicated that in no uncertain terms Malky Fraser would deny the allegations of breaking into Harry's flat. Trial was set for 3rd of March 1980 and, given his previous record of crime, he was remanded in custody till that date.

Harry put his house in order and returned to his studies. Somehow he thought Malky would come to terms with his temporary incarceration and agree to the charge in March but that was a long time away.

At Christmas, Harry took Kofi to his mother-in-law's home in Wigan where Maggie's father was a medical practitioner.

'Telephone, darling,' said Maggie's Mum.

'There's no one at the other end,' replied the good doctor but the phone rang again as he held the silent receiver.

What chaos Kofi caused making the telephone ring at all hours of the day and mimicking the sombre response to the phone that doctors have in readiness to receive life and death news.

'I think we'd better hide the Christmas turkey from Kofi's eyes,' suggested Maggie.

'Stuff him. Stuff him,' was Kofi's response.

Mother-in-law never needed to be asked to prepare the trimmings but far less the command to get on with it. Of course every Christmas Kofi got a new toy or a treat of varied nuts and fruit. That year he was appreciative of a hard wooden bark with nuts hidden inside. Needless to say the resultant debris on the lounge carpet had to be swept up.

'Hmmmmmmmmmmmmmmmmm.' The sound of the Hoover started even before it was switched on.

He was on his best behaviour in Wigan most of the time but managed to master the Lancashire broad drawl. 'Let's be havin' ye... hey hey. Let's be havin' ye.'

More nuts at New Year and Kofi stole the show, time and time again, picking up the sounds of a new and temporary environment in Wigan. On New Year's Day, the family returned to London and Kofi resumed his position in the lounge enabling him to see the passing pedestrians of Pittshanger Lane.

In February two official envelopes lay on the hall floor when Harry returned from the university. One was addressed to him and he felt it was important. The frank showed it was from the Crown Prosecution Service. He opened it immediately.

'Crikey. A citation. Uxbridge District Court... Friday, March 7th, Harry Dynes a witness in the Crown's case against Mr. Malcolm Joseph Anthony Fraser.'

'Blimey. And a letter for you too, Kofi.'

It too was a citation. Kofi was required to give evidence in the case as well. This was with undoubted certainty a colossal mistake. The Crown Prosecution Service had made a real bloomer. But it did make Harry laugh. It was an easily made blunder if the police statements had only been given a cursory glance. Nevertheless, it was an error to be rectified with haste.

The following morning Harry telephoned the Crown Prosecution Service and made it clear to them that Mr Kofi Dynes was in fact an African Grey Parrot. That would, beyond doubt, lead to a prompt conclusion, and the citation would be withdrawn. Harry laughed down the line.

'Mr Dynes,' said the middle-aged, over-serious and overweight Miss Helen Clark, a lady prosecutor. 'This is a serious matter. He's not just a parrot. He's a crucial link. The defence will claim it was a prejudice the police had against his client and so the case must prove beyond all reasonable doubt that there was an uttering by a real parrot which led to the sequence of events to trace the alleged culprit.' She spoke with authority and dignity, seeing no need to recall this witness. Indeed it was not a mistake. Kofi Dynes was cited as a witness.

'Mr Dynes, without Kofi there would be a break in the chain of events. The Crown's case would be damaged, perhaps even beyond repair.'

'But I have no control over Kofi's outbursts whether they are animated noises or narrative.'

'That is a risk I must take. He may not squawk "I Belong To Glasgow" but at least, Mr Dynes, it proves the police did see a parrot and you can tell the court, too, what he said,' she said with no illusions.

Harry accepted the situation as described in disbelief, marvelling at the perspicacity of the English Courts but cleared his commitments for Friday 7th March.

Spring had not yet sprung by March so Harry, wearing the red, white and blue of his university scarf and his knitted Christmas-present gloves, carried Kofi's cage to the court in good time. Over the cage was a cover so that Kofi would not be frightened by his journey, or exposed to the cool damp London air, let alone to some unsavoury characters that tend to lurk around courts. The anteroom to the court was selected as Kofi's temporary abode.

'This will prevent some of our awkward clients interfering with him,' said Mr Nicolson, the court clerk.

'Would they?' asked Harry.

'Poking a pen at him through the wire cage would not be out of their minds, I fear, and it might intimidate this witness,' said the clerk.

'Just let them try it. He'd break a pencil in less than the time it takes to blink and should any unfriendly finger threaten him, he'd snap at it and draw blood, causing a painful wound,' said Harry.

'You mean he's aggressive?'

'Can be, if you annoy him. But not to friends and he's got many.'

Harry was called to take the oath and gave his personal information. The details of the burglary were recalled with accuracy and his evidence was not seen as anything to challenge. The prosecutor then called for Kofi Dynes. There was a moment of delay before Harry brought in Kofi in his cage, placing it on the table in front of the bewildered Judge Nigel Ravenscroft QC.

'Is this a prank, Madam Prosecutor?'

'No, my Lord, this is Kofi, the property, already mentioned, of Mr Harry Dynes. This is the parrot to which both police officers referred in their evidence, as did the crime officers who saw the bird when they arrived at the locus.'

'At the locus,' repeated Kofi.

'Hmmm... at the locus indeed. I rather think this bird cannot be seen as a witness. And I shall consider whether the parrot may have been coached. But I will allow you to continue and I'll reserve judgement on the bird. I suggest he becomes a production at this stage. Production one, not so, Madam Prosecutor?' suggested the Judge.

'Yes, indeed. But it will be a little awkward attaching a label so near the parrot's beak, Ma Lud.'

'Point taken, Madam Prosecutor. But I have the production noted, I do assure you, and I await his responses with eager anticipation.' The Judge turned to smile at the smirking defence agent, Mr Des Green.

'Have you any objection to this witness?' the learned Judge asked.

Mr Green rose from his seat with the aches and pains of a man three times his age and stared at the bird in the cage over his half-mooned glasses.

'As long as it's a bird in a cage and not in the hand, I have no objection, Ma Lud.'

Mr Green sat down satisfied with his remark, staring at the bird. As he did so, Kofi returned the compliment with a neck-bowed stare and added for good measure:

'Don't do the crime, can't do the time. Don't do the crime, can't do the time.'

Harry shrugged his shoulders. He wasn't taught that expression. He must have heard it in the anteroom.

The proceedings drew to a close for lunch with the defence preparing to defend Malky's case when it resumed at 2 p.m.

'I think Exhibit Number One can be released, not, of course, from his cage but released as indeed you are, too, Mr Dynes, from today's court case,' intoned the Judge.

'Thank you, my Lord,' answered Harry.

As the Judge stood up, Kofi called out in repetition after the cry of the court official:

'All Stand!'

'All stand. All stand. Daaaa da daaaa da da da, Daaaa da daaaa da da da.'

The Judge stopped in his tracks. He turned towards Kofi.

'Hmmm, thank you, Mr Kofi Dynes. So you belong to Glasgow? I shall consider that as evidence in this case this afternoon, Mr Green. You have been warned,' said the Judge on his way out. Mr Green's wig slipped a few inches down over his brow. Then he placed both hands on his hips and turned to his client. Malky Fraser raised his shoulders in disbelief and shook his head as he was led out of the court by officials, insulting them as he was led away. Mr Green, whose face had turned red, looked at the Prosecutor.

'Ma'am. I have never had a case like this before and I hope and pray from the bottom of my heart it's my last like it. I can't cope with an unpredictable bird.' He threw down his pen and retired to the faculty room to eat his cheese sandwiches.

Miss Clark took off her wig and motioned for Mr Dynes to approach her. She leant over to whisper into his ear.

'Mr Green said that he "can't cope with an unpredictable bird". Of course he can't; that's his trouble. You see, he's gay. Now, shhhh, don't tell anyone I said so.'

Harry knew Fraser's defence was crumbling as Kofi added to his impending gloom once more from his store of large shop sayings.

'Going down... going... down.'

Elly-Ann Jones laughed as she continued to scribble.

'This will take some time. I had no idea that there was such a colourful backdrop to your bird.'

'You see why I miss him so much?'

'Yes, I certainly do. It's looking like a few more visits will be needed to complete this novel. Or perhaps it's a biography.

'No, it should be a novel,' said Harry. 'Kofi can say "novel" but can't say the "phy" sound as in biography.'

15
On Speaking Terms

David Conway was a handsome thin young man of twenty-three with blond hair and piercing deep-set blue eyes. Visibility restricted a further description because that was all that could be seen of this patient. Some regarded him as a human vegetable. He was in a room of his own in the Edinburgh Infirmary. To all intents and purposes he was brain dead following a horrific car accident almost five years ago. His family lived for the day that medical advances would enable his mind to return, and then perhaps his speech. His doctors had a different, more pragmatic, if perhaps somewhat heartless and pessimistic, approach and agenda. They saw no real prospect of amelioration in his condition. Nor could they expect one. Medication had long since been relegated as the desirable cure. Yet it was not appropriate to mention the alternative to his parents, given their constant devotion to and vigil with their son.

Kofi was wary about unknown people who might grab him again but his beak was his protection and it gave him confidence. He noted David spent long hours motionless only to be turned from time to time by nurses. After that was done, he was left for long periods. Kofi had not seen such a still person and it intrigued him.

Winter morning light came late. The hospital sounded active with ambulances and people arriving and departing. Much movement was observed by Kofi around the building.

A group of nurses and doctors came to a nearby back door to smoke. The doctors stood on one side, the nursing staff and auxiliaries on the other. He noted the division. But there was no movement in the patient's room. Kofi saw David's window was open. He flew on to the window ledge and grasped the metal frame. Still David did not move.

Kofi made some car braking sounds. Then an F1 starting grid sound. Then came the Hoover sound and the police car, ambulance and fire engine sounds. Each had a distinctive tone. He whistled the Ghanaian national anthem, which he had learnt in his last few days in Ghana. Then he took a break. He watched but still David was lifeless. His repertoire continued. This time it was more verbal.

'Who's a pretty boy then? Who's a pretty boy? I am, are you? I am, are you?

There was still no response from this statuesque body.

Mr Ralph Auerbach was a bespectacled Glasgow dignitary of the Jewish community. His parents had been Glaswegians since their escape from Vienna in 1938. Ralph studied medicine at Glasgow University, then specialised in neurology. He was one of three consultants in this sphere at the hospital. That afternoon at 3 p.m. in his medical office, this neurological surgeon had the most distressing of meetings. It was a meeting that was overdue in his opinion but one which had to be faced by the family.

'Mr and Mrs Conway, your son David has been with us for almost five years. In that time as you know we have kept a careful eye on him and his condition. Sadly we must confirm that there have been no signs of any improvement over this period of time.'

'But medications and procedural progress are always being mentioned on television, Doctor. David needs time, if nothing else: time,' said his mother.

'Time is what we have given David, I do assure you,' he said with quiet authority.

'You want to free the bed, don't you? It's about targets and money-saving, isn't it? It's not about our son, is it?' said Mrs Conway in an angry voice which trembled and snarled at the same time.

'Dear, listen to the doctor. He knows what he's saying,' said Mr Conway, trying to pacify his wife.

'You want to kill him, don't you?' she cried.

'Mrs Conway. That is not what doctors do.'

'No. I know your Hippocratic Oath but I also know what DNR means.'

'I assure you there is no Do Not Resuscitate notice near David's bed. I assure you.'

'Then you'll starve him, give him a hospital-acquired bug or something to end his life. That's what this meeting's about. Isn't it, Doctor, isn't it, I said... ehh... isn't it?'

Mr Conway embraced his wife and patted her on her back as hysterical bouts of tears made her makeup run.

'I'm sorry, Doctor. She's emotional,' said an embarrassed Mr Conway.

'It's understandable, Mr Conway. Such crucial decisions must be made in the clear light of day and under no emotional pressure. Today is not the day. We'll leave it there.'

'But you are thinking of turning David's life-support machine off, aren't you?' asked David's father.

Dr Auerbach's nod was just enough to be seen.

'I'm Kofi Dynes. I'm Kofi Dynes. I'm no a wee sparrow I am no a wee crow; I'm a grey parrot I want ye to know. I'm Kofi Dynes, I'm Kofi Dynes, I am no a wee sparrow I am no a wee crow. I'm a grey parrot I want ye to know.'

The door opened. In fright, Kofi flew away to the warm tower on the roof. There he watched until the body was alone again. Once more Kofi returned to keep an eye on the rigid patient. He was intrigued. This patient offered no nourishment and Kofi was hungry. So he set off in search of a local garden to find an offering of fat balls and nuts. Someone had attached food onto glass windows. That must be for small birds, he thought. No purchase on a window there. Yet it did not take long to spy a net of nuts on a branch at the bottom of a garden. There he satisfied himself and once more there was no shortage of puddles to quench his resultant thirst in Edinburgh. This was indeed a land of plenty.

Kofi returned to the window ledge of the hospital room once more, where with some alterations, he gave a second performance, and two hours later an afternoon matinee. He seemed to be transfixed with this inactive young man.

David's parents had visited him every second day since his accident until the confrontation with Dr Auerbach. Now they visited their son every day without fail, no longer trusting the staff to keep their son alive. They increased their interaction with him. Sometimes they played the music he loved as a young man not long out of school. They recalled what they were doing as a family before his horrific road accident and talked about it to him. But his sister and brother had long since left his bedside for regular visits. His aging parents were seen to be caught in a religious grip devoutly attending him as if he was lying in State. They had run out of ideas, run out of inspiration, and they were clinging to the thinnest of threads of vanishing hope. Their ability to sustain this vigil impressed some of the nursing staff but frustrated others of the medical staff beyond reason.

Two days later they returned as usual. They sat at David's bedside in a daze. His mother held his hand but this time, after more than four years of silent devotion, David turned. He opened his mouth.

'I...m... no... a...'

'David darling, it's Mum. You are speaking again. Speak to me, darling!'

'I...m... no... a... wee...'

'Listen, do you hear him talk, Ian?' she said to her husband.

'Let him speak then, for God's sake. What is he saying?' his father asked.

'I'm no... a wee... sparra... I'm... no a wee... crow. I'm... jist a grey parrot... I want ye tae know.'

David's mother leant forward to hug David and kiss him. David, for the first time in more than four years, gave a weak smile. It was a definite smile and it could not be denied.

Mrs Conway opened the door of the room and called to a nurse.

'Nurse, come quickly. David is speaking, it's a miracle, he's talking! You must come and listen!'

The nurse felt sure Mrs Conway was grasping at straws. Perhaps David had sighed but he had done that many times before, both in his parents' presence and when the staff were present.

'I'll be with you in a minute, Mrs Conway.'

'But it's true, nurse, you must come and hear him,' she begged.

The nurse had not heard Mrs Conway speak with such convincing veracity before. Perhaps she had heard something different. Just in case, she thought against her better judgement, she would come to his room anyway.

But David was in a deep sleep. He could not respond to his mother's nudging.

'Mr Conway, did you hear him speak?' asked the nurse.

'I guess you don't believe us. But he did, nurse. Honest, he did.'

'What did he say?'

'I know this is hard to believe but he said a poem.' Mr Conway spoke as if his powers of persuasion had evaporated.

The nurse concluded that their outburst was the evidence. They were surely delusional in their wish for David to get better and return to be the handsome loving son he must have been. It was a tragic case as David's condition was making his parents mentally ill.

'I'll leave you now, Mr and Mrs Conway,' she said.

'But believe us, nurse, David spoke to us, as my husband witnessed.'

'Yes Mrs Conway. I hear what you say.' The nurse's forced weak smile offered her paltry understanding or apparent empathy.

The Conways stayed for another four hours by David's bed but he was exhausted and so were they. No one believed them. David failed to come out of his sleep. When his parents left the ward late that night, it was with mixed feelings and heavy hearts. True they had heard David for the first time and that gave them hope but it might be the beginning of the end when he seemed to be improving, before his final breath on earth.

The following afternoon Kofi sat on David's window ledge for his repeat performance of sounds, then dialogue. David listened with interest and then smiled. He tried to copy what Kofi was saying. Kofi was a patient teacher. Little did they know that the same nurse back on duty was now outside the door with her ear against the keyhole. With great caution she turned the handle. Her eyes met Kofi's on the window frame. He panicked and flew away. But David continued to speak.

'Who's a pretty boy? I am. Who's a pretty boy, I am.'

'Yes, you are, David. You are a pretty boy, aren't you?' said the nurse.

David's eyes opened.

'Yes, nurse. I am...' He looked at her. 'And so are you, nurse.'

The nurse approached David. She sat on his bed and held his hand.

'This is remarkable, David. You have made a great effort to talk again. I must tell the consultant. But you must also be aware you might be starting all over again. You might not recognise your family and that will be distressing for them as well as you. You realise this may be the start of a lot of hard work? And I mean a lot of very hard work.'

'I'm no a wee sparrow, I'm no a wee crow. I'm a grey parrot, I want ye tae know,' said David.

'David, think now, who taught you this poem?'

'The bird at the window, of course.'

'You mean the bird I saw on the window ledge?' she asked.

'Kofi... Kofi a bird. A grey parrot. Yes, that's right, he taught me.'

The nurse's brain rummaged through her training. It drew a blank. If she was not careful, she might be seen as cranky. Then it dawned on her that this might have been the missing Dumfries parrot David had encountered. And he said its name was Kofi. Corroboration was needed nevertheless before the consultant got hold of this remarkable development.

16
The Tarnished Duke

Amy Nixon was eighteen, and a straight A student of Knightswood Secondary School in Glasgow. She was the first of her generation to go to university and was soon to embark on a German and Business studies course at Glasgow University. She knew exactly where her future lay. So too did Ewan Errol, a lad of a similar age from Ayr. His father was an air traffic controller at the busy Robert Burns airport of Prestwick but aviation was not Ewan's thing. It was medicine, and he had been awarded a place to read the subject at Aberdeen University next term. His other interest was developing; it was in Amy. She was four inches smaller than Ewan, who was six foot two inches in height, but her flowing chestnut hair, her buoyant personality and a smile as wide as the Firth of Clyde were so appealing, and had captured Ewan's attention. Her teenage body had recently changed to a delectable wasp-like figure with a bosom almost out of proportion to her lean frame. She was beginning to show signs of interest in this rugby, beer-drinking hulk of a teenager, which was Ewan.

They were part of a party of eight, marking their rites of passage in the Duke of Edinburgh's Gold Award scheme. Their final task was to orienteer from the picturesque town of Killin in Perthshire on the River Dochart at the end of Loch Tay to the Falls of Connel overlooking the Firth of Lorne. It was an arduous trek through Glen Dochart to Crianlarich and then through Strath Fillan to Tyndrum. On through Glen Lochy to Loch Awe and finally via the Pass of Brander and Taynuilt, to the former ferry port at Connel now served by an architectural marvel of a bridge. It would take three and a half days to complete the hike at a steady pace and to meet the supervisor's van at Connel. That would be the most welcome sight offering comfort and refreshment but above all confirmation that their Duke of Edinburgh Gold Award had been accomplished. They set off on the road just outside Killin in twos. Amy and Ewan took up the rear. They were the only couple to hold hands.

The country opened up for Kofi to see once more. Everywhere he went nourishment was available and so he decided to continue his travels north-west. His flight brought him to Aberfeldy on the banks of the river Tay.

Immaculate gardens reminded him of how Harry used to place his cage outside in the summer where he could enjoy the warmth and observe the birds, cats and dogs which came into view from his vantage point of safety. But now he was free to meet and greet whomsoever he took an interest in. It was a most gratifying experience for this social bird. The town was compact with what seemed like a multitude of different dogs being led on leads. None were like the red brush-tailed fox Kofi had encountered at Wanlockhead but he suspected, given the opportunity, some of these beasts might like to get the taste of him.

So to the hills he flew in search of secure accommodation after he had dined on the generosity of the good people of Aberfeldy and their wonderful selection of different varieties of ripe apples, suet blocks, sprouts, kale and nuts.

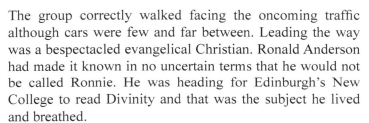

The group correctly walked facing the oncoming traffic although cars were few and far between. Leading the way was a bespectacled evangelical Christian. Ronald Anderson had made it known in no uncertain terms that he would not be called Ronnie. He was heading for Edinburgh's New College to read Divinity and that was the subject he lived and breathed.

'Ewan, don't fall behind,' he said out of jealous spite. If this final group task was to succeed Ronald expected everyone to pull their weight and pull it together in the same direction. The lagging, hand-holding couple at the end did not meet with his approval. Nor was such open physical friendship known to his life's experience and his glowering eyes told them so.

It was agreed that their first night would be encampment near the village of Benmore overlooking Loch Lubhair. They reached that destination at 6 p.m. and three tents were erected in next to no time in a semi-circle. Amy, Carol and Angie would occupy one tent while Jim, Ewan and Mike the second tent. Ronald would have the third, leaving Bruce, the holder of the boys' short straw, to join the Bible reader.

Mike Nelson, the electrical engineering student to be, gauged the wind flow and then prepared the ground to light a campfire. His studious attitude showed his methodical way of working. His T-shirt emphasised this with his compartmentalised attitude to life. On his chest it read WORK-EAT-REST, in blue, red and green, on an orange background. He excelled in all three statements, being the hardest worker, the fastest eater of the group and the loudest snoring and farting member.

All sought suitable dry sticks to get the flames under way except Ronald who had unpacked his guitar. He sat on a nearby stone singing *Morning Has Broken* from his New Life songs and hymns songbook.

'Don't you know any by the Killers, Ronald?' asked Carol, the aspiring English language teacher with an Alice band restraining voluminous black waves of luscious hair. She was the tiniest of the group but packed a punch in her fiery responses and Shakespearean quotes.

Ronald did not answer but sang more loudly:

Praise with elation, Praise every morning,
God's recreation of the new day.

The beans were bubbling and the sausages heating up.

'Meal's ready,' said Angie, the second medic. Angie had been nominated the first-aid member. She came from the hamlet of Carnduff a few miles out of Strathaven, where her father was also a general practitioner. She was a gangly lass who wore tight jeans making her seem even taller than her five foot eleven inch frame. Being last born with four elder brothers, her tomboy experiences and her self-confidence moved the trek along.

All gathered round with their plates and Bruce doled out the contents of the pot. Bruce would soon be studying chemistry at Strathclyde University. He wished to teach this subject in a secondary school and be the Duke of Edinburgh organiser in that environment. There was not a sport he had not tried which he did not love or accomplish to a satisfactory standard. From hang-gliding to scuba diving and many ventures on land activities, Bruce was the action man. No one doubted this position of strength, yet he was also spectacled and had an occasional stammer.

As each recipient grabbed a slice of buttered bread before finding a spot to sit down to supper, Ronald stood apart.

'Blessed art thou oh Lord God, King of the Universe, who brings us forth bread from the Earth. Amen.'

'AAAAMEN' repeated the others in unison, sniggering as they filled their mouths with sausage.

After washing their plates, they sat around the glow of the fire on a cold clear night. Ewan lay back looking up at the sky.

'Canis venatici,' he said, pointing to two stars. Then almost with his eyes closed he continued, 'Pegasus; Vega, the Milky Way…'

'Hmmm, Milky Way? If you've got one to spare, I'll have one,' said Bruce. They all laughed.

By this time Amy had joined Ewan stargazing with small talk. Time passed by in a fire-dazed stupor, with academia set on hold for everyone that night.

'No more wood on the fire. Let it die out,' said Mike Broadfoot, the only member not heading for higher education. But that did not worry him. He would be entering the family undertaking business and that meant earning straight away while the others would be starting to accrue debt. Mike was the funniest group member, making puns and remembering jokes that had flown from the minds of the others. He told them that humour was a skill all undertakers must have and the group nodded at his wisdom. The group drew nearer to the alluring dying source of heat.

Bruce got out his harmonica. He began to play *Kum ba ya*. Ronald began to sing as if possessed, holding his arms out with palms pointing heavenward. His eyes were closed.

Ewan's eyes were fixed on Amy's.

'Let's go for a dauner,' he said.

'Where to?' she asked.

'It's such a bright moonlit night. Do you think we could… make it to the top of Ben More?'

Amy looked up to the sky. It was lit as if the attic lights were on.

She smiled. Then she looked around. The night seemed to be content and settled. No noise came from the village and in the silence her heart pounded more strongly. Feelings of expectation were filling her receptive mind.

'C'mon, let's go.'

The fire had been doused by water from the nearby stream. They made sure everyone was tented in preparation for playing cards or retiring for the night. The only murmur was from Ronald reading from the scriptures while his tent-mate fumbled in his pockets for change. Bruce had just lost the first game of brag. It was time to set out.

The night light showed the path leading towards the 3852 feet of Ben More. A hoot of an owl seemed very near.

'Frightened?' asked Ewan.

'Hmm... with you here? No,' she replied.

Ewan smiled and turned to face her. He held her shoulders and bent forward, still smiling, and kissed her lips. They lingered for a moment before disengaging.

'The top. We'd better make some progress,' said Amy.

In the middle tent the games were coming to an end.

'Your luck's not in today,' said Carol.

'Not tonight anyway,' said Bruce.

'Once a knight always a knight. Twice a night and you're doing all right,' said Mike.

'That reminds me. Do you think it will be a case of Not Tonight Josephine for Ewan and Amy then?' asked Jim.

'God knows, they've only just met,' said Bruce.

'Not so. They met a while ago at a D of E meeting in Glasgow. Don't you remember Angie?'

'Not sure if they were an item then, Carol. But as soon as we knew who was on this programme I guess we all knew things might perk up... I mean develop.'

'It will never last. It can't,' said Jim.

'You're a pessimist.'

'Don't think so, Carol. Body types not right. More Laurel and Hardy than Ginger Rodgers and Fred Astaire, if you ask me. And if he's going to be in Aberdeen an' her in Glasgow, it does not augur well.'

'I reckon it will a' go well, 'said Jim.

'Augur well, I said,' said Mike.

'*How should I, your true love know, from another one? By his cockle hat and staff and his sandal shoon,*' said Carol.

'What?'

'Shakespeare, Jim. Hamlet.'

Bruce took out his harmonic and played Bach's Air on the G string, the accompanying music of an old Hamlet cigar television advertisement.

'Ahh I get it, clever that,' said Angie.

'Get what?' asked Jim.

'Nearly there. I can see the top.'

'Ewan pet, at least it'll take less time to get down.'

'Get down? We mustn't wake them. Fancy a night on the mountain?'

Amy stopped to catch her breath.

'A night on the bare mountain? Are you serious? You mean stay out all night?'

'No?'

'We'll see. Let's reach the top first,' she said.

Seventeen minutes later, Ewan raised his arm in triumph.

'Made it. What a sight. Speckles of domestic light. Huge fluffy clouds just out of reach beneath us. Not a bird in sight but the flicker of bats. It's magic, Ewan,' said Amy.

Ewan towered over Amy in a clinch. They turned a full 360 degrees together marvelling at the darkness, the deepness and the softness of the night sky. Beneath them the land was dark. The hills looked like shrouds of angry black hooded night travellers stopped to see what they were doing at this late hour. A sprinkling of light from homes in the village looked like glow-worms flickering here and there as lights were extinguished by bed-seeking residents.

Ewan sat down. Amy did the same a moment later after lingering on the wonder of the darkness above and below. It was an encapsulating feeling: one she was glad to be sharing with Ewan.

Ewan brought her close to him and their kisses began in fun. Then their hearts grew impatient. Hands explored and tensions grew. Their emotions struggled to come to terms with what each other had achieved in such a relatively short romance. The point of no return fast approached.

'Darling, can we...?'

Amy knew instantly what Ewan meant. He fumbled in his pocket and raised a condom for her to see.

'Thank God. That's reassuring,' she said, taking hold of him.

The stars shook gently as they formed a heavenly bond. Oblivious to anything except each other, the act began and the participants experienced a particular overpowering joy that neither had known before. It was a powerful force. As they discovered in the aftermath, it had been the first time for each. Lost in each other's embrace, they had each lost their virginity.

'Where the hell are they,' asked Jim.

'Shhh, you'll wake Ronald. You don't want him to know they're out,' said Mike.

'Just thought they'd be back by now.'

'Angie, I hope Amy doesn't wake us when she comes back,' said Carol.

'You know, the pair of star-crossed lovers.'

'Yes, *in her first passion woman loves her lover, in all the others all she loves is love.*'

'Wow, that's profound,' said Angie

'Lord Byron,' said Carol

The night grew warmer as if the evening embers had risen to comfort them. But it was the gathering cloud from the west which gave them cover. That they had both crossed the threshold together made it such a special moment on top of the mountain.

'I never thought it would happen on top of a mountain,' said Ewan, smiling. 'The perfect setting.'

'On top? I was under a mountain!' said Amy, chuckling.

After a half hour when their bodies were relaxed and comforting each other in a loose embrace, the first few rain drops were felt. They stirred.

Ewan looked at the gathering sky. They would get drenched if the rain-bearing clouds did not clear the mountain top; no matter what they did, they could not escape the rain.

'Well. We could keep most of our clothes dry if we took them off and made a pile. We could dance naked in the showers or we could start the descent right now. Your call,' Ewan joked.

Amy laughed. She opened her waterproof and laid it on the ground. She gathered all their clothes under the covering.

'Come on then,' she teased.

In circles they danced naked like the dancers in the musical Hair. They did not mind standing on twigs or loose stones. Their gaze was on each other and the beauty they had discovered that night as the rain fell more heavily and washed their exhausted bodies.

Then Ewan stood on a sharp stone and gave out a loud groan and fell to the ground. His footing collapsed and he began to roll off what seemed to be an insignificant drop onto velvet moss beneath. The width of this soft landing was however insufficient to support his body. As his anguished cries grew louder, he fell down onto a ledge eight and a half feet below.

Amy rushed over to see where he was.

'Ewan. Where are you?'

'Ahh, over here… Amy… it's my… ahhhh.'

'Are you all right?'

'It's my ankle… and a few scrapes I've picked up. I think it's broken.'

'God, no. Are you sure?'

'I've seen these in Casualty's A&E when I got a porter's job. It's broken, no doubt about it. Aaahhh.'

'Hold on. Let me think.'

'I think… you'd think better, with your clothes on.'

Amy struggled to get her damp jeans on again and feared the dampness around her might lead to a severe cold. But uppermost in her mind was Ewan shivering naked on a ledge just below reaching point. She gathered his clothes and approached the drop. Ewan was focussing on her arrival. That was a good sign. He was grateful to see Amy had brought his clothes. Item by item she dropped each garment beside him and over time Ewan struggled alone in distress to dress, save for one sock and boot.

Amy could not bear to see him struggle this way. Sense left her for a moment, but duty prevailed.

Sliding over the ledge, like a toddler leaving a parental bed, she lowered her body as her grip loosened. The rain made her purchase impossible. The root she was holding gave way and she felt herself slipping.

'I'm falling, Ewan, I can't help it, I'm falling...'

Down Amy came almost on top of Ewan.

'Well, that's two of us marooned. I can't see how anyone will find us now,' said Ewan in a pained voice.

Amy smiled. She opened her mobile and raised it for Ewan to see. She dialled her friend Carol. She waited... and waited.

'Oh God... There's no signal, Ewan.'

'Here, try mine,' he said, handing over his mobile phone from his top pocket.

'You've got, let me see Craig, Neil, Andy stored...'

'Further down, further down.'

'Greg, Tony, Alison. Alison? Amy enquired.

'Yes, Alison... Alison Errol, my sister, but don't phone her.'

'Here's one. Ronald. Our Ronald?'

'Yes, don't ask me why I've got his.'

'At least we'll have someone praying for us,' smiled Amy.

'Come on... ring it. This leg's hurting.'

'Here's hoping this time... 07753... oh dear. No signal again.'

Before lying down to comfort Ewan, Amy filled her lungs. 'Heeeelp. Heeeeeeeeelp.'

Kofi was awake early enjoying the constant rain. It was before most people had risen. Alert as ever, he heard a faint call. It sounded again. It was so unusual coming from a mountain top that it was worth investigating.

He flew to a height above Loch Lubhair and on to the crossroad village of Crianlarich. There he saw climbers getting ready to assault Ben Oss. He was surprised at the human race's ability to come to terms with its environment. He had discovered people in homes and towns, in crowds and in hospitals, in prisons, and now, on the wild mountainside, he was finding more adventurous human beings. The air was as chilling as an open freezer. That meant more flying as his wings could generate warmth. Soaring into the territory of the golden eagle, sparrow hawks, kestrels and falcons, Kofi was aware of meeting an adversary. He decided to fly lower, clinging to the contours of the high, deceptively soft-looking mountains.

Then something different caught his eye. At first it seemed to be a moving collection of clothes but as he flew nearer he could see it was two people huddled together. He circled around them without their awareness. Then he heard the cries of pain coming from the larger human. It seemed that all was not well.

Kofi assumed they were in difficulty. They seemed unable to return home, their natural habitat. This situation was not normal and that alerted his mind to a solution. He flew to the ledge above them and greeted them.

'I'm no a wee sparrow, I'm no a wee crow

I'm an African Grey Parrot I want ye tae know.'

The couple looked up in amazement.

'Wow, an African poetic parrot, up here in the mountains? That's impossible. I must be seeing things. Amy, I think I must be going crazy.'

'No, you're not. I guess that's the missing parrot I've read about. Let me think, now, what's its name... ah... I remember! Kofi, Kofi?'

Kofi was delighted to have met humans who knew his name. He flew down to meet them.

'Hello, Kofi, I'm Ewan, Ewan, Ewan.'

'Hello Ewan, Ewan.'

'That's amazing. He understands.'

'Yes, Ewan, but can he help us get help?'

Kofi realised there was a degree of urgency in Ewan's voice. He strutted around them. Neither had the confidence to approach or touch him. Then he saw a glove. A bright pink glove. He dawdled up to it. He lifted the glove in his beak and seconds later flew off with it.

Amy looked at Ewan.

'Just what was that about? He's taken my glove.'

When the tents began to open, it was clear that neither Ewan nor Amy had passed the night where they should have been. This caused alarm.

'Amy, Ewan,' Jim shouted but there was no response.

Angie lifted her mobile telephone. 'I'll see where she is and give her a bit of my mind into the bargain.'

The group gathered round.

'There's no signal. I'll try again.'

'Let me try too, I might have a stronger battery,' said Carol.

Neither phone responded.

'Oh my God. They must be up on the hills,' said Jim.

'Aye but which one?' asked Mike.

Kofi flew back round the mountain to Crianlarich. At the hostel tearoom a group were preparing to set off orienteering. Kofi flew above them. Then he let the glove drop. It caused the group to look skyward.

'Look, that bird. It has just dropped that glove. Anyone missing a pink glove? Ladies? What the heck was that all about?' asked Tosh McGregor, the lean, grey-bearded leader of the group. He had the look of a haunted man with deep-set eyes and sideburns that extended down each cheek from his white-speckled, red-knitted, woollen toorie hat.

'What kind of bird was it?'

'I didn't see. Quite big I think. Like a pigeon I think.'

The leader stooped to pick up the pink glove.

'I'll leave it in the tearoom. Whoever lost it is sure to get back here, at some point in the day. Right, all ready? Then off we go.'

Kofi set off to the couple once more.

'I say we contact the police at Killin,' said Mike.

'You got their number?' asked Angie.

'I reckon it's a 999 job, don't you think?'

'I guess you're right. If they stayed out all night, then they'll be in some condition,' said Carol.

Mike turned towards the town of Killin. When he got through to them his grid points were relayed and he informed the police when they last saw the couple.

'They are sending the mountain rescue boys in, and putting a helicopter on standby but the ground is not best suited for a flight.'

'I guess that's all we can do. There's no point us going in all directions and getting lost. I think we should wait and see what the Mountain Rescue team suggest.'

'There's always...' said Jim, turning towards Ronald who was already on his knees seeking mercy, comfort and spiritual assistance for the couple.

Kofi returned to Ewan and Amy and they smiled at his return. However Kofi was active and not wishing to entertain. He swooped down and looked at the second pink glove.

'Whatever is it doing with these gloves, Amy?'

'I've no idea but if he steals any more clothing, we'll die of exposure.'

'Hey, grab that glove, quick!' said Amy.

Ewan rolled over and gathered it while Amy found a pen in her anorak.

'Have you any paper?'

'Don't think so. No, I haven't. Have you?' asked Ewan.

'Just the ordinance survey. Anyway, it's all we have.'

Amy began to write on the torn-out piece of the map. She then placed the note in the middle finger of the glove. She offered the glove to Kofi who waddled forward to collect it.

Kofi seized the glove and instantly flew away.

'I could almost see him wink, Ewan. I think that parrot may be our saviour.'

'Wait till you tell that to Ronald.'

'Your foot, is it feeling any better?'

'I'm in a restful position for it, but it is swelling and when I move it, it's very painful. It's almost confirmed now as broken.'

'But I love you, Ewan. Surely they have found us missing by now. They surely won't proceed without us. I think I should shout again. It may attract someone.'

'Either that or perhaps we should accept Ronald's prayers.'

'Do you think he's praying for us?' she asked.

'Can't you feel it? I'm sure he's praying.'

'You start thinking how to tell the medics how this happened. And let me know when you have. We need a plausible story.

'True love is never plausible, is it?' asked Ewan.

Kofi returned to Crianlarich where the car park by the tearoom was becoming the centre for the rescue party. He circled the gathering without being noticed at first. Then he dropped the glove in the centre of the encircled rescuers as they studied their ordinance survey maps.

'Hey, that's the parrot back,' shouted the tearoom lady. Jean came running out in excitement. 'Here, this is the matching glove. The pair came from that bird, you know,' she said, concerned.

Tosh stooped to pick it up.

'There's something inside this one,' he said, picking out the message.

'Not a long message.' He turned the paper over. 'Written on an ordi map. It says: Help. On top of Ben More. Injured man with partner. Stuck on ledge.'

'What are you thinking, Tosh?'

'Which way did that bird come from?'

'Over there, I think,' said Hamish.

'That's between Stobinian and Ben More.'

'Aye, but the parrot says Ben More. That sounds a good starting point.'

'Hamish, yes you're right, either that or a wild goose chase. We've got to find out if the gloves are from the missing girl.'

'I suspect they are. And that's a little less warmth for the pair. I hope they know each other well, 'cos they'll need each other's heat to keep warm and survive.'

The Mountain Rescue jeep set off and the trekking party began their assault on Ben More.

Their truck made good progress and stopped at its limit. Six of the team, helmeted and numbered, progressed at a good pace.

Meanwhile Kofi had returned to the couple to give them comfort.

'Hey, no more clothes please Kofi, if that's still in your mind.'

Kofi cocked his head.

'Oh, Ewan, he's so cute.'

'Oh Ewan, oh Ewan,' said Kofi in sympathy.

For a moment Ewan and Amy forgot their troubles. Here was a comforting parrot. Like a teddy bear to a sick child, like a carer for an injured soul, and that was Ewan.

'Listen, Ewan, I hear talking.'

'I can't hear anything.'

'I can… Help!' she shouted.

'Did you hear that, Tosh?' asked Hamish.

'Shhhh, a moment silence,' requested Tosh.

'Heeelp.'

'Yes, we are pretty near the top. No sign of them yet. Give me the hailer. Thanks. *Mountain Rescue on its way. Stay calm. Mountain Rescue on its way, stay calm.*'

'Yes, I heard that this time. What a relief. Are you okay?'

Amy supported Ewan's head and lightly brushed her hand over his forehead. Kofi looked on and walked closer to them.

Voices sounded nearer and Amy stood up.

'Over here, we're over here.'

'Coming, on our way,' said Tosh.

Tosh walked over to the ledge and peered over.

'Okay, we'll get you out of this. I'm Tosh. Who have we got down there?'

'I'm Amy. I'm okay but Ewan's leg is in a bad way.'

'Okay, dear, I see you are all right. We'll get you out first. Ewan, stay still and calm, we'll be with you soon, laddie. Right, Miss, let's get you up and out safe, then we'll have more room to see to Ewan. Okay, young man?'

'Great, just great,' said a relieved Ewan.

A short ladder was dropped down and Amy was instructed to climb up it. Before she did, she bent down to kiss Ewan.

'A night on the mountain, a most memorable night. Take care. I'll stay with you.'

'You mean a night on the bare mountain? A most unforgettable night, you mean.'

They laughed and their voices drifted upwards.

'What's got into you two? C'mon, Miss, let's get working on Ewan.'

Amy climbed up the ladder and was covered with a warm blanket without ceremony and taken down to the jeep.

The ladder was once again lowered and this time Tosh and Hamish came down with a restraining stretcher.

'C'mon, Ewan, we need you to roll over on your side, then we'll get this stretcher under you. Hamish will keep your leg still. Okay?'

'Yip.'

'One two, three... up... that's it.'

'Aaaagh!' cried Ewan

'It's more than his leg. He's got a lot of superficial scrapes on his face and arms. You're a lucky man. This is not a broad ledge. If you had gone over here, you would have fallen almost a thousand feet. It would be a sheet we'd be covering you with.'

Ewan reflected on the rescuer's words. It was a near thing and a sobering thought, of that he was sure.

'Crikey. That bird's back,' said Hamish.

'Back? It has been with us for quite a while, keeping us company. It's Kofi, you know,' said Ewan.

'Aye, it brought us pink gloves. And we got your message in one of them. Amazing, isn't it?' said Tosh.

'You are a clever bird, Kofi, a clever bird.'

Kofi cocked his head. 'Clever bird, ohhh yes, clever bird.'

'Right now, let's hoist you up. It's not going to be easy but we'll manage.'

'Hamish, we've got to strap him to that ladder. Get the rope round the stretcher.'

Without ceremony Ewan was stood up on the stretcher, which somehow eased the pain in his foot for a few moments. Colleagues above them pulled the petzel rope clamp and Ewan began to rise. Without warning the motion stopped with a jolt.

'Ahhhh, oh God… ahhhhh…' said Ewan in agony.

'Hold it there. There's a stone blocking the ladder step. Down a bit. Hold it… hold it. There.'

Hamish took his ice pick and hacked away at the protruding stone. Each blow made Ewan gasp but after a dozen well aimed blows, the stone gave way, dropped to the ground and then rolled over the ledge.

'Right, up again… pull!' instructed Tosh.

When the stretcher cleared the precipice, it was lowered with care to the ground and Ewan began to hear a gentle purr. It grew stronger and louder.

Amy looked up at the sky. A helicopter was about to descend to the mountain top where there was a patch of flat land: the patch of flat land that the couple knew so well.

'I must be with him,' she said.

'Wheesht, lassie,' said the rescue team's first aider, Merle.

'Can I go with him?'

'We'll have to wait an' see. It's the fella that's injured, no you.'

'I know but…'

'Is it yer man?' asked Merle.

'Aye,' said Amy, 'my boyfriend.'

'Yer boyfriend? Well, I suppose… I wis young once too.' She took her walkie-talkie out.

'Bravo Mike to Tango One, do you read me? Over.'

'Tango One, go ahead.'

'Is there room in the 'copter for the girl?'

'What condition is she in?'

Merle looked at Amy who was sitting drinking hot chocolate.

'I'd say suffering. Yeah, emotional suffering. Think she should be checked out however,' said Merle, winking at Amy.

'I'll ask. Hold on.'

Merle turned towards Amy. 'Do you think you can make back up to the helicopter?'

'It will take a mountain to stop me,' she replied.

'If ye can laugh aboot it, yer well on the mend, lass.'

The line opened again.

'Go ahead, Tango One.'

'Pilot accepts. Send Amy up.'

As the helicopter set off for Glasgow's Western Infirmary, the green light was given for the Duke of Edinburgh's contingent to proceed, two down.

On board Amy held Ewan's hand. Ewan was given a comforting injection by the paramedic Bill, whose body was encased in a well-insulated suit, but under his helmet was a very full black beard.

'This will mean you will be both missing out on your gold award. It's a pity about that,' said Bill.

Amy smiled at him. 'We can do it later. After all it's the last part. We've completed so much already. In fact when you are fully fit, Ewan, we can do it together. How does that sound?'

'That's a deal then, on one condition.'

'Being?' she asked.

'No climbing without Kofi.'

Amy smiled and when Bill wasn't looking she gave Ewan a kiss. 'You've given me a lot to remember today.'

'Yes, sorry it turned out this way.'

'Me too but... it was wonderful before, wasn't it?'

Ewan beckoned her forward once more. They kissed again.

'Caught you this time,' laughed Bill from within his bushy beard.

'I can't understand them, irresponsible, that's what they are,' said Ronald.

'It's what love does,' said Angie.

'Yeah, what do you know about love, Ronald?'

'How wayward is the foolish love. Yet in its place, love so amazing is so divine,' he replied.

'If you ask me, love is a universal migraine and they are giving me one right now,' said Bruce.

'We'd better get used to two down then,' Angie remarked.

'Just make sure no one else falls by the wayside,' said Ronald.

'Then we'll need your prayers,' said Mike.

17
No Such Thing as Bad Publicity

Harry had been home for almost a week and his strength was rallying. The empty cage was sparkling clean awaiting its rightful owner. Harry remained hopeful that Kofi would fly back one day despite the length of his absence. He missed his company more than words could say. The telephone rang.

'Hello?'

'John here. How are you?'

'Not so bad. Early nights though.'

'Well, I hope not next week.'

'Why? Are we going somewhere?'

'No, but I've just had a call from the BBC. They are doing a programme about our travels and aboot Kofi's antics. Remember giving Kofi's life history and oor motorcycle experiences and meeting Reevel?'

'Yes, sort of, over breakfast I remember.'

'Well, believe it or not they are going to put on a special programme about us and Kofi.'

'When?' asked Harry.

'Next Wednesday, 8.30 in the evening.'

'That's prime time.'

'Yes and no wonder. There will even be a hospital consultant speaking aboot the lad who had not spoken for five years. They are claiming Kofi broke his silence. Alec Salmond will also be interviewed. It keeps the focus oan our searches, no doot aboot it,' said John.

'How did you hear all this?'

'A BBC researcher telephoned. She called me tae confirm some facts she had gathered. Some I did not know aboot but she seems tae hiv a good list of them, so she does. Should be good viewing, not so?'

'It sure will. And Kofi was back at a hospital again? It would be great if Kofi and Morag came home for Christmas though, that would be a real celebration,' said Harry.

'It would, yes, of course it would but it is not realistic, is it? I've got my doubts. What I would like though, Harry, is for you to join me for Christmas lunch. Or would you have other plans?'

'The girls will be here for New Year but I'll be alone for Christmas.'

'No you won't. Have Christmas Day with me. Come for morning coffee and watch me cook the turkey. Don't make any other plans for the whole day.'

'That's very kind, John. I'll lend a hand too.'

'No need to, I'll have everything under control, as I say, so I will,' reassured John.

David Conway sat up in his bed looking out of his window. Kofi was nowhere to be seen but he knew this parrot had reached his mind like no medication ever could. He hoped he would see the bird again soon.

His parents arrived with smiling faces.

'Darling, how are you today?' asked his mother.

'I'm feeling fine although at times I just cannot understand what happened to me. It's crazy to think how so much time has passed by. I can't believe I've been here so long.'

'I know, son, but the great thing is that you will have a future. It's been hard over the years. There were times I felt you'd never speak again but I must admit your mother never gave up hope,' said his father.

'Darling, I hope you can see the programme the BBC is doing about that parrot next Wednesday. It's an amazing parrot as you know, and you'll see just what it has been doing around the country. I saw the trailer about it last night.'

'You mean Kofi?'

'Your memory is better than mine, it seems,' said his mother.

'What else has it been doing?' asked David.

'Wait and see. You won't be disappointed,' said his father, smiling.

A tear came to his mother's eye. She dabbed it with a handkerchief.

'David, you are the most wonderful Christmas present I've ever had.'

There was a knock on the door.

'May I come in?' enquired Mr Ralph Auerbach.

'Ah, Doctor, please do come in,' said Mrs Conway.

'Am I forgiven?'

'Doctor, I am sure you meant no harm. I know you must have so many difficult decisions to make each week. I am just glad you got this one so wrong.'

'Judgement is a very fine balance. Yes, sometimes we get it wrong, you might say. But my faith leads me to accept there is a greater judge than I. He gave us all time to reflect and that is what has saved David.'

Mr Auerbach sat at the edge of David's bed and smiled at him.

'How are you today, David?' he asked.

'I'm fine, Doctor.'

'He's not a doctor, David. Mr Auerbach is your consultant, your neurological surgeon,' said Mrs Conway.

'You can call me whatever you want, David. I'll not be offended. Now, can you tell me what day it is?'

'Er... no... or is it... Tuesday?'

'It's Friday, David. Do you know which month it is?'

'Umm... it's cold outside so it will be winter.'

Consultant Mr Auerbach smiled. He turned to David's parents.

'There will be moments of great clarity and then moments when David will not make much sense of his surroundings. He has gone though such a traumatic change. The mind is a law unto itself but there must have been something about that bird, the parrot. It may have been the repetition or the fact it was a bird speaking but something triggered something in David's mind. It did so in a way which none of our drugs could. And in a way none of us could have predicted. Tell me, Mrs Conway, is there a bed awaiting David at home?'

'Oh yes of course, it awaits him when David comes out.'

'Well, since David's voice returned we have given him an Electroencephalogram: you know, an EEG examination.'

'And... what did that show?' asked Mr Conway.

'There are millions of signals crossing over our brains. Some of them come apart and that's when we suffer a loss of motor activity. David's road accident caused much damage to his brain. The cortex protected some areas of his brain while other brain cells went into remission. But now they have been reinvigorated. How, I cannot say. But I will tell you this. We will need to monitor David for some time yet. And that will mean spells back here in hospital in all probability. But I think I need to give him more experiences to bump-start those lazy brain connections further, and also for him to discover the technology in our homes which seem to change every six months. Mrs Conway, do you wish to take David home for Christmas?'

'Of course. Yes please… darling, that is beyond our wildest dreams!' said Mrs Conway, turning to her husband.

'Of course we will, but Mr Auerbach, are there any preparations we will have to make?' asked Mr Conway.

'The best advice I can give you is pretend you have a new baby in the house. If he goes to sleep, and this is quite likely as he'll sleep quite a bit, make sure he is safe and when he is awake make sure you know where he is. You can take him for a walk outside by all means but he must not go out on his own, not just yet. If for any reason you cannot cope, then bring him straight back in. Am I making myself clear?' asked Mr Auerbach.

'I understand. And when will he have to return to hospital?'

'You'll get a letter. It may be an outpatient's appointment or it may require him to come in for longer reviews. But you won't receive that before the New Year.'

'Thank you, Mr Auerbach, thank you so much. We'll keep an eye on him,' said Mrs Conway.

'Oh and I'd not give him any alcohol yet, even though it's Christmas. It's a bit too early for that. But I'm sure you'll manage him quite well,' said Mr Auerbach.

'We'll take great care of him, I assure you,' said Mrs Conway, with Mr Conway nodding in total agreement.

'And can I remind you, the story of the parrot will be on television. I urge you to see it and please take a note of how David reacts to it. That might be interesting.'

'We will. David will make sure we don't miss it, won't you David?'

'Yes, Mum. I must see the parrot again.'

At 8.30 p.m. the following Wednesday, five days before Christmas Day, record viewing figures were recorded by BBC TV. Although Sally Magnusson was the reporter, the programme went out to the whole of the UK and mainland Europe for those tuned into the BBC worldwide.

The programme began by Professor Dr Alan Kimber of the Zoological Gardens at Whipsnade Zoo speaking about the African Grey Parrot generally. He explained that it was indeed a remarkably interesting bird.

'As Mr Dynes had the bird from such an early age, it bonded particularly well to him. They had been inseparable, since the bird was a chick I believe. There were few if any similar bondings in the animal kingdom between an African Grey Parrot and a human. Of course many rural families had kept caged parrots but the interaction between Harry and his parrot was unique. His handling was daily and his nourishment varied. Kofi was kept in prime condition.'

Dr Kimber sat down at a table where a stuffed African Grey had been placed. He stroked it.

'Unlike other parrots, wild African Greys have been documented imitating the calls of several other species,' he continued.

'Parrots have been your speciality?' asked Sally.

'Indeed so. Research with captive African Greys, most notably with a bird named Peter, has scientifically demonstrated that they possess the ability to associate simple human words. This was part of my doctorate studies, at Oxford,' said Dr Kimber.

'Just to make it clear, these abilities are attributed to the African Grey Parrot and not the family budgerigar in people's front rooms?' asked Sally.

'That's right. Budgerigars have less than an eighth of the parrot's abilities. We are talking purely of the Grey Parrot. They intelligently apply the abstract concepts of shape, colour, number, and zero-sense. According to

Professor Pepperberg and other ornithologists, they perform many cognitive tasks at the level of dolphins, chimpanzees, and even human children.'

'But Kofi interacts with adult humans too, not so?' asked Sally.

'This is what makes Kofi quite remarkable and again I refer back to the relationship between Mr Dynes and his parrot. Many pet Congo African Greys learn to speak in their second or third year. I suspect it was more like a matter of months or even weeks when Kofi started. Their vocal ability and proclivity may range widely among individual birds.'

A camera focused on a poster of a New York apartment. Then it entered a lounge revealing parrots and chimpanzees on the wallpaper.

'One notable African Grey is Paul who in 2004 was said to have a vocabulary of over 950 words and, like Pepperberg's parrot, was noted for creative use of language. When Jane Goodall, the primologist and anthropologist, visited Peter in this New York home, he greeted her with "Got a chimp?" because he'd seen pictures of her with chimpanzees in Africa. This was typical of Kofi's encounters.'

'He's a truly remarkable bird, isn't he?' asked Sally.

'Indeed he is. A study by Dr Dalia Bovet published in 2011 demonstrated that African Grey Parrots were able to coordinate and collaborate with each other to an extent. They were able to solve problems set by scientists: for example, two birds could pull strings at the same time in order to obtain food. In another example, one bird stood on a perch in order to release a food-laden tray, while the other pulled the tray out from the test apparatus. Both would then feed. The birds in question were observed waiting for their partners to perform the necessary actions so that their behaviour could be synchronised.'

'Thank you, Dr Kimber. That was a very interesting talk about the character and nature of this parrot species.

We now have in the studio Councillor Goodie from south Lanarkshire. Councillor Goodie, how did you come across Kofi?' asked Sally.

'Yes, hello, well, it was quite by accident. We were campaigning and fund-raising in Larkhall when I ran out of flyers! That's when I made contact with Kofi.'

Viewers learned of Kofi's aerial antics and his distribution expertise in the south Lanarkshire town.

'Thank you, Councillor. Dr Kimber, was that usual behaviour for an African Grey?' asked Sally.

'It was interesting that you say the leaflets or more appropriately the flyers were yellow. These parrots like bright colours and there's none as bright to a parrot as yellow.'

'From the Scottish Parliament, I think we can hear from the First Minister, Mr Salmond?' said Sally.

'Hello, Sally,' said Mr Salmond.

'You must have been pleased about Kofi's antics in South Lanarkshire?'

'Pleased, yes delighted, but we could do with a few more to get our leaflets around the country. But seriously, this is a heart-warming yet very sad story. Mr Dynes, who lives in Dumfries and is a good age, has lived with his parrot since it was a chick. To have lost it must have been soul destroying, indeed devastating and my sympathy goes out to him.'

'Then, should there be attempts to capture this stray bird?' asked Sally.

'Easier said than done, Sally. This is a truly remarkable bird that is one step ahead of us all. It is also helping people in so many ways. That is most satisfying to everyone. But we must ensure it comes to no harm or is frightened by well-meaning captors.'

'Thank you, Mr Salmond. Now in one of Kofi's most amazing feats, we turn to Mr and Mrs Conway in their home in Lenzie. Are you there, Mr and Mrs Conway?'

'Hello, yes we're here, Sally,' said Mr Conway.

'You are the parents of David who has been in a coma for four years, not so? Tell us about that,' said Sally.

Mrs Conway took a handkerchief from her handbag and dried a tear from her eye. Her husband noticed her distress and responded for her.

'Our son David was involved in a serious car crash over four years ago. For all that time he has been in a deep coma... but the parrot spoke to him... and why hear it from me? Let David tell you himself.'

David entered the lounge and sat down beside his parents. Polite applause came from the live television audience.

'It may seem hard to believe but I don't remember being unconscious for four years. I remember a bit about the car crash and then fell asleep. I awoke two or was it three weeks ago...'

'It was almost two weeks ago, David,' said his mother.

'Yes, two weeks ago. I was aware of a noise at the window. In fact it was a series of noises. Ambulances, police cars, Hoovers, telephones and even coughing noises. Then I heard speaking. The bird told me his name was Kofi and he recited a poem he must have been taught. Somehow this source was speaking to me from a different side of the room. A side no one ever spoke from. I told him my name was David and he repeated that. It was the start of the long road back to normalcy. It was that surreal encounter which brought me life once more. That was a wonderful moment for me,' said David. 'What a parrot!'

'Thank you, David, a remarkable story indeed. We are delighted with your recovery too. Now my colleague Reevel, you interviewed Mr Dynes fairly early on in the story, didn't you?' asked Sally.

'Yes I did, Sally. Very much a chance meeting, in fact. Mr Dynes is a delightful old gentleman. He's clearly devastated by his loss despite knowing the parrot is alive and doing so much good. Yet he's being helped by a retired wildlife police officer with his own mission to find his missing daughter. They are indeed an unusual couple, yet most likeable. What's more they have a surprising mode of transport. Here's a photo of them.'

The photo of the pair on the motorbike was shown on screen.

'Yes, we must not forget John Reid. His daughter Morag aged almost sixteen suddenly went missing four years ago and there was no clue as to what happened to her. You may remember we reported on the story at the time. John has identified with Harry in his search for clues about what happened to Morag. The only difference is that every now and then Kofi is found making himself known one way or another. That must give Harry some hope but Morag Reid's case remains no nearer solving. But I do admire their stubbornness. I hope they might both get what their hearts desire. It's a gripping story and one which will run for some time yet,' said Reevel.

'Well, we all know about the missing parrot Kofi and the intrepid twosome. I suspect the men will be taking it easy over Christmas and this cold spell but if any viewers come across Kofi, please report the sighting to the police. They have wildlife officers all over the country who are trained to deal with such situations. Likewise anyone who can shed light on missing Morag Reid should also call the police or this missing person's number on screen now... So from the studios here in Glasgow, after what has been a most intriguing story which, as Reevel said, is sure to roll on, it's goodnight from us all. Goodnight,' said Sally.

As the programme's credits rose and a strident number of descending chords were played in the background, a helpline remained at the foot of the screen together with Police Scotland telephone numbers. Both missing loved ones were given full prominence. The numbers were in a bold font.

Harry got up in stages to turn off his television and unplug the set from the wall socket. He opened the curtains to see the shadowy branches of a lime tree caress each other lovingly and wave to him in the glow of a street light. Then darkness. He turned off the lounge light. He climbed the stairs chuckling to himself. Ah dear, lost souls indeed but nevertheless, on the telly. He just could not imagine what response might be brewing in the land in either case.

He entered his bedroom and closed his curtains. He set the 'snooze' button to ninety minutes of Radio 2. As his head rested on the pillow, Willie Nelson's distinctive voice sang *Funny How Time Slips Away*. Harry realised that was true. Was he ready for yet another Christmas?

18
The Bells of Bishopton

Kofi found the west coast milder and damper: a lot damper. East and west Scotland were like being either inside a fridge in the east or in the kitchen in the west.

Bishopton settled near the banks of the River Clyde and had two large buildings in its midst. One was a residential girls' school, which sounded boisterous as Kofi flew by. It brought back bad memories of Barlinnie Prison, although voices were high-pitched and less numerous. He crossed the main Glasgow road and headed for a very old building with a tower. Inside that building that afternoon there was a meeting, a strategy meeting of the Kirk.

The Reverend Ron Boggle, a thirty-five-year old family man with three girls and a boy, was in the chair. He swept back his black locks revealing a white streak of a few very noticeable strands of hair. It was hard to believe, but his collie dog had a similar streak of white on his pitch-black sheepdog's coat. It was as if a painter's brush had accidentally run through the hair of them both. This peculiar marking had led Ron to call his collie Tache. The word was French for stain, although the less educated would remark that the dog had been named after its owner's moustache. Tache sat under the table, by his master's feet.

'Now we come to any other pertinent matters. Are any such matters forthcoming?'

'Well, times have changed,' said eighty-seven year old Jim Matheson leaning on his walking stick. This widower had been a member of Bishopton Parish Church since 1942 when he came from Birmingham to work in the ordinance munitions factory in the village providing ammunition for the Allied cause. The church made a particular impact in his life. He was the deputy: in fact he was the deputy organist, the deputy church officer to lead the Bible into church before the minister arrived, and the deputy fabrics convenor. But he was also the church's archivist, which had no deputy.

'Changes for the worse,' he said in reply, reflecting his long service.

'In what way?' asked Ron.

'We've lost our way. The church bell has not rung for ages and the youngsters are running away from church.'

'The church bell was rusted. It cannot be repaired without expensive scaffolding. We've got used to being without it.'

'Perhaps a wee drop of WD40 is all it needs to get it clanging again. But I mind a time when we didn't have a bell and every pew was full here.'

'When was that, Jim?' asked Ron.

'It was a Watch Night Service. There had not been a bombing of the nearby shipyards of the Clyde for forty-eight hours and it was generally felt that a Christmas truce was on the cards. At that time, the Church Officer was Sam Hall, a conscientious and very particular Church Officer, but one who wore a serious and sad countenance. The only times he had been known to be cheerful were on the days his beloved red and yellow striped Partick Thistle Football Club in his native Maryhill had won a match. These Saturdays were numbered on the fingers of one hand that season.'

'Yes, I remember that name,' said the Minister, engrossed in Jim's story.

'The Minister at that time was the erudite Rev. Dr. Stewart Thomson, one of your predecessors. He decided to go home to his manse and not wait for the Watch Night Service. You see it was customary for the Youth Fellowship to hold a Xmas Eve dance in the hall. The dance would end at 11 p.m. and the Youth Fellowship would go over to the Church for the start of the Watch Night Service at 11.30 p.m.'

'Some still do, you know,' said Ron.

'As you might know this church has seating for well over a thousand in the nave and another thousand five hundred in the main church. Dr Thomson gave his assistant the Rev James Harvie an Order of Service with instructions as to the conduct of the service and left for home. There would be little ceremony about the service as it was for only the Youth Fellowship, you see. There would be no office-bearers on duty and no offering was to be taken. Sam Hall and James were left in charge.'

'This sounds a very interesting story, Jim. One I am thinking I could use in a sermon perhaps.'

'Aye but wait, it's about to get more interesting. This church had been built with a bell tower without a bell at that time. Consequently, they used a gramophone recording of a carillon of bells, attached to a basic amplifying system. When the wind was in the right direction, the Bishopton carillon was clearly heard across the River Clyde at Dumbarton and Cardross. Sam came to James Harvie and told him, "We're on our own. We're going to have a great service." And they did just that.

"Get back down these stairs," he ordered. "What's wrong?" James asked. "The Chapel's full," he said. "I'm fitting in extra chairs. I'll come when I'm ready." So back James went to the vestry and waited. Just before midnight, Sam appeared and said, "Right! We're ready. Now speak up. The Chapel's full! I've jammed in another fifty chairs."

"Then why didn't you let them overflow into the transepts? They might not see as well but at least they could hear," James suggested. "What do you think I've done?" asked Sam. "The church is full and the rest are all standing."

'The back gallery and transept gallery were full.

'"There's two thousand in the Church. You'll no see them all, but they'll hear you."

'My goodness. But how did that happen?' asked Ron, taking notes about the memory.

'I'll never forget that service, Ron. The heartily sung carols and the way Jim's hand was wrung when the service was over. There was a mass of wonderful people who attended. Protestants, Catholics, but for the most part, people who normally would never enter a church: men and women in the forces uniform of all three services representing many different nations, and men and women in the green uniform of Corporation bus drivers and conductresses, shipyard workers, young and old, respectable and some less respectable, sober and the not so sober. And many were preparing to join the advance into Europe, that coming spring, for the final victory.'

'Those were difficult days. Sadly, the masses you referred to are no longer here,' said Jim.

'Aye, but hear me out. There'd been no collection taken, but that happy congregation that morning wanted to give – and nothing would deter them. Money was left all over the place. They found collection plates and filled them. They left coins on the pew seats. What's more it took several hours to count the collection that night; I should know, I helped them. But now you want to know how it happened?'

'I certainly do.'

'Well, Sam was still smiling in the early hours of Christmas morning. He had gone to the Youth Fellowship dance, you see. There, he asked the young folk if they had any good Christmas records and someone brought him Bing Crosby, singing *Silent Night*. That's when the idea struck. Bing Crosby had drawn people like a magnet. So Bing sang to them: *Silent Night*. But of course with the amplifier up at full, Bing was heard in Partick and Anniesland and even Dumbarton. They came from all the tenements around too. Sam's inspiration had worked a miracle,' said Jim

'But did the membership increase?'

'No but the next morning, Christmas Day, was Christmas communion. The Rev. Dr. Stewart Thomson arrived and heard about the Miracle at Midnight.

'"Put on that record again for the Communion Service, Sam," was the order. Sam did but the miracle didn't happen again. You understand, Christmas Day in Glasgow 1944 was an ordinary working day.'

'The collection that night must have been the reason we were able to get our bell in 1945. The proceeds from that night raised the capital. It's all making sense now.'

'It is indeed, Minister, but our bell is rusted as you say and that's the problem with the church in general now. Rusting away.'

'Do you think the bell would really attract folk?' asked Max.

'Well, maybe not, but it would be the church shouting out that it is alive and welcoming.'

'Hmmm, true. Shall I now close the meeting with prayer?'

Kofi enjoyed his time in Bishopton, the home of the marmalade king James Robertson, Sir William Arrol who planned the Forth Road Bridge and John Witherspoon, a signatory of the declaration of the American Independence. All that history was lost to Kofi as he headed for shelter. The rain was a misty penetrating cloak and Kofi had had enough showers to last him several days. It was to the Bishopton Parish Church tower he flew. This square column was open at the top and a large bell stood suspended from the roof.

The structure sheltered Kofi from the intermittent windy showers which assaulted the tower as he stood on top of the bell. But it was not a comfortable stance. He slid down to the lip of the great bell. He noticed he had not been the first to visit this construction. As he looked into the bell, he noticed a stick was lodged between the clapper and the resonator. It formed a spar and he managed to get on top of it and perch. There was evidence that other branches had been there, forming a nest but its occupants had flown away some time ago.

Kofi's weight was slight but sufficient to make the spar move. As he adjusted his stance, the spar fell to the bottom of the tower. Kofi jumped on the bell circumference and the bell began to swing. Then the most deafening sound was heard around him and startled those in the town. The Bishopton bells were ringing after a fifty-year silence.

Kofi did not like the deafening loud sound they were making and so flew away as fast as his wings would permit.

In the church hall below, Ron's recessional prayer stumbled to a conclusion.

'So... God Lord... who maketh... the trumpets to sound... the cymbals to clash and the bells to chime, come to us and share the joy of announcing you are alive and with us. Amen.'

'It's a miracle,' said Jim.

On hearing the bells for the first time unsettled Tache. He sat up, opened his jaws and howled wolf-like to wake the dead in the churchyard. AWWWWWWOOOOOO.

No one ever found out why the Bishopton bells rang out that day. But it did start the regular ringing each Sunday morning. And to Ron's delight the townsfolk responded and began to fill some of his pews once more.

Ron wondered how he could explain the strange campanology to his wife that evening. His eyebrows unfurled when he reached his conclusion. The resumption of the bells after their discussion and prayer that afternoon meant only one thing. It was further evidence that God moved in mysterious ways.

19
A Christmas Cruise

Christmas Day dawned quietly as ever. It was dull, mild and damp. White Christmases were a thing of the past. In his childhood in Kirriemuir in Angus, Harry had always had a deep white Christmas to trudge through and fall in the cold cotton wool. But in Ghana on the festive day he and Maggie had had fresh coconut cut from the shading trees on Busia beach. He recalled these Christmas memories with fondness and perhaps rose-tinted spectacles from an imperfect memory.

All spruced up with a bright red tie resting on a new cream shirt, Harry felt good. There was no public transport this day so he knew it would be a fifteen-minute walk but that prospect delighted him. Dog walkers gave a cheery 'Merry Christmas'. Many asked if there was any news of Kofi or Morag. Strangers he knew only by sight were asking. If only he could give a more positive reply.

Harry arrived at John's front door in Georgetown, Dumfries, and was met by a halo of bright festive lights. He rang the bell, clutching a box wrapped in festive paper.

'Come away in, Harry, ma man. Merry Christmas,' said John.

'Happy Christmas to you too. It was kind of you to invite me.'

'Not at all. Here, let me take yer coat. Now is it a sherry or a coffee?'

'11 a.m., then it must be a coffee. That would do me fine. You know how I like a mid-morning coffee, even on Christmas Day.'

'Right, you sit yourself doon in the lounge while I put the kettle oan.'

Harry entered the room and placed his present under the Christmas tree. A fresh scent of fir pines filled his lungs. The tree sat beside the fireplace masking three rows of deceased relatives, mainly in sepia, which John had displayed in dark stained wood on a crimson wall. Quietly in the background, John Barker's trumpet was playing O Little Town of Bethlehem. Harry kept time by nodding the beat with his head as if a stroke had struck him.

Cards lay on the sideboard and on top of the piano. Tinsel hung from the central light to a curtain rail. The scene reminded him of family Christmases when his girls were young in those days in Troon in Ayrshire. The unbridled excitement of finding the contents of their stockings at the foot of their beds made him smile. The inevitable tangerine peelings and the wrapped presents of varying sizes destined for specific recipients reminded him of a regular family festive time. But many other details had faded from his mind. A more current thought hit him. This was also the first year he would celebrate the special day without Kofi.

'Here, take a mug. Help yourself. There are some crisps and nuts aroond.'

'We always had nuts at Christmas and all through the year as you can imagine. I'll have a few crisps, just a few, as the turkey's still to come,' said Harry.

He pointed to the piano.

'Do you play?'

John smiled. His eyes glazed over.

'That piano has not played one note since Morag disappeared. It was hers. Grade 6 she had reached. In that piano stool is all her music, untouched. Thirs Grieg, Liszt, Beethoven, Sondheim, Aarne... and so many more besides. Prefer the older masters personally, so I do. But there will come a day, I don't know when. Either she will return to place her fingers on the keyboard or I'll have to pay for its removal. It's a damned heavy piece of furniture to move.'

John moved towards the tree and knelt down. He produced a present.

Harry took hold of it, thanking him.

'Let's see, a book I think.'

'No, it's nae a book,' said John.

Harry continued to open the packaging. He turned the present over.

'It is a book, isn't it John?'

'No it isn't. I said it wasn't a book. Read the card first and you will see it's noo really a book.'

Harry opened the envelope. 'Love Film.com will send you two DVD films from the collection in the book each month for a year.'

'For those long nights when there's nothing oan the telly,' suggested John.

'For those early mornings when I can't sleep either,' said Harry. 'But really, that's a super present for one as old as I am. Thank you, John, very thoughtful of you indeed. I shall definitely look forward to that. In fact I've not seen a Western for some time. You know a John Wayne film or even The Lone Ranger with Tonto.'

He laughed and gave John a hug.

'There will be nights ahead when spirits will get me low. It's in the nature of our searches. That's a good time to be distracted and films do just that... Now, where is it? Ah... here it is, your present. I hope it is at least as interesting.'

'Thanks, Harry. Seems quite heavy, I think,' said John.

He released the Sellotape from the neatly folded ends with the precision of a parrot's beak. He discarded the Christmas paper. A blue box appeared. He took off the lid and saw tissue paper covering his present. He separated the paper and lifting it out by its lugs he looked at the Quaich. He noticed the inscription on the side.

> *'From Harry to John.*
> *Both in search of their loves.'*

'How appropriate, Harry. I like that very much indeed. It will always remind me o' oor friendship. Let me place it oan the mantelpiece, with yer inscription for a' tae see.'

'If you look on the other side...' said Harry.

John turned the silver Quaich around. Indeed there was more writing.

> *'A Father's love for a daughter*
> *Exceeds the realms of love.*
> *A daughter's love for her father*
> *Will remain on Earth and Above.'*

John's throat went dry and Harry could see his eyes were moist.

'I doubt if the Sassenachs wud ken whit tae dae wi' a Quaich, Harry. But a love bowl with joint handles might spark a few romances sooth o' the border.'

'Aye, John, we can learn from each other.'

'You are a sensitive poet, Harry. You have cleared ma thoughts so well. I have a feeling it will all be resolved in the coming year. That is, one way or anaither.'

'Closure. I agree. That's what you're ready for. That's what we both need.'

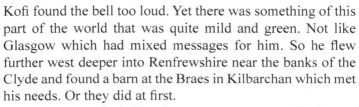

Kofi found the bell too loud. Yet there was something of this part of the world that was quite mild and green. Not like Glasgow which had mixed messages for him. So he flew further west deeper into Renfrewshire near the banks of the Clyde and found a barn at the Braes in Kilbarchan which met his needs. Or they did at first.

As usual a fat ball and some nuts were on offer but no matter how much his head was tucked under his wing or his neck telescoped into his body, he found it much colder that night. Where could he secure some heat to see him through the long winter nights?

Two days later on a bright keen winter day, Kofi flew north over the River Clyde. He noticed a large cargo boat sail down the river with dignity, leaving behind it a ripple that brushed the shoreline like a parental caress.

The container ship had set sail that morning from the Broomielaw docks in Glasgow. Its destination was the port of Antalya, in Turkey. The bill of lading recorded its cargo in stacked containers, as an order of miscellaneous white goods. That was the official list.

Kofi approached the vessel from the stern and felt the warm air expelled from the engine rooms. Heat was guaranteed from this source. He boarded unnoticed. He was surprised to find some healthy pickings of seed on the roof of some of the containers and a recent shower of rain had produced sufficient water to quench a parrot's thirst in the dents of the aluminium boxes. He waddled along towards the great funnels of the vessel finding the source of warmth of this apparent lifeless ship.

Flying around the ship he came to an unusual funnel. He landed on the lip of this much smaller metal protuberance which had a perpendicular orifice. But this one was unique.

It emitted unseen voices. Sobs and crying subsided and then resumed. Kofi realised there were humans aboard, unseen but present deep within the bowels of the ship.

For the next eleven hours this was Kofi's dwelling. During that time he heard much. The accents were unusual to his ear but not all of the words. He liked the sounds they were making and so he remembered them. But there was no audience for him on board, or anywhere for that matter. It was only the ship's warmth that kept Kofi a passenger.

Little did he realise that when he decided to leave the ship the following day in search of nourishment, he was back in Dumfries & Galloway but very much at the coast, on the extreme west, seventy-five miles from home. It was a largely unknown fact that it was exactly seventy-five miles from Dumfries to Edinburgh, Glasgow and Stranraer. Kofi had made an impact in the two great cities of this arc. How could he make an impact in a quiet coastal town?

20
An Eagle, a Birdie, a Parrot

Harry had not heard or read anything about Kofi for a while and was now thinking the winter could have taken its toll on him. No one in Scotland had reported any sight of him. He presumed that Kofi was still in the capital of course but the fact that no one had seen him there was both surprising and disappointing.

The overnight frost had lifted. Play resumed. On the fifth tee at the Stranraer golf course, there is a dip and wild, wild rough containing the thorny west coast prickly gorse. A golfer must clear this spot. It was not a long drive that was needed, more a five iron to clear the trap and head towards the green. But the dip and the impenetrable gorse was a psychological trap in the mind of many a golfer. Those new to the course rarely escaped its evil charm. Many lost their balls here together with their patience.

Adrian Murphy had come to Stranraer from his native Northern Ireland across the narrow North Channel for the weekend. A keen golfer at the peak of fitness for a thirty-five year old, he now sported a cap. It was not to shade his eyes but for protection as he was prematurely bald. A family man, he had left his home in Ballymena to join his golfing partner Sean McGonagall, from Cushendall, for a weekend of golf. Their wives were enjoying a shopping spree with tickets to see Hairspray that night in Belfast. The mutual breaks would serve them all well.

Sean was also a bus driver along the Antrim coast. He was pleased not to be sitting today. He placed his ball on the tee. He took a few relaxed swings of an iron in preparation. With a quick nervous tug of his lilac lamb's wool sweater sleeves upwards on each arm, he approached the white sphere. He was the shorter of the two but that meant power and he had been showing Adrian his heels on the previous two holes. He addressed the ball, bending slightly over it, his feet apart. He raised the club over his right shoulder and swung through. The ball went high into the air and landed on the fairway, leaving a pitching club from where it settled to the iron hard green. His jovial face smiled, revealing a gold tooth on his upper row of teeth.

'Nice shot, Sean,' said his partner.

Adrian, wearing a clashing mauve Pringle sweater, placed his ball on the tee without any preparatory idiosyncrasies. He addressed his seven iron. He swung the club over his right shoulder but when he followed through, the club hit the ground before the ball. The ball was hit on the upward swing of his club without power. The resultant action made the ball move hesitantly to the height of a man, but it had no velocity. It made its departure from any further activity and sank out of sight into the lush spiky gorse.

'Bugger it. I've lost that one.'

'Bad luck, Adrian. Take another ball. Play it again,' said Sean.

This time Adrian would not make the same mistake. He loosened up, looked up towards the green in the distance and dismissed the graveyard of his last ball from his mind. He swung his club to and fro this time to relax arm and shoulder muscles. He chose a different club, opting for a five iron to give him greater distance. He addressed the new ball and silently prayed to the God of Golf to make the ball fly down the fairway.

Whoosh! The ball was on its way. A perfect example of Newton's Third Law of a force equal and opposite then followed. His ball struck a prominent boulder set in the fairway. The momentum was reversed. In abject agony Adrian watched as the second ball bounced backwards on the firm turf and landed in almost the same spot in the gorse as his previous ball.

'That's it. No more bloody shots on this blasted hole. Play yours out. I can't keep losing balls at this rate,' said Adrian, wiping his brow with his heather-purple sweater sleeve.

They began to march off the tee with Adrian muttering about never having lost two balls to a gorse bush before, but Sean ignored his self-chastisement.

'Hey, did you see that, Sean?'

'What?'

'The bird, the fricken bird. Flew into the gorse. What was it? A gull?' asked Adrian.

'Possibly, or a pigeon perhaps,' said Sean.

The men continued down the path to the fairway. They looked back at the scene of the ball-swallowing dip but there did not seem to be any ornithological movement beneath the spiky yellow gorse flower buds and certainly no sight of either of the two white golf balls amid the specked clusters of frosted lace-like spider webs.

The couple proceeded. They laid their golf bags outside the smooth putting surface.

'Play another ball on the green, Adrian. Good for putting practice.'

Adrian went to his bag to find the third ball this hole had required.

'Play yours out then, Sean.'

Sean stroked the ball with elegance and his golf ball rolled towards the hole. It stopped three inches from the lip.

'I'll give you that, Sean.'

'How kind,' he laughed.

Kofi then flew out of the gorse towards the green. Clutched in his powerful claws were the two missing golf balls. As Adrian stooped with his putter to hand, Kofi let go and the balls landed at Adrian's feet.

'Holy Mary. Can you believe this?' said Adrian.

'Looks like a parrot to me,' said Sean.

'But that's hardly believable, I tell you,' said Adrian.

'More like a retriever. How did it know I was the daft golfer who lost two balls at this hole?'

'Parrots must sense the senseless,' joked Sean.

'Joking apart, wow, look at it fly. It's definitely an African Grey Parrot. Hey, wasn't there one in the papers recently? A missing one?'

'Yeah, mind you I thought it was in Edinburgh, myself. But better be quiet about it, or they'll just say it was the luck of the Irish. Either that or that you've kissed the Blarney Stone as well.'

Sean and Adrian finished their round. They made for the nineteenth hole and ordered two Sawney Beans, a locally brewed lager from the bar, tended by the burly local and popular barman, Ian Sharpe.

'A good round, gentleman?' he asked

'Most... enjoyable,' said Sean taking his first sip of his cool lager, leaving him with a prematurely white moustache.

'Lose any balls then?' asked Ian.

'As a matter of fact none! On a course we're not familiar, quite remarkable, I'd say,' said Sean.

'Not even at the tricky fifth tee, the one over the gorse?' asked Ian. 'It catches many out.'

Sean looked at Adrian as if they somehow knew the incident at the fifth had been seen. Adrian thought the best policy was to come clean.

'When I say we did not lose any balls, we were technically right to say so. But an incident at the fifth hole, which you have mentioned, caused quite a commotion. Did you see what happened?' asked Adrian.

'No. Something happened?' questioned Ian.

'Yes, it was quite remarkable. I lost my first ball to the gorse so took a second ball. It went further but you know that boulder on the left of the fairway?'

'Ah, the Ailsa Craig? That's what we call it. It catches a few out,' smiled Ian.

'Well, with the second ball, as you say Ailsa Craig caught me out as well. Back into the gorse it went. Now we have gorse on some of the links courses on the Antrim coast across the water as you might expect but nothing like this in Stranraer. Back home I could use a club to tease out a stray ball, but here it's impossible,' said Adrian.

'As we left the tee,' said Sean, 'I saw a bird fly into the gorse. I wasn't sure what it was at first. A quite big grey bird, I thought. Probably a pigeon or a gull, you know that sort of size. Anyway I assumed it might be nesting in the infernal growth. It seemed a safe place to do so. So we proceeded to the green. I had just about played out and Adrian took up his putter from the edge of the green.'

'That's when it happened. This parrot appeared with my two golf balls in each of its claws. It dropped the balls beside me and flew off. I've never seen anything like it before,' remarked Adrian.

'Now by any chance have you, out of interest as it were, kissed the Blarney stone?' asked Ian.

Adrian smiled at Sean.

'I thought you might ask. It was… um… yup… the luck of the Irish, I'd agree. And as a matter of fact, I have kissed the said stone but this was no Celtic myth. It was an African

Grey Parrot beyond doubt and it found my golf balls,' said Adrian.

'Then it sounds like you must have met that missing parrot, Kofi,' said Ian. 'I didn't ken it was down this way.'

'Kofi, that escaped bird?' asked the players in unison.

'Aye, we have a celebrity bird in Scotland they can't catch but it has taught many of us a few home truths.'

'Then someone must be missing this bird,' said Sean.

'Aye and I'd better let the cops know he's doon here in Stranraer noo.'

The telephone rang as Harry sat in his lounge reading his Dumfries Courier newspaper.

'Coming, coming, coming, hold on, I'm coming,' said Harry as he got up from his favourite soft chair and moved as freely as his knees would permit.

'Mr Dynes?

'Speaking.'

'Constable Stan Harris here, in Stranraer, Wildlife Officer. There's a parrot around the town, a grey parrot. I reckon, as I don't know of any others on the wing, it might be your missing parrot, Kofi. I thought I should let you know.'

'Stranraer? That's a long way off. And... er... you must have succeeded John, not so?'

'Aye, that's right. I've already informed John. He gave me your number. I've been following Kofi's progress but I reckon he's on our patch now. I don't want to let you down. I'm pretty sure it is Kofi. At least I've had no reports of any other African Greys. I hope we can catch him.'

'Well, you're right. I suppose there can't be many loose grey parrots, but I last heard of him in Edinburgh,' replied Harry.

'Maybe so, but don't you think it's worth a look over here?'

'I most certainly do. I'll see what John's doing and maybe we can set off soon,' said Harry.

'I've got a feeling this is Kofi. It's rare to have anything of significance happening in our town. But I just feel it in my bones; things are about to change.'

'What's the weather like in Stranraer?' asked a concerned Harry.

'If you get to Stranraer you'll get the benefit of the gulf stream. It's quite mild for this time of year here. It's the last forty miles into the town you have to watch. There it's higher ground and likely to have a few icy spots. But John knows what he's doing on that bike of his. Safe as houses they say. That's John.'

'Then we'll see you soon. Thanks, bye.'

John was eager to get his bike on the road after what he had hoped would have been the worst of winter. He had polished his machine in his garage on dreich days to keep himself occupied and keep his black dogs of depression, booze and fags at bay. He knew that soon the boys would be back in their leathers. When Harry confirmed what Stan Harris told him, John dropped everything and went round to Harry's home in a flash.

'Hold on, Harry, we're aff again,' smiled John.

'Kofi, we're on your trail again and this time...' But Harry was not about to utter the words to tempt fate.

Harry was glad to be on the back of John's motorbike again. He'd even admit he was missing his regular rides. He also felt that this was the first time Kofi was back in Dumfries and Galloway. It must be a good omen. Perhaps he was finished with his travels, in need of giving his wings a rest, indeed of returning home.

The bike slowed down and then stopped by the hamlet of Carsluith. They relieved themselves while gazing out to

Wigton Bay and the Baldoon sands. Time for John to light up again and reflect on life.

'Shall we stay at the North West Castle in Stranraer?' asked Harry.

'Sounds a good idea to me. They let families bring their dogs into the bedrooms, so they will be sympathetic if we catch Kofi,' said John. 'But that's a good half hour's ride from here. We'd better get going.'

'Aye, you're right. But we should also keep an eye out. Kofi can travel some distance in no time at all,' confirmed Harry. 'And the roads… take care, they might be slippy.'

'You do the lookout then, Harry. I'll keep my eyes on the road.' John stubbed out his fag under his leather boot-heel.

The bike rose and fell over the tar macadam hillocks as if they were meant for each other and swept around the long curves of the A75. With conviction John selected the right time to overtake Irish-bound lorries and Harry felt the thrill of rapid acceleration once more. He realised without meeting John, he'd never have had the rides of his life.

The motorcycle drove into the drive of the North West Castle hotel that looked splendid at the head of Loch Ryan. This popular family-run hotel was set in a walled garden and its walls were as white as the bobbing flecks in a choppy bay straight ahead. The riders booked themselves into single rooms for an undetermined length of time.

After showers and donning non-leather clothing, Harry and John went out for a walk. It was a very short walk indeed. The police station was the next building in the street to the hotel. As soon as the couple arrived at the station, the desk staff gave them a great welcome.

'Good afternoon, good to see you all again. Is Stan Harris in this afternoon?' asked John.

'Hello, John, long time no see. How's retirement?' asked the receptionist.

'It's never been as busy right now.'

'I guess not, not with your searches going on. It was a great story on the telly about you. Anyway, Stan has been in all afternoon. Shall I get him for you?'

'I know his room, just give us a pass and we'll go up and see him,' said John.

He placed a visitor's pass around Harry's neck and they proceeded through a side door and upstairs. John knocked on his former colleague's door.

'Come in,' said Stan.

The two men entered.

'John Reid, my friend. Great to see you again. And this must be Harry Dynes. Not so? We meet at last.'

'Aye, it's my partner in crime, as it were,' laughed John.

'Not the best of sayings around here, Mr Civilian Reid,' joked Stan.

'Pleased to meet you,' said Harry.

Stan was a man of around thirty-five. His finger supported a marriage ring, and two children with his wife stood facing Harry in a nearby photograph. There was also a dog lead and a copy of the biography of Marley. Stan's wardrobe door was slightly ajar and Harry noticed the lapels of a Boys' Brigade captain, and the forage cap of black-ribboned tails lying limply over the shelf lip.

'Delighted you have dropped by. We've had several sightings of Kofi in recent hours. It's very much a Stranraer story now.'

'The last we had heard, he was in Edinburgh,' said Harry.

'We suspect he's taken to water. There's a steady flow of ships coming down the Clyde. I reckon he's managed a lift on one of them. No one would have seen him on these mountainous cargo ships. The crew are all indoors down in the dungeons and the containers are stacked up on the decks like Lego bricks. In winter Kofi would not find much by way of food there. I guess that's why he jumped ship. That's my theory anyway.'

'Are you sure it's Kofi and not another parrot?' asked Harry.

'If a parrot had gone missing anywhere in the country, we'd have an update in our briefings and I mean any missing parrot in the UK, and mainland Europe too actually. I assure you Kofi is the only reported missing African Grey Parrot. Budgies, canaries, cats and dogs by the hundreds are on our missing cards. All gone missing but an African Grey on the run is as common as a one-legged robber outpacing a police cadet.'

The telephone rang.

'Hello... yes... at the golf club? How long ago? Okay... yes... be there in five. Bye.' He hung up.

'Okay, gentlemen,' said Stan, turning to them. 'Let's go. My van is round the back. Follow me. We're off to the golf course. It seems Kofi is playing around there.'

'Aye, playing a roond himsel,' said John.

'Um, an eagle, and albatross... perhaps there should be an African Grey Parrot too!' joked Stan.

The police van pulled up at the clubhouse. Stan went inside to speak to the Irish golfers while Harry and John scoured the skyline and looked over the first hole.

An electric caddy was brought out for their use and John took to the controls while Harry sat beside him covered by an autumnally coloured Buchanan tartan rug. They went round each hole in turn and once again Harry shouted out Kofi's name. But it was getting dark. There were many trees to focus upon. Could some movement be seen? Was that a parrot, or a crow?

'It's no use, John. We'll have to set out early tomorrow. But I still feel him around. I can't say why, it's just a feeling I have,' said Harry.

That night they sat down in the hotel dining room. As they were served, Gerald McLean, the retired music teacher at Stranraer Academy, took to the keyboards. His silver hair reflected a time gone by and his musical selection covered that era. He played with his eyes closed as his mind drifted. He played his eclectic repertoire each night to the diners. Even on some rare occasions when no diners were at the tables, he played. He played because he was a widower. The smiles of his attentive audience were more than a conversation for him and when he was asked to celebrate a special birthday or play a particular melody, his eyes lit up and he felt the most valued member of the community. He was often offered a drink but he never accepted. He was tee-total and had been so ever since his wife was killed not five miles from home by a drunk driver speeding so as not to miss the last sailing of a boat over to Ireland that night.

Moon River was played as the Ecclefechan tart arrived on plates with a scoop of ice cream. But neither of them finished their meal with a coffee. John had a mug of hot chocolate. Harry was pleased to have been served a huge mug of hot malted Horlicks, the elixir which guaranteed sound sleep. It had been a long day and an early start was essential if they were to capture Kofi. John managed a quick smoke in the gardens of the hotel breathing in the salt air as much as the tobacco.

Harry retired to his room facing the sea. He kept his window two inches open from the bottom and the curtains slightly apart, ostensibly to enjoy the early morning view from his bed, but also to enjoy the healthy breezes from the Irish Sea. He cleaned his teeth, attended to his ablutions and then entered his clean cream sheets, removing his spectacles and placing his head on the marshmallow pillow. He laid his watch on the side table. It was 11.12 p.m.

Sleep came to him within three minutes. Half an hour later, there was a knock on the window. It was not loud enough to waken Harry. It became a constant knock and somewhere in Harry's mind it sounded familiar. But was he dreaming? Of course he must be; he turned over. Yet the knocking continued.

Harry tossed and turned once more and realised the noise would not go away. He resented this disturbance. He opened his eyes. The room was dark except for the light through the separated curtains. He could make out the port lights as lorries moved about with their goods, some preparing to embark over to Ireland and some arriving from the Emerald Isle from the docked Stena Superfast VII. There was movement at the port but there was also some movement at the bottom of the window. He searched for his glasses. He needed focus.

Once his glasses were on, he realised it was Kofi at the window.

'Kofi?... Kofi...' he called with the voice of an excited child. 'Kofi's a good boy. Kofi's a good boy. Come here, my friend, come on, come here, come on Kofi pet, this way... that a boy.'

Harry brought his face to the window. Kofi pecked at it with the speed of a kettle drum roll.

'Stay Kofi, I'll let you in. Don't fly away now. That's it. Easy... easy… come in, in you come. Steady now.'

With very great care Harry raised the window sill. As he did so Kofi waddled over the wooden window frame into the bedroom, then flew across the room and perched on a chair by the mirror. Harry closed the window smartly. He turned to his friend beaming as wide a smile as the harbour's mouth. He switched on the light so that they could recognise each other and see the happiness in each other's eyes.

'Kofi, my dear friend. How I've missed you. Oh this makes me so happy. We're together again. Yes. No more chasing around the country. It's all over now. We're going home my friend, back to our home in Dumfries. Your holiday is over, Kofi. We are back together.'

Harry moved his stroking hand from his appreciative head and placed it under his chest. Kofi walked over his arm. He pecked at his pyjamas lovingly as if to apologise for his lengthy disappearance. Harry threw the day's Dumfries Standard under the chair and took Kofi over to perch on the back of it. He cleaned out the soap dish and filled it with fresh water. He presented it to Kofi who drank with his usual pecking action. Harry lowered himself and came eye to eye with Kofi.

'Well, my friend. We're back together and it makes me happy. I hope it's the same for you. Soon be home again, Kofi. Now whatever happens, you must not go missing again. Hear me? Must not go missing.'

'Must not go missing again,' said Kofi. 'Must not go missing again.'

Harry looked at his watch. It was now a quarter past midnight. No, he wouldn't wake up John.

'Sleep well Kofi, we're going home tomorrow. Back home to Dumfries, young man.'

Creeping so as not to disturb his feathered friend, Harry returned to make sure the window was tight shut. He thought through what he had just said to his feathered companion. How could a parrot and two men ride a motorcycle to Dumfries? Anyway, that was a problem for tomorrow. One solved problem a day was sufficient in Harry's mind. It was time to enjoy the moment he had been waiting for all those weeks. It was at last the moment he had caught up with Kofi. He felt wonderful.

'Sleep well, Kofi, you rascal. We'll be home tomorrow.'

'You rascal, you rascal,' replied Kofi.

21
A Scoop for Stranraer

The alarm bell sounded at 7 a.m. Harry woke and turned it off without thinking. Yet still it rang. It rang without a break from the back of a chair. Kofi was in his element once again. Harry shook his head from side to side.

'Same old you,' he said with a warmth Kofi recalled.

Harry got out of bed and sat in front of him.

'I don't blame you. You wanted to explore and I gave you that opportunity. And I almost found you in the grounds of the hospital but anyway, that's in the past. I just wonder if you know how popular you have become. And when we get back to Dumfries, I'll have to let everyone know you are home once more and for good. But not till then. I want to make sure you do get home and back to your normal environment. I won't count my chickens.'

'Count ma chickens; count ma chickens,' said Kofi.

'It's like you never went away, old friend.'

Harry lifted the telephone with the broadest of smiles and dialled internally.

'Good morning, Reception. Room 207 here. Could I have a breakfast tray in my room?'

'Certainly, sir, of course you can. Do you wish for the full breakfast?'

'No, just some toast and cereal,' said Harry.

'It will be with you in ten minutes, sir.'

'Oh and one other thing please…'

'Yes?'

'A bowl of nuts if you have any,' he requested.

'Would that be raisins and nuts, sir?

'No nuts, just nuts. Thank you.'

'And not salted nuts, either?'

'No, plain and any variety of nut will do.'

Harry still had to break his happy news to John. Another task to do with enthusiasm.

'John, I'll be having breakfast in bed this morning.'

'Oh dear. Not feeling so well, Harry? Or was it something I said last night?' asked a concerned John.

'No, no no. Nothing you said. And I'm fine, honestly. But come up and see me after you have had breakfast and don't forget to knock on the door.'

'Sounds like you have company, Harry?'

'Yes, I do.'

'What! You old rogue. You don't surprise me,' said John.

'Knock, John, that's all I ask of you, please knock.'

John had a full Scottish breakfast at a table on his own. As he drank his Assam blend, his mind swirled round trying to make sense of Harry's strange request and stranger behaviour. He returned to his room to brush his teeth, still contemplating the early morning discussion. It seemed surreal. This was not normally Harry's modus operandi at all.

He knocked firmly on Harry's bedroom door. Harry opened it enough to see who it was. John's eyebrows were furled. They met Harry's warm smiling face.

'Come in when I open the door, John.'

John did as he was asked. When he entered, he looked straight at Harry, assessing his demeanour.

'Are you okay, Harry? You are acting very strangely.'

Harry smiled at him.

'Look over there, by the mirror.'

John turned round.

'Gosh... good grief... Is that Kofi? How on earth did he find his way here?'

'Kofi, meet John. What do you say?'

'Hello John. Hello John. Hello John.'

'Well hello, stranger. We meet at last. Tell me how you got him here, Harry.'

'He flew to my window last night. I spoke to him and he knew it was me so all I had to do was open the window and in he came.'

'As easy as that?'

'Yup. Just like that. He must have sensed I was here. You know just like a dog. Kofi must have had the powers of a bloodhound sensing a trail.'

'Will he bite me if I stroke him?'

'I don't know. But I doubt it. Here, let me show you what to do. Come up to him with confidence. Hold out your hand like this and place it above his feet resting just below his chest.'

John clenched his fist and brought it towards Kofi.

'Come on, Kofi, let's be friends.'

Kofi cocked his head and then stepped on John's fist. He looked him in the eye.

'We're friends, Kofi,' said John.

'We're friends. We're friends. We're friends,' said Kofi.

'Now I ken jist what ye mean tae Harry,' said John, relaxing with the target of his recent search.

Harry's face looked puzzled.

'So now, we have a problem. I'll stay with Kofi while you try and find a metal cage.'

'Okay, got that.'

'By the way, the hotel already knows. The waiter who brought my breakfast was first to see Kofi. He won't keep that a secret for long.'

'I suppose so, because after I get a strong cage in Stranraer, if I do, I go next door to alert the police so that they stand down all the wildlife officers in the land. That'll soon be picked up by yon press. I think we'd better get oot o' town as quick as we can and git back to Dumfries,' said John.

'But we can't travel by bike with him.'

'Don't worry, Harry. I'll sort that oot, so I wull.'

John set off on his chores as the hotel manager Mr McMillan came to visit the room of the reported avian discovery. The knock was firm. Harry opened the door and the knocking continued.

'Ho, ho so it's true. You do have a parrot. I see he's very much at home here in the hotel,' remarked Mr Hamilton.

'Oh I am sorry. I'll clear up as much mess as I can. He's not the cleanest of guests.'

'Don't you worry about that, sir. It is an honour that this bird has been reunited with you here in our North West Castle Hotel. This will bring us good publicity and that's more than an overnight stay. So, Mr Dynes, for you and Mr Reid, we are going to waive the charges,' said Mr McMillan.

'Thank you very much indeed. That is most kind of you. Er... but shall I pay for Kofi's night and morning breakfast?'

'Mind the gap, mind the gap,' said Kofi

'He's right, you know, I have made a gaff, I meant all of you, none of you need pay,' said the engaging hotel manager.

'For Gaff hear Gap. He's not good on his F's,' said Harry.

'Too many are these days. Foul-mouthed F word utterings everywhere you go. Now, it's a matter of time before the press arrive. Do you want me to hold them off?'

'If you could, until John purchases a cage. That would be great. He should be back before long, I hope,' said Harry.

'We're a bit cut off here in Stranraer. It will be our local journalists that will get the scoop. The others will follow soon though. I hope you can get away before the others arrive,' advised Mr McMillan, with some insight.

'Yes, but that's all in John's hands. When the local journalists come and I am pretty sure with a photographer too, send them up and I'll speak to them. It will be good for the town here to get the scoop of course,' said Harry.

'Get the scoop! I'll do that later,' joked Mr McMillan.

'Oh, I get it,' said Harry.

'Giving the local paper the scoop will be appreciated,' said the manager, leaving the room. He placed a 'Do Not Disturb' notice on the door handle.

'Get the scoop, get the scoop,' said the mischievous bird.

John arrived with a large circular wire cage and some news. But when he entered, Harry was seated in the armchair with Colin Patterson, the senior journalist from the Galloway Gazette, and Tony Park, the photographer. Perched on his bed rail was Kofi.

John listened into the conversation and did not interrupt, until Harry was unable to answer.

'So how will the two of you and the parrot get back to Dumfries on a motorbike?' asked the seasoned Stranraer reporter.

'A good question. I'll ride back on my own. Harry and the parrot will be chauffeur-driven,' said John.

'And who will be driving and when will you be leaving?'

'You are a good journalist but I can't tell you oor plans other than to return tae Dumfries. Harry needs time tae recover fae the past six months and so does Kofi. Now you can take pictures o' Harry wi' his bird in the room where he was reunited but that is a' we can say at this time. So Mr Park, the photos now please,' said John.

'I appreciate what you are saying. I'll have more than enough to write and I can send it out to Reuters. But once I do, and we appreciate the dividend this gives us for a change, the big boys will come along with their cameras and microphones. Mr Dynes, you may have got Kofi back but hold onto your horses, the circus will be coming to your home,' said Colin, who could not wait to inform his wife about this breaking story, let alone his readers.

Tony clicked a hundred snaps to the minute. Kofi responded with clicks at a rate of fifty to the minute. He was no match for Tony's expensive black professional Nikon D800 (936MP) Digital SLR camera. But Kofi appreciated the attention. He lapped up the clicks and saw Harry approve of the adulation.

Kofi was placed in the cage, the best John could get. It was not a parrot cage of course, more a large budgerigar cage with narrow perches and thin wire.

'He may get out of the cage, you know. He could twist the wire before we get to Dumfries. That worries me,' said Harry.

'I think it will be alright. Superintendent Barry Petit will be going to Dumfries in thirty minutes so we'd better get ready. He's agreed to take you and Kofi. His car will drive up behind the hotel and the manager will notify us that they have arrived and lead you to the car. Remember, even if Kofi gets out of his cage, he'd still be in the car,' said John, as organised once more as he had been during his days in the police.

'I suppose so. After all we can't make alternative arrangements. You've been on the ball, keeping busy. But I've got some news too,' said Harry smiling.

'Really? What's that?' asked John.

'Mr McMillan has waived our bill. That's why he let the local journalist in. It gives him good publicity. The photo of the hotel window where Kofi arrived last night has already been taken. It's a great story for Stranraer,'

'It sure is and they deserve the scoop,' said John.

'It's a tired joke now, the scoop.'

'Maybe, Harry, but don't lose your sense of fun.'

'Kofi's not back home yet. I'll relax then. Now don't mention the Superintendent's name again.'

'Why? You mean Barry Petit?' clarified John.

'Shhhh... yes, pet it. Kofi will expect to be caressed by the Superintendent.'

'And that's likely?'

'With Kofi, you know by now, John, anything is possible, yes, anything.'

22
An Agent Appears

Harry packed his overnight bag. Kofi had been fed, watered and entertained. He would be placed in the cage at the very last moment. That moment now arrived.

Mr McMillan came to take Harry's bag, his leathers and crash helmet. A chambermaid stood ready to hold the door open for Harry to proceed with Kofi in his temporary cage. They followed the manager along a corridor to a service lift. They descended to the basement and when the lift doors opened, a dark-blue shining new BMW police car awaited their arrival. Superintendent Barry Petit came out to shake Harry's hand. Barry was indeed a man of slightly restricted height but his effervescent personality made up for that. Barry was a local Stranraer man and knew the people and every blade of grass in the town. He was proud to have the highest rate of detection in the authority and his men almost worshipped him. Barry had been earmarked to go far in the police force but his loyalty to the town kept him local. He was so well appreciated as an officer that he had been given the police service medal three years ago and on the Queen's birthday that year he'd received the OBE. He said the medal was for the town and not for him, of course. However the townsfolk felt he had deserved it for himself: such a humble man.

'Delighted to meet you at last, Mr Dynes. Let me open the back door. You can sit with Kofi there and I'll sit in the front. The driver will take you home,'

'Thank you very much for resolving this problem,' said Harry.

'When Stan told me about John's motorbike, I knew there would be a problem. There was a need to get you out of Stranraer as fast as a bolt of lightning and so I was left with this option. I've business I can do at the Dumfries HQ with my boss, Cathy Ronson, anyway. But of course, I'm glad to be of service.'

As the engine started, two escort bikes arrived to lead the way. They swept round the front of the North West Castle hotel, with the car following on. They did not stop at the entrance. A traffic warden waved the procession through onto the main road. Harry was having the smoothest ride of his life. Kofi was bewildered with the sirens and horns. He soon overcame that problem.

'He haw; he haw; he haw; he haw,' he said.

The police cycle outriders peeled away from the car just after Glenluce. Meanwhile John was already twenty minutes ahead of the car on his bike riding within a shade of the maximum the road and the law would permit.

After an hour and a half the saloon drove down Harry's drive and Kofi returned home again. It was as if Kofi's adventures had never happened. It was very familiar for Kofi to be placed back in his cage and the way he quenched his thirst and pecked some seed enhanced Harry's view that normalcy would return very soon indeed. Harry made a cup of tea, took off his shoes, and sat down to the quiz programme Pointless, and then the telephone rang.

Kofi just had to ring in unison and perform a solo ring after Harry had lifted the receiver. Kofi was very much home again.

'Good afternoon. Mr Dynes?'

'Speaking.'

'I'm Neil Scott. I'm a literary agent for many celebrities, authors, actors and poets at the Clova Agency.'

'I think you have the wrong number. I'm not an author. I may do some poetry but I'm in my late eighties, and I'm no celebrity or an actor either.'

'It's not the wrong number, I assure you. One of my authors spoke to you, I believe?'

'Ah, you mean Elly-Anne Jones?'

'Yes indeed. Now we're on the same wavelength. You see it's my job to get the best terms for each author and organise their commitments, make sure they are there when they should be, you know that sort of thing.'

'Oh, I see. But I'm going nowhere. I don't need an agent,' said Harry, confused by this call out of the blue.

'I appreciate your response, Mr Dynes, but perhaps you don't appreciate how your life is going to change,' said Mr Scott.

'Change at my age? And how's that, may I ask?'

'As you know, my colleague Elly-Ann Jones is writing a book about Kofi. I am in the early stages of seeking film options too. Now at your age, I can imagine you just want to get back to normalcy as soon as possible.'

'Yes, you've hit the nail on the head. By the way, the story's ended. You've heard the parrot is back home with me?' said Harry.

'You mean Kofi's home with you at last?'

'Yes, just arrived back from Stranraer with him a few minutes ago.'

'That's wonderful news, wonderful. But the public will want more. They can't get enough information about you and your parrot. So I guess you'll want to know what my charges are?' asked Neil.

'Charges? Whatever for? Anyway I may not be able to afford you, had you thought about that?'

'Oh, yes, I have and you will find me inexpensive. It's painless. I'll take 10% of your profits. That's my charge for all my clients. I'd like you to be one too. If you agree I'll add you to the list.'

'Well, you have taken me by surprise but 10% sounds very reasonable, if I am making any money from this situation. But I assure you any money that's comes my way over this search story will have to cover our petrol and living costs which we have been spending over the last few months. I doubt if there would be much left after that.'

Neil laughed down the line.

'I'd not be so sure. I think you'll make a tidy amount more than you could imagine.'

'So you have a different idea? Anyway, it's all over my head,' said Harry.

'I'll send you a contract in the post and if you agree, sign and send it back. By all means seek your solicitor's advice but make no mistake, Mr Dynes, you are about to come into some real money.'

Harry replaced the telephone, shook his head in astonishment and raised the television's volume. He needed some distraction.

'How many words do you know ending with -ENT?' asked Alexander Armstrong. Before any of the contestants answered, three words came to Harry's mind. Puzzlement, amazement and bewilderment. One of his answers was a pointless score. But Kofi got the dreaded maximum hundred points with his effort.

'Important, Important!'

'No, Kofi, that's ANT, not ENT. But you are right about one thing. That telephone call was important.'

Before the end of the programme, Fiona rang her father. Harry was quick to start the conversation.

'Darling, Kofi's back home.'

'That's great news, Dad. Delighted to hear Kofi is back at last. I can hear him still ringing.'

'Yes, darling. Same old tricks. Isn't it wonderful? You must come home and see him again. He'll have missed you too.'

'Maybe next weekend if that suits you.'

'Yes, that's good. I'll let Kofi know you will be visiting.'

'Okay, put me in your diary. Of course now that you have Kofi back there's no need for you to have any more cycling excursions, I hope,' Fiona said.

'Well, one search is over but there's still the mystery of Morag and that might mean a trip or two.'

'Don't you feel you deserve a break? Anyway Morag is not like Kofi. You knew where Kofi might have been all the time, you were on his tail, but you have no idea which direction to go to find this missing girl of some four years.'

'I know but darling, I can't let John down at this stage,' said Harry, trying not to dent his daughter's genuine concern for his health and wellbeing.

John visited the following day and was glad to see Kofi ensconced in his cage looking contented.

'How are you today, young Kofi?' he asked.

'He's been a bit quiet this morning. Perhaps getting used to having lost his freedom,' suggested Harry.

'Have you told the press yet?'

'About Kofi's capture?' clarified Harry.

'Yes. They are bound tae find oot,' said John.

'No, not me I haven't yet but oh... I must tell you... I've got an agent,' said Harry.

'You've an agent?'

'Yes, me at my age, I've got an agent.'

'What agent? A Pools agent, a secret agent? What kind of agent? How come?'

'Mr Neil Scott of the Clova Agency, no less. He manages my affairs. You know, speaking engagements, a book about Kofi and even the possibility of a film. Can you believe that?'

'Speaking engagements?'

'Not that I have any yet but if they come, he makes sure I get there and get paid.'

'Wow, this is some development. And how much will that cost you?' asked John.

'Ten percent on all profits. But I can't see how there's a story without you, John, and I know only too well that finding Kofi is only half the picture.'

'I think it was always going to be easier finding Kofi but I'm satisfied we gave as much publicity to Morag as we could.'

'Someone somewhere knows what happened to Morag and you have the right to know.'

John looked at Kofi in his cage.

'It's all over for you, Kofi. I must carry on alone,' he said.

'No, not as I see it, young man. I'll do anything you want me to do to solve Morag's disappearance. You know that, John.'

'Harry, you can't be oan a motorbike as much these days. I've valued yer support an' made good use of you oan two wheels but let's remain as friends and let me face ma demons alone.'

'I suppose so. You are right. There's not much I can do. But I can be your sounding board perhaps?' suggested Harry.

'You know what? You make a lot o' sense. A sounding board is jist what I do need. Someone tae listen tae my frustrations and my disappointments. Someone tae keep me away fae the door of depression and the whisky an' ony other demon up ma sleeve.'

'And the fags perhaps?'

'Aye, the fags as weel. I should cut down more.'

'And someone to share your successes too, I hope.'

'Aye, if there are ony,' said John.

Harry grabbed hold of John's shoulders.

'Sure, we'll keep together through thick and thin.'

'Thick and thin; thick and thin.'

'You said it Kofi! Thick and thin,' said John.

'Ohhh yes. Thick and thin,' said Kofi once more.

The next day Harry received an e-mail from Neil Scott. He wanted to visit Harry and show him some papers. Harry was keen to meet the man who was going to take 10% of all his future earnings.

Neil Scott was a tall man with a pencil-thin beard. He wore his spectacles at the tip of his nose, only returning them to its bridge when he was reading papers. His black hair was brushed straight back. He reminded Harry of his French teacher all those years ago. He worked tirelessly seven days a week for his clients. Harry was client number thirty-seven.

'It's a pleasure meeting you at last. I've been following Kofi's story since Day One,' said Neil.

'Day One for me was thirty-five years ago when I first met Kofi,' replied Harry.

'Indeed and that's where the book starts.'

'So Elly-Anne has completed the book?'

'No, not yet, but I have been busy. We have two authors already working on draft copies.'

'That's a bit lavish, isn't it?' asked Harry.

'On the contrary. One author, Katy Ritchie, is preparing a children's version. I'm told it might be a cloth book, a cardboard book, even a waterproof bath book, but it is too early to say. You see, each event can make a series of Kofi's adventures for children.'

'But I've not met Katy Richie. How does she know the stories?'

'Elly-Anne Jones has shared her knowledge of the story with her. They felt it wouldn't be fair on you to go through the process again with Katy.'

'Very thoughtful,' said Harry.

'Now I managed to get Elly-Anne a contract with Netherholm Publications to publish both the novel and the children's book. I'll be meeting with them next week to finalise the small print.'

'The small print? Is that for the children's book?'

'I'm not falling for that joke, Harry. It's the small print that will make you some money for your retirement.'

'Retirement? I thought I'd reached that point twenty years ago. Anyway, I can see that you have been busy.'

'You have hardly been retired over recent months, Harry. And you seem to be thriving on it. We have to keep one step ahead in this business. Anyway, here's the pleasant bit about it.'

From his folder Neil produced a chequebook. He tore the cheque from the stub and gave it to Harry.

Harry looked at the amount and then at his name on the line above.

'Five thousand pounds. Good grief. What's that for? Hang on, the book hasn't been written yet so it can't be making any sales money. And is that after you've taken ten percent?'

'5K is all yours. You've earned it. It is for two reasons. This money represents your part in the bargain. It means now that we have an author assigned to the book, you cannot accept any other agent or author to work on publishing the book if they come knocking at your door.'

'Well I never. This has come right out of nowhere. But what about the papers wanting a story about Kofi and John?'

'That's the second reason. We are presently in negotiations with two daily nationals. We play each other off raising the stakes as we go. But I'll send an e-mail as soon as we reach an agreement. Oh, and by the way there will be another cheque. But I don't know yet how much that one will be for, yet.'

'Your job is becoming only a little clearer for me to understand,' said Harry.

'Yes, it's me being a negotiator, a deal maker, and facilitator. In summary, I'm the oil in the engine perhaps. Not so?'

Harry looked at his cheque once more. He shook his head.

'You're more like Father Christmas I'd say.'

'Father Christmas is a good boy. Father Christmas is a good boy,' said Kofi.

'I think he likes you,' said Harry.

'That's just as well. Because I'll be seeing you quite a bit, Harry... oh and you too Kofi,' said Neil.

'But the book will take some time I suppose?'

'I've got the illustrator working on it. Katy Grimes. She's a brilliant illustrator. You'll be impressed by her work. You'll find her at www.kittydinners.co.uk. I'm also making progress with film rights and that's another development. Early days there but they like the crossover genre. They don't get many.'

'So now I get the picture. If I get a call from the Disney studios, I tell them to call my agent,' said Harry.

'Exactly. But there are a few exceptions. Local or national radio might want to interview you. They will probably send a journalist. Television might want you too. Again it might be an interview here in your home with a camera or you will be taken to the studio. That's fine. They'll settle their account with you. Nothing to do with me in the normal sense, unless you want to check out any arrangements they have made. In fact if you have any doubts or issues please let me know. Of course you are still bound by the book agreement. Is that clear?'

'Yes, I'm sure I'm getting the hang of it, Neil. Confusing at first but by and by it will all make some sense.'

Three days later Harry opened his computer and sent an e-mail to Neil.

'Hi Neil, just had a telephone call from the BBC. They want me to appear on the Graham Norton Show. Is that okay?'

Neil was quick to respond.

'Harry, are you up to it? I guess you are. So go out and buy a new shirt.'

23
The Graham Norton Show

The BBC 1 London studio of Graham Norton paid for both Harry's and Kofi's flight and accommodation in London. As he waited in the Green Room, Harry could hear the audience being warmed up to fever pitch by Graham. Sitting beside Harry, who was in his new olive suit, pink shirt and a pink and mauve striped tie, was the singer Carla Grey, in a low-cut orange dress, and retired footballer Frank Rushton in what looked like an expensive shiny blue suit with a thin neck tie like a strand of spaghetti. The opening music announced the start of the show.

Graham was standing in an aisle amid the audience. The camera panned in to his position.

'And action!'

'Gooood evening, television viewers and lovely audience. Have we got a show for you this evening? Hmmm... Oh yes we have! Now one of our guests this evening, wait for it, is an African Grey Parrot! Hmmmm... I know, I know, yes, I know. I know what you are thinking. I do have some of the oddest guests. So now, if you were a parrot, what would you say? What will Kofi's first words be on the show? Pretty lady over here. Yes? What do you think Kofi's first words will be?'

'I'd think he'd say: Who's a pretty boy then?'

'Hmmm, I guess even a budgie says that,' said Graham. (Laughter.) 'Let me try over here now, the gentleman with the gorgeous beard, what do you think a parrot would say, sir?'

'AAAAArsenal. Come away the AAAARsenal,' the man said.

There was a riotous response. Some supporters cheered, while other team supporters booed. The din increased and Graham held his hands aloft.

'Righty right. Okay, okay, okay. Well then, we'll have to wait and see what Kofi says first. Now one of the most beautiful sights, I am sure you agree, is a parrot's tail, at the end of its bum...'

On the screen suddenly appeared the snooker player John Parrot bending over the snooker table with his red shirt protruding from his trousers. The audience let out wolf whistles and applause mixed with shouts of shoulder-rippling glee.

'All right, right and what a line-up we have this evening. We've got singing diva Carly Grey...' (Applause.) 'And retired football player Frank Rushton...' (Applause.) 'And as a special guest, Harry Dynes with Kofi the parrot!' (More applause.) 'Yes, what a programme, what a line up,' said Graham, descending the stairs to the stage. The applause continued with some whistling.

'Alright, mmmm, love you all, yes, yes. Okay right and our musical guests this evening... the group, yes they are here... the one and only One Direction!'

The younger members of the audience shrieked like a platoon of escaping mice while their parents' age-group followed with more muted applause, many of them not having heard of this sensational group.

'Now Frank has retired. He's no longer playing ball with his friends.'

The screen showed a defensive wall facing a free kick with Frank protecting his manhood like all five others in the defensive wall.

More uncontrolled laughter followed.

'And finally the lady with the golden voice. A lady with a great following and an expressive persona.'

The screen showed Carla being chased by the photographers and her heel being caught in a drain. Her anguish belied her expressive persona as she hobbled away shoeless, mouthing a profanity.

'Let's bring them all on... Carly Grey... Frank Rushton... and Harry Dynes.'

Graham shook the hands of the males and pouted his lips to touch both of Carla's cheeks, while the celebrities greeted each other on the couch. It was as if they had not made each other's acquaintance in the Green Room earlier.

'Now first Harry... and I should explain. Kofi is in fact here but you thought it wise not to bring him out just now, is that so?'

Graham made eyes at the cameras and mouthed 'Language!' (Laughter.)

'No, Kofi won't swear, it's just that he interrupts. He's not a socially good guest really, 'cos he's always chatting and repeating himself,' said Harry.

'Good heavens but this is a chat show. You mean he could do my job?' Graham looked shocked. (More laughter from the audience.)

'Carla, did you ever have pets at home in Newcastle as a child?'

'Ooh not birds. Cats. They would eat birds. We had three cats... Salt... pepper and... mustard. Mustard was the ginger cat,' said Carla.

'Don't tell me, don't tell me. Salt was a white cat and Pepper a mingy mouse colour perhaps,' said Graham.

'OOOh Graham, you are naughty. I loved my cats as a child.'

'Now Frank, did you have pets?'

'Still do, Graham. Dogs. Two black Labradors at home,' said Frank.

'Don't tell me, um… They are called Bristol Rover and Chelsea.'

'Very good. Almost! The bitch is Chelsea and the dog is Brov, short for Bristol Rovers.'

'Yes, Frank, we all know Brov is short for Bristol Rovers. Just because you are a footballer with a law degree, you must think we are all morons!' laughed Graham. 'Anyway, retired from playing, you are now the legal advisor to the FA. That's a step up isn't it?'

'I always thought I'd stay in football and I guess many knew that, but I had always said I would never be a manager. When I was offered the post, I leapt at it. It's an interesting post at an interesting time.'

'You mean extending that goal line technology to the side lines… that sort of thing?' asked Graham.

'Yes and controversial issues like the length of bans, crowd control, policing issues,' said Frank.

'Actually, Ping Pong is my sport,' said Graham to smirking laughs.

'Well, Ping Pong is something I like to play too. We must have a game or two,' said Frank.

'Hmmm, I'd love to ping pong with you Frank!' (More laughter.)

'I'd ping pong with anyone these days, I don't get the opportunity,' said Carla.

Graham led the applause.

Carla's interview seemed to fly by. She was a fading star whose re-releases of her oldies were making a comeback in the charts with a younger generation. But the songs meant little to Harry. Classic FM was his regular station.

'Right now. Sitting quietly on the settee is a man who is in his eighty-fifth year. You can hardly believe it, not so? That's right, isn't it Harry? Eighty-fifth year?' (Applause.)

'Yes, thank you.'

'Harry, this is a turnaround for you. Becoming a celebrity at your age?'

'Maybe it's because of my age. You know, on a motorbike for the first time, detained in a mental hospital overnight... they thought I was delusional, you just could not write about it, but they have.'

'Ho ho, tell us about that Harry,' asked Graham.

The audience listened keenly...

'Wow, what an experience that was, Harry. But now, if we can, let's meet Kofi himself. And let's listen to his first utterings,' said Graham.

A stagehand arrived with a stand. Harry slipped off stage and came back on with Kofi on his arm. The audience applauded.

'Now then. So this is Kofi. Can I touch him?'

'Yes, just put your arm under his chest and he'll mount it.'

Graham did what he was told. Kofi mounted his arm and looked him straight in the eye.

'Well, young man, we were wondering what your first words on television might be?'

Kofi was aware of the audience.

'Ohh a lotta people. A lotta lotta people,' he said.

Carla laughed the most loudly, putting her hand to her mouth.

'Gosh do I speak like that?' she asked.

'Parrots don't lie, Carla, but who would have guessed that would be his opening line? And Harry, you have not been alone in all of this. Tell us about John Reid,' said Graham.

'Yes. It's John's bike of course. A great experience.'

'First time on a bike then?'

'Yes, Graham, you bet, it was. I've got the leathers too.'

'Hmmmm, I just love leathers… anyway John is now retired and is trying to get to the bottom of his daughter's disappearance.'

'Yes, that's right. We've no idea how she disappeared,' said Harry.

'Well, John cannot be with us this evening but we all wish him luck. It must be very hard for him,' said Graham, showing his sombre side for a change.

'It is indeed,' said Harry.

'Now one of the particularly poignant stories about Kofi was when he brought someone out of a coma, a young lad who hadn't spoken for four years after a car crash. And we've got him in the Edinburgh Studios. Hello David, do we have David? Oh yes there he is. Hmmm… handsome young man. Can you hear me?'

'Yes, Graham, loud and clear,' said David.

'Now it was Kofi that brought you out of your coma. Wasn't it?'

'Yes, quite remarkable.'

'Quite remarkable, Quite remarkable,' Kofi said.

 (Laughter in the studio.)

'There he goes again,' said David.

'Tell us, David, how did it happen?' asked Graham.

'I'm told I was out cold for four years but sometimes I could hear voices…' David spoke with confidence for another four minutes.

'Well, it seems to me that you've fully recovered now, not so?' asked Graham.

'Yes and back into my studies.'

'Tell us what you are studying?'

'Well, I had a place at Strathclyde University to study electrical engineering before the accident. So I'm going over all my advanced physics school notes and I'm glad to say it's all coming back. I will probably reapply to the university. Again, it's all thanks to Kofi,' said David.

'Thank you, David, it's a wonderful story and we wish you well in your studies,' said Graham. (Generous applause.)

'Now before the red chair, it's time to hear One Direction.'

'One Direction, One Direction,' said Kofi.

24
Hollywood Comes Knocking

Kofi and Harry returned home and saw a reference to their television appearance in the Dumfries Standard lying among the mail on the hall carpet. John rang to congratulate them and for mentioning his case on television too. He would call round soon. Harry slept well that night after the flight. London was not far away. But travel exhausted him more than ever.

The following day after lunch, the telephone rang.

'Harry, Neil here. Great show last night, I thoroughly enjoyed it. Well done. Now have I got some good news for you! We've just taken out a film option. I'll send the papers down to you with orange markers to show where I need you to sign.'

'Is it like the book?' asked Harry.

'Almost, yeah. But they may consult you about the script to get their facts right. That type of thing.'

'Then why don't they wait until the book is out to sort that out?'

'It's all about momentum, keeping the story fresh.'

'But Neil, John's quest is far from over,' said Harry.

'John's quest, in my opinion, is bound to fail. I know these are harsh words but I think it's realistic. You have given him much publicity, yet there's not been a murmur about what happened to his daughter. Now that you have

Kofi back, you'll not be so keen to travel so far and wide and I can't see you being able to help him. Not so? Anyway the circle is complete as they say in the film world. Start with a problem, work on the difficulty and hey presto, the resolution. That's why they are interested in the parrot film. '

'I see.'

'Now with Morag, you've only got the first arc. She's missing. See, not part of the film.'

'Many know about his quest to find his daughter. He needs only one reply. That's all it needs and it could start a series of enquiries. Maybe then he can conclude whether there is any likelihood of finding her. But I understand him. It will be in his bones for as long as he lives and there's no trace of his daughter,' said Harry.

'Yes, sadly I think you are right,' said Neil.

The RDA Picture Studio of Los Angeles had appointed Daniel Guardino as their scriptwriter. Harry signed the papers where requested, not fully believing what his signature would launch. What they might do with the story would be beyond Harry's editorial understanding. Any bonus which might accrue from this film venture would be welcome but he would let them get on with it and one day perhaps attend the Dumfries picture house to see the film. Then he remembered. That was no way to launch a film. Perhaps it would be at a glittering evening at the Cannes Film Festival. He would strut down the red carpet with Fiona and Laura on each side. He made a note to make that the start of his dream that evening in bed.

John arrived later at the front door.

'Harry, are you in?'

'Come in, come in.'

John opened the door but Harry was nowhere to be seen. A quiet humming came from the bathroom. Harry was almost asleep in a warm bath concoction of fragrant bubbles listening to Vivaldi on Classic FM.

John mounted the stairs.

'Kofi invited me in, Harry.'

'What?'

'I said Kofi invited me in.'

'Oh I see. I'll be down in a minute. Make yourself a coffee,' said Harry, rising from the cooling water.

John made two cups. Harry arrived down in his dressing gown. He lifted his mug of coffee.

'TV personalities have long lie-ins. I see you are following their example.'

Harry laughed.

'I'd put it down to ageing. You know, all this travel and interest in Kofi is taking its toll. I'm not as fit as I thought I was. I spend too long in that bath these days.'

'Anything more than aging and tiredness?'

'Breathlessness, I'd say. No more than that. But it does slow me down.'

'Have you had a check up at a Well Man's clinic?'

'Hmmm... perhaps I should. Not today though.'

'Sure?'

'John, if your bike's not broke, you don't fix it, do you?'

'I get your point. But you know the NHS is there fur ye at the point of need.'

'So they say. But is it? I mean, I hear of people needing a new knee and they offer it to be done in Belfast or Sunderland. Now there's nothing wrong with either of these delightful cities but who would look after Kofi if I was treated in one of these far-off places?'

'Okay, I hear what you say, but don't be stubborn. If it requires investigation, don't hold back.'

'To be honest I don't feel able to ride the bike again, sorry.'

'Don't worry, your quest is over; but mine's still on the go,' said John.

'That's what I mean. How can I help you find your daughter?'

John sipped his coffee, his eyes fixed on the ceiling.

'I've come tae realise, I'm no ever going tae find oot what happened to Morag. I'll look a lot less noo. I need to get on with my life. With your help I have done as much as I could. I've been raising her profile and gaining universal awareness. But you're right. That's over now bar the one thought that she might come intae my life again, but it will be more likely at her bidding these days, and no due to my efforts.'

The telephone rang in the lounge. Harry answered but of course the ringing went on.

'Be quiet now, Kofi, I'm on the phone. Hello?'

'Hello, Andrea here of D&G Life. Can we come over and take photos of you and Kofi the parrot and ask some questions too?'

'And when were you thinking?'

'If it suits you, this afternoon?'

'Kofi, me and John? We're all here. There's more than one story, you know.'

'Yes, that's so very true. It would be great to see all three of you. Three pm?'

'Three it is. I guess you know where I live?'

'Oh it's very much on the tourist trail now, Harry,' said Andrea.

Harry replaced the phone.

'Stay for some soup,' he said to John. 'D&G Life is coming at three. Let's get the place ready for them.'

'I think you'd better get dressed first,' said John.

At 3.05 p.m. the front door bell rang. Andrea introduced herself and her photographer, Pete White. Andrea had a warm pleasing smile framed by a bob of dark hair, not black but a deep dark chestnut colour. She was petite while Pete was tall and angular. The camera had a longer strap than usual to accommodate his size. He had the face of a seasoned outdoors photographer. They both put Harry and John at ease but Kofi took exception to the visitors.

'Snap snap, goodbye; snap snap, goodbye,' he said.

Andrea and Peter laughed.

'Looks like he wants to get rid of us,' said Andrea. But Harry was no longer in the lounge. He had gone into the kitchen to attend to the griddle. He returned with a pot of tea and a pile of warm golden pancakes.

'My my! Don't tell me you are a baker too, Harry?'

'Well, Andrea, we've been inundated with press, TV, radio etc but after all, you are our local magazine, a special service to you, you might say,' laughed Harry.

'Most impressive,' said Peter, 'but before we enjoy the pancakes, let me get a shot of you two in discussion over the tray.'

'Beginning to look like one of these house-hunting shots,' said Harry. 'Just the bread-making aroma and the smell of ground coffee missing, I think!'

The D&G Life edition was published three months later. It showed Kofi in a cocky pose with a more sedate John and Harry. The story was becoming familiar and the local magazine seemed to Harry to be the final media interest. Autumn was not so far away. The nights were getting longer.

The humming lawn cuttings of the season were being announced by hard-working gardeners. Kofi listened with his head at an angle.

'You know I think I need a gardener, John,' said Harry. 'After all, I can afford one now.'

'A regular gardener?'

'Surely no one would grudge me that perk? Someone to cut the lawn in summer, see to the vegetable patch and the fruit trees in season. Tidy up the garden in late autumn, you know that sort of assistance. I'm sure to find someone before long.'

'Harry, no way. You are not doing that. It's Pay-back time. I'd be more than happy tae keep an eye on your garden. Oors is no that big a job. It will give me an additional purpose in life. I'd be more than glad tae do it for ye, Harry.'

The gardening discussion came to an abrupt halt. It was a telephone call from Harry's agent.

'Harry, there's been a bit of a problem.'

'In what way?'

'I got a message from Daniel Guardino. You know the scriptwriter in California?'

'So the film is off?' Harry enquired.

'On the contrary, Daniel is a little unsure of the timing of some events and he wants to speak to you.'

'That's fine, we can arrange a suitable time for him to call, can't we?'

'No, he'd prefer to meet you. He'll perhaps even identify some shot venues around the place. He'll be over in a week or so.'

'Setting the film in Scotland, is he?'

'Where else?'

'I see. Well I'd better welcome him. Will he be staying with me?'

'No, that's not necessary. He'll be staying at the Cairndale Hotel. I've arranged that already. He doesn't want to inconvenience you.'

'Very thoughtful of him, I'd say.'

'Okay. I'll be in touch. Bye.'

'Bye.'

Harry replaced the telephone.

'My, that Neil's a busy chap. You'll never guess what, John.'

'Then I can never guess I suppose. Your life seems to be full of surprises these days.'

'Daniel Guardino, the scriptwriter. He's coming to Dumfries.'

'Wow. Things are taking off for you.'

'Yep, they are. Not so much on Morag's front though. You know, John, I think after all this time, you must prepare yourself to face the music, face the worst. I think you are coming to realising that, aren't you?'

John's anger rose unexpectedly. 'What do you mean, Harry?'

Harry sensed the atmosphere. John had changed his tune yet again. He tried to clear the air.

'Maybe it's because I feel we are getting on together, John. I can be more frank with you. So the truth is we're not really making much progress with Morag, are we?'

'Harry, damn you, you must realise I will never give up the hunt for Morag. You know that. I know you do. You have two daughters. Would you have ever given up if either Fiona or Laura went missing?'

There were a few seconds of silence as their tempers abated. Harry nodded and touched John's arm. 'You are right. I mustn't forget that, it's so true what you say. I've never been in your situation. And if I had lost either of my girls, I'd be just like you. Okay, Morag lives until we can no longer say that for sure. You agree?'

'That's the way it is, Harry, that's the way it has tae be.'

Harry said no more but reflected on his friend's volte-face. It was irrational to accept then deny anything, especially a missing daughter. Mood swings and depression: same source, he thought.

25
Kofi Goes to School

Sheila Steed was the headmistress at Ae village primary school on the outskirts of Dumfries. Always dressed to perfection, this mother of two grown-up boys and wife of a civil engineer husband lived in Edinburgh Road, not far from Harry. She was a regular squash player when darkness came early, and in the summer months she could be seen playing tennis at the Nunholm sports grounds. Hers was a fit and alluring body for a fifty-one year old who had no trace of grey in her chestnut hair. The evening walk with her golden retriever always ended her working day. On such occasions she met Bobby out with Frank Dunbar. Their conversations were social; after all, teaching and estate agency work were mutually incomparable professions.

Harry's phone rang as he opened his kitchen window to let a fly escape.

'Hello?'

'Hello, Harry, it's Sheila here, Sheila Steed.'

'Oh hello. Sorry about the delay, I was just coaxing a fly to leave the kitchen.'

'Ah...'

'Yes, life goes on even after Kofi's return,' remarked Harry.

'Yes, some of my pupils have been asking me about Kofi. The class have been following his antics and would love to meet him. Would that be possible?'

'Hmmm, you mean bring him to school?'

'Yes, that's what I had in mind. How do you feel about that?'

'You see, he has escaped once and I fear in a classroom he might find an open window.'

'I fully understand. I can promise that the room will be sealed, as it were. I can even drive you to the school. That way you can keep an eye on him in transit.' Sheila was trying to ensure the pupils would not be disappointed.

'Well... when do you want us to come?'

'Wonderful! Perhaps at the end of the week? What about Friday? How does that suit you?'

'I'd rather make it Thursday. I've got my Probus meeting on a Friday.'

'Then that's settled. Can I come to collect you at 9.45 a.m. on Thursday?'

'Yes please. We'll be ready.'

Harry informed Kofi that he was going to school, and that he'd meet small children and some teachers too. He'd also be going into a classroom. But above all he must not try to escape again.

'No escape... no escape again, please.'

'No, no, no escape again,' said a contented and informed Kofi.

Thursday morning was bright and sunny when Sheila's car drove up to Harry's home. Kofi had been put into a smaller heavy wire cage to make travel without his stand possible. Harry sat in the back of Sheila's C-RV Honda 4 by 4.

'I think I should have a car like this, Sheila,' he said.

'Why's that?' she asked.

'There's no need to bend down or mind my head when I enter or leave. It's like stepping into it instead of stepping down to it.'

'Yes, we like it although some think it's a petrol-guzzling cattle-chaser of a car.'

'Moooo... mmoooooooooooooooooooo,' said Kofi.

'Is he alright. Harry?'

'Oh yes. Very much so. You said "cattle" and that prompted a memory in him.'

'Oh, then I'll be very careful what I'm saying from now on,' Sheila laughed.

She engaged the engine.

'Brooom... broom.'

'I think he has come across a new engine sound too.'

It did not take long to get to the Ae village school just out of Dumfries. The car drove into the playground and approached the back entrance with care.

'The pupils are in their classes at present. That's why I collected you when I did. If not, you would have had a welcome like a pop star in the playground.'

Harry carried Kofi's cage into the empty classroom.

'Well, best behaviour now, Kofi. This will be a new experience for you, lots of little people.'

A thundering of feet was heard to come to a sudden stop in the corridor. Then excited voices were ordered to be quiet.

'I don't want anyone to shout or make a noise. You might frighten Kofi. Now, let me see if we are ready to enter the classroom.'

A boy began to chat with excitement to his friend.

'Kevin, I said, H U S H.'

Not a fallen pencil could then be heard when thirty-two excited nine-year-old children took their seats in the classroom.

'Right, class. This is a very special day. You have seen them on television, read about them in the newspapers and heard about them on radio. Now at last Kofi has been returned to his rightful owner and we are so very lucky to have them both with us today.'

'Miss, can we take a photo of Kofi?' asked confident Sally, lifting up her mobile phone.

'Well, Mr Dynes, would that be possible?'

'Yes, provided not all at the same time.'

Seven minutes went by as a column of pupils approached with raised phones to take a picture of Kofi. Some took a second shot of Harry.

As the last pupil returned to his seat, a loud ringing of the bell was heard.

The children immediately stood up and formed a column by the door.

Mrs Steed looked at her watch.

'Can we see him after break, Miss?'

'Back to your seat, it's not time for a break yet.'

'I'm afraid that was Kofi,' said an embarrassed Harry.

Mrs Steed laughed.

'Well, boys and girls, do you see how Kofi tricked us into believing it was our school bell?'

'I thought it was the real bell,' said Annie.

'Yes, that just goes to show you how intelligent parrots are. Right, after that, who's got a question for Kofi or Mr Dynes?' asked Mrs Steed.

'What other sounds can Kofi make?'

'He hears everything. For example when I'm in the lounge with my Hoover...'

'Hmmmmmmmmmmmmmm Hmmmmmmmmmmmm,' said Kofi.

The children laughed.

'And I am sure you all know the sound the ice-cream van makes. Well, he sings that one too. Then of course there is the ambulance...' said Harry, looking at Kofi to take his cue.

'Dida Dida Dida...' said Kofi

'The police car...'

'Paaapeep Paaapeep!'

'And the fire engine too... the fire engine too, Kofi... come on, the fire engine... Well, he's not wanting this game to go on. But he says lots of things. Often twice, it's a parrot thing.'

'Can I come and touch him?' asked Neil.

'Well, not all at once. Neil, come forward,' invited Harry.

Harry opened the cage. Kofi was keen to step out into the classroom and onto Harry's arm.

'Now he has a very powerful beak but he uses it to break Brazil nuts or to solve a difficult problem. He will be very gentle with you. He's happy to be here. Now, Kofi, this is Neil.'

'Kneel,' said Kofi with the loud instructional voice of a market stallholder and Neil dropped one knee to the floor. Everyone laughed.

But this placed Neil's face in front of Kofi's. They eyed each other up.

'Hello, Neil. What's up?' asked Kofi.

Neil laughed.

'Well, reply to him,' urged Mrs Steed.

'Hello, Kofi. How old are you?' asked Neil.

'I guess that's a very difficult question for him. In fact I'll have to work it out myself. Let me see... um, he's thirty-six years old.'

'My mother's thirty-six years old, too,' said Avril.

'Well, that's something you can tell your mother this evening. She's the same age as Kofi,' said Harry.

'Yes and Dad calls her ma Bird too,' Avril informed everyone.

'That's enough. Now the first row, come out to stroke Kofi,' ordered Mrs Steed.

'Neil, you sit here and keep Kofi on your arm. Let the pupils touch his head or his chest; he likes that best. But not his back,' said Harry.

'Why is that?' asked Neil.

'Well, you might like me to stroke the hair on your head or pat your back but you'd not be so keen to let me stroke your toes, would you?'

Neil laughed. 'No, not my toes.'

'It's the same with Kofi. But you can touch his feet. He doesn't mind.'

Neil was the lucky pupil who held Kofi most and Kofi seemed to bond with him.

'Can I kiss his head?' asked Neil.

'Yes but approach him slowly. He likes that from those he trusts.'

The lesson was over thirty minutes later and the pupils went out into the playground. Harry was invited to bring Kofi, in his cage, into the staff room for a morning coffee.

As the teas and coffees, fruit drinks and herbal teas were being served, the teachers all seemed to have a word or a question for Kofi, and many questions for Harry about how he was coping with celebrity status.

'Does he eat ginger nuts?' asked Judy McLean, the Primary Seven teacher.

'Offer him one and see, but I suspect any food with the word nut in it will interest him.' said Harry.

Kofi took the round hard brown biscuit in his left leg and turned it around like a card trickster. He examined it and then began to crunch it, dropping crumbs as he did so.

Suddenly, there seemed to be a bit of a rumpus in the corridor. Mr Wright, the janitor, was trying to keep Mrs Brenda Bell from entering the staff room, but there was no holding her back.

Eyes burning in a head full of pink rollers, this portly figure (in crimson above the waistline and navy blue below) had her sleeves rolled up and sweat on her brow. She had come hotfoot from her home. She was ready for battle and would take no prisoners.

'The Director for Education is going to hear about this and that damn parrot. As for you, Mrs Steed, your job's on the line, I can tell you that for a fact.'

'Please, can we discuss this with the head teacher and not here in the staff common room,' suggested a flustered Mrs Steed.

'Oh, I see you want to hide your dirty washing from your colleagues do you?' she snarled.

'Easy now, easy now...' said Kofi.

'Shut yer bloody mouth, ya cocky bird.' Mrs Bell's eyes flashed towards the powerful beak.

Harry felt most uncomfortable. This was an experience he was unfamiliar with and most certainly unprepared for.

'Then at least take a seat, Mrs Bell. Let's get to the bottom of this.'

'You know my Neil. You know the condition he has. He has missed many weeks of schooling because of his allergy. And you bring a parrot into his midst. Not only that. You let my son hold the bloody parrot longer than any other pupil. You let him kiss the stupid bird too. Oh yes, my facts are right. Neil just phoned to tell me about it.'

'Neil enjoyed the experience. Did he tell you that?' asked Sheila.

'Enjoy the experience? If he had an allergy to ice cream, he'd nevertheless eat one. You cannot be too careful with kids. His allergy is to feathers, Mrs Steed, and you know that. It's in his school file, underlined, in bold black ink. This bird has feathers, no skin. It's a bloody bird, for God's sake, what else do you expect? Do you hear me, f-e-a-t-h-e-r-s.'

'But he showed no signs of distress, I can assure you. There was no allergic attack.'

'No, not yet. But how would you like to waken at four in the morning with a wheezy child gasping for breath, gasping for life? Eh? How would you feel then? I'm surprised he's no gasping right now. It usually takes only a few minutes before it starts after he's been with feathers.'

There was no reply forthcoming and Brenda Bell had released all her venom. She held her head up and through gathering tears spoke only once more.

'I'm taking Neil to the doctor's surgery right now. You will be hearing more about this, I assure you all.'

Brenda Bell banged the staff door shut, making the glass windows shake and rustling some wall-pinned notices. She left calling out for her son as she marched down the corridor.

There was a moment's silence in the staff room.

'I should have known,' said Sheila. The tears began to flow from her eyes. 'I should have known he had a feather allergy, it is, as she says, in my class pupils' notes. It was my fault.'

'That's it. No more school appearances for you, Kofi, or for me. Too stressful. Far too stressful.'

John consoled Harry. 'It wis nae your fault, Harry. You were responding to an invitation.'

'Maybe. Yet I've never known anyone to suffer after touching Kofi.'

'Harry, maybe it's been a problem with duck feathers in a quilt or a pillow she's had. I'm sure she's no had real bird feathers to contend with.'

'But feathers are feathers, aren't they, John?'

A few days later there was a knock on Harry's door. Inter Flora handed over a bunch of flowers for Mr Dynes. Harry signed for them and took them to the kitchen to find a vase. As he cut through the cellophane, he cut round the small white envelope. He was intrigued as to which admirer might be sending him flowers.

He cut the flowers an inch from the end and put them in the peelie waste bin. He did not have the artistic flair of his widow but the flowers were displayed to his satisfaction. He opened the envelope and took out the card. It was blank on both sides.

That evening Sheila came round to visit Harry.

'At last some good news. Indeed some very good news,' she began.

'That sounds as if you have not lost your job after all then,' said Harry, smiling.

'Far from it. I've even had a letter of apology from Mrs Bell.'

'Really? Well I never.'

'Yes, you see Brenda did take Neil to the surgery. They found nothing untoward but made an appointment for Neil to be seen at the allergy clinic at the hospital. There they did extensive tests.'

'My, I didn't think she's go that far. There was no sign of Neil suffering when he held Kofi as far as I can remember.'

'I know. But wait for it...'

'You mean you got the test results?'

'I did indeed. They tested him with all sorts of feathers yes, including imitation and bird feathers. And they found no allergy. They said he was now clear of allergies. You can imagine how happy Mrs Bell is.'

'I can indeed! And Neil is back to school?'

'Yes, as happy as can be.'

The following afternoon, Harry answered the door to Mrs Bell. He did so not sure if he was about to face a battleship or perhaps more likely, in view of what Sheila had told him, a canoe.

'Mr Dynes, I'd like to apologise to you for my outburst. And I've brought a box of Brazil nuts for you and Kofi. I know he'll like nuts, perhaps the chocolate too.'

'Yes, he'll enjoy them as much as I will. I think you should come in,' suggested Harry.

This was not the woman he had seen in a vile rage at school. Her hair was neat and freshly trimmed. Her face was soft and pleasing to observe. Her peach blouse was low cut to tease, her tight skirt exaggerating her femininity and as she sat down in the lounge Harry noticed her stockinged legs were shapely too. Gone was the image that had met his eyes that Thursday morning.

'I like the flowers,' she observed.

Harry lingered on her pleasing comment.

'Did you forget to sign the card then?' he asked.

'No, I thought about it. I wanted to be sure you knew about Neil before receiving flowers from a demented angry Brenda Bell. Sheila told me she would visit you and tell you about my good news.'

'Ahh, it's all falling into place.'

'You cannot know how happy I am. Almost since his birth, Neil has had an allergy to feathers. They have been life-threatening and severe. It caused us a lot of worry, we had to cancel holidays some years and so his illness affected all the other members of our family too. But his recent tests were thoroughly comprehensive. For the very first time in his life he is free from feather allergies, indeed all allergies.'

'I am very pleased to hear that. It's such good news for Neil.'

Brenda rose and went over to Kofi's cage.

'So you are the star. You really are. They said it might be the holistic affect. In fact I'm not sure if I wish to investigate it further. All I know is that I'll not be up at all hours. I'll not be rushing Neil to the hospital or worrying what might happen to him at school... you saw how it affected me... but these days are over now and it's all thanks to you, Kofi, you really are a star. Sorry I upset you, parrot, but you are a star. Yes that's what you are, a star.'

'A star... a star... you are a star,' said Kofi.

26
Bless You Bishop, Bless You

Daniel Guardino was a New Yorker born and bred. Italian blood pumped through every vein: Sicilian, perhaps. Bronzed arms and face led to that assertion. Surely a Mafia link somewhere, thought Harry. Over the next few days Scotland was unlikely to top up Daniel's tan. He was a hard talker and even spoke when inhaling his next breath. His voice was peppered with short staccato bursts as his active mind brought thoughts into speech. He was at the top of his profession as an experienced scriptwriter. His word was final and his colleagues knew that. If it were legal, he'd do it. And if not, he'd do it unseen. He was also some four inches shorter than Harry.

They had arranged to meet at the Cairndale Hotel in a side room; Harry arrived moments after the appointed time of 3 p.m.

'Great to meet you, Harry.' Dan extended a hand to shake Harry's, while the other hand slapped Harry's shoulder.

'Very pleased to meet you too, Mr Guardino.'

'Hey, call me Dan or Gino, whichever you feel comfortable with, but not Mr Guardino, okay? You sound like you are speaking to my deceased fadder.' Dan laughed, causing the light bulbs above his head to shake.

Harry smiled wishing he were thirty years younger and more able to cope with this dynamic machine-gun rattling-tongued New Yorker.

'And how long will you be staying in Dumfries?'

'I just arrived last night and you're wondering how long I'll be here? Hey, you gotta be kidding. I've never been to Scotland before. I gotta see much more. I'll be following Kofi's route wherever he went and seeing the countryside. It's mighty green in places here. Great for filming.'

'Lots of rain, that's why it's green,' said Harry.

'We film in any conditions. Ooh, and thanks for the London Court case. We'll find a Sheriff court in Scotland to play that one out. I'd like to meet some Scottish actors too. Someone to play you, for instance: a man of fifty perhaps.'

'You flatter me. I'm a lot older than that you know,' said Harry proudly.

'Sure. But you're much too old, too slow for a film with a lot of action. I gotta make it believable, so Harry's fifty, okay?' said Dan, unconcerned.

His cutting remark seared Harry's soul.

'Now, any more stories I need to know? Gotta flesh out another ten minutes; that's ten pages for script purpoises.'

'Well, now, let me see, when I was a... younger... man, of course,' said Harry, taking stock of this ruthless dealer, 'there was Kofi's encounter with the Bishop. Does that ring a bell?'

'Sure haven't heard about that one.'

'Well, after London we moved to Stirling. Kofi settled there in more ways than one,' said Harry.

A waitress with a tray entered. The hotel silverware supported afternoon tea with chocolate fingers, and circles and triangles of traditional shortbread. The waitress smiled as she poured the tea for Harry.

'Got any iced tea, ma'am?' asked Dan.

'Iced tea?' queried the waitress. 'Just a moment.' She was wondering if anyone had ever been as brash enough to ask for iced tea in Scotland.

'So you were in historic Stirling. Tell me about dose days.'

Harry started to sip his tea. He took a bite of his sweet biscuit and began to recall the story.

Parkdyke
Stirling 1983

Parkdyke was a newly-wed's paradise. It lay near Cambusbarron in a quiet cul de sac of the university and administrative centre of Stirling. Wimpy Homes in Parkdyke were where first mortgages had been secured. Harry and his wife were made most welcome. Everyone knew their neighbours and Kofi knew everyone too. Many young families came in to see and greet Kofi. He always had a word for them.

The World Championships of the Highland Bagpipe Society took place in Kings Park, Stirling, beneath the castle on more than one occasion when they lived there. Pipe bands from all over the world arrived to play battle and secure the silver platter. But practice took them to secret locations so that the competing bands could not eavesdrop on selected airs, stirring tunes and the syncopated beats of the drummers. They came from Canada in droves, from Australia in strength and New Zealanders felt on home territory as the band came from Dunedin, the most Scottish of New Zealand towns. But from India, South Africa, Norway, The Netherlands and Belgium, bagpipers and drummers descended on Stirling.

Kofi began to hear a new sound. He got the pitter patter of the side drum down to a tee. The boom boom, boom of the bass drum to sheer perfection too. But what amazed Maggie and Harry was his ability to blow up, in stages, the sheep's stomach before the first notes emerged hesitantly out of the drones of the Highland bagpipe from Kofi's lungs.

Harry took Kofi to work at the end of the second term. He thought the children at St Modan's High School might be interested in seeing him and his antics. Sure enough there was a steady lunchtime queue waiting to see the parrot. The pupils knew he could perform and thought of ways in which they could try to make him speak. In no time at all Kofi had become the pupils' friend.

'Boring algebra; boring algebra.' Another saying came from the mathematics teacher who sometimes doubted the work presented to him had been done by the pupil himself. At such times he would ask:

'Is this the work of a pavement street artist?'

It became part of Kofi's language store.

But once a year on St Modan's Day, the Bishop of Edinburgh would come to the school. This was an important day and one which would find Kofi kept in the locked guidance room and not near the assembly hall or the staff common room in which the Bishop would be taking lunch. Harry was confident that Kofi would keep a low profile until the Bishop left to return to the capital.

However the Bishop was not only a very learned gentleman, he also had oodles of compassion and enquired about the work of the guidance staff.

'Pupil poverty, truancy, discipline, that kind of matter. How do you approach these issues?' he asked.

'The guidance suite is there to give space and privacy to the pupils who need to address their difficulties with our help,' replied Laura McKenna, senior Guidance teacher.

The Bishop was intrigued. Harry sensed a degree of concern.

'I'd like to see this resource myself. I think this is such valuable work you are undertaking,' said the pious Bishop.

And so the entourage of Bishop, his aide and the school chaplain, the two other guidance teachers, the Rector and Harry set off to the Guidance department. There were three doors in the corridor. The nearest room was for the fifth and sixth year pupils and a bird that had been left alone a little too long.

'Are all the rooms similar?' asked the Bishop.

'Indeed, they all are, except for their colour scheme,' replied the Rector.

'And what colours are they?' the Bishop enquired.

'The faraway room is green. I'd say as true a green as the grass of Dublin's Croke Park.'

'Hmmm,' said the Bishop.

'Well worth a visit,' Harry said in a bid to keep Bishop and bird apart.

The Rector continued. 'The middle room is an attractive cream with a warm hint of yellow. His Holiness the Pope would approve of the yellow room, I am sure you will agree.'

'Both very traditional Catholic colours,' the Bishop remarked.

'Then there is the last room, the room for the older pupils. It gets a bit tatty at times. It's not had a facelift for some time,' Harry said, before uttering a silent prayer.

'Let's see how bad it is,' said the Bishop, placing his hand on the door handle. The Rector unlocked the door. Harry placed his hand on his chest as his heart started to beat more strongly. Please God, he prayed earnestly, shut Kofi up or make the encounter go well.

'Ah, an African Grey Parrot! Psittacus erithacus,' the Bishop remarked.

'You are obviously very familiar with the breed, sir,' commented Harry.

'Very much so. I was brought up in Nigeria. When I was a young boy we had a Grey Parrot. Quite a talker, I recall. So what does this parrot say?'

'I think he's on his best behaviour today,' said Harry, grateful that Kofi had remained silent as he observed this crimson-gowned man with a matching biretta.

'So he's yours, I am told Mr Dynes?'

'Yes, I occasionally bring him in. He can make pupils relax. He has proved his worth recently when a sixth-year pupil learned that his father had died unexpectedly. Kofi sat on his arm for over an hour until we could arrange for a relative to take the poor lad home.'

'A gift from God indeed, Mr Dynes,' the Bishop said approvingly.

Kofi seemed to welcome the attention in the eyes of the gathered crowd. But he could hold his tongue no longer.

A wolf whistle emerged.

'He's mistaken my robes for a dress, I think!' laughed the Bishop, and all echoed his sentiment.

Kofi got into his stride.

'Who's for tea? Who's for tea? Not for Harry, he's fifty-three.'

The Bishop laughed.

'He's a cheeky fellow at heart, I would say, Mr Dynes.' But then the Bishop abruptly stopped laughing. 'Oh excuse me... I'm going... to... to... sneeeeeze.' He struggled to get his handkerchief out in time. His explosive sneeze echoed loudly around the bare walls.

'Bless you Bishop,' everyone said.

Then Kofi joined in. 'Bless you Bishop, bless you Bishop, aaaatichoooooo, aaaatichooooooooo, aaatichooooooooo.'

The Bishop approached the cage. He put his hand to the parrot who offered his head to be massaged.

'And bless you too, Kofi.'

Harry breathed a sigh of relief as the Bishop left the room on amicable terms with his unpredictable parrot.

'Gee, great script. We could even use St Modan's school with the layout you describe. How would you like to go back to Stirling?'

'You mean me travelling around the country with you?'

'If you feel up to it,' said Dan.

'I'll give it some thought.'

'Sure, think about it. I can go alone but I thought you might like to tag along. But sure, you take your time on that one.' Dan gulped the last mouthful of his cold lemon tea.

Harry resisted the temptation to tour with him. Dan was a hurricane; he was a fair-weather traveller.

27
But That's in Arizona!

Harry's decision was made for him. He was asked to report for tests at the local hospital. He would be required to be in a ward for a couple of days.

'So can you look after Kofi while I'm away?' he said to John.

'Sure, Harry. I think Kofi trusts me to feed, water and clean his cage. I'll even make you a promise to have all the windows and doors closed when I'm doing it.'

'I trust you, John. Anyway it will only be for a couple of days.'

'Yea but the tests, what are they about?'

'I'll let you know when I've had them.'

'Peoria, mhhhh, mhhhhhh. Peoria, mhhhh.'

John understood almost all that Kofi said. But this made no sense at all. Kofi's arrival, however, kept John busy and his guest did much to keep his spirits high. There was no peace in the house. Yet John could see how his friend Harry could be so attached to his feathered companion.

'He'll be back soon, Kofi, back soon,' said John.

Kofi tilted his head and turned around on his spar.

'Harry gone; Harry gone. Back soon.'

Three days later Harry returned from hospital and telephoned John.

'It's a fraud,' said Harry.

'What?'

'They found nothing sinister. They said I had a shadow in the left lung. They had to investigate of course. Thought I'd need chemo. But whatever it is, it is benign. No big C there. So I tell you, it's a fraud.'

'Great news. But I guess they didn't say it's a fraud.'

'No, not exactly these words. But it left that impression. Something about growing older not coming without its aches and pains and at my age, needing to take it easy. So they told me. To me it was a mountain out of a mole hill.'

'But the tests, what were the tests?'

'They took a skin graft and the usual bits and pieces, urine, cholesterol, X-ray, that sort of thing.'

'They'd do that to me as an outpatient. So why not you?'

'Well, they gave me some brown oral medication at night too and then took all those tests the next day. But anyway they found nothing. I've nothing to hide.'

'Okay but I'll leave you a day or two to recover. I'll drop by with some eggs and a quiche which you can eat hot or cold, a few slices of roast chicken, bread and some salad items. You've got tea; I'll bring fresh milk, and you were getting low on coffee so I'll get some more. You have quite a bit of mail. Not much that looks of any importance. That's my initial impression but that's for you to decide. I didn't open any of course. I'll bring Kofi back on Friday morning. How does that suit you?'

'Well, why don't you come round on Thursday night for a meal and bring him then? I'll surely have recovered by then.'

'Provided you have recovered, sounds a good idea to me.'

On Thursday night Harry looked forward to having Kofi's cage back in the lounge. John arrived and Harry took Kofi from him.

'Kofi, pet, you see I can go missing for a couple of days too. So now you're home. Home sweet home.'

'Home sweet home. Home sweet home,' said Kofi.

The oven opened. Out came the roast chicken and, after a few minutes cooling, it was carved. Roasted potatoes, broccoli, carrots and a sauce that Harry had made from garlic, onions, a tin of chopped tomatoes, some tarragon and curry powder awaited the hot plates.

'Harry, you're a great cook,' said John as Harry poured two glasses of Domaine la Bégude, a French red from Vaucluse. 'Cheers. Welcome home. That's you officially back in the rudest of health.'

'Yes, it's good to be back. Have you heard anything from Dan?'

'Yeah, didn't ye get his card?'

'Something about heading to the Trossachs. Must have been after he'd been at Stirling.'

'Other way aroond. He's recovering in Stirling.'

'What do you mean?'

'Dan had an accident. A deer ran in front of his car.'

'He wasn't driving, was he?'

'No, he's got a driver. But poor Dan ended up in Stirling Sheriff's court as well.'

'Good heavens, but you said he wasn't driving, so whatever for?

'When the police got to the scene, they could see the damage the deer suffered but Dan's injuries would have been fewer if he had been wearing a seatbelt.'

'Surely it's compulsory in the States too?'

'Aye, it was a moment of madness. He saw the deer approaching and thought he'd get a good shot of it.'

'You mean shoot it, like dead?'

'No, Harry. Shoot with his camera, you dope. So he took his belt off and whack, his head cracked the windscreen.'

'Is he badly injured?'

'Mainly his pride, which needed a pinch anyway, as you well know. Got a £60 fine but he had no license to give him points so he got the wiggly finger from the Sheriff aboot common sense.'

'And his injuries?'

'Your man Neil says he's chatting up the nurses. Sounds like a full recovery to me.'

'I wonder if that'll put the script back a notch.'

'Doubt it. I reckon Dan can write a script with his eyes closed and in a plaster, in no time at all. Mind you, the nurses might enjoy the distraction.'

'But how come, John? I mean, how can he write a film script so quickly? It's taking Elly-Anne some time to write this book.'

'It's because it's a film, Harry. Not a book. It's visual. It's not only the words but also camera instructions. Fading here and there, cutting at other places. I guess they know what they are doing.'

'I see,' said Harry, impressed.

'The viewer needs time to interpret what they are seeing as well as hearing,' said John with surprising pertinent knowledge.

'How do you know all that then?'

'Until recently I guess I've been watching aboot twenty films a week. Thirs not really much dialogue in them. Ye soon learn.'

'Peoria, Peoria, Peoria, Peoria, mhhhh mhhhh,' said Kofi.

'There he goes again with that expression. I don't know where he got it but it's been a fairly constant refrain since you left.'

'What is it again?' asked Harry.

'Peoria, that's what he's been saying.' said John.

'Peoria... Victoria... Ramona... Peoria... no, it's pretty meaningless to me,' said Harry.

'Sounds as if he's crying afterwards. Perhaps it was because he was missing you.'

'Maybe, but I can't pinpoint what he's saying. I'll keep an ear out for it and think about this wail at the end.'

'Hang around. You'll soon hear it again.'

Kofi said many things but every now and then he returned to his mysterious word. Two days later the problem returned.

'Peoria, Peoria, mhhh... mhhh,' he said.

Harry could not think why he hadn't done it before. He went to the computer and entered Peoria into the search engine.

Peoria City, Arizona. Harry didn't know anyone who had been there. He scrolled further down.

Jury deadlocked in mall-shooting, Peoria. The local news of Peoria seemed like that of the Wild West and two more pages were occupied with vivid details of the shoot-out. After that came the advertisements. Peoria, the best university in Arizona. Car Dealers in Peoria. The list of Peoria-related businesses, sports clubs and more mundane news continued for another six pages.

Harry scrolled down two more pages. There he came across a new entry. MV Peoria.

Harry had a new subject to investigate. He discovered that the MV Peoria was a Turkish-owned and registered cargo ship. A rather massive container ship, in fact, as the photo showed under 'Images of MV Peoria'. Harry entered its current voyage. Goodness. It was becoming clear. It might be a missing link. The MV Peoria had left Glasgow the day before Kofi was spotted in Stranraer. He must have cadged a lift on it.

Quick, the telephone! John would be interested to have this mystery solved at last.

'John?'

'Hi, Harry.'

'I've solved the problem.'

'What problem?'

'The Peoria problem,' said Harry

'Really?'

'Yes. I looked up Peoria on the internet,'

'So have I. It's jist a toon in Arizona, isn't it?' said John.

'Well, yes, on pages one, two and three, it's a town alright. But did you get to page nine?'

'No.'

'Well, I did and guess what? It's also a Turkish cargo boat and what's more, it sailed last week from Glasgow on its way to Antalya in the Mediterranean. Am I making myself clear?' Harry asked.

'You mean Kofi was a passenger?'

'Oh, yes... an un-paying passenger, yes, a stowaway you might say.'

'Then Dan will have to get that into his script somehow. So where's Antalya?'

'It's a port in Turkey,' replied Harry.

'Well, well, you are a better detective than me these days, Harry. But as a former police officer I must caution you that stowing away on a ship is an offence.' said John.

'Go on, charge Kofi,' laughed Harry.

'Whatever will that parrot come up with next?'

'Time will tell, John. Time will tell,' said Harry.

'You said that twice. Was that you or was it Kofi?'

28
Film Rights and Illusions

Neil phoned from his Glasgow office.

'Good news for you Harry.'

'What this time?'

'Just heard from Dan Guardino.'

'Is he better?'

'A few bruises on his head but with that tan they are hard to see. Could have been much worse. You don't mess with deer on those highland roads.'

'I'm glad something stood up to him. That would be a new experience for him,' laughed Harry.

'What's he saying, Neil?'

'Well, bottom line is that he's now got the finance to proceed with the film rights and is starting to cast already. And they will be filming in Scotland. I gave him that Turkish boat suggestion. He likes that as a link from Glasgow to Stranraer. So he's able to pay you a cheque for the first instalment. It's a dollar cheque, but after it's been converted, expect a cheque for around 20K.'

'Really, that much?'

'Just wait till the public get to see it. Remember you also get the two percent net of box office sales.'

'And what about John?' asked Harry

'He's on the book royalties. I've given him 3K. Same conditions apply.'

'Why the big difference?'

'Kofi is seen as the main protagonist; you know, it's his story and he's yours. You started it off, remember?'

'It was Kofi that really started it. What I must remember, though, is to change my will,' said Harry.

'Young girls... Young girls... Young girls...' said Kofi.

The words encouraged Harry to sing the Beach Boys song as he replaced the handset.

> *Some girls like to run around, like to*
> *handle everything they see.*
> *My girl doesn't run around because*
> *you know she'd rather be with me?*

'You heard that on Radio 2, didn't you, Kofi? I heard it on Ken Bruce last week.'

Kofi looked studious with his head tilted to the left. It was a pose he often adopted when he was listening or thinking hard.

'Young girls... Peoria... Young girls... Peoria.'

Why would some girls be on the Peoria, Harry pondered. A cargo boat? Not a cruise liner. Was thinking outside the box valid with such a morsel? A thought strayed into his mind. Was he thinking rationally? Ah possibly not. Hmmmm. No harm in sharing it with John.

He lifted the telephone hesitantly.

'John, are you busy?'

'Not really, why?'

'Then come round for a coffee. I've some thinking to share with you.'

'Thinking? So now you're a philosopher!' laughed John.

'Yes, a philosopher, I like that idea, mind you... either that or a crackpot.'

Within half an hour John was round in Harry's kitchen helping him pour the coffee.

'Well, Harry what's this insight lurking on your mind?'

Harry brought his coffee through to the lounge.

'You know a man approaching his eighty-fifth birthday doesn't have all his marbles. Does he?'

'Some do, some don't. I'd say you have all yours. Well, maybe a few have gone missing.'

'Okay, I'll be happy to admit that. Yes, but sometimes my thoughts run away from me and I thought twice about this one before deciding I should share it with you. Let me pass it over you. I'll tell you what I've been thinking. Promise you won't be offended, or more likely laugh at me?'

'Of course not. This sounds intriguing, my friend. I'm a' ears.'

'Maybe it is or you'll reject it straight away but this is what I thought: a bit like Joseph had a dream, eh?'

'Don't tell me, a book, a film and now a musical?' suggested John.

'No, no, it's more about your troubles than mine. You see it took us a long time to work out that the Peoria was a cargo ship. And we deduced that more likely than not, Kofi was a passenger on this container ship, at least to Stranraer.'

'Got aff when he was hungry, we thought, aye,' said John.

'Yes, probably. But recently he's been chanting "young girls" and "Peoria" in the same breath. Now I thought it might be the wives of the crew at first but from what I know of cargo ships, they don't usually take their wives on board. Are you following me?'

'Yes, but not sure where this is taking us.'

'Well... hear me out anyway. Remember Kofi has been crying too. Not crying in reality, but you know, mimicking sobs? The "hmmmm, hmmmm" sobbing? Could it possibly be... some girls sobbing... like the white slave trade?'

John's brow became furled. What thoughts had entered Harry's mind?

'What do you mean?'

'Maybe… well, you see, young girls are in demand in the Middle East. The Peoria might be trading them, as well as legal cargo.' Harry awaited John's reaction to what was now entering his mind as a far-flung, mad delusional thought.

'You've got me thinking, my friend.'

The tension eased from John's face and the excited expression of a young boy emerged.

'If I went tae see my old colleagues with this suspicion, they could trace the ship tae its port of docking and oversee the unloading activity. If it's a human cargo, it might be a lead. Harry, you've given me something new tae think about. You really keep ma mind active, ye ken.'

'So you are not angry with me?'

'Good heavens no. Why should I be? Morag's a cold case. You might have given a cold case a bit of a warm up.'

'Then I think you should thank Kofi. It was his explanation.'

'That Kofi of yours is turning oot tae be a quite remarkable bird.'

'Peoria, Peoria… hmmm, hmmm, young girls,' said Kofi once more.

That afternoon Harry had an appointment at the local surgery. Dr Sabur saw him.

'Tell me, Harry, where is it hurting?'

'It comes and goes. I get a bit breathless at times but I put it down to my age. I've been taking some aspirin at night as I'm running a bit of a temperature.'

'And what about your stools?'

'Loose. Diarrhoea most of the time.'

'I'm going to refer you to the hospital. They'll make an appointment for you in the next couple of weeks. In the meantime, I'll prescribe some antibiotics and take things a little easy; lay off the aspirin too for the time being. It's not necessary for you. You have a strong heart,' said Doctor Sabur.

'But I had tests recently at the hospital. I'm surely not needing to go back there?'

'I don't have any chest reports. That's where they need to investigate now,' said the wise doctor.

John returned to Police Headquarters for the first time since his retirement. He asked to speak to any available inspector. Inspector Brian Gibson came down to meet him.

'Hello, John. Nice to see you again. Social call?'

'Well, aye and no. It's always good tae see old friends but on this occasion it's sort of business, actually.'

'Okay, let's go into my office.'

They made their way along a corridor and entered the room at the end overlooking the police car park.

'Fire away,' said Brian, opening his desk drawer and taking out a pad of paper.

'We, that is, Harry Dynes and me, have reason tae suspect the MV Peoria of trading in young girls. You know, an educated guess: a hunch.'

'Intelligence is what we call it, as you know. Not a hunch. Surely you hadn't forgotten?'

'Oh no, I hadn't forgotten Brian. But when the intelligence is fae a parrot, that's when it becomes an educated guess, I'd say!' said John.

Brian laughed. 'Okay, the ship, where is she now?'

'I believe somewhere on the high seas heading towards a port in Turkey,' said John.

'Do you know the port of embarkation?'

'It was Glasgow's Broomielaw. We believe the ship may have taken on some young girls.'

'Hmmm... I see,' said the Inspector.

'Brian, have you any cases of trafficking?'

'There are some in Glasgow and elsewhere in the UK. Those caught are in prison. If you are right and we find girls in transit, they could be interviewed as part of the ongoing inquiry, Operation Enfield.'

'Enfield... Essex?'

Brian smiled. 'No, the Enfield is a fictitious creature sometimes used in heraldry, having the head of a fox, forelegs like an eagle's talons, the chest of a greyhound, the body of a lion, and the hindquarters and tail of a wolf.'

'Oooo... a dangerous beast, that one. So who thought that one up?'

'Someone who realised human trafficking was a complex matter, I suppose.'

'So you think this modern-age slavery has never stopped?' asked John.

'Does crime ever stop? Anyway, leave it to me and I'll make some inquiries.'

'Thanks, Brian. But do you think it might lead somewhere?'

29
Turkey Trap

Harry looked at his index finger. The mallet finger was out of its retaining support but it was reluctant to stand up completely straight. It showed a come-on bend that Harry could do without. It also reminded him of the day he went to hospital and returned to find Kofi missing. It would never quite be straight again. A letter arrived from the hospital later that day. He had an outpatient's appointment in four days time.

'This time Kofi, you wait for me in your cage, okay?' Kofi bowed his head. He knew when he was being reprimanded.

John came to Harry's home with his news.

'I've heard from Brian. Latvian and Estonian girls in Glasgow have gone missing, completely disappeared. Local prostitutes are very concerned aboot them and what's happened tae them. They are really quite scared. They fear they are murdered. Police HQ told me their handlers would nae report them as missing. The police in Ankara have been notified aboot oor suspicions and they know that they are no more than that, yet they want to co-operate with us. They will set a trap when the ship docks.'

'Then I hope they get the girls repatriated,' said Harry.

'Better still if we could get those involved back here to be charged. Then we might even know how long this trade has gone on for and what they dae with the girls once in Turkey.'

'Yes, that would be something,' said Harry.

John walked over to Kofi who was preening himself.

'You know, Kofi, if you had never gone missing, we'd never hae met. You have made me so happy, pretty bird.' Kofi waddled forward on his spar and offered his neck to be scratched. John obliged.

'Caw... caw... caw...'

'Steady, John, you are getting him aroused.'

Now passing the southern coast of Crete, the MV Peoria had had an uneventful voyage. The stacked seven-high containers had not slithered an inch since leaving Glasgow. It was just as Captain Tayyip Tabakov had wished. The tricky part lay ahead but he had been in this position before and knew the Turkish authorities were lax. After all it was a Turkish ship returning home. Trade was necessary and although customs checked the cargo with some degree of thoroughness, it was a cursory affair for a few hard currency dollars or pounds sterling to change hands regularly.

The next day Captain Tabakov approached the harbour at Antalya. A pilot boat came to guide him carefully into the quay. From the harbour master's tower Inspector Halis held binoculars to his eyes. On the bridge of the Peoria he could see Captain Tabakov and the first mate. Neither seemed agitated. It was a watch to last as long as required.

The Inspector focussed on the laid-back checkpoint. A log was being raised and lowered between two oil barrels as vehicles passed by. Each departure found the duty policeman approach the driver, followed by a prolonged handshake; then the officer placed his hand in his pocket afterwards. That was normal and the officer and his family now had dollars to spend.

Containers were being dispatched by two gigantic cranes. They were then gently eased on to flat rail wagons. The locomotive inched along to make ready the next container. Customs took note of their contents and made sure each container was watertight and sealed. No one could have survived the voyage in a container. Consequently it was a relaxed operation undertaken by poorly dressed and lowly paid casual stevedores.

At four twenty in the afternoon, a black van arrived and made its way towards the ship. Its rear doors were opened and it reversed slowly to the covered gangway. It remained there for almost half an hour. The driver remained at the wheel. Inspector Halis's interest grew. During this time, some fair-skinned girls were ushered speedily off the ship into the black-windowed van, under close supervision. Inspector Halis strained through his binoculars to gain vital information.

Then the doors were closed and the vehicle made its way towards the twin barrels and freedom. The driver would make good money provided he could get through the barrier.

Two detailed officers stood up at the barrier. One greeted the driver and shook his hand.

'Salaam Alikum,' he said.

'Alikum Salaam,' came the reply. Both smiled.

The other officer returned from his patrol around the van.

'Please,' said the policeman to the driver, as he approached the driver's window. The driver offered a closed fist. The officer's hand went to shake his. The lingering handshake brought a smile to the policeman's face, and a larger one beamed from the van driver. He could now proceed without an internal inspection but the widest smile was on the face of the other policeman who had walked around the van.

They nodded simultaneously and the barrier was raised.

As the van went through and out of sight, Inspector Halis rang the officer's number on his mobile.

'Tracking device secured?' he asked.

'Like tar on your fingers, sir,' he replied.

Upstairs in the police station at Antalya the detectives were tracing the movements of the van. Initially it proceeded north-west to the town of Isparta. It stopped there but only sufficiently to fill its tank. Then it moved off again, this time taking the Dinar road. For a few seconds, contact was lost. It returned moments later.

'A tunnel,' said the Inspector.

'Then they are on the Afyon road. I know the road well,' said Kamil Borazin. 'They will now be on the main road to Ankara.'

'That will make our task much more difficult. If the van enters a shanty township, it will not be so easy to trace them,' said Inspector Halis.

'Wait... no... they are not heading to the capital. They have taken a minor road leading to Emirdag,' said Kamil.

The van proceeded much more slowly on uneven terrain.

'Let's hope the tracker doesn't fall off,' said Halis.

'No way, sir,' said the policemen.

The tracking device noted another deviation. They were now leaving the minor road.

'This one leads nowhere. Look, the van is stopping. Quick, get a satellite view of the locus,' said Inspector Halis.

The screen focussed on a rural hideaway surrounded by trees. In the centre was a large barn with a smaller building by its side.

'This is too dangerous for us. I must get the Special Forces to take the buildings and then we come in with the back-up.'

Recip Tayyip Erdogan, the Turkish Prime Minister and head of the parliamentary coalition, was advised of the Special Forces preparation. He called an emergency meeting of the inner cabinet.

'Gentlemen, the police in Antalya have been tracking what they believe to be a human kidnapping operation. It may have been taking place for some time,' said the Prime Minister.

'For how long?' asked Malik Rashool, the Home Affairs minister.

'We had no information before the last couple of days that this sort of thing was happening,' replied the Prime Minister.

'With leaky ports and corruption by the police and harbour officials, no wonder this crime is taking place beneath our eyes,' said Malik.

'I'd rather not call it corruption. You know the Government cannot pay either the police or the port officials well. They regard it as part of their pay to get a bribe, or a tip, as they prefer to say. But not so much money changes hands and at this time it is not something we should try to change,' said the Prime Minster.

'I'm concerned with corruption and our EU ambitions,' said Malik Rashool.

'Yes, I understand.'

The stakes were high. If the operation ended in disaster it would be seen as an inept attempt at rescue with the likelihood of great loss of life. The Prime Minister asked that they proceed with care and caution.

Harry was becoming quite breathless and John had started to go to town to collect his friend's weekly shopping. Harry sat with a rug over him watching afternoon television with Kofi. Countdown on Channel Four taxed his mind, to come up with fewer and fewer words over five letters. Of course it did help when the thirty seconds were up after the clock ticked downwards. It ticked down a second time, every time note perfect as Kofi orchestrated.

John telephoned.

'Harry. I've just had a meeting with the Chief Superintendent, Cathy Ronson. She has re-instated me into the force on a contract. I start tomorrow!'

'Are you kidding me?'

'No, deadly serious.'

'Then I won't be seeing so much of you as you spin around the countryside with your wildlife hat on.'

'No, Harry. Not as a wildlife officer. They are sending me to Turkey. Ankara has given the boss some interesting information. I'll tell you all about it when I return.'

'Okay, Constable Reid, and when will that be?'

'It's open-ended. I'm there to give them a hand.'

30
It's English, But Not as I Know It

Final preparations were made in Ankara. The Special Forces codenamed the operation 'Sivas'.

Six highly trained commandos stood ready. Camouflage hid their faces and, to ward off the cold October night air, they all wore dark gloves, bullet-proof vests, and khaki scarves. Emblazoned on each scarf was their operational logo, Sivas.

At the Afyon police station, four vehicles were being prepared. Tyre, fuel and equipment were attended to. Eight police officers were armed and their communication with the Special Forces was in place. A strict embargo on calling the Special Forces now came into force. They would give the code to the police as soon as they had made the premises secure. Only then would the police arrive and take over. The coded signal they would give was KARAMAN, a district in the Taurus Mountains where the Special Forces trained. Watches were synchronised. As Siva personnel boarded an army Aerospatiale Alouette II helicopter, the police boarded their blue jeeps and each set off for their agreed rendezvous.

For Sivas, that meant landing near the Emirdag junction. From there, it was a slog of five miles to the target. Within 750 metres of the target, a dog's bark was heard. One soldier quietly made friendly overtures to the dog and the dog obligingly approached. He held his hand out with a piece of dried biscuit. The dog approached gratefully, confidently, sniffing the offering. Suddenly it was grabbed by its neck and with a swift arcing movement a knife crossed its throat. It had no time to gasp. It was dead. Sivas Number 2 threw the animal into the ditch beside the road while others strained to hear any disturbance from the direction of the house. For two full minutes no one moved. Every sinew was alert.

Then the elite solders approached the outhouse. A brief reconnoitre gave them a degree of confidence. There were no external guards. Access to the smaller of the two buildings was gained silently. No one was there. They assessed its contents by torchlight. Tables, desks, chairs and filing cabinets, of which they counted seven, were all that was to be seen. It was disappointing. It was not a place with any evidence of night-time staff or captives. Troops prepared to breach the second building. They burst into the building firing above all heads. Waking up from his soporific guard duties, Nadil Oman tightened his grip on his rifle. But before he could aim at the intruders the gun was forcibly knocked out of his hands and he was pinned to the ground

'Don't move or I shoot you,' the lead officer growled in his native Turkic language.

'Don't shoot, don't shoot, please don't shoot!' said Nadil.

'How many are here?'

'Just me and Gokayan and the girls,' said Nadil.

'Where's Gokayan?'

'Here somewhere.'

'Locus secured. We've got Gokayan outside,' a Sivas voice announced.

The lead officer was pleased the operation had gone flawlessly. No loss of life had been reported. He held his radio to his mouth. 'Silva 1, KARAMAN, KARAMAN, over.'

The barn was then lit up. Six girls sat up with blankets to their chins. They were unsure of their new status. Fear was etched on their faces. The police arrived and reassured the girls before ordering them to bring their clothing and blankets with them. They were led out of the barn and placed in one of the police trucks. The police driver looked at the six blonde women. 'Where you from?' he asked.

The girls were reluctant to answer.

'It be okay. We make you safe. Where you from?' he asked again.

'We are two from Latvia, three from Estonia, one from Russia. We work in Scotland, in Glasgow.'

'What work you do?'

'We get no work. We try hard to work but none. So we left to work at night with men.'

'Why are you in Turkey?'

'We were taken off the streets in Glasgow by a Turkish businessman, offering us work here. He promised a better life in Turkey. It was a better choice.'

There were many files in the smaller building. They were for another day. The premises were sealed and the Turkish employees were taken to the police station for interrogation.

Three hours later the police were back at the police station in Afyon where they were debriefed.

'Any problems?' asked Inspector Halis.

'Only the barking dog, but the special troops dealt with that,' said one officer.

'So little resistance on entering the barn?'

'Just the sleepy women and two men meant to be guarding them but at that hour they were very much asleep too.'

'No casualties?'

'None sir,' said one officer.

'Just me,' said another. 'I twisted my ankle.'

'But nothing else?'

The man shook his head.

'And the girls?' asked Halis.

'They are being detained until we can make a decision. They may become witnesses. They seem to be mainly Eastern Europeans,' said the sergeant.

The Sivas specialist team flew back to Ankara, where they were debriefed. Within minutes they slipped into the night, dressed as civilians returning home after a long day's night.

Harry worried if this venture eastwards was giving John too much hope all of a sudden. Even if the ship did have human cargo how could that relate to a missing daughter some five years ago? Each worried about the other. Neither of them mentioned their concerns in their e-mails.

The Turkish capital was surrounded by mountains. A careful descent into Ankara was mandatory. When John cleared customs, he was met by Inspector Halis.

'Salaam Alikum, Inspector Halis,' said John confidently.

'Alikum Salaam, Eid Mubarak. By the Grace of God you have arrived and it's a happy Eid time too. They just call me Halis. You should too. But I mislead you a little, I am not a Moslem. I am a Christian. I am a Turkish Anglican to be precise,' said the Inspector.

'My apologies, it just goes to show how little knowledge I have of Turkey.'

'We are a proud people with much history and at times we get too excited in our politics. We have a radical Moslem sector and a laidback all-comers-welcome Anglican tradition, with countless religious views in between. Turkey is a very diverse country.'

'Just like in Scotland at present,' said John.

'So tell me, what do you do?'

'I have recently retired. I, too, was a police officer.'

'Retired? You look too young!' said Halis.

'We can retire after thirty years of service. It's the nature of the job. But for this inquiry I have been re-instated.'

'I agree it is a hard job. But we suffer longer, it seems. So what department were you in?'

'I was the wildlife officer for the region,' said John.

'Wildlife... wildlife... Was that a full-time job? I don't think we need that post in our force,' remarked the Inspector.

'I am sure you dae the work onyway. There are many birds of prey in your country. Do they steal their eggs?'

'Yes, of course they do. They eat them or sell them.'

'And is that an offence?

'Ah, it is too common to make an issue of it.'

'Well, what aboot theft of farm animals or machinery?' asked John.

'Theft is theft whether it is of a car, boat, or grain from the fields. We investigate.'

'Whit aboot tobacco and cotton? Are these no smuggled oot o' the country?' asked John.

'Oh yes. Tobacco smuggling especially. We had some of your officers over here explaining how they trace the tobacco cargos.'

'But it's no general police work you have in mind for me tae dae, is it?' asked John.

'No. We have found out that the trade in girls from the UK has been steady over the past few years. We were told you had an interest in this type of crime so we're happy to have you on board.'

Inspector Halis arranged for John to stay at the Aktif Metropolitan Hotel in Ankara.

'We'll collect you at 9 a.m. and explain everything to you. By the way, you have your British uniform?'

'Yes, packed in my case. My Police Scotland gear.'

'Scottish? Hmm, then wear it all the time,' said Inspector Halis.

'All the time?'

'Yes, then I won't have to explain who you are so often. It's a morale booster for us too. It shows we're serious about work and our international relations.'

'I see.'

'That accent of yours. Is that Scottish? Is it English you speak?'

'Aye, I guess so. It's the way I talk onyway. I'll try nae tae make it ony stronger. Bit let me ken if I'm no makin' ony sense, will ye?'

'Ken, is that not a man's name then?' asked Halis.

'Aye, Ken's a man's name a' right but it also means Tae Know. I ken; they ken; we ken. Ye ken?'

'Ayiii kennnn,' said Halis, trying the Scottish accent out. 'A bit like Alaikum, I think.'

'Aye, Salaam,' said John.

31
Harry's Will and John's Hook

The following morning John was driven to Police Headquarters in Ankara. He was led to Inspector Halis's office.

'Good morning, John.'

'Good morning, Inspector.'

'It's Halis. Call me Halis. You were comfortable last night?

'Very much so, thank you. The hotel is very comfortable indeed.'

'That's good because I can't promise such comfort in the days ahead. Missing girls, especially from the UK: it's something we need to end. It's a big problem.'

'I know too well. I have a missing daughter too. Of course she may not be alive and she may not have been in Turkey, but I agree it's a trade we must stop.'

'You lost a daughter some years ago?'

'Yes, some five years ago now. No trace of her at all,' said John.

'I hope I'm not raising your hopes falsely. But we have found out that the trade in girls from the UK has been steady over the past few years.'

'The police haven't heard much of it in Scotland though. Missing people are usually children in care homes, troubled teenagers and the rare murder, but rarely is there no trail left at all,' said John.

'No, it is the girls on the periphery of society that are caught in their evil net. Girls from the former eastern communist countries, who now live in the west, seem to be their target at present. Many are brought over land. Others come by ship. Less suspicious. Only one border to cross, as it were. They know the jobs they came for are no longer available in the west. Their dreams are squashed. They stand out and they get picked up by this trade.'

'But my daughter was not like them,' said John.

'No. No, I didn't mean she was. Do forgive me. They are not all taken in groups. Some of the women are coming in one at a time. It seems they disappear from the streets. It is very difficult to trace them because they are soon out of your country. They can be driven miles to ports with Turkish boats ready, about to leave. Some girls are doped and placed in crates. Once aboard they are taken down into the galley to work preparing meals. When the ship approaches port again, they are doped and taken ashore and driven away to a secluded spot from where they are sent to families paying for them.'

'You seem to be on top of it then, Halis.'

'Scratching the surface, I guess. Destitute, they settle into a family. They feed and care for them. Yet it started with abusing them. It's a terrible trade and one we want to stop. The girls we have found are almost all from UK ports but are not all UK citizens. Others come across mainland Europe through Germany, as I said. That may make finding your daughter difficult. That is, if she is in Turkey at all,' said Inspector Halis.

A firm knock on the door interrupted them.

'Come in.'

'Three this morning, sir.'

'Thank you.'

Halis looked the three photographs. He dropped them in front of John.

'Murdered?' asked John.

'Drug deaths, I presume. Post mortems will determine but we get a few each day.'

'That's a high level. It is a potent strain of drug that's around just now?

'Look more carefully.'

'Not Turkish girls?'

'No. Girls who see no future. It's a last resort. No, not all Turkish.'

'But why this trade in Turkey?' asked John.

'In Asia we are all dark-skinned. Admittedly some are darker than others, or should I say some are lighter? Your people are white and try to colour themselves brown. We are the opposite and it's more difficult to do. There is a market for European hair on a girl. They assume the girl will marry into a family and so the gene is planted for future generations.'

'But my daughter can't have children. What would they do with her then?' asked John with a furrowed brow.

'I am not sure.'

'No, I am not sure either, and you can't be sure, but what could happen to her?' John persisted.

Halis hesitated. Reality was not always pleasant to convey even for an experienced police officer.

'The worst would be she would be disposed of somehow. But if it is a wealthy family that has her, she might be a secretary for the family business. I don't know. If it was a true Muslim family, then she would be well looked after, I am sure.'

'I can't see how a true Muslim family could buy a stolen European and think that was not a crime.' John thumped the back of a chair with his fist.

'I hear what you say. It goes to show it is a difficult crime to understand. But we are gaining experience.'

'It's the dilemma with drugs, isn't it?'

'You mean legalise?'

'It's not as easy as that, Halis. Cocaine is grown and manufactured in rural areas of Columbia and Peru, and weed in Afghanistan. Give them lucrative jobs and the crop dies. Leave them with no work and no support and they'll grow the crops, and they need a market.'

Halis nodded. It was a universal conundrum.

'Drugs are one thing. Several British Pakistani girls have been sent home to marry in their Asian country against their will. Some do not wish to defy their parents and so they go reluctantly but they have all been schooled in British schools and have lost many friends. Nor do they wish to be burdened with children at their young age. We are beginning to intercept these ships if they dock in Turkey before their onward voyage to Pakistan, especially to Karachi.'

'Most would fly to Islamabad or Karachi, I would have thought,' said John.

'Oh, don't misunderstand me. By far, most travel by plane but there is still a considerable number that go by sea, I assure you. Indeed it is easier to go by sea. Airport security is seen as much tighter than our cargo sailings to ports. Governments are looking out for such cases there. '

'You have certainly got my full support in what you are doing.'

'Then let's be on our way. There's something happening at Afyon. I want you to be there.'

Harry opened the brown envelope that was propped up against the marmalade pot. Inside was a letter bearing the hospital frank mark. It confirmed his appointment and required him to fill in a form listing the medication he was already taking by name, frequency and strength. He was to bring this completed form to the appointment. The kitchen wall calendar confirmed his increasing appointments. He had little enthusiasm or energy to make his hospital trips but knew they were in his best interests. Although he had not thought about it, even Kofi saw signs of him slowing down.

'Move along there... Move along. Mind the gap; mind the gap,' said Kofi, watching his master's demeanour.

Harry realised he missed his friend John and worried about him. His was possibly an obsessive quest, diminished a little over the weeks spent tracing Kofi, but now that Kofi was home the full force of single mindedness must have overpowered John. He was placing all his hopes on this final threadbare link, based on the hunch of a parrot. It did not make sound investigative planning sense. But maybe that was where creativeness could succeed. After all had Sir Alexander Fleming that night looked at the dirty Petri dish and binned it, we would have heard no more. But he didn't. He thought creatively and that dirty Petri dish led to the discovery of penicillin.

The doorbell rang. This was the appointment Harry was expecting.

'Come in, Arnold.'

Arnold Hilton was a Glaswegian but his accent was much more rural. He lived on an out-of-town former manse with his teacher wife. As a lawyer the hustle and bustle of Court work was not for him, except when he was called to fatal accident inquiries that had befallen his clients. He had a slightly receding hairline and the athletic build of a long distance runner but he was more often seen running around in his top range Audi. His area of expertise was wills, and he knew how to put his clients at ease. His glasses had an austere frame, as black as his polished shoes.

'Good afternoon, Harry. I trust you are well.'

'Good afternoon Arnold... Good afternoon Arnold.' Kofi never ever missed a trick.

'Ah and I hope you are well too, Kofi,' said Arnold Hilton, solicitor of Hiker & Blunt.

'Take a seat. Let's get this over with,' said Harry.

'Come, come. A will is not such a difficult task but it is important to get it accurate. It solves many a problem after you've gone.'

'Yes, after I've gone. A lovely euphemism. But I agree, I do see the light at the end of the tunnel now. And to be honest, Arnold, it's not something I fear. The older I get, the more death becomes a friend to me.'

'That's a fairly common and realistic feeling but is your health not what you'd wish it to be?'

'After the motorcycle chase around Scotland, I felt that was the watershed. I'd never do that again. Now I've got breathing problems. Something they will try to attend to next week at hospital.'

'They may well find a bacteria and treat it promptly. Then you could be a new man. If that were the case you'd not be seeking my expertise today,' said Arnold.

'There's never the right time to update a will. Too early and it's out-of-date, too late and... you said it... it causes problems.'

'You're right, Harry. So let's get on with it. You ready?'

'As ready as I'll ever be. So then, as you know, I had a will made many years ago. Have you still got it?'

'Yes. Perhaps we can start by checking it and making adjustments as we proceed. A codicil as we call it. '

'Arnold, I think we should start again. It's a different situation now.'

'If you wish.'

'The house when sold should be divided equally and the proceeds go to my two daughters.'

'Yes, that's already there,' said Arnold.

'Then my charities. 2K to the Dumfries Burns Club to keep it running; 2K to the Shannon Trust to help make prisoners literate; 2K to Rescue Collies; 2K to Dumfries Probus; 5K to Morag Reid if she is found; 5K to John Reid and 5K for each community in Dumfries to have safe playing parks; and I'd better give the girls 10K each in addition to the sale of the house. That should leave me enough in case I get placed in a residential home before too long. Have you noted all that?'

'Wait a moment. I'm trying to add this up. You are a pensioner; are you sure this money is available?' asked Arnold.

'It's a funny thing. Had you visited last year, I'd not be talking like this. But it seems every week I'm getting news of royalties that get paid every second month for the books about Kofi. You see I get monthly statements. Also I get advances from the film company in California. They tell me I'll possibly be even on my way to being a millionaire when the film is released in so many countries. Can you believe that? I can tell you it's a golden egg that I'm sitting on and that's a comfortable place to be.'

'I see.' Arnold tapped his pen on his clipboard.

'Don't worry, rest assured, there will be enough to pay your fee,' Harry smiled.

'That is the least of my concerns,' said Arnold.

John had a cup of hot Turkish coffee brought to him.

He looked up.

'Hmmm, thanks.'

He sipped it and then laid it down. Halis sat with his cup held in his hands.

'John, we were able to find some Eastern European girls last week. They were in some state. They had no idea what was happening to them. Two of their guards were captured but they were of little importance. Mind you, they will be prosecuted. We are still interrogating them but I'm not sure if they really know much about the operation. We need to find the organisers behind this outrage, the middle man as well as the bosses.'

'That does not seem easy,' said John.

'No, but in an outhouse we found filing cabinets. They may give us a few more clues. Let's get over there and see what's happening.'

John was driven to the outhouse secured by the Special Forces earlier in the week. When he arrived he noticed lights on in the building.

'I see you have a team in.'

'Yes, they've been busy over the last twenty-four hours. There's much intelligence to sieve through,' said Halis.

John entered the building. Tables were laid out at which female police officers and administrative staff members were reading through the papers of each drawer to try to gain an insight into the minds of the gangs. Stones were laid on top of piles of papers denoting they offered little intelligence. But there were four demarked areas. John asked what they were for.

'They have made four categories. These are the ones which are shedding most light.'

'Can I see what they are?'

'Yes, come with me.'

There were two rows of papers. The ones at the back were marked geographically. It showed that this was a country-wide operation. The ones at the front were classified by activity. The fishing industry, domestic service, textiles and clothing, and finally the pharmaceutical industry. It seemed that the trade in modern slavery was heavily engaged in the Turkish economy.

'When you say domestic service, what do you mean?' asked John.

'Some girls are forced into marriage. Others may see this as a satisfactory solution especially if it is to a wealthy family. In both cases they service the home and the master of the house. That's the domestic service category.'

'But such girls could be free to contact the police or run away if they wished,' suggested John.

'True but remember some of these girls have left an Eastern European country to find work in the west. None was available. So they often prostituted themselves to make ends meet. The opportunity of marriage to a wealthy man might not be such a bad option for these girls. They are more ready to adopt a moderate Turkish lifestyle.'

'What about the pharmaceuticals?' asked John.

'You see they are not so many in that category. I'm sure that's because the industry is very well administered. The Government must ensure high standards are in the pharmaceutical industry at all times. They are inspected frequently from home and abroad. Too risky to employ such girls there,' Halis replied.

'I'm surprised that any are sent there then.'

'Money, John. They pay well in that sector and that means their handlers get a good cut. Some of the girls may have a qualification in the industry and they would be pleased to get into one of these firms. But there are not many in this category, I agree. Probably textile and clothing will be where most of them are, in sweatshop factories working under guards. It's a miserable life but there's a demand in mainland Europe for cheap clothing and that's what they do. It's your High Street shops which buy them.'

'I suppose that just leaves the fishing industry.'

'Yes, it does, the final category, John. Let's hope we get a nibble,' said Halis.

Harry's appointment at the hospital fell on a Friday. He took the bus there from Great King Street as he had done for his broken finger. But this time, before leaving the house, he not only secured Kofi's cage but also made sure the conservatory was closed and locked. Of course it had to be; the first winter frosts had arrived.

Mr Kwabena Nkansa was the specialist he had come to see. This Ghanaian chest and respiratory disease consultant, with shoulders as broad as an American defence back fielder, had a smile showing a row of perfect top teeth. The lower gum, however, had so many small gaps between each tooth that he spoke with a whistling lisp. It did not suit such a large figure. He was married to Mary, a Scot who had been a VSO teacher in Abetifi when they met some fifteen years ago. Now they had twin girls in their last year of primary school. He took Harry's blood pressure and a sample of his blood.

'We will have this analysed to check for any strain of bacteria which is making you breathless and of course it will give cholesterol readings too.'

'Cholesterol? Hmmm, that again. Ah well. That's the least of my worries at my age, Doctor,' said Harry.

'Standard, Mr Dynes. We don't miss opportunities to see if the engine is working to full capacity.'

'When will I get the result of the tests?'

'It will take a few days. We will give you a call to discuss the findings.'

'You mean come back to hospital?'

'Yes, it's better to have a face-to-face talk than a telephone conversation. You can ask more questions that way.'

'I suppose you're right. Is it something I should be worried about?'

'Let's see the results of the tests first.'

Harry nodded. He could have anticipated that response. He did not need to have asked the question.

'So, Mr Dynes, off you go. We'll be in touch.'

Harry was partly relieved. It seemed whatever was slowing him down was not as serious as to detain him there and then.

Inspector Halis came to see John on the Friday afternoon. He found him seated making his own notes on what he was finding.

'John, you need a break. Your eyes will be popping out of your head and you'll get a headache.'

'Yes, but it's satisfying work. I feel I am on the right track. I might as well go till the end.'

'No. You'll work better on Monday morning after a restful weekend at our summer house.'

John saw the value in what Halis was saying. He did not require a second asking.

The Halis family had a holiday house facing southward on the outskirts of Bolvadin. It gave an extensive view over Akseher Golu, a deep lake with good fishing. Several boathouses were dotted along the shore. It was no longer summer. A wintry sun shone on the lake reflecting the azure cloudless sky. They would pay for it in the early morning after the evening's roaring log fire had ceased to burn.

Inspector Halis drove John down to the water's edge. John took photos of the beautiful landscape.

'It's like Scotland you know. High mountains sheltering deep lochs,' he reminisced.

'Where your monster lives?' asked Halis.

'Ah yes, you've heard about the Loch Ness Monster. A most mysterious beast indeed.'

'So the monster exists?'

'In Scotland, monsters take over the lives of so many. Drink and drugs fuel their experiences and that's when some of them actually believe that the monster is real. They have seen it and know it well. It is a story that lived in the lives of our ancestors but it's such a good story, it's a financial winner. Some Americans come in the hope that they can be the first to prove the monster exists.'

'I have some of the monster with me,' said Halis.

From his knapsack he brought out two cans of beer. 'Have a Carlsberg.'

'I thought alcohol is not sold in Turkey.'

'It's sold in Turkey but Moslems don't drink it. Anglicans don't mind. Even the communion wine is alcoholic here,' laughed Halis.

They walked along the shoreline with their cans. John could not have felt more relaxed after a week straining his eyes over files and papers.

They came to a couple of boathouses.

'That's ours. Second one along. That's where I keep my fishing rods. Do you want to come fishing with me tomorrow?'

'From the shore?' John asked.

'No, that's my boat over there.' He pointed to a twenty-foot almost flat-bottomed boat with an outboard motor attached.

'I haven't fished for years,' said John.

'Then I hope you get your catch, in more ways than one.'

John looked at Halis and smiled.

The summerhouse was small but had a kitchenette and a dining come seating area. There was a fireplace with a stock of chopped wood. There was only one bedroom in which there were two single beds. But John did not find a toilet.

'That's outside. Take a torch if you need to go, otherwise just piss on the nettles over there at the side of the house,' smiled Halis, looking apologetic about the standards of hygiene.

Both men were tired and wanted a good start to their fishing day. But as they lay in their beds their minds were racing.

'So your daughter went missing very suddenly?'

'Yes, just vanished one night between visiting a school friend and returning home. We can even say where she disappeared,' said John.

'Then that's a great start, isn't it?' asked Halis.

'No, not really. Between the friend's front door and the bus stop. It's not far.'

'The road the righteous travel is like the sunrise, getting brighter and brighter until daylight has come,' said Halis.

'Let's hope it's a bright day tomorrow then.'

'When hope is crushed, the heart is crushed, but a wish come true fills you with joy.'

'Profound words, Halis.'

'You should read the Book of Proverbs, John. They speak to me in all situations.'

'I like the words you've said. They touch my heart. I'll sleep soundly now.'

'Good night, John.'

'Good night, Prophet Halis.'

The morning sun made their eyes smart. There was warmth in its rays. After a breakfast of bread and ham, washed down with tea, they dressed in warm clothes and set off down to the boathouse.

After collecting their rods and spinner lures, they proceeded to launch the boat. Halis started the motor at the rear of the boat and John sat at the bow, mesmerised by the waves breaking as the boat proceeded. After twenty minutes the engine was cut and the boat drifted quietly to a floating stop. It was so peaceful. There was something after all about the colossal number of weekend fishermen at home who were doing what John was about to do, on lakes, lochs, river banks and reservoirs. He breathed in the silence and the peace provided by this setting. He recalled he had not been in a real depression since he met Harry and he was not sure how much of that was also due to Kofi. But the parrot had led him to this stress-free paradise and his ailments seemed so far away.

Halis's hand entered his breast pocket.

'Do you smoke, John?'

John smirked. 'I'm trying to give them up.'

'Keep trying! Meanwhile have a Djarum.'

'Djarum?'

'It's an Indonesian clove cigarette. They're quite refreshing. Try one.'

John bent forward to receive a light from Halis's lighter. He sucked in the unusual but surprisingly pleasant vapour. As he sat back down again, the boat wobbled from side to side. The more John tried to correct himself the more exaggerated the movement became.

'Steady, John. Hold both sides of the boat and lower yourself. Forget about the ciggie.'

'Okay, okay, that's better. Phew that was a scare.'

Halis laughed. 'You would have been the biggest fish I'd ever caught if you went over.'

'Well, I'm glad I didn't. I'm still catching my breath. Now where's that fag?'

'In the water on this side, out of reach. Here, I'll light another.' Halis handed it over to John, who filled his lungs in an effort to calm himself and felt the adrenalin subside.

'You have a taste for the unusual blends?'

'No, I usually smoke 555 but I've found the Djarum best for keeping the flies away when I'm fishing.'

'I see,' said John, reflecting on his colleague's perspicacity.

'You fish on the port side; I'll take the starboard. Always remain seated, or the boat could capsize. That would be a sad way to end your life. That water is so cold at this time of year you would not survive long.'

'What if a large fish pulled me in?'

'Then it was good to know you, John.'

They laughed.

'We'll tell my wife it was sooooo big,' said Halis, stretching out his hands. 'In reality we might get a few trout. There's no lake monster here.'

It was chilling thinking of being thrown into the water but John was able to cast some distance. He let the lure drop a moment or two and then started reeling in. Halis was doing the same on the other side.

'What do you do to relax, John?'

'You know, when I was a police officer I kept fit by running, playing badminton and swimming once a week. Now, to be honest, I've given up all sport. Not even the occasional swim. I ride my bike and keep it clean but that's aboot the energy level I'm up tae these days.'

'I'm surprised. I thought you'd be keeping fit,' said Halis.

'I've found only one real activity. It's mental. Exercising the mind. I suppose many would say I live night and day to find my daughter or learn what happened to her.'

'Even if you don't find her, you have identified a weakness in our service. Our port borders are not secure. They are open to corruption. That is unforgivable in this day and age.'

'Halis, you know, it was a parrot that led me to Turkey?'

'What? You said a parrot?'

'Yes. Amazing isn't it? Let me tell you about it.'

'Please do. But first a coffee?'

'Oh yes please.'

Halis poured a cup from a flask he had concealed in his knapsack.

'No sugar in your coffee?'

'Aye please, a spoonful if ye have it. Ahhhh, this is the life,' said John, taking the fag from his mouth and lifting the coffee to his lips.

'The parrot?' asked Halis.

32
Everyone Catches Something

Mr Kwabena Nkansa's letter arrived a week after Harry's last appointment. It invited Mr Dynes to come in to the hospital as soon as he could. He should also be prepared to stay in hospital for a full three days.

Harry had not expected to read this. He rang the hospital to confirm when he'd arrive. This gave him time to clean Kofi's cage and leave sufficient food and drink for him. He'd also leave Radio 4 on quietly while he was away. Kofi needed something to occupy his active mind. Harry noticed a few feathers on the cage floor. Moulting was usually a feature in the spring but he did not question what he saw. Noticing that Kofi's eyes were a little more tearful and crusted than usual was again a sign that the bird knew he'd be on his own for a few days; that, too, was a reasonable evaluation in Harry's mind.

At hospital Harry did not have to wait long before Mr Nkansa entered the consultancy room and closed the door behind him.

'Well, Mr Dynes, the results are back from the lab. May I ask you, do you have an aviary?'

'No, not an aviary but I do have a parrot.'

'Oh yes, of course you do. How could I have forgotten?

What I am trying to discover is whether he is kept in the house. You keep him inside?'

'Yes, in the lounge.'

'It's an African Grey, of course. Very talented birds.'

'Yes, he's an African Grey who thinks he's human too,' said Harry.

'Tell me, has the parrot been off-colour recently?' asked the consultant.

Harry contemplated the signs he had seen before departing. 'He does seem to have moulted prematurely and his eyes seem to be more glazed over than usual. Perhaps he has a cold.'

'I rather suspect your parrot has psittacosis. And he's shared that with you.'

'Oh dear. Well… what will that mean?' asked Harry.

'Parrots with psittacosis usually die within three weeks of becoming ill.'

Harry gasped. 'Usually?' Maybe the consultant was mistaken.

'Septicaemia eventually develops and the bacteria becomes localised in epithelial cells and macrophages most organs. Usually the eyes have conjunctiva and the disease spreads to the gastrointestinal tract. This rapidly triggers a rapid death.'

'Oh dear. Poor Kofi. That's a very grim reality,' said Harry, realising the consultant was on top of his game.

'Yes it is. Psittacosis Serova A is endemic among psittacine birds and causes sporadic zoonotic disease in humans too. Mr Dynes, this is what you have.'

'This comes as a big surprise. A real shock in fact. Can I be treated for this, Doctor?'

'Yes, treatment is usually via doxycycline or tetracycline and can be administered via drops in water or by injections. Your blood analysis shows leucopoenia, thrombocytopenia and moderately elevated liver enzymes. Are you following me?'

'Just about,' said Harry.

'I want to admit you for three days. During that time I wish to treat you with doxycycline intravenously. Remission of symptoms is usually evident within forty-eight to seventy-two hours. However a relapse can occur. If that happens, treatment must continue for at least ten to fourteen days after the fever abates. Is there anything else you wish to know?'

'It's all come as a shock to me. It doesn't look good, does it?' asked Harry.

'You are not as young as you once were. You may take a longer time to recover,' said the consultant.

'Well then, I suppose there's a bed available today?'

'The ward sister will be down in a moment. She'll have you admitted.'

'Thank you, Mr Nkansa. You certainly know about parrot disease.'

The consultant smiled. 'You will have recognised I have an African name.'

'Not only that, I recognise a Ghanaian name,' said Harry. 'I found my parrot in Ghana where I worked.'

'Yes indeed. When I was a young boy in Bekwai, in the Ashanti region, I had an African Grey. It became ill and I lost my sister to that. There were no antibiotics strong enough for a young girl in those days. That has made me a bit of an expert in this field. I am often consulted from around the UK, when people fall ill with psittacosis.'

'And are there many cases of this parrot disease these days?'

'Not as many as there used to be. It was pet-shop owners and people who had had their pets for a very long time who used to be referred. No, not nearly as many now,' said Mr Nkansa.

'Then I'm in good hands... but Kofi... oh dear. This will be so sad, so very sad.'

Halis caught two 4lb trout. John caught a cold. After three hours they had enough fishing. It was time to go to Halis's home.

Halis's wife, Nadine, cooked the brown trout. She wore western clothes and she was slim with dark hair, well-groomed, and wore noticeable eye makeup. To John's eye not even a grey hair was discernible but in Turkey it was still a woman's duty to disguise her looks and her age to appeal to her husband. A bowl of incredibly hot soup was served first but as John politely drank it the heat seemed to invade his body. The soup seemed to seek out the cold symptoms and banish them.

'You can have no idea how much better that soup has made me feel,' he said.

'Then it's an omen for next week perhaps,' said Nadine.

'May I comment on your English accents? You both speak incredibly well. Um, to be honest, you speak better than I do, much better than me, so you do... and that despite it being your second language,' said John.

'English is the international language but I must confess my grandfather was an Englishman,' said Nadine.

'Really!'

'Yes, a very good man. He was captured in the Gallipoli campaign during the First World War and taken prisoner by our Turkish army. He was taken to Konya to work but it was not hard work on the farm and they were not closely supervised. My grandmother, who was his age, took a liking to him as she had often seen him work on her father's land. She tried to bring him drinking water regularly to get to know him. When the war ended David Morgan stayed for a few weeks to get to know my grandmother even better.'

'And did he?'

Nadine smiled. 'He did. And so they married. They had two sons and one was my father. So I have English blood in me.'

'Perhaps even Welsh blood. Did David Morgan ever go back home?' asked John.

'I see why you are asking,' said Halis. 'There are similarities perhaps. David liked the land and the people and had a wife. There was nothing to go back to, he told his new family. The war had made him bitter but also thankful. He had found a new life while he kept his Anglican religion and tradition.'

The wine was passed round as they ate. It had been a very relaxing and memorable weekend. Only one issue surprised John. There was no e-mail from Harry. So he sent one asking how he was, and requesting him to reply soon. He also gave him an account of his whole week. By the time Monday arrived, John was more than content with life in Turkey, completely refreshed and eager to return to the quest in hand.

Monday morning, a working day once again and no different for John. Back to the room of boxes and photographs, but feeling refreshed from a marvellously hospitable weekend. Despite a full day working, he did not despair. His heart was in his work.

At the end of the day he checked his e-mails. Still there was no word from Harry. This was worrying. He contacted the main switchboard at Police Headquarters in Dumfries. The message was brief. Check on Harry Dynes... and Kofi, his parrot. Worried... no contact from him.

On Wednesday John carried on with shoulders bowed over the papers and photographs. A cup of tea arrived. He put down everything and cupped his hands around the hot mug. His focus seemed to waver. He sipped again. Then a chill travelled down his spine. He put his mug back down so quickly some tea spilt. He seemed to be gasping for air. Short bursts of panting aroused attention from the other staff present.

He lifted up the page of photographs and then an anguished smile came across his face. Tears welled up and then began to pour down his cheeks. His hands were shaking almost uncontrollably. He could no longer hide his secret.

'It's… it's… it's her! This is HER!' he screamed. Now tears were pouring down his face and his eyes were red and glazed. 'That's my daughter. Look. This is Morag. I tell you this is her, my missing daughter.'

The clerical staff came rushing over to see the cause of the commotion.

'That's her, my daughter,' John shouted again and again.

'The one in the centre?' asked a clerical worker.

'Yes, most definitely.'

'So when is that one dated?' asked the senior typist.

John turned the photograph over. Morag's name was crossed out and had been substituted by the name of Leila Ahmed. The name did not ring true but the date did: July 2009. July 2009 was six weeks after Morag disappeared from Dumfries.

Harry sat up in bed in Ward 6. He was able to see out of the window to the rolling hills of the Stewartry of Kirkcudbrightshire. The antibiotics seemed to be working well and his strength was coming back to him. In the afternoon, a uniformed Inspector Ewan Stevenson arrived.

'Hello, Harry, I'm Inspector Ewan Stevenson. I've come to visit and see how you are.'

'That's very kind of you. I'm actually feeling much better. I think I might get out tomorrow if the doctors agree.'

'That's good.'

'But I am surprised to have a policeman as a visitor. Not that I'm objecting, you understand,' said a flustered Harry.

'Relax. I'm here to tell you that John Reid was getting a bit worried about you. He hadn't heard from you for a while and wondered if you and Kofi were all right.'

'Oh dear, I've not been keeping in touch. Fact is that I was becoming so tired, I didn't have the energy to sit down at the computer.'

'We know. That's why we went round to see what was up. A neighbour, Bruce Harper, said you were in hospital. We managed to get into your house; don't worry, we caused no damage, Bruce had a key. Your parrot was not too pleased to see us, of course. Perhaps the uniform did not help. He was on the floor of the cage eyeing us up.'

'Did he speak?' asked Harry.

'Not when we were there. You had obviously given him his food but we topped up his water pot. It was getting low. He let us. I put my hand in his cage but he stood his ground and did not move. Anyway before we left he was back on his perch. I'm sure he's pining for you: missing you dreadfully, I'd say,' said Ewan.

'Well, I'll soon be home and much fitter.'

'That's good to hear. So how is my old colleague John Reid doing? Any news of his daughter yet?'

'No, I've not had any recent news yet, but he's following a lead as you boys in blue say.'

'But will it lead anywhere? I mean, wasn't it a very superficial tip-off that started his trip to Turkey?'

'I'd not say insignificant. Rather an inspired piece of thinking after taking into account an unorthodox ornithological point of view, is what I'd say,' said Harry.

'You mean your parrot told him to go to Turkey?'

'It seems so. Or perhaps Chief Superintendent Cathy Ronson did. Not sure which. Strange, isn't it?'

The Inspector knew when he was beaten. He was not privy to his Force's agreement. Nor was he aware that several Eastern European girls had been located coming from a Turkish cargo ship that had left Glasgow in the late autumn.

That very day an aeroplane arrived at Glasgow Airport with a Turkish police escort to deliver home the Latvians, Petra Stula and Elza Igaune, the Estonians, Evelin Kanter, Ingrid Talts and Anna Mandri, and the one Russian girl, Yelena Chavkin. The girls were taken to a secure compound but not as suspects. They were there to shed light on the illegal handlers, the men who'd forced the girls to work the streets while feeding them inadequately and depriving them of any free time or contact with their families back home. They relaxed between interviews and face-recognition sessions in a well-furnished lounge with a large TV screen and stacks of DVDs. None of the girls had lived in comparative luxury in the west before. But their evidence was crucial and the comfort ensured it flowed.

As a result of their co-operation, eight men from Scotland, three from Northumberland and two from Belfast were charged with kidnap and forced labour involving some twenty-three girls working in and around the Glasgow conurbation. These men would not see the full light of day for a total of one hundred and eighty-four years. That averaged out as fourteen years of imprisonment for each of them. More would follow.

33
The Parrot's Demise

Inspector Halis was delighted for John. It placed pressure on him now to find where Morag, or as she was now known, Leila Ahmed might be. He contacted the British High Commission to see if anyone knew about the Scottish girl or something about her present whereabouts. But that source revealed nothing other than support for what they were doing. Meanwhile John resumed work in the office an hour earlier than before.

'I've gotta scrutinise every sheet I turn over. Morag has been in Turkey. This is the closest I've ever been to finding her. I must not miss anything. Paid, paid, paid. Seems $1,500 secures a European girl. Disgusting.'

'You alright?' asked Halis.

'Talking to myself. Keeps me sane.'

'You carry on.' Halis wandered off to see how his staff was doing.

Only the wealthy had dollars; only the wealthy had such a quantity of dollars to spend on their investment. But was a blonde European a status item, a domestic servant, or now an Islamic wife? These were the troubled thoughts that filled John's mind now and he did not mind anyone who heard his blethering.

At 4 p.m. that Monday, Inspector Halis received some information by text. He learned that there were two large suspicious fish canning factories. Both were surrounded by barbed wire. Both were known to be labour intensive. Reports believed that the workforce had not been seen coming and going, thus raising concerns over employment conditions and status.

'John, there's been a development. We have sent two undercover police women into two fish canning factories to see if Leila Ahmed is there. First they must be accepted, of course.'

'But if they get in, maybe they will be trapped. Forced to work there too,' said John.

'Do you honestly think we'd risk our officers? Come on, John. They both have hidden tracking devices. We'd mount an attack if we didn't hear from them after twenty-four hours.'

'So where are these factories?'

'They're near the Dardanelles, on the north-west coast.'

'How soon can we get there?'

'It will not be that easy. If Leila is there, she is likely to be in a guarded environment. We don't want a gunfight. You have a saying don't you, "softly, softly catchee monkey"? Not so?'

'Indeed. And I don't want any harm to come to any girl even if she is not my daughter,' said John.

'Then we must plan for this. Let's go to my office.'

Mr Nkansa approached Harry's bed.

'Good morning, Mr Dynes. How are you today?'

'Haven't felt as good as this for several weeks, Doctor.'

'Then the antibiotics have given you strength. Enough to go home?'

'I hope so,' said Harry.

'What support do you have at home?'

'Support?'

'Yes, physical, emotional, you know, can you manage at home?'

'Physically, slowly. Emotionally, yes, I've got my parrot and the daily chores; I get through.'

'Hmmm... but it won't always be like that. I want to put in a request for a social work assessment to see if they can identify supports or devices to make your life a little more comfortable.'

'That sounds useful. I've seen others with them. I can tell my time has obviously come for them,' said Harry.

Dr Nkansa's face fell. Clearly there was something troubling him.

'But your parrot... Now you realise... he was the source of your ailment and of course a relapse of psittacosis is not out of the picture. You won't like what I am about to say but say it I must. You must get rid of your bird. He'll die soon anyway but the sooner he's gone the less likely you will be re-infected.'

'Oh no! Lose Kofi after all these years? That will be a disaster. How can I cope without Kofi?'

'I know it will hard, Mr Dynes. It will indeed. But as I told you, Kofi's days are numbered already. He gave you that illness, an illness which could have killed you.'

'I could get an outside aviary for him. Not so?'

'That would not really be practical. Being near an infected bird, you breathe its breath, and you handle it when feeding it. You could become re-infected. Worse still a visitor could pick up the disease. You couldn't live with that, could you? That is if your parrot does not die very soon, within a day or two perhaps. I remind you, Kofi was the carrier of your disease and he will inadvertently give it to those who come in contact with him from now onwards, don't forget.'

'You are making it hard for me to end his life.'

'I am sure your vet would attend to it but such matters must be undertaken immediately. I know this is a shock, although it probably passed through your mind. Wait till after lunch to give you time to sort your feelings. Then you can go home,' said Mr Nkansa.

'Well, you have made it very clear.'

'I'm not a vet, Mr Dynes. I can only cure you and that's the only way I can. I am sorry.'

The canning factories were located at the coastal town of Geyikli. It was a town not far from the Dardanelles but significantly it gave free access to the Aegean Sea and the hungry European markets.

'The fish are anchovies. Mainly Mediterranean people like them. But there is a significant European market for them too. They pay well and so there is a great need for them. Their factories are on an industrial scale,' said Halis.

'So when can we get there?' asked John.

'John, this is hard but I don't want you there at this operation at all. You would not be able to understand the Turkic orders. And if Leila, I mean Morag, is there, it's not the place for you to reunite with your daughter. It could be amid crossfire. We'll put you up in the town of Izmir, at the Kapari Hotel.'

'I'm becoming an expense fur you,' said John.

'The Kapari is a fine hotel of high standards. If we find her, she will need a lot of support, I imagine. Getting her away from the factory area will help her. Meeting you will also help. But that is also why I do not want you at the factory. You could compromise the operation. You must stay at the hotel until you hear from me. Is that clear?'

'There is heightened excitement in ma veins. But I'm trying tae be sensible and expect nothin'. The waiting will be difficult but aye, I understand. I'll stay at the hotel, I promise ye that.'

'Expect nothing. Yes, that's a sensible approach. Anything else will be a bonus,' said Halis.

'Agreed,' said John.

At Glasgow airport the flight to Riga was announced. From the departure lounge, Petra Stula stood up to embrace Yelena, Ingrid and Evelin. Eliza did the same as the two were called to Gate 3, a flight back home to Riga.

'Goodbye, I will always remember you,' said Petra. They exchanged hugs and kisses.

'Tell your story to the press. We will, and we will mention you too,' said Yelena.

'Bye,' said Petra.

Evelin's and Ingrid's flight was then called. 'Yelena, I would like to see you again but not on my homeland, you understand?' said Ingrid.

Yelena understood only too well. It had taken longer for Evelin and Ingrid to accept and trust her, a Russian, coming from the people who had populated their country illegally. But over time and necessity they had gelled well.

'Then one day when we are rich, we meet in Monte Carlo, no?' suggested Yelena laughing.

'Yes, why nut. Let's make it in tree year's time,' said Evelin.

'Tree years. We will be rich before that. We have a story to tell. We can use our voices to prevent others going the same way as we did. We can become politicians, we have a cause to declare. Nut so?' asked Yelena. Evelin and Ingrid embraced her without replying. She had been more political than the others.

'And now we speak better English, that is in demand at home,' said Evelin.

'Ah but with a Scottish accent,' said Ingrid.

The Tallinn flight was called next. Ingrid and Evelin in turn kissed Yelena.

'Till Monte Carlo, now do nut be late you girls,' said Yelena, and a group hug was seen by all in the terminal.

Yelena stood by the window as the Estonian-bound plane ran down the runway. She was the last of the group to leave. She followed the flight as it took off and soared into a blue winter sky. The plane became a speck over the Campsie hills.

Yelena felt no bitterness towards the land which had trapped her in slavery. It was the criminal gangs she hated with disdain.

The aeroplane was now turning over a snow-capped peak. Then the plane disappeared from sight. It was a journey she was soon to make until...

'This is a passenger announcement. Flight Number FTG 224 to Moscow is delayed due to freezing fog at Moscow. Further announcements will appear on the departure board. Flight Number FTG 224 to Moscow is delayed.'

Yelena walked towards WH Smiths in the terminal. She browsed the bookshelves. She selected the Pocket Poets edition of Burns. Then she took the last of her British twenty-pound notes and bought a hot Scotch mutton pie, a Tunnoch's caramel wafer and a large bottle of Irn-Bru. This was a diet she had gratefully devoured in earlier Glasgow days. She knew how to absorb Scottish culture and cuisine. It was a country she would be leaving in due course with mixed feelings, but almost above all she knew she would miss what she was eating. She sat down and enjoyed her nourishment in body and mind. She flipped though some of the familiar poems of Burns, which she had learnt in Russia as a schoolgirl.

That Thursday, a convoy of police set off for Geyikli. It took them six hours to drive to the seaside town. They stopped at the police station at nearby Ezine where they ate a meal and gathered to confirm the plan of action. The local police identified the layout of both canning factories. They were on the south side of Geyikli with the road leading to a dead end at the town of Gülpinar. Both buildings were surrounded by an eight-foot-high chain fence with razor-sharp blades at the top, facing both ways. Access to the sites was by one way only, straight down the drive. The gate guards had to be removed first. To prevent one factory tipping off another, the police would make simultaneous raids on both factories.

Halis received a text.

'Officer Avci reports no word of Leila Ahmed in Factory One. Officer Erkin has yet to report.'

Blankets and mattresses appeared in the police station. The time to leave would be 5 a.m. That gave them five hours to rest.

At 4.45 a.m. plans were finalised. Officer Erkin sent a text message saying that there were several European female workers in Canning Factory Number Two. If Leila Ahmed was anywhere, it would be in this factory. Significantly the officer spies confirmed both workplaces had around one hundred and twenty workers.

Halis arranged for eight police buses to take the workforce away. Four buses were earmarked for each site. Staff would be detained on site and taken away by police to the buses then onward for interrogation.

Muslim officers bowed down facing Mecca in prayer as dawn broke. Their incantation echoed around the police station:

Allahu Akbar x 4
Ash-hadu an ilaha illaha x 2
Ash-hadu ana Muhammadar-rasulullah x 2
Hayya ala-salah x 2
Hayya ala-falah x 2
Allu Akbar x 2
La ilaha illallah.

God is the Most Great. I Bear witness that there is no God but Allah. I bear witness that Muhammad is the Prophet of Allah. Come to prayer. Come to success or salvation. God is the Most Great. There is no God but Allah. It is better to pray than to sleep.

John had prayed more in the last year than in most of his adult life. Others would describe it as talking and dreaming. But if not that, what was prayer?

Harry ordered a taxi from the hospital. When he got to his house, a tear was already in his eye. Putting Kofi out of his misery would break his heart. Harry had known Kofi for thirty-seven of his eighty-five years. Kofi had known Harry all his life. He placed his key in the door. The door opened and Harry stooped to bring in his hospital bag. There was no welcome from the cage. Harry visited the downstairs bathroom and as he urinated, he called through to Kofi.

'With you in a moment, Kofi, I'm home again.' A lump came to his throat as he spoke.

Harry could not be sure if there was a response as the loo flushed. He washed his hands and looked at himself in the wall mirror. He had never looked so sad and it aged him terribly. He entered the lounge. Kofi was in his cage, on the floor. Harry approached. Kofi's eyes were glazed and almost shut, his beak wide open to receive his last gasp some hours before. Gone was that vital life, that life-long friend, taken by psittacosis. Perhaps it was better not to have seen him suffer. But Harry also felt guilty that he had died on his own. There was no ill-feeling that Kofi had caused Harry's recent ailments but the stark warning of Mr Nkansa had given Harry time to confront reality and make the necessary arrangements. There was no longer a need to call the vet. Nature had attended to that service, as nature does, at a time of its choosing.

Harry dug a hole three feet deep. It faced south against a wall in his garden. Kofi would enjoy the sunny spot in summer and would be facing the land of his birth. Harry took Kofi out of his cage and wrapped him in soft white kitchen paper. Before placing him into his grave, he kissed him and retained one of his red tail feathers. It was an act of love but foolishness too.

Harry stood over Kofi at the burial ground but before placing him down for good, he lit the covering paper. The flames soon reached Kofi's feathers. Harry placed Kofi in the grave and the flames took hold. As the feathers burned, the stench of burning skin caught Harry's nose. He stood back, the smoke and his emotion drawing tears in a steady flow. Then, as the embers died, Harry took a trowel and covered Kofi's featherless body. He returned to the house. Then he cleared and cleaned the cage outside with disinfectant. He took Kofi's NHS play splint to the bin. And he left the cage outside to air in the last two hours of daylight.

A hot bath was run and Harry lay back in the warm soapy suds where he reminisced over Kofi's life. It brought the occasional smile to his face and when he recalled that motherless chick when it came into his life, he was grateful that his feathered life was longer than that of his parents. But tears also flowed for his recent demise. And it brought painful memories of how his wife had grown to love Kofi after an unsteady start. How Kofi had endeared himself to her and mourned her passing when she sadly died. Harry thought of Kofi's recent escapades on the wing. It had caused him frustration and sadness but now, on reflection, it was an experience that Kofi had enjoyed to the full and he had come home. Yes, he had come home a hero in the eyes of so many grateful people. A smile broke through the tearful face. He shook his head. 'Yes, Kofi's life was truly remarkable,' he told himself.

Once dry and dressed, Harry lost no time in searching for old albums featuring Kofi. Selecting the best photographs, he put them aside to take them to the photographer's shop the next day. He was going to remember Kofi in his own special way. He prepared the stairway wall with ruthlessness, removing landscape and seascape pictures which left a shadow to be dusted. Kofi would have a wall to himself.

Tomorrow he must also get to grips with the season and get the Christmas decorations out of the boxes in the attic.

34
A Bird in the Hand

John woke up to a frustrating day. So near, yet so far. It was potentially a day to savour, but also a day which, if it turned out wrongly, might set his depression into overdrive. A telephone call at any time might resolve his search. He paced his room. He opened his laptop to check his e-mails. At last one from Harry. There was no subject heading but anyway it was a welcome letter to distract him.

John read on with incredulity. He learned that Harry had been hospitalised having succumbed to a bout of psittacosis. Thankfully he had recovered sufficiently to be allowed home but then he read how he discovered Kofi and how he disposed of him. It sent a shudder down John's spine. Kofi, John's guide and inspiration, companion and friend had died. But how much more than for John would the sorrow be for Harry? Kofi had been priceless for him. John was possibly on the eve of his greatest feat, being reunited with his daughter. He had so much to thank Kofi for but it was too late to do it. An uncomfortable hard lump stuck at the back of his throat and he bit his bottom lip to delay the tears. Eventually he could not prevent them escaping from red eyes.

It was difficult for John to reply. He deleted his reply three times before he was satisfied with the right tone of his message. It took his excitement down many pegs on his fevered anticipation of the day.

A low heavy cloud lay over the town in the morning. It was a drizzly day, one so familiar to all Scots. But it seemed darker and colder than a cold winter back home.

Halis ordered the boarding of their vehicles. They set off for the town of Geyikli wrapped in warm blankets. It was 5.20 a.m.

On approaching the first factory, the stench of rotting discarded fish came from a large blue uncovered bin. Scavenging vultures picked at the entrails and in their excitement created much noise. The noise of the birds disguised the police activity as they approached the gatehouse. The barrier remained down.

A gate guard left his small office and approached the unmarked police van.

An officer grabbed the man and forced him into the van. They questioned him about the point of entry, the security arrangements, the staffing levels, the number of employees and the number and type of any weapons. The man was so scared that the information flowed from him incessantly. He did his utmost to divorce himself from the evil employers who paid his meagre wage. He also told them the manager Jakub Kutlar did not arrive till after 10 a.m. most days. That gave Halis some comfort. He had some breathing time but the sooner he acted the better.

The vehicles sped into the compound and up to the side door. A padlock secured the doors. Large metal bolt cutters appeared and released the locks and before the chain fell to the ground, the police were already in the building. They were met with looks of astonishment by women sitting at long benches with anchovies in one hand and tins in the other, even at this early hour of the day. A bowl of oil greased the anchovies before they were sealed in their final position in tins, awaiting Spanish, French and Portuguese housewives and chefs.

Halis spoke with a calm voice in his native dialect. 'Turkish police here. Do not be afraid. We are here to free you and help you. Please answer my questions honestly. How many of you are forced to work here?'

All who understood raised their hands.

'How many enjoy working here?

There was no response.

'How many of you are Turkish nationals?'

Fifty-eight hands were raised.

'And why have you chosen to work here?'

A lady stood up.

'I speak for all the Turkish women. We have been disowned by our families. We have run away from forced marriages and violence. We know we are not well looked after here. We sleep where we work, but we are not criminals. We do not earn much. We are fed. That's all. But we are all sisters.' She sat down.

Halis smiled. 'I know you are not criminals. You are victims, all of you.'

The women noticed a woman leave her table and come forward to the Inspector. She removed her sari to reveal a police uniform top.

'Let me take over the questioning, sir. Woman to woman is best,' said Officer Erkin.

Halis stood back.

She spoke slowly. 'I have worked with you. I know you are all good women. I am also a policewoman here to help you. But many of you have been forced to work here in very poor conditions and this must end. To help us, can the Turkish women move to the top end of the hall. Thank you. All the other women come to the front.'

Then, in perfect English, Officer Erkin repeated what she had said in Turkic.

The women stretched as they rose from their tables. They needed no second asking. How long they had been seated in front of the fish was unimaginable. A head count followed.

'I make that one hundred and twenty-eight.'

'Are there any missing women?'

The self-appointed Turkish spokesperson rose to her feet once more.

'A sister died at her bench two days ago. They took her away but we were not allowed to attend her funeral.'

'Are there any other women missing?'

'No, sir, that is all of us.'

'Do you have any access to the outside?'

'We are allowed out one hour a day into the yard. But we cannot escape. The yard has wire on two sides. This building is on another side and the wall and the steep mountain behind it make it impossible to escape. We work seven days a week.'

'These are appalling conditions,' said Halis.

'See the conveyor belt? It leads outside so we see if it is day or night but you cannot leave that way. See how small the gap is. It's the only natural light we see, apart from our hour in the yard.'

A number of foreign nationals in the front rows caught Halis's eyes.

'I know some of you have been kidnapped from Europe. How many of you are Russian?'

Eight hands went up.

'Let me do it another way. Let's start from the right side and go along the rows. Tell me your nationality. You understand?'

Most heads nodded. Those who did not nod were bound to get the hang of the question as each gave their response in turn.

The first girl fidgeted. She had lost her voice.

'La... Lat... via... Latvia.'

'Latvia. We are six from Latvia.'

'Poland.'

'Russia.'

'Latvia.'

Latvia.'

'Russia.'

'Poland.'

'England.'

'Where in England?'

'I'm from Harborne, in Birmingham.'

'Scotland.'

'Belgium,' said a black woman.

Halis raised his hand. The next girl's mouth was open ready to answer but she awaited the Inspector's instruction.

He looked again at the girl from Scotland.

'Are you Leila Ahmed?'

She looked up at Halis. Not a word came from her lips. She nodded.

'Are you also Morag Reid from Dumfries?'

Leila could not digest at first what the Inspector was saying. What would be the consequence of saying more? She froze.

'Officer Erkin, take Leila away from here. Speak to her in the confines of a police car.

Leila offered no resistance. Officer Erkin placed her arm around Leila's shoulder.

'Now I want all of you to come outside and go into the buses provided. We will look after you away from here.'

'What will you do with Leila?' the spokesperson said.

'It's all right. We will send all the foreigners home as soon as we can. That will take time so I ask you to be patient,' said Halis.

The women filed out into the daylight. Their eyes were strained. They followed like sheep.

'Where are we going?' they asked.

'I think a clean-up first,' said Halis. 'You all smell, no, not smell, you all stink of fish.'

In the police car Officer Erkin consoled Leila.

'It is not your fault. Some terrible things have happened to you. We will get you away from here. We want to get you back to Scotland. You are Morag, aren't you? Morag Reid from Dumfries?

Morag nodded. 'Yes, I am.' But it was the voice of a child answering to please, and not a woman's voice thrilled to be away from the scene of such misery.

The hotel carpet was losing its pile. John looked at his watch as he paced backward and forward. It was 7 a.m. Both factories would be secured by now, surely. The computer gave him some comfort. With no news received and none to tell anyone, he entered Solitaire and played his first game. After playing five cards, he had drawn four aces. Was that a lucky omen or not?

There was a knock on his door.

'Come in.'

A waitress brought in a tray of breakfast.

'Is there anything else you wish?' she asked.

'Is there an English language newspaper I can have?'

'Of course, today's Zaman. I will bring you a copy,' she said.

True to her word, not two minutes later the Daily Zaman arrived. John looked at the front page as he ate his breakfast. A serious train crash was reported at Mardin on the Syrian border. Seven travellers had been killed as was the train driver and the tanker driver who had collided with the train. Graphic pictures of the carnage filled the front page. On the second page was a report about the Sivas raid. John was surprised and disappointed to see this appearing before the conclusion of the current activity and the pending court cases. It disgusted him how reporting of the raid could have been divulged so soon.

He turned another page and found the daily crossword. He took out his pen and poured himself another cup of tea. It did not take him long to make a good start to this easy crossword and he was pleased to see his watch had recorded a full half hour since he answered the first clue. But he was anxious to have current news. Meanwhile he settled to read the 8-3 thrilling football match result between Istanbul team Galatasaray v Bucaspor of Ismir. The photos were excellent. Football in Turkey was the vital escape from daily life. As the match report engrossed John, the telephone in his room rang. He threw down the newspaper.

'John?'

'Yes, Halis. Any news?'

'Yes. We've found Leila, I mean, Morag.'

A silence prevailed. John could not find a word to speak in reply. He dropped his pen on the floor without thinking.

'Are you there John... John... hello?'

'I'm crying, Halis. Tell me again. You have Morag with you? You have found Morag?'

'Yes, she's with us and safe.'

Halis waited as the sobbing continued.

'Really?' stammered John. 'You're sure? I can't believe it. I can't believe this day has come. That's... that's ... that's wonderful, wonderful, really wonderful. Ohhhh, all my prayers have been answered! You have no idea how happy I am. Oh... vindicated... ah, Halis, are you definitely sure it's her? Definitely? Is she okay? Can I speak to her?'

'Hey, steady John, too many questions. Yes, it's definitely Morag. You must realise how much of a shock it has been for all the girls. At present, I must warn you, Morag cannot cope. She can't speak to you yet. She's been through a lot, you need to know that and she's lost all her confidence. She'll need psychological support. That should of course start with you. But not quite yet.'

'Has she been told I'm here, here to take her home?'

'Officer Erkin is with her. She'll tell her in good time. We must take it slowly. It takes time for her to understand what is happening this morning and time to place her trust in what we're doing. It takes time, John.'

'I see. But she is coming here today?'

'Yes. But possibly not for an hour or two at least. So please be patient.'

Officer Erkin arranged for Morag to have a warm bath with lots of bubbles and soap with a friendly instruction to take her time and unwind. New western clothes would be brought to her when she was ready. And Officer Erkin was not finished.

'How long will this take, Officer Erkin?' asked Halis.

'Sir, this is women's work. It could even take another couple of hours.'

'A couple of hours? You do know that her father is waiting to see her after years of pain and anguish? He's only a few miles from here. He's jumping up and down,' said Halis.

'Sir, I can send a fish woman whose clothes stink to meet him. Or do you prefer a freshly bathed young woman looking the best she can in the circumstances? Perhaps looking more like the day she went missing and her father heard of the tragedy.'

'Officer Erkin. You know what's best. Carry on.'

And Morag's pampering carried on. A hairdresser made suggestions for her. But Morag had no idea what she wanted.

A conservative blow-dry and cut shaped her hair beautifully. The sheen brightened her face. Her golden blonde locks fell free of fish odours and her face was given a light bronzing to mask a pale sun-starved face. Morag looked in the mirror. She smiled broadly for the first time.

'Is that really me?' she asked.

'Yes, Morag. You look great.'

A Turkish coffee was served to them. Morag sipped and visibly relaxed.

'You know we want to fly you back to Scotland?'

Morag sipped more coffee.

'When?' she asked.

'You do want to go back soon?'

'It's been a long time. It's where I was abducted,' she replied.

'Yes, I know. People like the ones who abducted you, the crew who brought others to Turkey, the taskmaster at the factory and his brother who ran another fish factory, are all arrested and now await trial. You understand?'

She nodded.

Officer Erkin followed up the conversation as best she could.

'Who would you like to accompany you back to Scotland?'

'You?'

Officer Erkin smiled. 'Perhaps that could be arranged. I must ask the Inspector. But if a family member could come to collect you, would that be good?'

'You mean my parents?'

'Yes, would that be good?'

Morag smiled.

'Well, prepare yourself for a really pleasant surprise, Morag. Your father, John Reid, is in Turkey. And he's come to collect you.'

Officer Erkin awaited a response. Morag smiled again as she digested the news.

'Isn't that good?'

'Yes, my father? Really? Ohhhh my God, I cannot believe this is happening. Dad in Turkey? But why is he here? I don't understand. That's good, yes, that's great. But my father in Turkey? How is this possible?'

Officer Erkin felt Morag could not understand all that was being said. Even the officer could not adequately explain why her father was in Turkey.

'Your father is a policeman.'

'Yes, that's true,' Morag replied.

'He has been working in Turkey for just over a week. He was brought out to detect illegal human trafficking.'

'Yes... I think I understand. But Dad, why him? Why was he chosen to come to Turkey?'

'Morag, I have no idea. I've really no idea. You will have to ask your father when you meet him.'

She seemed to be still in part denial. The officer poured more coffee and offered Morag another piece of sponge cake.

'That tastes good, doesn't it?'

'Yes, this tastes good,' said Morag.

'I can take you to see your father now. Do you want to do that?'

'My father is really in Turkey?'

'Your father is in Turkey, yes. He's in a hotel at Izmir. We can take you there.'

Morag said nothing. Her shoulders began to shake, then the sobs were heard and the tears followed. Officer Erkin sat beside her and comforted her with her arm round her shoulders.

'All is well, Morag. All is well. You have nothing to fear anymore.'

They retained that clench until the sobs subsided. Officer Erkin then gave her a tissue to dry her tears.

'Let's make that a happy face again. That's the face you want your father to see. Not so?'

'Yes, I want to see my Dad,' said Morag.

Officer Erkin telephoned Halis.

'Sir, we're ready now. Transport to Izmir required.'

The road to Izmir hugged the coastline. Morag saw much of this beautiful part of the country for the first time from behind a rug, which she clung to like a young child in the back of a family car. At lunchtime, a hummus wrap was brought to the car for her, as well as a fruit drink. Afterwards Officer Erkin led her to a local hotel bathroom.

'Are we really going to see my father?' she asked.

The officer smiled. 'Yes Morag, it's really true. Your father is expecting you. He will be so pleased to see you.'

'Really, really pleased?'

'Yes, Morag. You will see him soon now.'

It took a further hour on the road before the car entered the outskirts of Izmir. During this time Morag put aside her doubts about the reality of meeting her father. She began to tell the officer about her life in Dumfries before the kidnap.

The car drove to the centre of the city and parked in the car park of the Kapari Hotel.

'Morag, your father is in this hotel. We will take you up to his room to meet him. I'll stay with you a while. Is that clear?'

'Yes, thank you.'

Officer Erkin led Morag up the outside stairs of the hotel. They approached the receptionist who was aware of the sensitivity around their guests.

'Good afternoon. Can you tell us which room Mr John Reid is in?' asked Officer Erkin.

'Fourth floor, Room 422. Shall I ring him and say you are on your way?' asked the receptionist.

'No, er... no, thank you. I think it best that we meet him at his door,' said Erkin.

The lift took them to the fourth floor. With Inspector Halis staying on the ground floor, Officer Erkin and Morag made their way along to Room 422.

'Do you want to ring the bell or shall I?'

'Give me a moment. I'll ring it,' said Morag.

Taking a deep breath, hoping that everything she had been told since her departure from the fish factory early that morning was true, she rang the bell. Almost instantaneously the door opened.

Her father stood before her with his arms wide open. Morag rushed forward to be hugged by him. Officer Erkin slipped past them into the bedroom and sat down. All she could hear were the sounds of mumbled joy and sobs coming from both father and daughter. Their tears flowed copiously like large oyster pearls.

'Darling, darling, darling. I've missed you so dreadfully much. I've longed for this day, Morag. I thought it would never come. I thought I'd never see you again. Oh darling, this is wonderful. You are coming back to Scotland with me, aren't you?' John asked cautiously.

'Yes, Dad, I will. I've missed you and Mum terribly. I want to be with you both again as soon as possible.'

John hesitated. Too quickly had Morag mentioned her mother. This was a test. No, the time was not right. He could not tell her now, yet the words were forming in his mind.

'Morag, in the past five years much has changed. But one thing is for certain. You are more beautiful than I've ever seen you. Mum will be so pleased. We must let her know as soon as we can.'

'Yes we must.'

'Your disappearance made me difficult to live with, I can tell you. Mum suffered. But it's all worth the effort. I'm so pleased,' said John.

Morag released herself from her father. 'I'm divorced,' she said.

'What?'

'Well, you knew I could not have a family of my own but the man I was forced to marry did not believe me. When he found out, he divorced me. That was when they put me into the fish factory.'

'Come sit down. Can you tell me more?'

Father and daughter sat on the bed.

'Mr Reid, Morag was working in the fish factory this morning. She needs time to adjust. Don't overexcite her or ask too many questions this afternoon. There will be plenty of time now. The answers will emerge in due course,' Officer Erkin cautioned.

There was a knock on the door. The hotel staff brought a tray of tea with a selection of sandwiches and biscuits.

'I'll leave you now,' said Officer Erkin. 'I know the English always enjoy their afternoon tea.'

'Yes, but please stay. I'd like you to,' said Morag.

Officer Erkin looked at her father and then at the tray.

'If I stay, then I will pour the tea.'

Morag smiled at the service but her father was anxious to find out more.

'So Morag, who were these fish people?'

'They are a wealthy family running a fish company. They export anchovies from the Sea of Marmara. They treat their womenfolk at home quite well but in the factory we are under a very threatening Mr Ahmed's control. He was the one who divorced me.' Morag turned to Officer Erkin. 'What will happen to them?'

'The Inspector says by the time Mr Ahmed learns any of his women are missing he will be on his way to a police cell. Before you leave, Morag, we will want to get a full statement from you. Perhaps we can do that tomorrow? There is no rush.'

'I think tomorrow would be a good idea, as long as it's o'er quickly. I must get Morag back home, so I do,' said

John. 'I'll arrange that then. So I'll be on my way. May I say I am so happy for both of you,' said Officer Erkin.

John stood up and shook her hand. 'You have taken good care of my daughter today, thank you.'

Morag stood up and gave Officer Erkin a hug.

'It's been some day, Morag. Thanks for sharing it with me,' said Officer Erkin.

As the door closed, leaving them together for the first time, John stood back from Morag and admired her.

'Darling, I last saw ye as a child. Now ye are a beautiful woman... but I'm so upset that you lost yur childhood so early.'

Morag came to him and held both of his hands.

'Daddy, don't be that way. I may look a young woman but deep inside, I know I'm still a confused child.'

The room had an adjoining room in which Morag could sleep but neither went to bed until late.

'It wis no like you bein' twa minutes late fur onythin. That's how I got the police tae look into yer disappearance promptly. Ye must have bin taken awa' only twenty minutes before I called them.'

'Well, of course, it was the day before my birthday, remember?'

'Aye, how could I forget, dear?'

'I'd gone to visit Gail who had turned sixteen a few days before. I left just after 8 p.m.'

'Gail... that's Googy, isn't it?'

'Yea, that's right. You've got a good memory.'

'Aye,' said John, recalling his day at Morrison's store.

'Then I went to see Susan in Moffat Road. I was there till almost nine at night when I went for the bus home. As I was walking up Moffat Road to the bus stop, there was nobody about. Oh hang on... I think I saw that man, Frank, the manager of Your Move but he was a fair bit away. He was out with his dog, a black Labrador, I remember.

Anyway, then a car, I think it was a blue Fiat, slowed down and stopped. A man wound down his window with a map in his hand and asked if he was on the right road to Castle Douglas. It seemed an honest request. I was thinking how best to tell the driver how to turn around their direction. I was not really concerned when the driver had got out of the car and came round to where the map was being studied. Then I got a fright. I was bundled in a swift movement into the back seat of the car. They put a blanket, smelling of oil, over my head. I was terrified. I didn't have time to think or scream.'

'You pair wee girl.'

'The car moved off slowly, presumably not to draw any attention to it. The men in the car were not angry, but more anxious that their deed had not been seen. I could tell we drove south, past Annan and then Gretna, and soon the car was heading south on the M6,' said Morag.

'No wonder we had naithin tae go on. Ye were oot o' the country in half an oor.'

But that was as much as Morag wished to recall that night. By 10 p.m. she was sound asleep. John slipped into the bathroom, guilty that he had not done it sooner.

'Thrilled to report Morag is alive and well. Returning to Scotland soon with her (Glasgow Airport flight TBA in due course). Mo asleep will get her to speak to you tomorrow. Search over. Obsession over and out. John.'

The text message was successfully sent the second time after John opened the bathroom window and held his mobile outside. To hell with the cost. He'd never sent such an important text. Surely Alison was still up and about. It was around two in the afternoon in Dumfries. She was bound to check her phone some time that day and certainly before she retired for the night but that would be some time off. John ran the bath water. His shirt was dark with sweat. He placed his mobile phone on a towel on a chair by the bath.

He lay down in the bath with his head in the soapy water. He was aware of the broadest of smiles on his face. The water was warm and relaxing as he cleared his mind of five years of anguish, five years of bitter mistrust: almost five years of separation and four years of marital distrust. A new chapter was emerging. But the pages were blank. He lowered his head once more.

At first he thought it was a faint ringing in his ears but then he realised it was his phone vibrating softly in the pile of towels. He sat up and let the water drain from his head. It was a text message that had arrived.

'Hi. Wonderful news, wonderful wonderful news. Just told Granny who wants us to move back together as a family for the sake of Morag. Forgive me John. I got it so wrong. Send my love and kisses to Morag and hope to speak to her soon. Please let me know about flight times to Glasgow. I'll be there. Love Alison. Xxx Xxx'

John read the message twice. In fact he then read it again. It was a text full of promise and forgiveness. The first page of the first chapter had been written already.

The following morning Morag and her father were taken to a room in the police station at Izmir where Morag was shown photos of the human traffickers. She was able to identify several of them. She then recalled once more how she had been taken off the street in Dumfries and sent by ship to Turkey from the port of Liverpool. She did not know the fate of others she met on that ship. Some had come from Glasgow and were on the boat already. She recalled with no delight the conditions in which she worked for years. She soon became resigned to the forced labour régime. There was no escape. No means of communication. At times she wondered if her parents had died. That feeling grew to the point she believed they had and so she was hesitant to believe the events of the previous day. It also made her accept her life was the one dealt to her as she could not change the conditions. Her statement was concluded at noon and signed.

That left sufficient time for her and John to board a flight to London from Izmir.

'Time to go,' said Halis.

'Are we leaving now? Where are we going?' Morag asked.

'We are going to the airport. Time to go home,' said John.

'So how did you know I was here in Turkey, Dad?' asked Morag.

'You won't believe me if I told you,' he said.

'Really, why not?'

'Because it was a parrot that made me come, so it did,' said John, smiling as he remembered Kofi's vital message about the container ship.

'Dad, no really, don't joke. Tell me, how did you know I was here?

'I have much to tell you, Morag. But please believe me, yes, it was a parrot. Now I must put you through to Mum. You tell her we are on our way home. The line will be so-so. Try it anyway.'

Harry received John's ecstatic text as he ate his lunch. It was short but clear. *'Found Morag – bringing her home c u soon. John.'*

Harry choked on his scrambled eggs. Thoughts battered his mind.

What, Morag found? How pleased must John be? His search over after all these years has paid off. I can't believe it, he thought. And Alison, I'd love to see her expression, a mother again. And they are on their way home. Ummm... what homecoming was required?

Harry reflected how the media had dominated his life while John was kept in the shadows. Perhaps the media should be told of Kofi's death and the return to Scotland of Morag after being kidnapped almost five years ago. Yes, that was bait the press could not ignore. Harry replied:

'Wonderful news; where and when are you returning? Must meet you at the airport. Harry.'

They finally boarded Turkish Airlines Izmir to London, Flight TKA 384. It may not have been their last visit to Turkey. That would depend on the progress and development of the court cases for Mr Jakub Kutlar, Mr Ahmed and others being detained. But now they were in the air and away from the life of slavery she had spent in the fish factory. Morag smiled at her father and placed her hand on his. He placed his hand over hers and then Morag placed her head on his shoulder and promptly fell asleep.

John could not wait to see Alison's reaction and get back as a family once again. He would be there in no time. Surely there could not be any complication at their Heathrow stopover?

35
The Reunion

Four hours later the plane landed at a very busy, frantic Terminal 3 at Heathrow. People of many nationalities mumbled as they threaded their way to gates and cafés. John and Morag made their way to Departures through the security procedures. Their main baggage was already checked through to Glasgow. They had a little over an hour to wait in transit. Morag asked her father to finance some more western clothes. She lost no time heading for Monsoon for a skirt and trousers with three coloured tops, ideal for Christmas. John was happy to use his card to pay for the westernisation of his daughter. But then Morag wanted to go to M&S where she knew her more basic clothing requirements would be in stock. John was quick to realise this was a department he'd not feel comfortable in so he gave her three twenty-pound notes and waited in the expansive foyer near an electronic Boots billboard. She took her time.

'John Reid?' enquired a man with a camera at his eye and two behind his back.

'Yes,' he replied.

'You just arrived from Turkey?'

'You seem to know my movements,' said John.

'Then I hope you don't mind a photo or two for the papers tomorrow? They want a photo of you. By the way, you found your daughter, Morag, didn't you?'

John did not want the prying attention on his fragile daughter. He did not reply. But he did agree to his photo being taken to appease the snapping cameraman.

As John suffered under the photographer's constant clicks, passersby took out their cameras to catch the unknown celebrity. Morag, who had her new purchases in her M&S bag, came out to find her father the centre of attention, surrounded by press cameras. She moved to the back of the crowd. Her father was being snapped from all angles.

'Excuse me. What's happening?' Morag asked a young woman standing on tiptoes holding a phone camera.

'Not sure. Probably some soap star, I don't watch soaps but I've taken a photo of him to show my mother when I see her. She'll tell me who it is,' she said.

'I can tell you who he is,' said a dapper young man dangling his overcoat on his shoulder, 'I've read the book about him and that parrot Kofi. That's John Reid. I heard that he went to Turkey to search for his daughter, it was in the papers.'

'Really?' said Morag.

'Oh yeah, they've been in the papers regularly. Anyway, where have you been over the last year or two? In outer space?' he asked.

'Probably,' said Morag, moving away.

She walked round the back of the growing crowd and signalled to her father. John saw the hand movement but did not immediately recognise his daughter in her new attire. She beckoned him once more.

'Okay, that's all the photos. I've a plane to catch,' said John. Three other photographers had arrived by now. They were disappointed.

'Did you not find Morag?' one camerawoman asked.

But John ignored her too and set off. As he approached his daughter, he lowered his voice.

'It's Gate 12 for the 5.30 p.m. to Glasgow. The press will follow us.'

'Must they?'

'They've got a sniff of a story and they'll be on our tails until we board.'

Morag's approach to the gate caused an anxiety which smouldered in John's mind. Sitting there, vulnerable, they would be unmercifully pecked at by the news crews. It was not a welcome development in his thoughts nor Morag's that day.

She kept two arm lengths to the side and two to the rear of her father until they reached the gate. At Gate 12 they sat almost opposite each other two rows apart in the waiting area, awaiting the flight to be called. The press followed like an unruly family. They ventured along the seated passengers at Gate 12 asking five young women if they were Morag Reid. Eventually they asked Morag.

'Morag who? Reid? Don't know her. I'm going to meet my friend in Glasgow,' said Morag.

John smiled when he saw the reporters move on. They looked like lost sheep wishing a collie would round them up towards this enigmatic girl.

The press were dumbfounded. John's daughter was nowhere to be seen. They had no photograph to compare her with. It made their search rather impossible. Perhaps reports were wrong. He might have returned empty-handed. Anyway, they had a few good shots of John.

When the flight was called, a formal queue built up. All had their tickets at the ready, all except Morag.

She sauntered back and forward catching John's eye. When John was next to show his ticket at the counter, he nodded at her to come forward. Morag walked up to him smartly, apologising to the family behind.

'There she is. It's that one,' shouted a cameraman, running to the front to snap her as she turned away from the kiosk. John and Morag moved off together. John placed his arm round Morag as they walked down the gangway to the plane. Any photo taken from behind would show a sugar daddy with his trophy wife. But the press let them go. They knew that they were covered further north.

Harry sat in the arrival lounge at Glasgow Airport. He had been driven up to Glasgow by the Times journalist, Peter Harkness, who had Harry agree to story rights on behalf of John. Harry tried to relax. He stood up and paced up and down the viewing area. He took a large breath in but the growing excitement and his shortness of breath held him in check. That this breathing condition had returned at this crucial moment displeased him immensely.

The bright lights of the plane could be seen over the Clyde on a darkened winter night as the plane circled into position. Harry followed its progress until the plane shot along the runway at a decreasing rate and taxied back to the terminal. He straightened his tie and unconsciously combed his hair. But this was not his story. This was the end of a double quest and this was John's moment in the spotlight with his daughter. He wondered how she would look and just how happy John might be at last.

The media gathered around, jostling to get a selection of pictures. John and Morag smiled at them as they proceeded through the concourse. As other passengers headed for the exits and the Glasgow streets, John and Morag were led upstairs to a private area reserved for special occasions and special guests. Harry's heartbeat increased.

On entering the room, John placed his bags down. He saw his old friend and embraced him.

'Harry, I'm so pleased tae see ye here. It makes the story complete. But what a shock aboot Kofi. My sympathy tae you fur the loss o' Kofi. I wull never forget him, I can niver, niver forget Kofi.'

'Nor can I. He was a very special bird, wasn't he?'

'Without him, I'd niver have foond Morag,' said John.

He turned towards his daughter.

'This is Morag, my daughter. Ma precious wee lass Morag. Come meet Harry, the man I've been telling you aboot.'

'Mr Dynes. I don't know how to thank you. I think you saved my dad's sanity from what I've heard, and helped to find me. I'm grateful for what you have done and grateful to your amazing parrot too, of course. '

Harry gave Morag a hug.

'I'm so happy for you both. Welcome home, Morag. It's the day we've all been waiting for. It's your parents' dream come true,' said a very happy Harry.

The door opened. Morag looked round.

'Oh, Mum, Mum over here,' she said, running towards her.

Alison embraced her daughter with a clamping tightness. Her eyes closed as if recalling the day before Morag's sudden departure. But closed too to shut off the stream of tears which were corralled behind her eyelids. A mother's embrace, so natural and so loving, satisfied John immensely.

'Darling, I've lived the past five years believing you lay somewhere in the ground and we'd never find you. Eventually we had to move on. I am sorry… I did not have the faith… the faith required… and the determination... of your father,' said Alison.

'That's all in the past, Mum. It's over. It's over. I'm here. I'm back home.' Morag withdrew an arm's length from her mother.

Then mutual tears, sobs and loving caresses of her freshly coiffured Turkish hairdo ensued to the partial embarrassment of outsider Mr Harkness. Eventually he stepped forward.

'If I may be as bold to interrupt,' he said.

Harry stood aside as the journalist encroached. Peter Harkness had the manners of an English public school boy drilled into a six-foot frame with a blond thatch on top. He wore a conservative blue tie sporting the faintest of speckled grey spots, a grey shirt with two Times logo cufflinks and a dark business suit of charcoal grey. To complete his appearance, he wore size nine and a half light tan leather brogues.

Peter was the Times senior reporter, a man approaching, if not clearing, the magical sixtieth year, when hesitations about retirement tease the mind.

'Peter Harkness from the Times,' he announced. 'We have arranged for you as a family to go to a secret hotel in the country this evening. You need to have some precious time together, alone as a family, and, if you would agree, I need to have a piece on John and Morag for tomorrow's Times. We can leave as soon as you are ready.'

Alison felt this was an arrangement which Harry must have made without her knowledge. It was time for her to depart and make her own arrangements to be with her daughter at a later time. She gave Morag a hug.

'Well, I am so pleased to see you back and looking so well, take care. I'll see you soon,' she said, turning away.

'The invitation is open to everyone, Mrs Reid: I mean the whole family, no exceptions,' said Peter Harkness. 'We've got two cars ready and waiting.'

'Yes, of course, Alison, you must come tae, come and share oor family happiness, some more,' said John.

Alison looked back at the group from which she had moved away a few paces.

'You mean that, John?' she asked.

John walked over to Alison. He laid his hand on her shoulders. 'Unless you have ony aither plans, an' I canna think yiv got ony mair important ones today, I'd love tae have a family weekend at a country hotel. It's no a family withoot you, Alison.'

Alison smiled at John, banishing the anger and vitriol of recent encounters.

'Put that way, then how could I refuse?'

'Right then. Why don't Harry and I have the first car and the Reid family take the second car?' said Peter.

'But surely, I'm just going to head back to Dumfries?' said Harry.

'Oh no, not another potential defector. Forgive me, Harry, of course the Times is paying for you too at the hotel and I did say everyone, didn't I?' asked Peter.

'But I'd prefer the family to enjoy the moment together. I'm for an early night,' said Harry.

'Not fine by me at all. Harry, you are family tae me, tae us a'. You are certainly no dropping oot now,' said John.

'But don't you see, it's your story now, not mine,' said Harry.

'Nonsense. If we're having a meal, you are at the table too. The ladies have tae get tae ken you tae, Harry.'

'Right then, that's sorted. We rendezvous at the hotel. Let's go!' said Peter.

'Which hotel?' asked John.

'The drivers know, and we don't want the press to know, do we?' asked Mr Harkness.

Harry arched his eyebrows. So did John.

'It's a mystery, folks,' said John.

36
Unwinding the Knots

The cars drove south to the Trigony House Hotel where the Times had secured all bedrooms on the upper floor. The hotel lay deep in the lush countryside of south-west Scotland, on the outskirts of Thornhill.

The gardens, shrouded in a winter veil, contrasted with the red sandstone hotel. When the sun shone brightly, it shared its colour with the red squirrels that scampered up and down the Douglas fir trees. Their antics would be seen at breakfast. The group arrived at 8 p.m. Half an hour later they were seated in the restaurant where John and Morag relived their experiences in Turkey. Peter Harkness sharpened his pencil and took copious notes, sipping a cool white Italian Foscana Pinot Grigio as he wrote.

It was approaching 11 p.m. when Harry begged to leave the party. It had been a very long exciting day for him. Peter Harkness had some seven pages of notes, which he was required to shape into a feature article by 9 a.m. the following morning. So he retired to his room. His light went out shortly after 3 a.m.

Both Alison and Morag lingered till after midnight as John shared the experiences and the activities of his most unlikely relationship with Harry and his enigmatic and resourceful parrot.

But John respected the need for Morag to have a girls' chat with her mother. Anyway he was tired too. He approached Morag who stood up. Alison also rose from her fireside armchair.

'Goodnight, darling, sleep soundly. Home tomorrow,' he said, kissing and hugging Morag. Then, standing before Alison, the years disappeared. He stepped forward. He held Alison's shoulders and gave her forehead a kiss. 'Good night, Alison. Sleep well... well… er...' But he could not formulate the right words.

'You too, John,' she replied with a smile which had attracted John to her some twenty-eight years previously when they met separating from friends on the beach at Rascarrel Bay one warm sunny day in June. She raised herself up on her tiptoes. Her lips approached his. Then they touched after too long an absence.

'And thank you John, for persevering,' she said. John's eyes lit up and a smile came over his face. To hear the words perseverance and thanks in the same sentence was a total vindication in his mind. It was not a time to gloat.

Alison and Morag returned to their fireside seats placing a log on the dying embers. The next couple of hours passed quickly as mother and daughter filled in the past five years of such different lives while sharing an equal level of anxiety. And Morag wished to know what had become of her school friends, where they were and if any had remained in Dumfries. The burning logs were dimming. The hall clock struck once. Morag turned to more personal matters.

'At first I could not believe you and Dad separated. Was it really because Dad had become obsessive in finding me?'

'Put like that it seems so simple. And it was. It was also so easy to move in with Gran, to be honest. She almost encouraged me. But when I heard you had been found, it made me feel very guilty, very guilty indeed.'

'Don't feel like that, Mum. Life is like that. Think about it. If you were as… well, I mean, if you put as much into finding me as Dad did, it would have been impossible. You would have argued and probably got divorced.'

'Yes I suppose that's true, dear. We would have clashed. But I am kicking myself about not supporting him now.'

'That's just the way it was, Mum. You can't blame yourself or do anything about the past. Can't you see? It's all about living from day one now for me and for you and Dad. Anyway, tell me about Harry. Do you know him well?' asked Morag

'Everyone knows Harry. He's a celebrity. He was even on the Graham Norton Show.'

'The what?' asked Morag.

'The Graham Norton show?'

'I've never heard it.'

'Well, how would I describe it…'

'Is it a comedy show?'

'Yes and no, no, not really. It's rather camp, I think that's the word. You know, gay. He's Irish and a chatterbox. It's a programme full of innuendos with several well known guests and some musicians. You might like to get used to it. First time it's a little bit over the top, I'd say,' said Alison who was not a regular viewer. 'Oh yes, Harry was very much the star of the show. Well, him and Kofi of course.'

'Kofi was on the show too?' asked Morag.

'Actually I remember now. How silly of me. I've got a video of it. You'll love to see it.'

'Yes, that would be cool.'

Their mutual smiles lingered.

'I am sure John must have mentioned the depth of his friendship with Harry. It's something special, you know. Dad needed John to pull him through. They are really very close friends. Almost inseparable it seems sometimes. Maybe that is what John needed, a listening partner in his quest to find you, but I was not that one.'

'Something must have made you decide to leave, surely?' asked Morag.

'It is so difficult to explain, darling. Yes I know, I suppose there was a tipping point. You see, when John retired, I don't think he knew what to do. But once the thought of your disappearance focussed his mind, he became obsessed. He was staying up late searching the missing person's blogs and internet sites, making notes and phone calls to the Samaritans and missing people's agencies all around the UK the following morning. He left notebooks and papers for me to tidy and then he would complain that I had moved his papers. No, it was not a single incident. It was a turning of the screw until I could take the pain no more. I made the threat to leave but because John was so obsessed, my warning made no impact on his thinking. I told him, his search was in vain. Sorry, I did because there was no progress being made and I felt none would ever result in finding you.'

Alison held Morag's hand.

'The final straw? Well, on this specific day we had one hell of an argument. I even threatened a divorce and he did not seem to stand in my way. He was so determined to find you but I'm sorry to say, it was based on no hunch. So the next day I left and went to live with Gran, who to be honest, also needed my help. Darling I'm not proud to say it but yes, it was not a difficult decision to separate at the time.'

'But Mum, he's no longer obsessive, he found me. Maybe had he not been so obsessive, I might never have seen either of you again.'

'Yes I know. Of course it's true. You are making me feel permanently guilty,' said Alison.

'No, you mustn't think like that, Mum. Let bygones be bygones. But looking forward, there is the question of my future. Dad seems happy for me to stay in the family home. So why can't you stay too? Is it out of the question?'

Tears welled up in Alison's eyes. Morag moved closer and placed her arm around her shoulders.

'I've been very lonely at times living alone in my mother's room. But I thought I was getting used to it. Now I'm not so sure. When your father kissed me this evening, I felt a certain warmth, a passion I once knew with him. It was a reminder of happier times,' she said.

'Well, why don't you come over to Dad's home tomorrow and start to make the preparations for a Christmas meal, just like you always did? I'll give you a hand, a meal for the four of us. What do you say? Would that be a good idea?'

'I almost forgot about Christmas. But I like what you are suggesting. Mind you, it should be you to bring up the subject to Dad at breakfast. The idea will have to come from you.'

'It will, but Mum, just imagine if his obsession is now for you.'

37
Justice for All

A thud on the hall carpet roused Mr Conway.

'Postman,' he shouted.

'Anything interesting?' asked his wife.

Mr Conway gathered the mail and entered the dining room where David was having his breakfast.

'Lots of Christmas cards. Oh, and a letter for you, David, from the University I think, yes, here it is.'

David put down his toast and took a quick drink of tea. He held the letter. He rose from the table and went in to the kitchen. He took a knife and retired to his bedroom.

In Ankara, a police van arrived at the State's High Criminal Court. Inside the van were five accused prisoners. Each was handcuffed as they were led from the van into a secure rear entrance of the courthouse. Their defence lawyer, Kadir Akasan, a man of severe gravity etched on his moustached face, spent an hour with each accused person and a further half hour was spent amongst them to get the best possible defence aired in court.

But no defence was required, concocted or established. All five men realised an acceptance of the charges before them might lessen their period in custody and even spare them a possible death sentence. Little did they realise this did not form any part in the mind of Judge Fethullah Kurnaz, delivering the sentences in the native Turkic language. The Judge had been sitting in the High Court of Judiciary for six years. He could be irascible in court but was a fun-loving father at home to his seven children.

'The accused Kamran Ahmed will rise.'

Kamran was a man in his early forties. His black lengthy beard made him a shadowy figure, dressed in an open necked shirt, dark grey trousers and sandals. His gaze was not at the Judge but at his footwear.

'Kamran Ahmed, you have admitted your guilt and therefore it is deemed you are guilty of trafficking an undisclosed but considerable number of young European women into Turkey illegally; in addition to this you kidnapped them and forced them into demeaning hard labour duties. You married a Scottish woman without her consent. You ran a fish factory illegally, employing destitute women. You treated them as slaves. The court sentences you to twenty-two years imprisonment. In addition the court will seize all assets accrued from the illegal kidnapping of the victims.'

Kamran was led out of court, his head hung low.

'Captain Tayyip Tabakov rise,' the court usher requested.

The captain was no longer a proud man. He was somewhere in his fifties with streaks of white hair. His open necked shirt revealed a white hairy chest and a protruding stomach hid his black leather trouser belt. He was perhaps something of a Father Christmas figure. But he was not smiling and his sack was empty. He anticipated a similar verdict and consequently the end of his life at sea.

'Captain Tabakov. You are the dignified mastermind of this illegal trade in trafficking. It was your responsibility for everyone on your ship. A position of supreme authority at sea. You showed scant concern for the women you trafficked and little concern for what happened to them while in your care. You are sentenced to eleven years with criminal assets seized. Take him away.'

'But I admitted my guilt. Can you not take that into account?'

'I have,' replied the Judge.

'If you had, you'd have halved the sentence, think again, please.'

'Bring him back,' demanded Judge Kurnaz.

Captain Tabakov returned to face the red-faced Judge.

'I will not have the decisions of this court challenged by the accused. There is an appeal process. Use it if you must. Now, for this outburst, you will serve twelve years and I warn you any further ill-thought contempt of court remarks will increase the tariff. Take him away!' The Judge's ruddy complexion eased.

'Jakub Kutlar, please stand.'

Jakub stood proudly showing his contempt for the court procedures. A smirk enhanced his attitude. His deep-set eyes and his prison-beard growth made him look the most sinister of the accused. He had much to answer for.

'You are guilty of slave labour and kidnap. I sentence you to fifteen years and warn you against any outburst. Your illegal assets will be seized. I note that in your case, these assets will be quite significant. The State seizes them.'

Jakub Kutlar's lips began to tremble. He began to sob. It was the first time emotion had been observed on this bearded face for a very long time.

'Rise Recap Sufar and Sadat Basbug.'

'I have a degree more sympathy for you two crew men. You were probably unable to resist the crimes of Kutlar and Tabakov. But there is evidence that you showed little regard for the victims and you made money from carrying out the

Captain's will. Each of you is sentenced to six years and any financial proceeds from the crime you have made will be seized. Take them away.'

The cases were to prove landmarks in the deportation and kidnapped of European girls to Turkey. That was exactly the message Judge Kurnaz had hoped to give.

David slipped the knife into the envelope. He opened the letter's contents.

'Yippeeeeeeee... I'm in!'

His parents came rushing up on hearing his delighted squeal.

'The university?' asked Mrs Conway.

'Strathclyde?' asked Mr Conway.

'Yes, September next year. They have given me a place.'

'Wonderful, David,' said his father.

'I'm so proud of you, son,' said his mother.

'So that's two letters I'll have to write now.'

'Two?' asked his father.

'Yes, one to accept of course,' said David.

'And the other?' asked his mother.

'I want to see if the Scottish Wind Farm Authority can give me a placement before I start the course. If they do, I can perhaps get them to take me on after I get my degree. I think wind farms and other renewable resources in Scotland are the future.'

'Boy, your memory problems seem a thing of the past,' said Mr Conway.

'We're going to have a great family Christmas this year,' said Mrs Conway.

'We certainly are, dear, eh David? Nothing can go wrong now.'

38

Kofi Dynes 1978–2015

Wafts of sizzling bacon along the ground floor from the kitchen could be detected by a man with the most serious case of nasal congestion. It led to the group sitting round the breakfast table with plates of sausage, bacon, eggs to order, black pudding, white mealy pudding, haggis and tomato. Almost all enjoyed this hearty winter breakfast except Harry who settled for a bowl of porridge and brown toast while Alison sipped herbal tea to settle her nerves and buttered an oatcake.

'Tell me, Morag, in Turkey, were you made to convert to Islam?' asked Peter.

'On the outside I conformed to their rituals. There was no other option but despite having no faith five years ago, I silently prayed every night to our Lord and Saviour and he answered my prayers, didn't he?' she asked.

'He seems to have. Religion I feel should be personal, meaningful to the individual and devoid of any State intervention,' said Harry. 'But Morag, I admire how you got through it all. And, you have certainly missed out on four Christmases too. We'll have to put that right, eh John?'

John nodded with a broad smile and a wink to Morag.

'Christmas is almost upon us. But I don't think you have had time to get any presents,' suggested Peter.

'Don't you think I've just had my present?' said Morag.

'Of course, no present could possibly have pleased your parents more but I have, as you say here, a wee present for you. Nothing much, but useful I think. Here, Merry Christmas. Something to place under the tree.'

Peter handed over a slim oblong package wrapped in Christmas paper.

'Thank you, Mr Harkness, that was a surprise. Yes, I'll put it under the Christmas tree. Dad, do you have a tree?'

'Er... it's not exactly up yet.'

'Er... you mean not exactly bought either?' teased Morag.

Her dad nodded looking like a sad bloodhound.

'Then we've a lot to do this morning. We'll need a Turkey for four, all the trimmings and a Christmas pudding. Not to mention the wine. I've almost forgotten its taste,' said Morag.

Alison studied John's response to the mention of four at the table.

'Then I think we drop ye aff at yur home, Harry, and we'll go shoppin' as a family jist like we used to oan Christmas Eve,' said John.

'Aren't you forgetting something then?' asked Morag.

Her parents looked at each other with blank faces.

'Is there still a 6.30 p.m. Christmas Eve service at the Easterbrook Church?'

'Yes, that's right. What a good idea. Perhaps you could pick me up from Gran's, John.'

'I was... assuming... you might want to come home with us, if that's in order?' he asked.

'Oh yes, Mum, please,' said Morag.

'Then I'd be glad to,' Alison said with a warm smile, realising it had been a considerable time since she crossed the family threshold. It would certainly give her an idea how John had been coping with his housework.

'Harry, do you wish to come to the service?'

'No, an early night will suit me better. And anyway, it's a family thing and that's the three of you.'

'A family thing is the four o' us, Harry, as you ken only too well but onyways you will be bright-eyed and bushy tailed fur Christmas Day, won't you?' said John.

'One word of warning, there is still a lot of interest in the three of you. Journalism will not stop for Christmas, quite the opposite in fact. People at home with not much to do the day after Christmas need a paper. While the children play with their new toys the older ones tackle the papers, the crosswords and the obituaries, the letters and the features. We never close. So even at the church service there will be nudging and some tittle-tattle. There will be much congratulating of you all too. My advice is to smile your way through it, but don't answer your door on Christmas Day. Now I've ordered a taxi to take you to Dumfries while I'll be run to Edinburgh for a flight to London,' said Peter.

'And don't forget to take that story to your paper,' said Harry.

Peter patted Harry on the back. 'The editor got it at 4.05 a.m. this morning. E-mail, Harry, it's faster than a blink of the eye.'

'It's a memory thing. Even faster to disappear than a blink of the eye. Silly me,' said Harry.

That afternoon, Harry was dropped off at his house. He switched the central heating on and made himself a cup of tea. He drank it by his computer, passing the spot where Kofi had stood all those years.

He was able to delete and in some cases unsubscribe to redundant messages. The interesting ones seemed to be from his agent, Neil Scott, and Dumfries & Galloway Council.

Neil announced that the film would have its official opening in London in March next year. He would give details nearer the time but hoped John and his daughter would be able to come to it too. It might interest scriptwriters to look at Morag's story now. But that was for the future. He was hearing, however, that Morag would be sought by BBC arts programmes and the religious affairs department. But that was at an early stage of planning, to visit again later next year. Neil ended his message with seasonal greetings, wishing Harry good health and happiness for the coming year.

Happiness abounded in Harry's mind. He had practically got over the reality of Kofi's sad demise and was delighted with the outcome of John's patient years of searching. But deep inside was a niggle. It was a shortage of breath once again, a stinging watering of the eyes and a stiffness of the limbs and a reminder of what had taken him to hospital not so long ago.

The other important message which pleased Harry so much came from Gavin Stevenson, Chief Executive of the Dumfries & Galloway Authority. The council had seen a popular tourist opportunity. Kofi had been created in a painted metal casing with all the correct feathering and a bright red tail, making him recognisable. The inscription in gold leaf stated:

Kofi Dynes, an African Grey Parrot who lived with Harry, his owner, in Dumfries. He captured the imagination of the public with his antics and insights into our lives. Now recorded in the popular book, 'The Parrot's Tale', it is also a Universal film of the same name.
Kofi Dynes 1978–2015

The statue would be unveiled on New Year's Day and Harry had been asked to do the honours of unveiling the amazing parrot and then join the Council members in the Council lounge to mark the occasion with drinks and snacks. The site chosen was in the High Street at the Loreburn Mall Shopping entrance.

'Ha... Kofi will form a bookend with Robert Burns at the top end of the High Street at Burns Statue Square. Marvellous,' thought Harry.

He forwarded this message to John. What a Christmas present that was to open!

39
Christmas Joy

Alison knew when she woke that there was no dust to be seen and the carpets had been swept. John had the Hoover moaning at 2.30 a.m. on Christmas morn. He had gone to bed an hour later with a satisfied smile on his face. The house was ready for Christmas. He had really pushed the boat out this festive day and she appreciated what he had achieved.

Harry sported a bright red festive tie with his olive suit and brown shoes. In his hand was a bottle of Macallan's malt whisky for John, a large box of soft-centred dark chocolates for Alison, and a dainty gold watch and a voucher for £1,000 for M&S, as well as a settling home cheque for £5,000, for Morag.

A full traditional Christmas lunch was enjoyed by all that day. Paper hats were on heads at rakish angles. Festive candles and sweet-smelling perfumes filled the air. Crackers were on the table and warm cinnamon sticks floated in a large bowl of punch on the sideboard.

Then Morag opened her cracker and asked:

'Okay, where does Tarzan go to shop for clothes?'

The others thought for a moment but heads shook laterally.

'Perhaps Jane's store?' suggested Harry.

They laughed, but were unsure why.

'No, not quite. A Jungle Sale, of course!' she replied.

Presents were opened by the pine-smelling tree. Harry received a coffee-coloured lamb's wool jersey from Alison, a bottle of Harvey's Medium Sherry from John and a packet of three pairs of socks from Morag.

Morag opened the envelope from Harry.

'Harry, this is too much. You have given me my present already. It's embarrassing. Here, let me give you a kiss.'

'You have to realise I'm at an age when I won't need all the royalties I am receiving because of the books and film rights. I've a pension too and I should be living on that. But a kiss? Any time, Morag, any time.'

'Have you seen this, Morag?' said her father opening the weekend Times arts pull-out section.

Morag peered over his shoulder. His finger pointed to the top of the page.

'Goodness. Bestsellers, Paperback Fiction, No. 1 The Parrot's Tale with 78,241 sales. That's amazing, Harry!' said Morag.

'Aye, and over here, look,' said John.

Morag took the paper in her hands and followed John's directional advice.

'Goodness. Bestsellers, Hardback Fiction, too. No. 1 with 23,792 sold. Harry, this is unbelievable!'

'I'm afraid it's true. That's why you have the cheque.'

Morag leapt up to Harry and once more gave him a hug and a kiss.

'Oh... enough... enough. An old man can take only so many kisses in a day.'

The laughter increased.

'Oh, and Peter's present. Look, it's a Parker pen with the Times logo on it,' said Morag with the excitement of a young child.

Just as Peter had prophesised, the Times had published on Christmas Day and in the centre spread was Peter's story of Morag with pictures of them at both airports in London and Glasgow. They took it in turns to read and then they tackled the Times Jumbo crossword.

It was a warm happy family atmosphere in the Reid household once again. The Christmas meal had all the trappings and all felt full even before the Christmas pudding appeared. By then the punch and wine had taken its toll and Harry was gently snoozing by the fire after a glass of Macallan in his cushioned seat.

'Look at him sleep like a child, Alison. Can ye believe that wis ma pillion passenger? The man in search o' his parrot.' John lowered his voice. 'The parrot who found Morag. The man and parrot that brought us back the gether.' He turned towards Alison and took her in his arms.

'Am I forgiven?' he asked.

Alison brought her lips to his and kissed him.

'Am I?' she asked.

John bent down and kissed her again.

'Sometimes we don't need words, do we?'

They both shook their heads as Harry stirred.

It was an evening no one except Harry wished to end. John eventually rang for a taxi. Harry stood in the hallway waiting for the car's lights, while John and Alison stood, arms entwined, beside him.

Harry was driven home by taxi at 11 p.m. after a very happy and successful Christmas day: the second he had shared with John. But this time the female company had added a certain extra charm and delight. Alison and John waved him away. Then John turned to Alison.

'If we get together again as I hope we dae noo, I've been thinking o' doing something, ye ken, to keep me occupied,' said John.

'What brainwave do you have in mind this time?'

'Well, I'd like tae start a gardening service fur the over eighties. I enjoy doing Harry's and it gits me oot in the open again. I think it will be well-accepted in the older community,' he said, smiling with confidence.

'It will depend on what you charge.'

'Aye but I've a good pension and the occasional royalty, so I needn't charge much' if onything.'

Alison brought John close to her and kissed his lips once more, then whispered into his ear.

'I think you've got your life back. I'm sure your depression has lifted. I've seen nothing of it since Morag returned. Make an appointment to check it out, then set the alarm for 8 a.m. each morning and 10 a.m. at the weekends.'

'Why so late at the weekends?' John asked naively.

'Perhaps we can stay in bed a little longer,' she said, winking with her left eye, and showing her double dainty dimples.

John smiled. 'Like the old days?'

'Loved the old days,' she replied.

40
The Days Are Short

That night Harry felt uncomfortable. He could not identify the source of pain. It was a general and debilitating over-all misery. He could not get to sleep. He knew something was seriously wrong. He was now gasping for breath. At three in the morning, he got up and dressed ever so slowly. He e-mailed John, Fiona and Laura as they slept. He told them he was about to go to hospital and might be away for a few days. He added his love to all three of them.

Then, with a degree of reluctance but with purpose, he dialled 999 and shared his symptoms with the telephonist. They informed him an ambulance would be on its way.

Seventeen minutes later, with blue lights flashing on the roof and a siren at every junction, Harry was taken to the Accident & Emergency Department of the Dumfries and Galloway Royal Infirmary. A few drunken revellers who had come to grief were singing off-key in their examination bays. The police were at hand to ensure the medics could concentrate on their life preserving work. But Harry was not detained there long. Instead he was removed to the quieter Ward 8.

Fiona arrived with her sister early the next morning, Boxing Day, to see how ill their father was looking. His temperature was high. His blood pressure was low and his heartbeat irregular. He looked pale. Further tests showed hepatitis, myocarditis and keratoconjunctivitis had returned to invade his body. Harry was in a sorry state and his daughters knew he was very ill indeed. An intravenous drip nourished a failing body.

At 10 a.m. John and Alison arrived looking anxious.

'Harry, Harry. Can you hear me?' asked John.

Harry opened his encrusted eyes. A duty nurse approached.

'Are you family?' she asked.

'Almost,' said John.

'Can I have a word with you?'

'Of course,' said John, following the nurse into the corridor and then into a quiet room where the atmosphere was solemn. John knew its real purpose.

'Mr Dynes is very ill, very ill indeed. He has had a relapse of his psittacosis but this time it is really much worse. Despite powerful antibiotics he is not responding. I fear he is not likely to pull through this ailment, especially as it's a re-occurrence. Can I have a contact number for you?'

'Oh dear, oh no. You mean he's aboot to dee?'

'Yes, possibly quite soon,' she confirmed.

'Oh God. I wis no expecting this. He was with us on Christmas Day, last night... phew... at least his daughters are with him noo. They live in Edinburgh and Birmingham, ye ken.'

'Yes indeed I know. Laura drove up straight away starting very early this morning. She phoned her sister who left promptly too. I have their contact numbers. But you are in Dumfries. That's why I need your number. As for his girls, it will be the last time they see him. Make sure you give them time alone with him.'

'Aye, yer right. Sure. Thank you for yer help,' John said, giving his personal card to her.

He returned to Harry's bedside where Laura was holding his hand. Alison sat at the end of his bed.

'Harry, we've had a great couple of years. I jist could nae have done onything withoot you. You have been simply wonderful,' said John.

Harry smiled weakly. 'No more... motorcycles.'

'No, no more motorcycles,' John agreed with a broad smile and a chuckle.

Fiona smiled.

'Well, Kofi played his part; he found Morag. And we had a great time oan the road, didn't we, Harry?'

Harry just nodded with a faint smile.

'There's something I haven't told you yet, my freend.'

'Wh... what's that?' Harry asked.

'The hatchet has been truly buried. Alison and I are going to live together again. We've settled oor differences. We'll have a wee party to celebrate later in the spring. When it's warmer and you'll be there.'

Harry smiled. 'I'd like that, John. I'd... like that.'

'And Fiona and Laura will be there too,' said Alison.

Harry smiled.

John and Alison left the ward hand in hand. Fiona and Laura sat closer to their father. They sensed the inevitable hour.

41
Once More in Ghana

Kwabena took off the cover to reveal a wire cage. In the cage, sitting on a perch, was a young African Grey Parrot.

Harry's mouth gaped open. His wife frowned. It was a most inappropriate gift in her eyes as they prepared to leave the country and Harry noticed her expression. Harry also knew it was not polite to refuse a gift.

'You wish me to have this parrot?' asked Harry.

'Please. Yes, it is our present to you. We came across it in the forest last Friday. Its mother had been shot.'

'Shot?'

'Yes, hunters use bows and arrows to shoot adult parrots for their red tail feathers. They say they use it for juju medicine.'

'Last Friday? Oh... I suppose that makes him a Kofi.'

'It certainly does. The Friday-born are always named Kofi in Ghana. And you know that a parrot often lives for eighty years?' asked Kwabena.

Maggie's attitude softened as the parrot stared at her with an air of intelligence.

'Eighty! Wow I'll be one hundred and thirty by then!' said Harry.

'I hope so,' smiled Kwabena. 'I hope so.'

And Harry smiled as his memory slipped. First Fiona bent over and kissed her father and then Laura did the same. Then his smile faded as his arms went limp. A nurse came to him and closed the curtain around his bed. Harry was not aware of her.

Harry was in warm Africa once more as a young man. He was getting acquainted with an inquisitive parrot. He stroked it all the way from its soft neck feathers down its back to its bright red tail. What a beautiful parrot! Then, bathed in the sunshine of West Africa and with his parrot on his shoulder, Harry went for a walk. It was a walk that never ended.

The nurse approached between the girls. She took his pulse, felt his brow, placed her hand on his chest and then closed his eyes. She recorded the time of death as 12:05 on 27 December.

'Girls, stay as long as you wish. Your father has slipped away. My sympathies are with you both… Let me get you a cup of tea.'

With tears in their eyes, the girls smiled at the nurse and silently thanked her.

42
Kofi Is Resurrected

New Year's Day was a day in which the sun shone brightly in Dumfries. A sharp coldness brought coloured gloves and scarves to the gathering. And the Canada Geese flew screeching overhead in intermittent waves, announcing the ceremony.

John Reid, dressed in his new three-piece suit, stood by the covered statue of Kofi outside the Loreburn centre, with Fiona, Laura, Alison and Morag at his side. A large crowd gathered in silence as the Rev. Dr. Maurice Bond gave a prayer of thanksgiving for the lives of Harry and Kofi Dynes. The First Minister of Scotland, Alex Salmond, gave a glowing tribute to the contribution Harry and Kofi had made to life, the communities and tourism in Scotland as well as their part in successfully solving one of the most difficult and serious types of criminal acts in the world today.

Chief Executive Gavin Stevenson gave the opening remarks.

'It was a time of sadness that neither Kofi nor Harry Dynes were able to see this day but we are here to celebrate their remarkable lives.'

The Provost then addressed the gathering and a piper played the Flowers of the Forrest. John was then asked by Gavin Stevenson to come forward and unveil the statue.

The crowds cheered and the photographers captured the moment when the veil fell. Morag held her mother's arm, then smiled at her, proud of her father yet still left in wonder about this quite amazing parrot that she had never met. When Fiona and Laura joined her, Alison took a transparent box from her pocket.

'This is Kofi's tail,' she said. 'I'd like you, Fiona and Laura, to have it.'

Fiona took the box and brought it closer to her eyes. Then she passed it over to Laura. She looked at it briefly.

'No, I am sure it means much more to Morag,' said Laura.

Fiona agreed.

'Thank you. Then I'll accept it and cherish it, of course. Yes, it's a special tale and one that's now been told,' said Morag.

At the reception at the Council Offices, wine and Christmas cake were served. The Chief Executive gave a glowing tribute to Kofi and Harry once more and Chief Superintendent Cathy Ronson spoke not of the obsession of John but the dedication he had shown in discovering his daughter's whereabouts. It was a stubborn investigation and one done superbly on his own, in the finest of policing traditions. The gathering also rejoiced in the unusual relationship of man and bird, and of older man with younger man together on a motor bicycle. It was a most unusual but joyful and above all successful venture, bringing such happiness to the people of Dumfries.

It was mid-afternoon when the reception came to an end. No matter how John and Alison wished the party to be over and Fiona and Laura thought of the long miles home, Morag remained the centre of people's attention. Everyone seemed to wish to speak to her.

At last the doors closed. With a couple of celebratory drinks on board, it was time to walk back home.

'Let's jist go back and see the statue one last time before Fiona and Laura heed aff. I'd like tae take a group picture, so a would,' said John.

'A good idea,' said Laura whose return trip to Birmingham would not be inconvenienced.

The group stood beneath the statue. They huddled close together for warmth as John placed them all in focus. He hesitated.

The winter sun glared penetratingly at a low angle giving the picture a warm wintry touch. Nevertheless, he thought he could detect a large bird on top of the fountain in the centre of the square. He was transfixed by it. It seemed to cock its head as if to speak. John felt a surge of happiness and warmth. He even imagined that the bird was talking to him.

'The End,' said Kofi.

'The End, so it is.'

EPILOGUE

After making a full recovery and enjoying a Caribbean holiday with her father and mother, Morag studied international diplomacy at St Andrews's University. This led to her appointment in New York four years later, with the United Nations Secretariat.

David Conway graduated BSc 1st Class Honours in electrical engineering and is now employed by the On Shore Whitelee Wind Farm Company.

John Reid runs a gardening project called Back Breaker for the over eighties overseen by Age Scotland. With more than seventy-five gardens to attend to, he has now employed twenty-three young people and retains half of them over winter. The other half is employed to keep senior citizens' minds alive over the long dark days, with reading sessions, poetry sessions, art groups and musical interludes. He no longer suffers from depression. His last strip of Lexapro was flushed down the loo.

Laura obtained her doctorate in clinical psychology and now works at the City Hospital Birmingham. Fiona left the Prosecutor Fiscal service to become a Sheriff for Lothian and Borders.

Acknowledgements

This is my opportunity to express my gratitude to everyone who has helped me to reach the last page. To Hannie Rouweler and Joris Iven for creative support; to my Dutch agent Pauline Vilain, may she rest in Peace.

To those who have kept me fit to write: Alan, Margaret, Stuart, Joyce, Danny, Katy, Morag, Mark and Ian. To friends Scott, Jane, Shannon and Ronan. To Frank and Christina, Lesley and Chris. It was a good year.

To Ayisha Malik at Cornerstones Literary Agency and especially Sara for her editorial expertise. To Spiffing Covers for the cover, typesetting and their friendship.

With special thanks to Stuart and Joyce whose front doorbell made me contemplate this novel while attending Dumfries and Galloway Royal Infirmary. To Jocelyn who knows what is true, what is exaggerated, and what has come from a place unknown.

Finally to Bobby and Buck. They know why they are mentioned. You need not know.

Reading Group Discussion Questions

Why do you think the author made the main character as old as eighty-five years of age?

Why did the author flash back to record events in Ghana in the 1970s at the end of the book?

Were Kofi's abilities believable?

For whom did you feel most sorry in the book and why?

What are the central themes of this book?

Did you prefer Harry's character as a younger or older man?

Did you enjoy the moments of humour? Which moments stood out for you?

Was the ending satisfying? Why or why not?

In what ways does the book explore the bonds of friendship?

Should the trade in African Grey Parrots to the UK be abolished?

Do you believe female kidnapping is becoming more prevalent in society?

Did the author need to end Harry's life or should he have ended the novel before he died?

In the final chapter, the origin of Kofi's early life is repeated. Why did the author do this?

How dignified was Harry's death?

How does this novel differ from Miller's other novels?

Note to Book Groups

Yes, it's true about my broken finger and Kofi the Parrot did exist and I received him in Ghana. There was a court case in London and I did work at St Modan's High School. What else is true? What inspired this novel? How long did it take to write? What questions would you like to ask the author? Perhaps you might wish to invite Miller to your book group meeting? There is no charge for book group visits but travel should be reimbursed where appropriate and the group should have read *The Parrot's Tale* in advance. Oh… and a cup of tea would be appreciated.

Contact Miller at netherholm6@yahoo.com

Interview with the Author

How did you come up with the idea of making the main character of your novel an eighty-five year old man who travels around the country?

Characters I have written about in my novels have been both young and middle-aged. I had never had an octogenarian protagonist before. I thought of him as I was sitting in A&E with a broken finger, having seen patients pass by of a much older generation. I wondered what they might find on their return home. For an eighty-five year old to travel, he requires a companion with his own needs. And so the idea of a double Quest was born.

How do you write a book with such a wide appeal?

Many of us have grandfathers or elderly relatives. I was writing a book for them in mind: one with which they could identify and enjoy as an amusing novel. Yet it's also the story of an amazing parrot and the British public do like their pets. The parrot is a particular favourite due to its mimicking powers. But it also has intelligence. As I owned an African Grey Parrot named Kofi during my time in Ghana, I can certainly speak with some authority about its behaviour. Kidnap and trafficking might seem juxtaposed and a very serious part of the book, yet it is the parrot that links the two themes. Kofi's story is quick out of the box while John's story smoulders before being set alight by Kofi. Kofi is the real protagonist. Now that is somewhat unusual don't you think?

Are you just as funny in everyday life?

A few might think so: a very few. My family are perhaps more honest and don't see me as a comedian in any way. Yet I have always been an optimist and if I see a different angle to approach a subject, like humour, I will use it, but only if it is appropriate. The dictionary shows that between the words Fun and Funny is the word Funeral. We only live once and as long as there are more funny moments than sad moments, then life will be enjoyed.

How do you see yourself as an eighty-five year old?

That's a hard question. I hope my royalties might pay for a regular gardener by then. But at that age I might be thinking of giving up driving. I am unlikely to have a pet of any sort, other than my wife. I know that doesn't sound politically correct but she sees me as her pet! I hope we can still play badminton at a leisurely pace with fellow octogenarians. I suspect my eyesight will be limited but I'll enjoy meeting family and celebrating their milestones as well as ours. I certainly won't feel eighty-five. I may look that age then but I hope others will see me as a sprightly author with perhaps thirty books written. And maybe someone, one day before I turn ninety, will ask me to ride pillion on a powerful motorbike.

What will your next book be?

Lawrence the Lion Seeks Work has now been published globally. Dutch and German editions are presently being illustrated. Hard copies will be published in six months. I am currently working on a new novel which involves a female double agent, as well as a book about all the dogs in my life. It is entitled Take The Lead.

Sadly Pauline Vilain, my literary agent, died suddenly on 30 April 2013.

Have you any regrets in life?

Regrets? I've had a few. But there again... I have been a humanitarian worker all my working life. I would love to meet again all the children I placed in care or under supervision at home, the victims of the Pakistani earthquake I managed in Mundihar NWFP, as well as the people I worked with to improve their lives in Ghana. But that makes me realise how fortunate I have been in my life. Non vraiment, je ne regret rien.

Parrot Tales

India
Mumbai

A talking Indian parrot named Heera has been credited with helping to catch an alleged murderer who has been charged with stabbing its elderly owner to death.

The body of Neelam Sharma, 55, was found at her home in the northern city of Agra. Valuables and jewellery were missing.

As police hunted for the killer the woman's family grew increasingly suspicious when her Indian ring-neck parrot, whose name means Diamond in Hindi, grew agitated every time the victim's nephew, Ashutosh Goswami walked into the room or when his name was mentioned. The family started mentioning various members of the family by name to gauge its reaction. The bird remained silent until Mr Goswami's name was mentioned, when it shrieked and became visibly upset. This information was passed to the police. Mr Goswami, 35, denied the murder at first but when he heard the parrot's evidence, he admitted his crime.

Shaalabh Mathur of the Agra Police said, 'We got a lot of help from the parrot to zero in on the murderer.'

Pet parrot Wunsy saves owner from park attack in London

A pet parrot saved its owner after she was pushed to the ground in a north London park, police have said.

Wunsy, an African grey, was being taken to fly in Sunny Hill Park, Hendon, when its owner Rachel Mancino was grabbed and pushed.

The bird, which was on its owner's shoulder, flapped its wings and squawked, causing the male attacker to run off.

Ms Mancino, 25, said Wunsy was a "weapon and lifetime companion".

BBC News Website: (accessed 11/04/14) *http://www.bbc.co.uk/ news/uk-england-london-26967945*

The Author's Other Works

Novels
>	Operation Oboe
>	Restless Waves
>	The Last Shepherd
>	Miss Martha Douglas

Self Help
>	Have you seen my… Ummm… Memory?
>	Ponderings
>	It's me, it honestly is (NHS booklet)

Biographies
>	Untied Laces
>	Poet's Progeny
>	7 point 7 on the Richter Scale
>	Take the Lead
>	Jim's Retiring Collection

Children's books
>	Chaz the Friendly Crocodile
>	Lawrence the Lion Seeks Work
>	Danny the Spotless Dalmatian